# THE RUNAWAY BRIDE

## A LYME PARK SCANDAL

## FELICITY YORK

Harper
North

HarperNorth
Windmill Green
24 Mount Street
Manchester M2 3NX

A division of
HarperCollins*Publishers*
1 London Bridge Street
London SE1 9GF

www.harpercollins.co.uk

HarperCollins*Publishers*
Macken House, 39/40 Mayor Street Upper
Dublin 1, D01 C9W8, Ireland

First published by HarperNorth in 2023

1 3 5 7 9 10 8 6 4 2

A catalogue record for this book
is available from the British Library

HB ISBN: 978-0-00-853573-5

Printed and bound in the UK using 100%
renewable electricity at CPI Group (UK) Ltd

For Steve

# AUTHOR'S NOTE

The story of Ellen's abduction is based on real events and real people. For the story, some timelines were altered, and some names changed to avoid confusion. Whilst most of the characters and events are based on reality, some are the product of the author's imagination.

# CHAPTER 1

*Tuesday, 7th March 1826*

*SHRIGLEY HALL, CHESHIRE*

*William*

William Turner stepped out of his carriage, weary and cramped from the overnight journey from London, but brimming with good humour.

Today, nothing could shake his sense of optimism. He had never considered himself a man given to bouts of self-satisfaction – he'd always been too busy – but as he looked at his home, the newly remodelled Shrigley Hall, he felt it deep inside. A sense of not only confidence but rightness, which buoyed his mood further. He sucked in a lungful of the reviving country air and nodded to his approaching butler.

'Ackroyd! How go things? Is my good lady wife at large?'

The man bowed. 'Welcome home, sir. Mrs Turner awaits you in her parlour, with your brother and Miss Davis.'

'Good, good, good.' William grinned as he strode out beside Ackroyd, the gravel crunching lightly beneath their feet. Miss Frances Davis was the former pastor's daughter, and she and Jane seemed to get along famously. 'They have been keeping her company, no doubt?'

Ackroyd smiled back and nodded. 'Indeed they have, but I should warn you, sir, there has been much planning and excitement in your absence. The work on the interior of the house continues at significant pace, and things might not be as ... organised as they ought for your return.'

'Just as well, my dear Ackroyd. One must expect a certain amount of upheaval if the place is to be fit for our imminent celebrations.'

Ackroyd's smile widened with a hint of relief. 'Indeed, sir.'

William ran lightly up the stairs to the grand portico and bounded inside. He might be in his fiftieth year, but he still considered himself in his prime.

Renovations to Shrigley Hall were almost complete, and the money he had committed to the project had wrought substantial benefits. One of which, to his wife's delight, was that many now compared it favourably to its close neighbour, Lyme Park. His heart swelled as he thought of Jane's pride in the house, which had every modern comfort she could wish for. It swelled too at her pride in him – she'd married a poor lad from Blackburn, and now here her husband was, High Sheriff of Cheshire. Three months since his investiture, and he'd been privately celebrating that fact daily. But once the house was truly immaculate, the family would hold a grand celebratory gathering that would confirm their place, finally, in the upper echelons of respectable Cheshire society. Now *that* would be the feather in his cap. It would make all his years of hard grind, of building his empire, worth it.

The grand entrance hall was usually a space of tranquil magnificence, but today William found himself confronted by a sea of workmen, ladders, sheets, hammering, and clattering. He picked his way through the hustle and bustle, pausing several times to admire the lofty ceiling. The dome with windows at the apex had been, in his view, a stroke of genius which gave the whole space an extraordinary sense of grandeur.

He stopped to speak to a passing footman, asking him to arrange for a light breakfast in his study, and greeted the workmen as they scurried about, paying no heed to the – admittedly rather alarming – noises their toil was yielding. It was going to be splendid. Truly a home that he, his wife, and their beloved daughter, Ellen, could treasure. Be proud of. At least until he secured the perfect husband for Ellen with an equally, if not even more splendid, marital home. He could scarce believe his daughter was about to launch into society.

He reached Jane's parlour door and gave a cheery knock before poking his head inside.

'Oh, my dear, you are home!' his wife exclaimed. She was ensconced in her favourite chaise longue by the window, with Miss Davis and Robert in comfortable armchairs on either side. The rest of the furnishings were covered in sheets spattered with the same duck-egg blue as the walls, which, judging from the sharp scent in the air, were barely dry.

All three set down their teacups to greet William warmly, as he strode over to kiss Jane's outstretched hands.

'Alas, this is a flying visit,' he said with an apologetic smile. 'I am expecting my legal advisor, Grimsditch, to call imminently. I trust I'll see you all at luncheon?'

Jane made a moue of unhappiness but nodded. Miss Davis leaned over to give her fingers a sympathetic squeeze. Miss Davis was an attractive woman, and Jane had confided to him she couldn't understand why such a beauty was yet unmarried in her fourth decade. He knew Jane was itching to ask, but had, to his relief, forbore from probing too far. Even she knew some things weren't polite to ask of one's newest friend.

Robert was well dressed as always, with his dark curls tamed à la Brutus. Robert was a bold and imaginative businessman, but as society required, he carried the look of languorous, idle wealth well. Much better than William did himself, he was forced to admit.

'We have been remarkably busy in your absence,' said Jane.

'So I hear …' William said, just as a thunderous crash accompanied by jumbled musical notes resounded from the hallway. He tried not to wince at the thought of what they might be doing to the grand piano. 'Has it been a terrible nuisance? You should take care with your health, my love.'

'You may rest assured that your wife is being most careful,' said Miss Davis.

Robert winked at William. 'You would be proud of Jane's fortitude. She has presided over the renovations with vigour!'

Jane confirmed this with a coquettish smile. His wife's health was often precarious, but – though he wouldn't dare say this out loud – it was seldom threatened by things that were pretty, expensive, or favourable to their position in society.

Once in the sanctuary of his study, William settled himself behind his large oak desk, where a simple meal of fresh bread and butter with some thick cut ham sat waiting alongside a cup of tea.

Happily, the refurbishment to this room was complete, and a maid had already lit the fire, which was filling the space with the comforting, warm scent of woodsmoke. Without delay, he took a bite of the bread, and picked up the small pile of post that was perched neatly on the corner of the desk. He glanced through the letters as he chewed, putting those that looked important to one side, and extracting the one from his solicitor, Grimsditch, first.

He was enjoying his first sip of tea when a scream rent the air. He started so badly that the cup leaped from his hand and shattered on the stone hearth, splashing his boots. The scream came again, and for a moment he thought it must be one of the workmen. The cries that followed chilled him to his soul.

Jane, it was Jane. Jane was screaming.

He raced to the door, tore it open, ran full pelt down the corridor. He flung open the door to her parlour and skidded inside, where he was greeted by a disturbing tableau.

Jane was staring at something in her lap, one hand clamped over her mouth, shaking. Robert looked on, wide-eyed, and Miss Davis was crouched by her side, uttering soothing noises. A footman was backing away uncertainly towards the door.

'What in God's name is going on?' William demanded, striding towards his wife. Miss Davis stood up, pressing a hand to her elegant throat. She shook her head in a startlingly sympathetic way.

'It's Ellen,' Jane whispered and squeezed her eyes tightly shut. William saw that the item in her lap was a letter.

Robert came to stand by his elbow. 'You should read it, William.'

He took the paper from Jane's unresisting fingers, as Robert saw the bewildered footman out. He scanned the missive and quickly mastered the content, his throat constricting furiously as he did so.

*6th March*
*Break House School, Liverpool*

*Dear Mrs Turner,*

*I hope my letter finds you as well as possible. Ellen was terribly worried about you when she left us this morning with Monsieur Thevenot, but she had every faith that your doctor would be able to restore you to good health.*

*Ellen's friends are missing her already, and are eager to welcome her back whenever suits you.*

*Sending all good wishes for your very speedy recovery,*

*Miss A. Daulby*

'Dear God,' he choked. 'Where the blazes is she if she isn't at school?'

Jane sobbed. 'Who is she *with*, William? Who is this Thevenot person? What does this *mean*?'

William's heart raced along with his thoughts. He could conceive of no satisfactory explanation for Ellen leaving school in the company of a man, or for the school thinking Jane was ill when she wasn't.

They were all silent save for the sound of Jane's weeping. Miss Davis was the first to break it.

'Do you know of anyone named Monsieur Thevenot? Has the school or Ellen ever mentioned him?'

William shook his head. 'Not to me. Jane?'

'Never!' She slumped back into the chair, mopping her face, moaning softly.

William's mouth opened but nothing came out.

Miss Davis stared up at him, a frown on her brow. 'Do you ... do you think she might have ... fallen in love and eloped with someone? This Monsieur Thevenot?'

Jane wailed inconsolably at the suggestion, and Robert all but glared at Miss Davis. 'Of course not. Ellen is far too sensible a girl for that,' he said.

William gripped the bridge of his nose betwixt thumb and forefinger. No. Surely not. Ellen wouldn't be so stupid, would she ...?

# CHAPTER 2

*Five days earlier*

*LYME PARK, CHESHIRE*

*Ellen*

Miss Ellen Turner peered up and down the corridor of Lyme Park, and let out a disappointed sigh. Where on earth could they all be?

Her small party had been enjoying a tour of some of the open areas of the magnificent house, and she had been distracted by an exquisite library, decorated in shades of red and gold. A library that housed a range of extremely interesting books on history and poetry, and what appeared to be a memoir written by none other than the current owner of the house, Mr Thomas Legh: *Narrative of a Journey in Egypt and the Country Beyond the Cataracts*. It wasn't the catchiest of titles, not like some of the novels that she liked to read, but she hadn't been able to resist pausing to investigate. Well, in fairness, she had become so engrossed, nestling in the perfect reading nook in the bay window, that when eventually she looked up, she'd found herself quite alone. She might have hoped her party would notice her absence, but, she realised with a distinct feeling of pique, they had not. They had clearly abandoned her.

Shaking her head, she picked up her skirts and ran lightly down corridor after corridor. The wretched house was enormous, and she was beginning to fear she was lost when, on rounding a corner, she let out an unmaidenly shriek.

There, facing her, tucked into an alcove, was a life-size stuffed bear complete with snarling teeth and upraised paws. She clutched at her pearl necklace instinctively, and laughed.

'Good Lord, who are you?' She examined the bear more closely. It was an incredible specimen, and she could imagine that meeting such a creature in real life would be enough to send the hardiest of souls into a decline. If, of course, they weren't eaten by the bear first.

Still smiling, she patted the creature on the snout, gave it a jaunty wave, and set off again in search of her companions. She tip-toed on the soft carpet until she rounded another corner, whereupon she let out a second undignified yell. This time, the bear grabbed her, and she really did scream.

'Miss … miss? I'm so terribly sorry, I didn't mean to startle you,' a deep voice told her.

Ellen dragged open her eyes and became aware of large, warm, slightly roughened hands holding her bare arms. She blinked up into a pair of cool grey eyes that held a good deal of concern.

She blushed, and pressed a palm to her forehead. 'I thought you were a bear!' she blurted. The concern in the cool grey eyes gave way to startled amusement and the corner of the man's mouth twitched.

'A bear?' Dark eyebrows lifted. He really was uncommonly handsome, and dressed in the very pink of fashion. A single lock of his dark wavy hair tumbled over his brow, a spotless cravat cradled his firm chin, and his lips were … Ellen coughed and pulled her attention away. He let go of her arms and as he moved, she caught a faint scent of sandalwood that emanated from him.

'May I be so bold as to enquire why you expect bears to be roaming the corridors of Lyme Park?'

'Well, I just bumped into one,' she said. 'He was lurking at the end of the corridor not far from here. He roared at me and made me start quite violently!'

The man's small smile spread, and he huffed out a laugh. 'He's a shady character, that bear.'

'He is indeed, so you can imagine why I feared I might have stumbled upon a relative.'

He nodded sagely. 'And might I ask who *I* have stumbled upon? I don't think we've been introduced.'

Abashed, Ellen looked down at her shoes. A well-bred young lady didn't rush around talking to men she hadn't been introduced to, without even the vestige of a chaperone. Her mother would be apoplectic if she saw her – either that or she would be plotting their betrothal. She wondered if he had a title. If so, her mama would definitely be matchmaking.

She cast him a speculative glance and dropped a curtsy. 'Ellen Turner of Shrigley Hall.'

The smile lingered in his eyes, but when she spoke, something sharpened in his gaze.

'William Turner's daughter?'

'The very same.'

He bowed courteously. 'Thomas Legh, owner of this pile, including the recalcitrant bear.'

Ellen brought her hands to her mouth. 'Oh, in that case, we *have* been introduced. I think it was a year or so ago, just after Papa bought Shrigley.' She smiled at him and, on an impulse, winked. 'I was much younger then, so you are forgiven for not recognising me.'

He lifted an eyebrow, as if she'd said something terribly surprising. 'In that case, all is well,' he said.

'It is indeed.'

A moment's silence passed, and Ellen was contentedly admiring Mr Legh's dapper square-cut waistcoat and modishly long trousers when he suddenly cleared his throat. 'I suppose it would be churlish of me to enquire as to your purpose,' he said. 'Perhaps there is something that I can help you with?'

Ellen had the grace to blush. 'Ah, well, you see, I was with my friends and my mother and her friends. We were being shown around the Elizabethan parts of your beautiful house, but I became distracted by your book.'

'My book?'

'In the library,' she confided. 'The one you wrote about your journeys into Egypt.'

He blinked, and to her surprise and delight, his cheeks pinked. He cleared his throat. 'Ah, *that* book. I fancy you are the first to pick it up in quite some time.'

'I was completely besotted with it. I couldn't stop reading, and when I looked up, *poof*! All my party had vanished.'

The handsome Mr Legh's eyes lit up at this, dark hair shining in a stray sunbeam that came through the window.

'As hard as I tried,' she went on, 'I couldn't find them. That's how I came to be wandering your corridors, jousting with bears.'

He laughed again. Ellen didn't think she'd ever made a handsome man laugh quite so much, and so genuinely, before in her life. She couldn't wait to tell Lavinia and Hester.

★   ★   ★

When they'd located her party in the drawing room, Ellen was in high spirits. Her mama embraced her, apparently convinced that she had met some dire fate in the minutes she'd realised Ellen was gone. *Such* was her mother's anxiety, in fact, Ellen began to wonder if she too had encountered the bear.

'Wherever did you go, my love? I was certain you were lost to us!' Her mother kissed both her cheeks then turned to dip her head at their host. 'Mr Legh.'

'I did get lost,' Ellen said as Mr Thomas Legh bowed politely over her mother's hand. 'But Mr Legh rescued me, and he very kindly restored me to you.'

Ellen cast a glance at Lavinia and Hester, her very best friends from school, who were staying with her family for the holidays. Lavinia's dancing eyes told Ellen she was itching to know what had passed between her and Legh. Hester, the more reserved of the two, was watching with quiet but pronounced curiosity.

Her mama, seemingly pleased at this development, took the opportunity to introduce Mr Legh to the entire party with some zeal.

'Mr Legh, may I introduce Miss Davis, who is new to the area.'

Ellen watched as Miss Davis gave Mr Legh three fingers with an appreciative gleam in her eye. He bowed and didn't return her flirtatious look at all, which further elevated him in Ellen's view. Miss Davis had recently become a firm favourite in her mother's circle. Quite old, probably at least thirty, but terribly pretty and funny. In that moment she struck Ellen as something of a forward female.

As the introductions continued, Ellen was pleased to note that Mr Legh was gallant to each of her mother's friends, in the quiet, rather pleasantly understated way he had about him.

Lavinia curtsied and fluttered her long eyelashes at him, accentuating her perfectly blue eyes. This performance was seemingly lost on Mr Legh, much to Ellen's delight. Hester managed a small smile that was returned nicely.

Mr Legh turned to her mother. 'Might your husband be home at the moment? Only I did intend to call on him. He wished us to discuss the upcoming celebrations for his elevation to High Sheriff.'

'He is most certainly here,' she said with dimpling smile. 'We would be delighted if you would join us for luncheon tomorrow, before Ellen returns to school?'

Ellen sighed inwardly at her mother's mention of her still being in the schoolroom, but hoped with quiet fervour that she would be allowed to join in this luncheon.

Mr Legh dipped his head in a small bow. 'You are most kind. I'd be delighted to accept.'

Arrangements made, and with a final flurry of chatter, Mr Legh bade them farewell and left them to enjoy the rest of the visit. But as he went, he glanced at Ellen and gave her a small but distinctly conspiratorial smile.

Ellen was still hugging that smile close to her heart when the small party headed outside into the sunshine. It was a splendidly crisp, sunny day, the kind that only March can deliver, and as the ladies sallied forth, Lavinia and Hester took Ellen's arm with purpose, and shepherded her away from the group.

'Tell us everything,' Lavinia said. 'How did you manage to find yourself alone with the dashing Mr Legh for so long? What did he say? What did he do? Did he try to kiss you?'

Ellen hugged her friend's arm, glancing over at her mother who was still engrossed in conversation with her bosom bows, and whispered, 'Of course he didn't try to kiss me, silly. He's definitely not a pond-slime man.'

The three girls giggled madly. Lavinia had taken to categorising men in the most inappropriate fashion and they knew that if found out, they would be severely taken to task. However, it was simply too much fun to resist.

'But was he a worthy type?' Lavinia intoned, and their laughter became so outlandish that it attracted attention from Ellen's mother, and they were forced to restrain themselves.

'Come to my chamber tonight and I'll tell you everything!' Ellen said in more subdued tones.

'What do you mean by *pond-slime man* and *worthy* though?' Hester said, apparently baffled.

Ellen rolled her eyes. 'We talked about this last week. Don't you remember?'

Hester just looked blank.

'I'll tell you tonight,' Ellen said and then straightened under her mother's commanding look.

# CHAPTER 3

*Frances*

Miss Frances Davis returned with the rest of the party to Shrigley Hall, where they took tea. She sipped from her elegant china cup and observed the small group whilst the young Miss Turner giggled with her two friends, all bright cotton dresses and bouncing ringlets. Ellen was a tall, striking girl with unusual good looks that belied her schoolgirl status. Her mother admonished the girls for hoydenish behaviour, and they settled down, but they were definitely plotting something.

Mrs Turner detached herself and came to sit with her.

'My goodness, what a day.' She fanned a lace handkerchief in front of her face. 'Fancy my dear Ellen having to be rescued at Lyme Park, and by none other than Mr Legh himself!'

Frances cast her a look of commiseration. 'Indeed, Mrs Turner, such an *awkward* situation to find herself in.'

Mrs Turner gave her a sharp look. 'He was very kind though, and most courteous in observing all the proprieties.'

Frances sipped her tea, widened her eyes, then smiled.

The response from Mrs Turner, not a lady steeped in society's strictures from birth, was immediate. 'Do … do you think that there was something untoward?'

'No, no, of course not. Your daughter is a sensible girl, but …' Frances leaned closer. 'I know the worries a mama has when her daughter reaches a marriageable age.'

'Indeed, indeed, but I intend for Ellen to have a London season to give her the best launch possible, and I don't want anything to put that plan in jeopardy.'

'I understand completely. She's a very beautiful girl. It's hardly surprising our local gentlemen are noticing her, particularly as she is an heiress.'

'You think Mr Legh noticed her? He doesn't have a title, but he is very well set up at Lyme Park.'

Frances gave a delicate sigh. 'Lyme is very lovely and it would appear that Mr Legh is well accepted into local society …' She hesitated and looked up through her eyelashes. 'Now.'

'Now?' Jane leaped at Frances's lure. 'Now? Wasn't he always? Is there something I should know?'

'Oh no, not at all, he's very well liked.'

'But … he's Thomas Legh of Lyme Park – there have been Leghs at Lyme Park for centuries. He must be the epitome of respectability, even though he doesn't have a title.'

'As you say.'

Jane pondered for a moment and then dropped her voice to a whisper.

'Do you have reason to suspect that he is not respectable?'

Frances too spoke in low tones. 'I'm sure it was nothing.'

Jane Turner sucked in a breath and looked around her. No one was paying them any heed, so she leaned in again.

'I beg you to tell me. I simply cannot afford for any kind of scandal to attach to her.'

'Oh, I couldn't possibly. It's not really a subject for feminine conversation.'

Jane moaned, and the ever-ready tears shimmered in her eyes. She was clearly about to entreat further when the door opened to admit William Turner along with his lawyer, Mr Archibald Grimsditch.

Frances patted Jane's hand. 'I'm sure all will be well,' she said, then turned her attention back to the girls. Grimsditch was bowing to them.

'When will you return to your school, ladies?'

'The day after tomorrow,' Lavinia replied with a sigh of unhappiness. 'We have had such a lovely time staying at Shrigley Hall we will be sad to leave.'

Frances ran the edge of her finger along the fine china of the saucer she held, appreciating its quality. She could see that Ellen was bursting to tell her friends what had transpired between her and Legh during her escapade. Despite the chit's apparent intelligence, the way she'd made eyes at Legh suggested a strong romantic streak, which might have its uses. Quite a clever move to get lost in the corridors of Lyme Park and then need to be rescued by the owner. And, if Frances's intuition was anything to go by – and it hadn't failed her yet – Thomas Legh had more than a passing interest in the young heiress. There had been a decidedly warm look in his eye when his gaze fell on her, in contrast to mere politeness with the rest of the party, herself included.

That would never do.

She watched Jane Turner take her husband by the elbow and whisper to him. He bent his head to hear her and frowned deeply.

'My dear, that's nonsense, there's nothing—'

'It's not nonsense; there is something, I swear.'

'Jane ...'

She hurried him into a corner, and Frances took another sip of her tea and smiled to herself. Perhaps the inestimable Mr Legh might not find his welcome quite so warm in this house once the Lyme Park scandal was revealed.

\* \* \*

## Ellen

Most of the household was in bed, and Ellen's maid long gone, when she heard excitable hands tapping at her chamber door. She pulled Lavinia and Hester hurriedly into the room, and they banked up the fire against the cold before huddling together on Ellen's bed.

'Do you have anything to eat?' Hester said, as she settled herself comfortably and pulled the soft bedding up to her chin.

Ellen grinned as she leaned out of bed and produced a plate of cook's famous plum cakes from the nearest cupboard.

Lavinia squealed and Hester laughed.

'Hush!' Ellen admonished as she balanced the plate on the quilt, and resumed her position between her friends. They each took a cake and ate.

'So,' Lavinia began, catching crumbs with her fingers and putting them in her mouth. 'Tell us all, and don't miss a single thing out.'

'Well,' Ellen said, chewing thoughtfully, 'it all began when I thought he was a bear.'

Hester snorted and sprayed crumbs across the counterpane. 'He doesn't even have a beard,' she said, ever the pragmatist. But by the time Ellen had finished regaling them with her adventure, embellishing only the tiniest bit, both friends had eyes on stalks.

'So, he's what?' Lavinia breathed. 'An archaeologist?'

'I believe so,' Ellen said. 'According to Papa, he was one of the first western travellers to reach the Nubian capital of Ibrim. That's what the book is about.'

'Goodness,' Hester said. 'Handsome *and* clever.'

'Not only that,' Ellen continued, 'he was in Brussels just over ten years ago when the Battle of Waterloo happened.'

'Did he fight? Was he a soldier too? Oh, my, he would look magnificent in regimentals,' Lavinia said, fanning her hand before her face.

Ellen laughed. 'I agree, but sadly he wasn't in the military. He was a volunteer who carried dispatches.'

'Handsome, clever, and brave,' Hester intoned. They all nodded.

'And he's a Member of Parliament ... *And* he's a magistrate.'

'Oh Lord, the man is a veritable saint.' Lavinia raised her eyes to the heavens, and shrieked when Ellen tickled her. 'Your papa seems to know a great deal about Mr Legh. Does he think he'd be a good match?'

Ellen grinned and took another cake.

'I have no idea. Mama is insistent that I shouldn't settle for anything less than a title.'

'Well, at least they are not trying to marry you off before you have your season.' Lavinia popped the last of her cake in her mouth. 'However,' she added with a note of mischief, 'Mr Legh might be a perfect reserve.'

'Or,' said Hester, 'don't marry at all, and keep your father's estate to yourself. You could be an ape leader and have the most remarkable life travelling the world, just like your Mr Legh.'

Ellen guffawed. 'You could both come with me! We could throw wonderful parties with no pond-slime men at all!'

Hester drew up the blanket again. 'Tell me more about pond-slime men,' she said.

'Well,' said Ellen, 'have you noticed how men seem to fall into various *types*? Lavinia drew the conclusion that all the men of our acquaintance are either a pond-slime man or awfully worthy.'

'What do you mean?' As the most serious of the three, Hester was the one most likely to need explanations.

'Well,' Lavinia began. 'There's the kind of man who looks at a young lady like a lizard does at a particularly fat insect.' Hester shuddered as Lavinia licked her lips.

'Or,' Ellen continued with relish, 'who stares at a woman's posterior when she passes, and ogles one's bosom when introduced.'

'No!' Hester clasped her hands to her chest. 'I can't bear that.'

'As both traits are about as attractive as pond slime … so, pond-slime men.' Ellen cocked her head to one side and held out both hands as Hester hooted with laughter.

'And the terribly *worthy* types,' Lavinia said, adopting a pious pose. 'So intent on observing every propriety, and behaving with such decorum, prating on about their accomplishments, their possessions, their perfect lives as though that is going to attract a diamond of the first water.'

Ellen and Hester nodded seriously, hands together in prayer.

Lavinia shook her head. Her hair was plaited, and the rags she was using to curl it danced about. 'When I marry, I want it to be someone who will adore me and ravish me on a daily basis.'

'Just what *does* happen when one is ravished?' Hester asked with a sniff and a hiccough.

'Well,' Ellen said, 'if you don't know, perhaps we should ask Miss Daulby to put it on the curriculum at school.'

Lavinia jumped to her knees, almost dislodging the remaining cakes from the plate. 'Oh yes! Monday afternoon – ravishment class!' She sketched the idea out with her hands.

Ellen laughed so hard she could scarce breathe, and Hester had a pillow over her face to stifle the crows of gaiety. Despite all this talk of men, Ellen thought, everything she needed was right here. Silliness at midnight, plum cakes aplenty, and two of the best friends on God's green earth … What more could a girl possibly desire?

# CHAPTER 4

The day before school resumed had dawned bright and sunny again.

Ellen had ventured exceedingly strong hints that she would like to attend her parents' luncheon with Mr Legh, but it was not to be. So she, Hester, and Lavinia had been out for a walk when they tumbled back into Shrigley Hall that afternoon, bringing in the cold with them. As they handed coats, hats, and scarves to a footman, Ellen fluffed up her dark ringlets and shook out her gown. She was laughing at Lavinia, whose fair hair had wilted badly under the pressure of a hat, just as her father and Mr Legh walked into the grand hallway.

Her father cleared his throat. All three girls jumped and then dipped curtsies.

'Legh, I believe you have met my daughter and her friends?'

Ellen's heart thumped. He was just as handsome as she remembered, and he looked unspeakably elegant in a dark blue coat and cream waistcoat. His shirt points were not too high, his cravat flawlessly tied. Those grey eyes sparkled as he smiled.

'Indeed I have. How nice to see you all again. I trust you have had an enjoyable walk?'

Ellen wished she could think of something clever or witty to say, but drew a blank. 'We did, thank you Mr Legh.'

'Most certainly, Mr Legh,' Lavinia chimed in. 'What a lovely part of the world you live in.'

'Well,' Ellen's father said, rubbing his hands together before any further conversation could be launched, 'we'd best let you ladies get warm.'

'Forgive me, but before we go …' Thomas said, glancing at Ellen's father. 'With your permission?'

'Of course.'

Legh turned to Ellen and gave her that small smile that quickened her pulse. He fished in a pocket to retrieve a small, bound book and handed it to her with a touch of awkwardness. 'As you were kind enough to show an interest, I thought you might enjoy a copy.'

Ellen's mouth was hanging open, she was sure of it. He'd brought her a copy of his *book*? She took it from him and turned it over gently in her hands, running her fingers over the soft leather of the cover, unable to hide her joy.

'That is … so kind of you. I will treasure it.'

'It is always gratifying to find someone has an interest in one's work. I'm honoured that you might consider reading it.'

The hallway, her father, and her friends were all forgotten as Ellen stared at the modest man in front of her. He was close enough for her to catch that elusive scent of sandalwood again and something else that, she wondered, might simply be … him.

They smiled at each other until her father cleared his throat again. Mr Legh made his farewell, and Ellen watched him go before her friends dragged her into the parlour.

'He's definitely not a pond-slime man,' Hester said, eyes wide.

'Not a worthy type either.' Lavinia nodded, knowledgeable as ever.

'So what does that make him?' Hester looked from Ellen to Lavinia and back.

Lavinia bit her lip and then smiled wickedly. 'Eligible. It makes him eligible.'

Ellen's hands were a trifle unsteady as she opened the book. *Oh Lord*, there was an inscription. He had written in it for her.

*For Miss Turner, a fellow adventurer. Yours, etc. Thomas Legh Esq.*

'Let me see, let me see.' Lavinia made grabbing hands. Ellen passed it over and she read it with Hester hanging over her arm.

'Oh my,' Hester breathed. 'Oh my *word*.'

\* \* \*

The journey back to Break House was arduous. The weather had taken a turn for the worse, with blustery rain rocking the carriage and chilling the girls to the bone, despite their blankets and warming bricks. However, Ellen was still glowing quietly inside.

'What I wouldn't give for a hot chocolate,' Hester said with a sigh.

Ellen pulled herself from her daydream and snuggled closer to her friend. 'Not long now; we should be there for dinner. I'm hoping for custard,' she said. But what she was really yearning for was the chance to return to Mr Legh's *Narrative of a Journey in Egypt*. She had shown it to Lavinia and Hester, but neither seemed overly interested in reading past the inscription. She, on the other hand, adored adventure stories, and could not wait to pick up where she'd left off.

\* \* \*

## THE OLD VICARAGE, POTT SHRIGLEY, CHESHIRE

*Frances*

It had to be now, thought Frances, from the comfort of her father's hearth. Turner was back in London making arrangements for his investiture, and the girl was back at school ... It was the opportune moment.

She tapped her lips with her fingers as she contemplated her next move. Ellen's mother was preparing to launch her into society – she'd listened long enough to the descriptions of the court dress, the balls, the parties that she had planned. It was also clear that Jane Turner was aiming for a titled husband. She even aspired to Almacks – in other words, she was shooting for the moon.

Indeed, Jane was planning everything with the military zeal of a general. And with Ellen's evident interest in Legh – which for all Frances knew might be mutual – they needed to act swiftly.

Not a single soul at Shrigley Hall had connected her, Miss Frances Davis, with her other name: Mrs Edward Wakefield. She smiled at the anonymity this granted her. She would announce her marriage after the plan had been executed successfully, of course ... but not a moment before. Her husband, meanwhile, would remain in Reading pretending he knew nothing of what was about to transpire. He didn't ask; she didn't tell. The marriage worked well that way.

She took a deep breath and began. First, she wrote a note to Brocklehurst's Bank with a request to withdraw one hundred and fifty pounds. Then she sent an urgent note to her husband's two sons, Edward and James Wakefield. Finally, she settled to write a letter of a very different sort. One that would catapult them all into the most daring of ventures.

When the letter was penned, and the plan in place, she carefully dusted the ink. She then held the paper up, scanned the content again, and felt a tingle of anticipation. Finally, she gathered the personal items that she had managed to remove from the Turner household: a hand-stitched, monogrammed handkerchief belonging to William Turner, and a small signet ring she had seen him wear on his little finger. She ran a finger over each with gratification. They should be enough. She dropped them in a velvet drawstring bag and put it in her reticule, ready for her next trip to Manchester.

# CHAPTER 5

*Monday, 6th March 1826*

*BREAK HOUSE SCHOOL FOR GIRLS, LIVERPOOL*

*Ellen*

It was a perfectly ordinary Monday morning at Break House, and with an hour to spare before lessons began, Ellen was writing a letter to her mother in the library. The school was a small establishment with only a few pupils, so she often had this room all to herself, which was how she liked it. Unfortunately, that meant it never took long for the headmistress, Miss Daulby, to find her.

'There you are, Ellen. You must come with me straight away.'

Ellen looked up to see that Miss Daulby had a pained look on her face, which prompted Ellen to think hard: what was she in trouble for now? Her headmistress was generally kind, but strict when she needed to be, and positively draconian when it came to etiquette and manners.

The picture of obedience, Ellen put down her pen and picked up her letter.

'Leave that there.'

Ellen put the paper down again, frowning, and followed as Miss Daulby bustled from the room and into her office. There stood a man Ellen had never seen before, staring straight ahead, and dressed like a servant. She looked from him to Miss Daulby and waited. Miss Daulby seemed unusually distracted.

'Take a seat, dearest Ellen.'

Ellen sat, heart beating faster. She'd never called her *dearest Ellen* before. What on earth was wrong? Miss Daulby's next words robbed her of breath.

'Dearest, I'm afraid your mother has been taken unwell. She would like you to return home urgently.'

Ellen's hands went to her mouth and her eyes pricked with sudden tears. *How ill?* she thought. 'Is she going to die?'

'Oh, my dear, no, I'm sure that's not the case, but if she is feeling poorly, she would no doubt welcome the presence of her beloved daughter.'

'Papa is in London,' Ellen said, mind racing. 'But her friends will be supporting her. If she is asking for me, then she must be terribly ill indeed.'

'Come now, Ellen, I'm sure … it's not too serious.' Miss Daulby was looking uncomfortable, and Ellen had the impression there were things she was not telling her.

'Might I see the letter?'

'I don't think that's necessary.'

Ellen begged to differ, but the urgent way Miss Daulby glanced at the mysterious man who still stood in the corner frightened her. 'Should I leave now?'

'You should. Go to your room and pack your portmanteau, then come back here. No need to take your trunk. Do you require one of the maids to help you?'

Ellen shook her head, curtsied, and exited the room before picking up her skirts and running through the familiar oak-panelled corridors. She found Lavinia and Hester together in the common room with some of the other girls.

'Come with me,' she whispered. Neither argued, so Ellen could only conclude that the turmoil she felt was showing on her face. They hurried to the dormitory which was, fortunately, deserted.

Ellen closed her eyes, then put her face in her hands to get hold of her emotions.

'Mother is ill, and I have to go home.'

'Oh no,' Lavinia said and gathered her close. 'Oh, love, what's happened? She was in the highest of spirits when we left.'

Ellen let Lavinia hold her and felt Hester's cool hand on her arm. She cried a little, but pulled herself together quickly, running her fingers beneath her lashes. Hester passed her a handkerchief.

'It might not be as bad as you imagine,' she ventured. 'You know your mama is prone to drama sometimes.'

That was true, Ellen thought.

'Come,' Lavinia said, 'let's get your things. The sooner you can return home and reassure yourself the better.'

Ellen nodded. With her friends' help, she put things into her portmanteau she thought she might need for the journey. It wasn't terribly far, but the roads at this time of year could be difficult, so she put in plenty of spare clothing, along with her personal things. She put in gloves and her favourite stockings and a night-rail. A few important items she put in her reticule, and after a moment's hesitation, she picked up the book Thomas Legh had given her.

'Good idea,' Lavinia said. 'Take something to read on the journey. Mr Legh will be a perfect companion.'

Ellen nodded again. She really didn't like carriage journeys, so a distraction would be welcome.

When her packing was done, she threw her arms around

Hester, then Lavinia. 'I will miss you both horribly. I wish you were coming with me.'

'And we will miss you. Write soon.' They each kissed her on the cheek, and when the footman came to carry her bag, Ellen left her friends with their arms about each other, looking miserable.

Ellen swallowed as she arrived back at Miss Daulby's office. She knocked and opened the door only to find it empty, save for the familiar smell of her perfume. She was about to leave and stand outside when she spotted a letter sitting on the blotter of Miss Daulby's desk. Heart thumping, Ellen peeked out of the door to make sure no one was about, then picked up the letter. It took but moments to discern that it was most definitely about her mother. She shoved it into her reticule, and slipped out of the room.

Moments later, Miss Daulby and the man arrived.

'Now, Ellen dear, let me introduce you to Monsieur Jacques Thevenot. He has been sent to escort you home.'

Ellen frowned. 'I don't think we've met, Monsieur. Do you work for my father?'

The man bowed. 'Indeed, Miss Turner, I do. I worked for Mr Legh of Lyme Park previous to that. I am requested by Dr Hull to take you to Manchester, where he will meet you and explain everything before returning you home.' His English was good, with a strong French accent.

'Oh, I see.' It was reassuring that Thevenot had worked for someone she knew, but if Dr Hull had sent this man for her, her mother must indeed be in a bad way. She tried to breathe evenly to quell the tremors that beset her, but it didn't really work.

Miss Daulby came outside with her and settled her into a green barouche. She sat back and looked about her with some concern; the carriage was nowhere near the standard her father would have ensured. It was certainly not Dr Hull's best carriage, either. There was an unpleasant, musty smell inside and stains on the upholstery. She shifted uncomfortably at the prospect of travelling all the way to Manchester in it. Miss Daulby gave her a paper of sweetmeats and patted her hand in such a kind way that Ellen was close to tears again.

Monsieur Thevenot confirmed he would sit outside with the driver, so as the door closed, Ellen was alone in the gloomy vehicle. Once they were away from the school, Ellen took the letter from her reticule and read.

*Saturday night, half-past twelve*
*Shrigley*

*Madam, I write to you by the desire of Mrs Turner, of Shrigley, who has been seized with a sudden and languorous attack of paralysis. Mr Turner is unfortunately away from home, but has been sent for, and Mrs Turner wishes to see her daughter immediately. A steady servant will take this letter and my carriage to fetch Miss Turner; I beg no time be lost in her departure, as, though I do not think Mrs T. is in immediate danger, it is possible she may soon become incapable of recognising anyone.*

Ellen squeezed her eyes tightly shut and put her hand to her mouth. *Incapable of recognising anyone?* She forced herself to read on.

*Mrs T. particularly wishes that her daughter may not be informed of the extent of her danger, as, without this precaution, Miss T. may be very anxious on the journey; and the house is so crowded, and in such confusion and alarm that Mrs T. does not wish anyone to accompany her daughter. The servant is instructed not to let the boys drive too fast, as Miss T. is rather fearful in a carriage. Mrs T. is very anxious that her daughter should not be frightened and trusts your judgement to prevent it. She also desires me to add that she, or I myself should she continue to be unable, will not fail to write to you by post.*

*John Hull, M.D.*

Ellen blinked, wiped her eyes, and read it twice more. *Languorous paralysis*, it said. Her mother had experienced bouts of paralysis before. She could only hope that she would make as full and happy a recovery from this bout as she did the others. For a moment, she wished she had not taken the letter, as sometimes it was better not to know, but then took a deep breath. At least she knew what to expect. Dr Hull would explain everything, and despite exhortations to drive slowly, the driver was taking them at quite a pace. There was nothing she could do but sit and wait, and – if she could find a way to concentrate on anything but her fears – read Mr Legh's book.

# CHAPTER 6

*The following day*

*SHRIGLEY HALL*

## William

'Mr Turner?' Ackroyd had appeared at the door. 'Mr Grimsditch awaits you in the … Beg pardon, sir?'

William whipped round as his ever-perceptible butler took in the scene. Jane was still sobbing quietly, Miss Davis wringing her hands, and Robert pale as death. There was little use trying to hide anything from Ackroyd, but it struck William now how important it was that they keep up appearances.

He managed a smile for Ackroyd and shook his head. 'Show Grimsditch to my study, Ackroyd. I'll be there presently.'

Ackroyd looked doubtful, but obligingly nodded and pulled the door closed behind him.

There followed a silence, in which William strove to gather his scattered wits. The news from the school was beyond anything he could ever have imagined. Ellen was a sensible girl, an intelligent girl. He knew, with a significant degree of certainty, that *she* knew how important it was that she marry well, as his sole heir. She would never, ever run off with someone. He couldn't believe it. Wouldn't believe it.

Unfortunately, the alternative was too terrifying to even contemplate.

'I'm sure there's simply been a misunderstanding,' he said, to himself as much as to the others. 'It will be something and nothing.'

Jane looked up at him imploringly. 'Do you think so? Oh, please say you do.' She struggled to sit upright. 'Perhaps it's a jaunt? Perhaps she has gone to stay with Lavinia, or … or …'

'Hester?' Miss Davis supplied.

'Yes, Hester!' It will be something like that, won't it, William?'

'Perhaps, between us and Grimsditch,' Robert said, taking hold of his arm, 'we can fathom what is going on and decide what to do for the best. Shall we?'

William nodded and patted Robert's hand. But as he prepared to leave the room, an awful thought occurred to him. He cleared his throat.

'Ah, Miss Davis … I am extremely grateful for your kindness towards my wife.'

Miss Davis smiled up at him from her post beside his wife's chair. 'It is my pleasure to render any assistance that I can, in such a difficult situation.'

William nodded and swallowed. 'I'm sure that under the circumstances, we can … rely on your utmost discretion?'

'Oh, of course,' Miss Davis said. The compassion in her face showed that she fully understood his dilemma. 'I know how precious a girl's reputation is. But I really do think …'

William waited for her to go on, but she subsided. He watched her fidget.

'Is something troubling you, Miss Davis?'

'No, not at all, Mr Turner, only …'

He stifled a sigh. 'Only what?'

Miss Davis bit her lip, then looked up at them all with anguished eyes. 'My dearest friends, I hesitate to say this to you, but you may need to prepare yourselves. If this *is* an elopement' – she paused to ensure her words sank in – 'however unlikely that may be, you will need to ensure that the match is acknowledged with all speed, lest a scandal attaches to her, and by extension to you.'

Jane's mouth hung open. William fixed his best social smile on his face and looked directly at the Davis woman, speaking as mildly as he could.

'My dear Miss Davis. If someone has married my child without my permission, I will first of all rend him limb from limb, and then have the—' he swallowed the epithet he wanted to use, hearing the northern tones of his voice edging strongly into his speech '... bounder thrown into prison.'

Jane slumped, and covered her eyes with her handkerchief.

Robert put his hand over his mouth.

Miss Davis swallowed.

★ ★ ★

'How long would it take to get from here to Gretna Green?' William demanded of Grimsditch the moment he and Robert were safely in the study.

'I have no idea, I've never travelled there,' Grimsditch muttered, staring at the carpet. 'Do you know there's tea and china all over the ...' Then he looked up and saw the expression on William and Robert's faces.

'What? What's happened?'

William recounted the whole and handed Grimsditch the letter.

Grimsditch read the missive slowly, and frowned at the floor for some time. He raised his head and gave William a long look. 'I fear you may be right. I fear she may have ... eloped.'

William felt every muscle in his body tense. 'All I'm clinging to at the moment is the hope that she's too intelligent for that.'

Grimsditch nodded cautiously. 'But she's also an impressionable, seventeen-year-old heiress to a considerable fortune – yours and your brother's. It could be the work of moments for an experienced man to convince her they were in love.'

Robert sighed and lifted one shoulder in a shrug. 'He has a point, old thing. And as for this Thevenot chap ... Well, Frenchmen are frightfully popular amongst the ladies.'

'Don't.' William's stomach lurched. 'I can't bear to think that.'

'Or,' Robert said gently, 'have you considered it could be ...'

William's heart beat heavily in his ears as his brother put into words the fear he hadn't voiced, even to himself.

'... an abduction?'

William squeezed his eyes closed. All he could do was nod, then move the conversation on. He needed to act decisively, not wallow. 'Grimsditch. Would you go and speak to Mr Legh, the magistrate, for me today? We'll need him fully apprised of the situation if it is an elopement or ...' he grimaced and waved his hand. 'I trust in his discretion, and we may need his support.'

Grimsditch nodded. 'Will you join me?'

William shook his head. 'The more I think on it, the more I feel that this ... fiasco will end up at Gretna, one way or another.'

'Could you have a letter sent to the chapel, warning them not to proceed with any marriage? Perhaps something from Legh alongside?' Grimsditch said.

A plan was crystalising in William's head. He thought, then rubbed a hand over his mouth.

'No, I can get there faster myself.' He looked at Robert and could see the glimmer in his eye too.

'Are you thinking ...'

William nodded. Robert had always been his partner in crime when they were young.

Grimsditch looked from one to the other. 'You can't be serious.'

'I am. The letter is dated yesterday. If they make an overnight stop, which surely they would do, we can overtake them.' He looked at his brother. 'Do you think?'

Robert's grin was conspiratorial. 'If we go hell for leather, I'd say with certainty.'

William nodded. Decision taken. 'We could be there by early morning.'

Robert rushed from the room to prepare, and William rang for Ackroyd. He felt charged with a genuine sense of purpose, now he was resuming some semblance of control over the situation.

Grimsditch rose too, and clasped William's arm. 'You are right. There's a possibility you could stop all this nonsense. I shall go directly to Lyme Park and keep an ear to the ground in your absence.'

'Good man,' said William. 'And could you do some detective work on this Monsieur Thevenot? We need to find out who he is, and fast.'

'Of course. And, Turner,' Grimsditch squeezed his arm once more. 'Good luck.'

Grimsditch closed the door behind him, and William crossed the study – stepping over the shards of china on the now wet carpet – to open his safe. He hesitated a moment before pulling out the contents: a beautiful walnut box that contained his brace of pistols. As he checked them over, the cold metal and polished wood felt heavy and reassuring in his hand. They were clean and primed, as always.

He raised one of the guns in front of him and looked down the barrel. He was a damned good shot, he thought grimly. Part of him hoped he wouldn't need to use it. As for the other part … well. He smiled and strode off to meet his brother.

# CHAPTER 7

*The previous day*

## THE ALBION HOTEL, MANCHESTER

*Edward*

'She's here!'

Edward Gibbon Wakefield glanced briefly at his younger brother, James, who had just burst noisily into the hotel room. Then he returned his gaze to the looking glass.

'How does she seem?' Edward asked.

James looked flustered and more than a little out of breath. 'Thevenot says she wants to go and wait for the doctor at her uncle's house. Apparently, he lives but a moment away on Oldham Street.'

Edward raised both eyebrows. 'Well, clearly, we cannot allow that. Is her uncle in residence?'

'I'm not sure, which is why we need to ensure that she doesn't go, just in case.'

'Keep her in the hotel.'

'Thevenot is trying, but she's a determined little thing. She wants—'

'Brother, calm yourself.'

'You are going to have to talk to her. You're the one with all the charm and persuasion at your fingertips, not me.'

Edward continued putting the finishing touches to his appearance – an infinitesimal adjustment to his shirt point, a stray hair secured – and looked this way and that, before determining that he would.

'Is everything ready?'

James nodded and tugged at his ear, a sure sign that his concern was increasing.

'I've arranged the horses, drivers, refreshment … I think we have thought of everything.'

'It's a long journey, so we must keep her fed and watered. The last thing we need is an out of sorts child on our hands.'

James came to stand before him. 'Are you sure about this, Edward? It's a hellish thing to do. Frances made it seem so straightforward, but how will we keep Miss Turner quiet? How will we keep her compliant? How in God's name will you get her to agree to even come with us?'

'Leave that to me.'

James looked profoundly unsure. 'Edward, she's only seventeen years old.'

Edward made an effort and smiled at his brother. He patted him on the shoulder. 'I know, and I will be the perfect gentleman. The gentleman of her dreams. I will be everything she thinks she wants. You'll see.'

'Christ, I wish I had your nerve.'

'Enough!' Still eyeing himself in the mirror, Edward attached the last of his fobs and allowed his quizzing glass to dangle at just the right length, before donning his smart brown frock coat. He spoke to his brother without looking at him and lowered his tone again. 'If you are faint of heart, I suggest you go running back to Frances. I'm sure she'll be delighted to hear of your cowardice.'

'But—'

Edward made a sharp move in James's direction and his brother flinched. He raised a hand but simply tweaked James's cravat and fixed him with a glare.

'I said, enough.'

★  ★  ★

## Frances

Frances sat in a small, private parlour of the Albion Hotel in Piccadilly, sipping a cup of tea. The tea, she noted, was not the same quality as Mrs Turner's, but not bad for the price she'd paid. She put the cup down carefully as the door opened to admit her husband's elder – and in her opinion, more intelligent – son.

'You made it?' Edward said.

She arched an eyebrow. 'Evidently.'

'How is my father?'

'In very good health, I'm pleased to say.' *And completely absorbed in his own little world*, she didn't add.

Edward took the chair opposite her without waiting to be invited.

'Ellen Turner is here. We will begin our journey in about half an hour.'

'Excellent news. I will make my way back to Pott Shrigley. I will be there in time to pay a call on my good friend, her mother.'

Edward laughed softly. 'If, as things unfold, you could assure the Turners of my excellent pedigree and profound kindness to children and small animals, I should be most appreciative.'

Frances inclined her head with a smile and regarded him. 'You will need to be very persuasive, my dear. You will find Mr Turner a cat of different stripe to people you have dealt with before.'

Edward shrugged and held her gaze. 'What papa wouldn't want to settle a generous amount on his daughter to keep the scandalmongers at bay? What else is there for him to do? Kick up a fuss? The damage to the family's reputation would be utterly irreparable. She would be beyond the pale even before her debut.'

'Yes, I agree, but you would do well to heed my words. Turner has a stubborn streak.'

Edward let his arm rest along the back of the sofa on which he sat, one leg crossed artlessly over the other. He really was the most confident of men. But his confidence often inclined to hubris, and he would need to learn a degree of caution if the enterprise was to succeed.

'I do heed your words, my dearest … Mama. After all, we wouldn't be here without your sterling planning, words of advice, and inner knowledge of the Turner family. But Turner is an industrialist from the North of England. He came from nothing, and he will do everything in his power to make sure he retains his position. Trust me.'

Frances considered him. If he thought that *northern* jibe would rankle, he was way off the mark. She did, however, acknowledge the words for what they were; a warning that she was as embroiled in this crime as he was.

'Be that as it may, my dearest one,' Frances purred, 'he still has rough edges that need to be … mellowed.'

'You and James.' He smirked. 'Always worrying. Any more pearls of wisdom before we go?'

Frances had to admit, Edward's infallible self-assurance was compelling. And what they were planning took fortitude, particularly when dealing with a family like the Turners. She hoped he would succeed. Not least because if Edward got his hands on the Turners's fortune, he would leave Mr Wakefield

Senior alone. She needed Edward out of his father's life before he bled the old man dry.

'Just' – she leaned in conspiratorially and took a final sip of her tea – 'don't make a dog's breakfast of this.'

Edward gave her an answering slow smile that anyone watching would have taken for flirtation. After all, she was not much older than his thirty years.

'Whatever you say … Mama.'

# CHAPTER 8

*Ellen*

Ellen was cold and uncomfortable by the time she reached Manchester. She dismounted the dreadful barouche eagerly, and felt a profound sense of relief when she saw they had stopped outside the Albion Hotel in Piccadilly.

'Oh, this is perfect!' she said to Monsieur Thevenot, who had handed her down. 'My Uncle Robert lives just around the corner. I will be able to go to the house and wait there. He only lives on Oldham Street. Do you know it?' She held up a hand to shield her eyes from the sun, enormously relieved by the idea that she could enlist her uncle's support. 'Where is Dr Hull?'

Thevenot, who had been peering over her head into one of the hotel's ground floor windows, looked momentarily lost. 'Pardon?' It was said in a terribly French way that made Ellen smile.

'I am supposed to meet him here. He is going to tell me about my mama.'

'Ah, of course, my apologies. If you would follow me inside the hotel, the doctor will meet you here.'

Ellen wanted nothing more than to run around the corner to her uncle's house, but she didn't want to appear rude, and she certainly didn't want to miss Dr Hull. So she drew herself up to her full height and strode with confidence, like she imagined a sophisticated lady would, through the doors of the Albion.

She'd never ventured inside a hotel before, and it was remarkable. She tried not to stare, tried to act as though she did this kind of thing regularly. There were high vaulted ceilings, and the most luxurious of fittings with an abundance of crystal chandeliers. The lobby was warm, and hummed with the genteel conversation of the guests. Ellen looked around her as Monsieur Thevenot spoke with the manager, and then guided her to a charming room that overlooked the old infirmary.

Ellen thanked him, took off her gloves, and sat in a comfortable chair by the fire.

'Could you make sure that a message is sent to my uncle?' she asked. She felt sure that Uncle Robert would come immediately, if he was at home. She was particularly fond of him, because he was always ready to help her with whatever scrape she'd managed to get herself into. And she was forced to admit, there'd been plenty over the years.

'I will arrange it, miss.' Monsieur Thevenot appeared to be very good at looking in her direction but not quite at her. 'Refreshment will be served presently.'

'I'm not sure I will need to stay for long. When will Dr Hull be here?'

'He will be along shortly.'

Before Ellen could ask further questions, Thevenot bowed and left, just as a maid arrived with a tray of food. She arranged the light meal of roasted chicken and vegetables on a table, and then brought a fruit tart and some custard. Ellen ate as much as she could and then, when there was still no sign of either Dr

Hull or her uncle, decided she needed to take matters into her own hands. It would be the work of moments to walk around the corner to her uncle's house. So close as to render a chaperone unnecessary, she assured herself.

On opening the door, however, she discovered a tall, fair-haired gentleman blocking her path. A very handsome fair-haired gentleman, dressed in a brown frock coat.

'Miss Turner?'

Ellen bobbed a quick curtsy. Handsome though he may be, she needed to get rid of him.

'I am Miss Turner. May I be of assistance?'

'I suspect it is I who can be of assistance,' he said with a kindly smile.

'We haven't been introduced, have we?'

The man shook his head. 'Allow me to remedy that immediately. Captain Wilson, at your service.' He bowed low.

'Pleased to make your acquaintance, Captain Wilson. Now, I don't mean to be horribly rude, but I have to meet with someone, so if you don't mind …?'

He moved closer to her, so she stepped back. He followed and that brought him into the room. Ellen swallowed and held up her chin.

'My dear Miss Turner, I have something that I need to tell you. A message from your dear papa that is sensitive enough for me to not wish to disclose it on your doorstep.'

Ellen's heart leaped. Her papa couldn't possibly be back from London yet. 'How do you know my papa?'

Ellen was a tall girl, but Captain Wilson was much taller. He looked down at her. 'Might you be so kind as to let me in so that I can explain?'

'Perhaps Monsieur Thevenot should join us, or the maid? I shouldn't be alone in a hotel room with a gentleman.' She felt awfully uneasy. She couldn't imagine any circumstance where she could be forgiven for entertaining a gentleman in her room. Nor could she imagine why any gentleman would ask it of her.

He paused, and then spoke quietly. 'My dear Miss Turner, you will not wish anyone to overhear. If you are concerned for propriety, perhaps we could leave the door open?'

Ellen hesitated, unsure what to do. She could almost hear her mother and Miss Daulby shrieking in her ear not to put herself in such a terrible position.

But it was no good, she needed to know what he wanted to say. She squared her shoulders. 'Very well, come in, but please leave the door open.'

Captain Wilson bowed again and stepped over the threshold, opening the door wide before looking at her for approval. Ellen went to stand by the window, and he followed. He stood close to her, too close. He was wearing cologne that was so strong it made her blink.

He looked grave. 'I would give anything to not have to deliver this message to you.'

Her heart fluttered in her chest like a wind-blown leaf. 'Please go on.'

'First, I have some good tidings: your mama is not ill.'

'Yes, she is – I saw the letter.'

Now it was his turn to blink. 'You did?'

'I stole it and read it. It was shocking, and I need to confer with Dr Hull as a matter of urgency. In fact, I was just on my way to see my uncle and enlist his support.'

Wilson licked his lips and nodded, a faint frown marring the perfection of his brow. 'The letter was sent to Miss Daulby to ensure that she allowed you to leave straight away. Your father and I did not want to disclose the real reason for your departure, as this would have caused significant embarrassment.'

Ellen gawped at the man. 'My *papa* sent the letter?'

'He did indeed.'

'But it wasn't his handwriting.'

Wilson paused, then nodded. 'He dictated it.'

Ellen was utterly unable to understand why her papa would do such a thing. Could this day get any stranger?

Wilson took a breath as though fortifying himself. 'The bank that had all your father's holdings has collapsed.'

The words hit Ellen like a blow. Her hands went to her cheeks. 'No, no, that cannot have happened to Papa!'

'I'm afraid it has, and … and … I'm so very sorry, but his fortune may be lost. He is keeping things as quiet as possible for the moment, as secrecy with these issues can, quite frankly, be life or death, but the situation is dire. He is even now fighting to see what can be salvaged.'

*All Papa's money was gone?* What would become of them? Shrigley Hall, the High Sheriff position … Ellen lowered her hands to her skirts, gripped them hard, and began to pace the room. She recalled the crash the previous year, and poor Miss Greenaway from school, whose father's business interests collapsed along with his bank. She'd been obliged to leave Break House for good!

Wilson came to stand near her again, and she could feel the heat from his body. She moved away from him, and tried to speak normally.

'Which bank was it?'

Captain Wilson regarded her intently. 'You know your father's banking arrangements?'

'I do. I pay attention. Is it Ryle and Daintry or Blackburn?'

Wilson raised his eyebrows. Most likely, it was extremely unladylike to know such things, but she was in no mood to play to the man's expectations. She needed to get home to her family.

'I'm afraid it is Ryle and Daintry of Macclesfield.'

Ellen could barely suppress a shudder.

'My dear, your papa has instructed me to take you to him in Huddersfield.'

'He is in London – why would I go to Huddersfield?'

'Your papa returned immediately he received the news but felt it unwise to alight to Shrigley Hall. Instead, he fled to Huddersfield, where, well, he is less likely to be recognised by his creditors. It is imperative that he remain undetected until we can see if his position can be restored.'

Ellen nodded and swallowed. 'Right. I see. Do we need to leave now?'

'We do. Your papa has asked that I take you to him with all speed, and he asked that you bear up as best you can until you are reunited with him.'

'I would like to go and see my uncle before we leave. He will be able to help us.'

'Sadly, Mr Turner is not at home. I checked before coming to you as I too had hoped to enlist his support.'

Ellen strained to remain calm. The main thing was her mother was not ill, and her father needed her with him. As terrifying as it might seem, there was nothing to be done other than follow the instructions he had given to the man standing before her. If her father trusted him, then she must too.

She looked up, sucked in a breath, straightened her skirts, and looked at Captain Wilson. 'Tell me what to do.'

# CHAPTER 9

Ellen gathered her things together with shaking hands. This was abominable. How would they go on? Everything in their lives had been splendid. The move to Shrigley Hall, and all the work to make it one of the most beautiful, welcoming houses Ellen had ever seen. Just as they were about to launch forth with the public celebration of Papa's success, the peak of everything he had worked for, it was all about to come crumbling about their ears. She couldn't bear it.

She closed her portmanteau and handed it to a young footman to take it to Captain Wilson's waiting carriage. Alone in the unfamiliar room, she looked at herself in the mirror. Her cheeks were pale and her eyes wide with shock. She closed them for a moment, squared her shoulders, and took a deep breath and set off to meet Captain Wilson in the lobby.

He spotted her approach and moved swiftly, flashing her a brilliant smile, far too brilliant for the circumstances, in her opinion. Her expression must have betrayed her feeling, because he moved closer to murmur in her ear.

'Might I suggest we put on a brave face? One never knows who is watching. If you could give me a pretty smile, and perhaps offer a little conversation as we take our leave, we should be able to allay suspicion that aught is amiss.'

Ellen immediately stood tall and summoned a bright tone of voice. 'Have you noticed the clock on the infirmary?' she said as she fell into step beside him. 'It's the most curious thing.'

He took her hand, tucked it into his elbow with a conspiratorial smile, and began walking. 'Do tell!'

She managed to rattle on about the odd clock, as a footman opened the door to allow them outside.

'You are doing magnificently, my dear,' Captain Wilson whispered, his breath tickling her cheek.

Ellen leaned away from him and kept a smile on her face until they arrived beside the green barouche, where Thevenot was waiting. The captain slipped him a few coins, and he bade them a good onward journey – still not looking either of them in the eye – before slinking away down the street.

'Are we travelling in this?'

'I think it best. No one will recognise it.'

Ellen nodded despite her sinking heart. She might have suggested procuring something more comfortable, if he hadn't looked the tiniest bit put out at her question.

Before they boarded, another young man approached them. He too was handsome, and dressed like a gentleman, but with a rather more timid countenance than her companion.

He walked up to them, offered a tight, anxious smile, and bowed.

Captain Wilson did the niceties. 'Miss Turner, might I introduce my brother, James Wakefield?'

She dropped a light curtsy and wondered why, if they were brothers, the two gentlemen had different surnames. She forbore from asking and boarded the carriage – she wanted to be on the way – but she was shocked when both gentlemen followed suit and sat opposite her. She shrank in her seat and clutched her reticule. If anyone found out she was doing this, her life in society would be over before it began. What's more, they were both large and the carriage felt small and crowded with them in it. But if they sensed her qualms, they didn't show it.

The carriage jolted as the horses pulled forward out of the yard, and Captain Wilson pulled down the blinds on the carriage windows, making the interior even more dingy than it already was.

'Gentlemen,' she said as they bowled along. 'Does either of you have a wife or a sister who could travel with us, for propriety?'

Mr James Wakefield gave her a sympathetic smile. 'I'm afraid I won't have a wife for another couple of weeks.'

'My congratulations on your impending nuptials.'

The captain lowered his gaze, and seemed to speak with difficulty. 'I am afraid I am a widower.'

'My condolences, sir.' The words came by rote, and she did feel sorry for his loss, but it didn't change the situation.

She tried again. 'The reason I ask is, I can't think of anything more guaranteed to draw unwanted attention than for me to be discovered travelling in a closed carriage, unchaperoned, by two unmarried, eligible gentlemen.'

The brothers glanced at each other.

'You are quite right,' Mr James Wakefield said. 'We will, of course, travel outside the carriage when we don't need to talk in private.'

Ellen nodded stiffly, wondering what more there was to say. 'And how long might it take for us to reach Huddersfield?'

Surprisingly, the captain smiled. 'You are an inquisitive little soul, aren't you?'

Well, there wasn't much to say to that. It came from being an only child to a rich man. He'd prepared her for the world. Or at least he'd tried to, but nothing could have prepared her for this. What she wouldn't give to be back in school with Lavinia and Hester, bored to tears in needlework classes!

She kept her tone even. 'I suppose I am.'

'My dear one,' the captain said, head tilted to one side, 'we will first arrive at Delph, where we will change horses. We will water the horses at Marsden, and, all things being equal, we will arrive in Huddersfield to meet your papa early evening. Will that do?' He arched an eyebrow at her, and the smile lingered. She had the distinct impression he was humouring her as one might a child.

Ellen nodded. 'That will do very well, thank you,' she said primly. There was something discomfiting about this man, and she wasn't sure she liked him above much.

'Miss Turner?'

The captain's tone was serious again, which made her nervous. 'Yes?'

'Now we are away from prying eyes, may I talk frankly to you?'

Anxiety pooled in the pit of Ellen's stomach. 'I thought you had been frank. You mean there is more?'

The captain smiled but his eyes were watchful. 'My poor dear, you must be wondering what on earth is going on, but we can't be careful enough with this venture.' He looked at his hands briefly, then back at her, his solemn gaze holding hers.

'My name is not Captain Wilson.'

'Oh, I see.' She didn't, not at all, but she waited for the explanation, feeling as though she had fallen asleep and woken up in the middle of a farce.

'My name is Edward Gibbon Wakefield. I am a very good friend of your father's, and I am deeply honoured that he has entrusted your safety, and indeed your safe conduct, to me.'

Ellen nodded and tried to hold on to her composure.

'I used a false name at the hotel so that no one would connect me to your father. I cannot emphasise enough how important discretion is until you are safely delivered to him. No one must know that your father has even the slightest qualm, until he is ready to reveal his position. There still may be the smallest chance that he can undo some of the damage.'

Ellen stared at the brothers who sat before her and tried to take in the enormity of the situation. How on earth could her father rescue the position with the bank if it had failed? Why was her father hiding? None of it made any sense.

She quashed the rising panic, because there was nothing else to do. There was only one way she could find out what was going on.

And that was to go with the Wakefields.

★   ★   ★

## Edward

By the time they reached Delph, Edward felt as though he might, just might, be making a modicum of progress with his heiress. She was a wilful one, that was for certain. If this was what education did to young girls, he was fast forming the opinion it should be banned, lest the fabric of society be grievously disturbed. Far too many questions, and far too many *opinions*, made wooing troublesome. He was loath to admit it, but there was probably something to be heeded in Frances's warnings. As they pulled into the yard of the Blue Ball Inn, Ellen had succumbed enough to laugh at his latest tale, but it had taken considerable exertion to achieve it. He was feeling pleased with himself when he got out to arrange the horses and the postilion. James followed, leaving Ellen alone in the carriage.

'I think Frances was right,' James said as he walked alongside him. 'She isn't like most girls I've met.'

Edward snorted. 'She is from the North.' It needed no further explanation. Frankly, was she not heir to the most phenomenal fortune, he would have abandoned the plan.

★　★　★

## Ellen

Ellen sat back in the coach with a sigh of relief. The Wakefield brothers had opted to sit outside for the next leg of the journey. It was stuffy and uncomfortable enough in the coach with just her.

She pressed her fingers to her temples, in an attempt to quell the headache that thudded behind her eyes. She was afraid and weary. Her head flopped against the squabs, and she looked out of the window at the passing scenery without really seeing it, until her mind drifted back to Thomas Legh.

She reached out and pulled her reticule to her, opened it, and took out the book that she'd hurriedly put in there.

She smiled. There was always something soothing about the feel of a book in her hands, and she settled herself by pulling her feet up onto the seat and tucking her skirts beneath her, with the book propped against her knees. Her mother would be beyond mortified, and Miss Daulby would have suspended privileges for the rest of her life had she seen her, but she didn't care. The circumstances were extreme, and she needed to take her mind off things. The light wasn't going to last for long, so she adjusted the blanket and read.

He had a lovely way of writing that made the reader truly feel like a companion on the journey. She let Thomas – boldly, she thought of him as 'Thomas' now – become her companion in turn, as she read of the terrifying plague that had affected the whole of Asia Minor in 1812, and forced him to quarantine in Malta for almost a month. She couldn't fathom what it must be like to have one's liberties so restrained, to be unable to go out and see people! Next, she followed him to the Gulf of Lepanto, just in time to witness the uncovering of a frieze that had been discovered in the Temple of Apollo in Phigalia. It was, frankly, fascinating, and as the unfamiliar places and names rolled around her head, she couldn't help but imagine Thomas in the intense heat, in his shirtsleeves, white linen clinging to his body. By the time she emerged from the book, as breathless as if she'd just taken a long swim in the glittering waters of the Ionian, it was sunset, and the sky was as pink as her cheeks. She sorely wanted to write to Hester and Lavinia and tell them of her newest fantasy, of mopping Thomas's tender brow and the rather vulnerable nape of his neck where his dark hair curled.

# CHAPTER 10

The carriage stopped sometime later to water the horses, and Edward Wakefield got back in. She sat primly on the seat whilst he sprawled opposite her.

'Saddleworth Moor has to be the bleakest place in Christendom,' he pronounced with such exaggerated disdain, the surprise of it made Ellen laugh.

'Have you travelled much?' she asked.

He waggled his eyebrows at her. 'My dear, I have travelled the world, and trust me when I say Saddleworth Moor on a dreary day is the worst thing to encounter. I'm impressed you have the fortitude to remain alert.'

Ellen laughed again, wondering how he would have managed with the plague in Asia Minor if Saddleworth Moor aggrieved him so much.

As the landlord made sure that the horses were watered, James Wakefield spoke to him at some length, leaving her alone with Wakefield the elder. She expected him to join his brother, but he settled himself comfortably and regarded her.

'You really are quite the bravest of young women.'

Ellen looked away, uncomfortable with the compliment. 'Hardly.'

'But here you are, embarking on this journey with nary a complaint. You've met everything with charm and grace. I must tell you: I admire you.'

'That is very kind of you to say.' She tried not to squirm in her seat, but her feeling of awkwardness intensified significantly when the carriage pulled away without James and she realised that she was stuck with Wakefield for the next part of the journey. He was still looking at her.

'You mentioned that you had travelled widely. Where do you call home now?' As conversational gambits went, it wasn't exactly scintillating, but it was all she could muster.

He smiled. 'I have several residences, but currently I can be found in Cheshire.'

'Really? Are you close to Shrigley then?'

Wakefield nodded, rested his hands across his midriff – which she couldn't help remarking was flat and firm – and let his legs spread wide. He regarded her through sleepy-looking eyes. 'Tell me, if you were to travel, where would you go?'

Well, that was much more comfortable ground. As Thomas's book quietly burned a hole in her reticule, she launched forth about all the places she would find fascinating. The faintly horrified look in Wakefield's eye didn't trouble her, and she had to own that she exaggerated her ambition to visit the Amazon. Just to see him blink but maintain a strained, polite smile.

\* \* \*

By the time they reached Huddersfield and the George Inn, Ellen had to bite back a sigh of relief. It was dark, and she strained to spot her father's carriage through the glass.

'Do you think Papa will be here already?'

'I will find out for you.'

With that, Wakefield opened the door and was gone. Fear had returned and now sat solidly in her stomach. Fear for her family, fear that she would be seen travelling with unmarried men, fear about what all this would do to her mother.

Suddenly she felt an acute need to be out of the dreadful barouche, and she was contemplating her escape when James Wakefield appeared, wearing a bright smile, and bid her accompany him into the warm tavern.

Ellen remembered the need to pretend that all was well, so she smiled in return and allowed him to lead her into a parlour. There, they found Edward Wakefield, standing by the hearth, his face a picture of commiseration.

'My dear, I'm so sorry. Your papa is not here.'

★  ★  ★

## Edward

Edward watched as the girl made a soft sound of distress and sank into a chair. She kept her eyes on the floor for a moment, and blinked rapidly. Edward steeled his expression to one of abject sympathy.

'Have you had word?'

Edward watched her carefully. 'I have,' he said, feeling his way with her responses.

'What did Papa say?'

Edward crouched by the chair so he could look into her eyes. He cocked his head to one side and went on in tones that were, he felt, soothing yet with just the right amount of fretfulness. 'He left us word to say that he loves you very much, that he's sorry you are in this frightful position, but … well, that he's heading for Carlisle. And he begs that we follow him.'

She stared at him, an edge of desperation in her dark gaze. 'Carlisle? But … that's miles away, days away! Why didn't he wait for me here?'

'I know, I know.' He patted her hand, but she removed it from under his, so he lowered himself into the chair opposite her and spoke gently. 'You must be so terribly disappointed. I suspect it was vital he keep moving, but if we travel swiftly, we may meet up with him on the road. He's not that far ahead of us.'

She nodded, seemingly struggling to contain the tears that made her eyes shine, her mouth a pinched line.

'May I see the note?'

Did *nothing* get past this girl? 'I burned it. It's too dangerous to leave something like that lying around.'

He could see she wanted to say something about that. Although she held her tongue and nodded, he caught a mistrustful look in her eye and, for a moment, heard Frances's barbed warning echo in his mind. *Don't make a dog's breakfast of this.* He felt his jaw clench. This girl was damned inquisitive, but *he* was damned if he was going to let her outwit him.

It was, he realised, time for something more to convince her. He relaxed his face and held up his hands, to signal he had nothing to hide. 'I can't show you the letter, but he did ask me to give you this.' He reached inside his coat and pulled out the monogrammed handkerchief that Frances had filched.

She took it tentatively, and traced the initials with her finger. It was a moment before she could speak. 'I made this for him,' she whispered. 'I stitched it all when I was ten. He was so happy with it.'

Edward's confidence came rushing back, and he risked a smile. 'He said you would recognise it. Fear not, my dear, we shall have you reunited before you know.'

She nodded and Edward said a silent *huzzah* at the success of the ploy. Not only was she won over, but for the first time she was even looking at him with *gratitude*. He decided he might rather enjoy the challenge of making her fall in love with him after all.

# CHAPTER 11

*The following day*

*NEAR HUDDERSFIELD*

*William*

William Turner patted his pockets as the carriage rattled along at a fair clip.

'I say, Robert, I don't suppose you have a spare handkerchief? I could have sworn I had one on me.'

Robert held tight to the strap as the driver feathered a particularly tight bend, then handed one over. 'Damn this weather,' he said, staring out of the window at the driving rain. 'It shouldn't take this long to get to Huddersfield. Perhaps we should have gone a different way?'

William shook his head. 'It is difficult terrain, but this is still the fastest route north.'

He couldn't believe that he was engaged in a dash to the border. And even if they made it in time, would they find Ellen there? Never in his life had he felt so ... desperate, or so helpless.

'Do you want stop at the George for lunch?' Robert said, doubt evident in his tone.

William shook his head. 'We need to keep moving. If the weather allows, we should travel through the night too.'

Without a moment's hesitation, Robert nodded. 'That might give us the edge. This Thevenot has no idea the plot has been rumbled, and if they *are* bound for Gretna, they may travel slowly. We shall have the advantage of surprise.'

William clapped a hand on his brother's shoulder, grateful that they were of one mind. But nothing could stop his anxiety from ramping ever higher. 'Do you really think it's an abduction?' he asked, unable to hide the pleading tone in his voice.

Robert sighed and ran a hand around the back of his neck. 'The more I think of it, the more I do. Something untoward must have been at play. Ellen must have been taken out of that school, by subterfuge or by force.'

William swallowed. He knew in his bones that Robert was right, but he didn't know if that made the situation better or worse.

'I hope Jane is bearing up,' William said after a few moments of silence.

Robert grimaced. 'It hit her terribly hard,' he said. 'The Davis woman seems like a good sort. If she remains with her, then I imagine Jane will come around.'

William nodded. He couldn't see Jane coming around until she had Ellen safely back home, and even then, it would probably take some time, but he kept that to himself.

'Fear not, brother,' Robert said. 'We will get her back. Just think, in a few weeks' time Ellen will be home, this nightmare will be over, and you will be celebrating your investiture as a family, surrounded by all your friends.'

William sat back in his seat. Robert's words sounded like wishful thinking. What's more, the thought of celebrating his success now was far from soothing. The investiture would involve a grand banquet, a ceremony, and a parade in front of all the local dignitaries and townspeople. Could such a celebration go ahead, if his name was mired in scandal? Would he lose his position as High Sheriff? Was that even possible? If it was, his family's fledgling place in polite society might be cast to the winds. All he'd worked for, snatched away by a mere rumour.

He swallowed. He must try to stop his head running away from him. God, if they could just overtake this Thevenot character. If they could just get Ellen home, safe and sound.

# CHAPTER 12

*The previous day*

*NEAR HALIFAX*

*Ellen*

Ellen had no idea at all what the time was; all she knew was it was dark and cold. The bricks they had put in the carriage at Huddersfield had lost their warmth, the wind had found every gap in the carriage, and she dared not move for fear she would bump into Edward Wakefield's knees. Her head thumped along to the rhythm of the horses' hooves.

She watched as James Wakefield's eyes fluttered, then drifted closed. His head lolled as the motion of the carriage rocked him to sleep. She wished she could do the same, but her mind seemed to have other ideas. She wished she could read her book, but it was too dark. She sighed and fidgeted.

'Are you terribly uncomfortable?' Edward Wakefield asked in a low voice.

'Not terribly.'

'Just a little?'

Ellen nodded and tried to smile. He shifted his position and moved his knees out of the way. 'I wish there was more I could do to offer you some comfort.'

'I'm fine, please don't worry about me.'

'But I do worry,' he said softly, looking at her intently. 'I worry a great deal.'

'Thank you, but truly, I'm perfectly fine.'

'So brave,' he whispered and gave her a long, searching look. He'd taken to doing that, and Ellen wasn't quite sure where to look, so she leaned her head back and closed her eyes. After a few moments, she slitted them open to see Edward Wakefield staring ahead, a sullen, almost petulant look on his face. She snapped her eyes shut before he saw her and endured the rest of the journey.

As they drew closer to Halifax, James woke up and made a production of stretching, so Ellen opened her eyes too. The carriage pulled up on Silver Street and drew into the yard of the White Lion. Ellen remembered it well from a visit with her father a few weeks ago. It was exactly where her papa would stop, and her spirits lifted considerably.

Inside the inn was noisy and busy. Staff bustled about, serving people who were talking and laughing. Ellen breathed in the familiar aroma of hops and malt and savoured it. The thought that she might be able to fling herself into her father's arms here, in just a few moments, made her eyes prick with tears.

Edward led them to a private parlour, and he and Ellen sat by the fire whilst James went to see what news awaited them.

'Where did you and Papa come to know each other?' She asked him. He'd said that they were good friends, but he'd never said how.

'We met quite some time ago,' he said, smiling at the fond memory, 'through business, back in the days when you lived in Blackburn.'

'Really? But we've never met before, have we?'

Edward shook his head. 'I don't think so. I tend to move around a lot. I've been working in Paris for the last few years.'

Ellen nodded and waited for him to go on.

'I think it's because I was his friend from the old days, before he came up in the world, that your papa felt he could trust in my absolute discretion.'

Ellen supposed that made sense. Edward then changed the subject, and tried to engage her in conversation about the sights of Halifax. She was nodding along politely to his rather lengthy description of the Piece Hall – *a veritable marvel of modern architecture*, as he put it – when James returned, closing the door carefully behind him.

'Any word?' she asked immediately, fearing she knew the answer.

James hesitated, tugged at his ear, then shook his head. 'I'm so sorry, Miss Turner. He's not here, and he hasn't left word either.'

'He probably travelled straight on without stopping,' said Edward, matter-of-factly.

Ellen did her best to appear unmoved, but she suspected it was a poor attempt. 'What needs to be done now?'

Edward ran a hand over his mouth and appeared to arrive at a decision. He gave her a strangely intense look and lowered his voice.

'Just how brave are you, Ellen Turner?'

Ellen blinked, shocked at the challenging tone and the use of her full name. 'Brave enough.'

He stood and loomed over her, making her want to shrink away, but she held her ground.

'Are you sure? Are you certain?' he said.

Ellen nodded and lifted her chin.

'Your papa must keep moving before his creditors descend upon him, because once that happens, any chance he has to rectify the situation will be lost. That means, if you wish to be reunited, we too must get to Carlisle with all speed.'

Ellen nodded again, heart thumping hard in her chest, mouth dry.

'Do you propose setting off at the crack of dawn tomorrow?' James asked.

Edward shook his head, not taking his gaze from Ellen for a moment. 'No, that's why I need to know how brave you are.'

Ellen swallowed. 'What are you suggesting?'

'I'm suggesting that we don't stop for the night.'

Ellen gawked at him. Spend the night in an enclosed carriage, with two unmarried gentlemen? It was a deranged notion, an idea so perverse she didn't know whether to laugh in Mr Wakefield's face or keel over on the parlour floor. But … on the other hand, how could she abandon her dear papa, when he'd asked for her?

'Well, my dear?' Edward said, snapping her out of her reverie. She looked at him. His gaze was level. Was she brave enough? Could she risk all to save her father? She thought of the handkerchief she'd embroidered for him, nestled in her reticule, and knew the answer.

She returned his stare. 'I agree. We should leave for Carlisle immediately.'

A slow smile spread across Edward's face, and as he looked down at her, something kindled in it.

'You are wise beyond your years, Ellen Turner.'

★　★　★

## Edward

As they walked back to the carriage, Edward made a point of taking Ellen's hand and tucking it into his elbow. She stiffened but made no attempt to remove it.

'Remember,' he breathed into her ear, 'no sad faces. No one must see you are unhappy or afraid, or they will start to gossip about the nature of our journey. We must protect your papa and your reputation at all costs.'

He watched as his words registered. The child wasn't stupid; she'd already articulated that she knew the perils of travelling with an unmarried man. But it might behove him to keep reminding her of it. She'd come far enough now that to make any kind of scene – in other words, to refuse to do as she was told – would be her undoing.

'We shall head for Keighley and then on to Settle. After that, we will make for Kirkby Lonsdale, Kendal, Shap, Penrith, and then to Carlisle.' He reeled off the places quickly, hoping this made the journey ahead sound less arduous than it would be. The last leg – *to Gretna Green* – he kept to himself. For now.

Edward could see that, as their journey progressed, two options lay before him. He could make more of an attempt to woo the girl, to convince her that he was in love with her, and that she was in love with him. Alternatively, he could persuade her that marrying him would save her father, and her, from ruin. He didn't want to labour that point yet – best to hold that in reserve for when he might need it. But if he couldn't make her fall in love with him, the notion that marriage might just save her reputation, and her father's fortune, would tumble her right into his arms.

As the carriage pulled away, he watched the little heiress try and squash herself into the corner of the carriage. James politely moved his knees, but this time, Edward left his where they were.

# CHAPTER 13

*Several hours later*

## Ellen

Ellen woke with a start. For a moment she couldn't remember where she was, but the musty smell in the barouche soon reminded her. It was pitch-black, and they weren't moving. 'Where are we?' she murmured in the dark.

James yawned in response as her eyes adjusted. 'What time is it?' he asked groggily.

Now Ellen could make out Edward, who was squinting at his pocket watch, tilting it this way and that to try and see the face.

'It's one in the morning,' he said. 'We've arrived at the Rose and Crown in Kirkby Lonsdale.'

Ellen must have been asleep for some time. As if he'd read her thoughts, Edward said, 'We stopped in Settle at 10 o'clock, but you both looked so peaceful, I couldn't bear to wake you.' He chuckled to himself. 'There we were, hell bent on a dash to Carlisle through the night, and you two were both sleeping like babes!'

Ellen looked at Edward and had to laugh. It wasn't that funny, but both Edward and James laughed with her. They were still laughing when they heard footsteps outside, and a knock came at the carriage window.

Edward opened the door. A maid and a stable boy greeted them, and the maid passed a plate of something that smelled delicious over and plonked it on Ellen's lap, much to her surprise. 'Gingerbread, on the house,' she said dozily. 'To keep the weary traveller's strength up.' The poor girl's cap was skew-whiff, and she looked like she was half-asleep as she wandered off. Ellen took the plate gratefully, and both Wakefields grabbed a piece, holding it between their teeth as they hopped out to help the stable boy.

Ellen sunk her teeth into the sweet, spiced biscuit. It was the first thing she'd eaten since luncheon in Manchester, and her stomach growled in appreciation. She snuggled down into her blanket, and listened as Edward and James chatted with the stable boy outside.

'By the way,' Edward was saying, 'you don't happen to have seen another carriage pass by here earlier tonight? We're travelling with a friend of ours, but we were delayed and have lost sight of him.'

'Oh yes, sir,' said a voice that must have been the boy's. 'A Mr Turner was here an hour ago, or thereabouts. A beautiful red carriage he had.'

Ellen's ears pricked up. Her father's carriage *was* red! *Dear Lord*, they were so close. If he could wait for her in Carlisle, she'd be able to see him. He would know what to do. She sat back and hugged the blanket close.

\* \* \*

## Edward

They reached Kendal in the small hours of the morning. When Edward handed Ellen down from the carriage, she leaned into him for a moment – a small sign that she had begun to rely on him, and was not wholly immune to his charms. That trick at the Rose and Crown had worked a treat – and the boy had sailed off whistling with coins in his pocket.

'You are so tired, my dear,' he murmured as she took his arm.

'Indeed, if I never see the inside of a barouche again in my life, I will be happy.'

Edward laughed. 'You truly do have the tenacity of a queen. But now, you must rest a few hours whilst I find out if there is word from your papa.'

'Do you expect any word?' The look in her eye told Edward she was sceptical. The last thing he needed at this juncture was her losing heart.

'We have almost caught up with him now.' He laid a hand over hers, and she allowed it to remain there. 'Have faith, angel.'

She looked up, a faintly quizzical look in her eye at the endearment.

They'd been travelling now for almost a full day and night, and he had to admire the girl's fortitude. Her hair was awry, her dress more wrinkled than a tweeny's, but she was still with them, still seemingly willing to join in with the silliest of jokes. Most young women would have been having vapours by now, and he'd half expected tantrums, but it seemed Ellen's spirit would not be easily crushed. He wasn't sure if that boded well for the future or not.

He took her inside the King's Arms, and once she'd disappeared with a maid, he turned to his brother.

'I think we need to act now.'

'In what way?' James looked as worn down as Ellen.

'Come, brother, stay focused!'

'I am, I am, I swear. I'm just hungry and tired.'

'Then we shall breakfast here.'

James sighed in relief. 'Thank God, I'm starving.'

'I think our little heiress may be warming to me,' Edward said.

James considered and nodded.

'I will allow her to rest to restore her spirits, feed her a hearty breakfast, and as we set off for Carlisle, I am going to put the solution to her.'

'You're going to propose? Now?'

'We are about to embark on the most difficult part of the journey. The road to Shap and beyond is steep and rough. She needs something to think about, to be resolute about, perhaps even excited about.'

James didn't look convinced.

'Trust me. By the time I have finished, she will be begging to marry me.'

'Edward, please be gentle. I've grown quite fond of her. If she is to be your wife, I'd rather it be of her choice.'

'You'd best not let your betrothed hear you say that.'

'Not in that way!' he blustered. 'In a brotherly way. She's terribly young.'

'That may be, but she's mature and has character.'

'A character that is stubborn,' James insisted, 'and not given to romantic flights. I'd counsel against pushing too hard too early, really I would.'

James was on thin ice now. Edward fixed him with a particular scowl, one that his brother knew all too well.

James retreated immediately. 'Of course, you should do as you see fit.'

# CHAPTER 14

## THE KING'S ARMS, KENDAL

*Ellen*

With her hair freshly coiffed, a clean dress on, and a breakfast of plump Cumbrian sausages eaten, Ellen felt marvellously restored. Strangely, she had found sleep elusive, but she'd had a couple of hours reading her book in a bed that was infinitely more comfortable than the woeful barouche. This time, she'd accompanied Thomas deep into Alexandria, then to Rosetta, then on towards Cairo and the Mokattam Heights. The mountains put her in mind of her own impending ascent of Shap, and the comparison made her smile a good deal. Perhaps she really was *a fellow adventurer*, as Thomas had called her in his inscription.

She was deep in thought about what it might be like to follow behind him, as he scrambled up a particularly precipitous slope, when she heard a small flurry of activity outside her room. She had already leapt out of bed and was stuffing the book back into her reticule when the door flew open, and Edward burst in.

'Are you ready to leave?' he said unceremoniously.

'I am,' she said, checking her reflection in the mirror. 'I have my coat and reticule here.'

'Then we must depart.'

'What's wrong?' Ellen said, noting a new tension in his voice. Edward took her arm and looked down at her with an oddly tender expression. He let his gaze rove over her features, then shook his head. 'I will explain once we are safely on the road.'

Ellen grasped his hand. 'Is it Papa? Is he here?'

Edward didn't reply and Ellen's heart beat faster. 'Please tell me.'

'I will, but first, I need to get you into the carriage as a matter of urgency.'

Ellen wanted to object. Wanted to refuse, but she realised that if her papa *was* somewhere near, she would need to play along with whatever plan Edward had engineered to see him. So, reluctantly, she left the inn and climbed back into the awful carriage. Moments later, Edward and James clambered in too, and Edward knocked on the roof with his cane. Immediately, the carriage lurched forward.

'What's going on?' she said, looking from one brother to the other. James stared at Edward, expectantly, and before he replied, Edward ran a hand slowly over his hair. Each action filled Ellen with foreboding.

'Your papa was there.'

'What? Then why are you taking us away? Stop immediately, I want to go to him.' She half rose from her seat, but was forced back down by a jolt in the road.

'My dearest one, if that were possible, you would even now be feeling the comfort of his embrace,' Edward said.

The words made tears spring to Ellen's eyes. 'Then why am I being borne away?'

'Yes, Edward,' said James, seemingly as confused as Ellen, 'do tell us why.'

Edward cast James a severe look, which softened when he turned back to Ellen. 'Because the situation is perilous, my dear. I'm afraid there is more to tell.'

Ellen slumped back against the squabs and fought, with all her might, not to break down and sob. Her throat ached with the effort, and when she spoke, her voice cracked. 'Please, just tell me what you know.'

Edward moved to take up a seat beside her, and as the carriage juddered from left to right, it felt like he'd lunged towards her.

'My dearest, bravest of girls,' he murmured. 'I have something to tell you ... and something to put to you.'

'Then please do, I can't bear this any longer.'

'Your father's already precarious position has been further compromised by the collapse of the Blackburn bank.'

Ellen moaned softly. She couldn't believe what she was hearing. If she did, then that would mean her papa's position was beyond rescue.

It took a couple of moments before she could speak. She opened her mouth, but nothing emerged, and she felt a tear splash on her cheek.

'My uncle will be affected too.'

At this, James's face convulsed with pity. Edward took hold of her hands and he ran his thumb gently over her knuckles. She held onto him tight – Lord knew she needed the support – and he took a breath, sending Ellen's pulse tumbling.

'James and I have an uncle, like you,' Edward said. 'Ours lives in Kendal, and I persuaded him to loan your father sixty thousand pounds to help him navigate the collapse of Ryle and

Daintry. To give him every appearance of weathering the storm.'

Ellen looked away, moved by the kindness. 'You did?'

'He agreed, but … there were terms. Terms that your papa accepted.' Edward hesitated and Ellen looked up at him. The anguished look on his face scared Ellen. She waited for him to continue. To tell her what her father had offered as security against the loan.

Edward bit his lip, then continued. 'He put up Shrigley Hall.'

Ellen's heart thudded hard. 'Wh— What are you saying?'

'At the time, your papa was confident he could repay the debt quickly, because he still had the Blackburn bank. But now with the Blackburn bank gone there is no possibility …'

'What will happen now?' Ellen needed it spelled out for her. Needed to know for certain.

Edward closed his eyes momentarily, then looked at her. 'He's asking for his investment to be returned immediately.'

'But … can he do that?'

'I'm afraid he can. He can … take Shrigley Hall from your mama and papa.'

Ellen could barely form words, she was so shocked. Then the wider ramifications of this news struck her with the force of a herd of stampeding horses.

'Are you saying that my mother is about to be turned out of Shrigley Hall? That's … that's cruel! What will she do? Where will she go?' Her voice was shrill, and close to breaking. 'Can't you ask him not to?'

'I … Oh, Ellen, dearest Ellen. There is a solution.'

Ellen gripped his hands tighter. 'Then please tell me what it is, tell me what I can do. I cannot have my mother put out of her home; it would kill her.'

He bowed his head and shocked her when he dropped a fervent kiss on the back of her hand. He seemed to be bracing himself for something, and Ellen wanted to scream at him to get on with it.

'First, you should know that I have become excessively fond of you these past hours that we have been together. Your bravery and your loyalty are utterly commendable.' He paused, and Ellen held her breath.

Edward's eyes closed and Ellen felt tears start to fall.

'There is a way out of this,' he whispered.

'Then tell me what it is! If you say that you are fond of me, tell me!'

'The money is, regrettably, gone. But as for the property … It could be recovered, if it were to become yours.'

The man was talking in riddles. She shook her head, unable to comprehend. Property couldn't become hers; she was a girl. 'That's impossible.'

'It can become yours by deed of marriage. Shrigley would transfer to your husband and be saved.'

'You mean I should marry? How can I marry?'

She looked at Edward and had a dreadful feeling she knew what he was going to say. She began to tremble all over and her breath caught in her throat.

'If … if you would be willing to lower yourself, to … accept *my* most humble suit …'

*Oh God, help me.* Ellen swallowed. 'I'm only seventeen. I can't marry anyone.'

She glanced at James, hoping he'd say something helpful, but he looked as overwhelmed as she. His brow was furrowed, and he was staring down at his shoes as if it was them, not her, that desperately required his attention. Edward squeezed her hands and regained hers. 'We are near Gretna.'

Gretna … get married at Gretna Green? Her head was spinning. Everyone would think they had eloped, that she had gone against her family's wishes, run away with Edward.

'There would be the most appalling scandal if we did that, for both our families,' she said, feeling on the verge of hysteria. She'd managed to hold on to her composure for most of the journey, but this? This was the very edge of enough.

'It would be more of a scandal for your family if you were all thrown out on the street.'

The brutal words hit her hard, so much so, she flinched. It was like being slapped and it helped her think.

'Where is my papa heading now?'

Edward looked at James, who at last looked up from his shoe strings. 'Still headed for Carlisle,' Edward murmured.

Ellen summoned every shred of courage she had, and shook herself. 'I am … deeply honoured by your kind offer. Let us go to Carlisle. We can speak to my father there and determine the best course of action.' She hoped she hadn't offended him. If her papa really thought this was the only way, she would marry him.

Edward hesitated, then he smiled graciously and looked straight into her eyes. He leaned closer, and for an awful moment she thought he might try to kiss her, but he didn't.

'Brave, brave girl. Let us head for Carlisle.'

# CHAPTER 15

*Later that morning*

*LYME PARK*

*Grimsditch*

Archibald Grimsditch marched across the courtyard, and up the steps to the grand entrance to Lyme Park. He held onto his hat with one hand as the wind buffeted him and was greeted at the door by Legh's butler.

He found the magistrate in his study, standing by a roaring fire. The mantel was of elegantly carved marble; at the far end of the room was an imposing mahogany desk; and mingling pleasantly with the woodsmoke was the scent of leather-bound books and ink.

'Mr Grimsditch, welcome. May I offer you refreshment?'

Grimsditch accepted, and the butler disappeared to procure tea as Legh offered him an armchair by the hearth. Although it was too early to break out the brandy, Grimsditch couldn't help but feel he'd have preferred something more substantial. He'd dealt with Legh in the past and had found him to be a good, sensible fellow: always willing to listen, and nobody's fool. But when speaking of matters as controversial as this, one never knew how kindly one would be received.

'I'm here on behalf of your neighbour, William Turner.'

Legh's eyebrows lifted in question.

'Indeed, this is a ... delicate matter, and one that Turner wishes you to hear in absolute confidence.'

'You are being tantalisingly mysterious, Mr Grimsditch.'

Grimsditch sighed. There wasn't any other way to approach this, so he took a breath and came out with it. 'We fear that Turner's daughter has been abducted.'

At this, Legh's eyebrows shot up. 'Ellen? What makes you think that?'

Grimsditch outlined what had happened, pausing only when the butler returned to serve the tea. They sat in silence, listening to the tea being poured and the ticking of the clock, and Grimsditch noticed that the look on Legh's face was one of real, keenly felt concern. When the butler had gone away, he did not pick up his cup, but left it to go cold.

Wishing to remain pragmatic, Grimsditch ploughed on until he had laid out all the facts, then gave Legh his own view. 'There seem to be two possibilities: first, the girl has eloped with some ne'er-do-well she knows her family will not accept. Second, and more likely, she has been abducted by a fortune hunter. Turner is a ... very rich man.'

Legh was frowning deeply now. As he opened his mouth to respond for the first time, his fingers traced a pattern on the arm of his chair. 'I met Miss Turner recently. She did not strike me as one who would succumb to the charms of a Lothario.'

Grimsditch nodded. 'Precisely. She's a clever girl, and not only that, she understands the family's position, and the need for her to make a good match.'

'I have to say,' Legh said grimly, 'I'm in agreement that this could possibly be a case of abduction.'

'The man who collected her from the school was a Frenchman, by the name of Thevenot. Our first task will be to discover who he is.'

Legh's eyes darkened abruptly, as he sat up straighter. 'I had a footman by that name until recently.'

Grimsditch sat up straighter too. 'You did? Thevenot is an uncommon name.'

'Indeed,' said Legh, a bitterness creeping into his voice. 'He was let go by my housekeeper for a petty mischief of some kind – the details escape my memory. But what does this mean? That Ellen Turner was abducted by a member of *my staff*?' He smacked a hand down on the arm of his chair with sudden force. Grimsditch was surprised by the violence of his reaction – this, from a man renowned for his mild, understated manners?

'All we know is,' Grimsditch said gently, 'he was the person who arrived at the school, presented a letter purporting to be from Mrs Turner, and left with Ellen in a green barouche.'

'Dear God.' Legh ran a hand over his mouth. The man clearly had an abiding sense of responsibility, and was wounded by the notion that a crime might have been committed by his former employee. But to Grimsditch's well-trained eye, Legh's pained expression at each mention of Ellen's name seemed to betray more than a sense of civic duty. Something more, even, than neighbourly concern.

'I cannot imagine that Thevenot has abducted her with a view to marrying her himself,' Legh went on – this time, with more decorum. 'I suspect that his involvement was just to remove her from her parents' and the school's orbit. He will be working on the instructions of another man.'

Grimsditch nodded. It was a reasonable assumption.

'What action has Turner taken? Does he have any idea who might do such a thing?'

'As yet, we haven't any more leads. But Turner and his brother are racing to Gretna as we speak.'

'And has he thought about what he might do if he is too late?'

Grimsditch scrubbed a hand over his jaw. 'I don't think he has thought that far ahead.'

Legh got up and began pacing the room. 'It's vital that nothing of this is reported in the newspapers. Any word would ruin Miss Turner, even if they get to her in time. It's imperative that no scandal attach to her name, or the family name.'

'Believe me, Turner is very cognisant of that fact.'

Legh stopped and fixed him with a determined look.

'What do you need from me?'

Grimsditch sighed with relief. As they swiftly discussed the practical issues that needed attending to from a legal standpoint, he became more and more certain that the magistrate was a thoroughly good sort. Legh's temper cooled to his usual competent, capable resolve, and they ironed out the logistics of a potential court hearing. Still, behind Legh's professional formality, Grimsditch couldn't shake the instinct that for him, something personal was also at stake here.

'Is there anything else?' Legh said, as their meeting drew to a close.

Grimsditch shook his head. 'No, you've been most kind.'

'It is not kindness at all. I simply cannot countenance the possibility that anyone in my employ might have been involved in such a vile conspiracy.'

'Of course not. But …' Grimsditch hesitated. 'Once Miss Turner is home safe, I'm sure she will be happy to see you again.'

To Grimsditch's surprise, Legh stiffened. 'Have a care, Grimsditch. If I am hearing the case against Miss Turner's alleged abductors, any personal calls will be out of the question, at least until after the legal proceedings are concluded.'

'Naturally,' said Grimsditch, taken aback by the abrupt turn in the magistrate's tone. 'But—'

'Will that be all?' Legh said again, his voice clipped.

'Of course,' said Grimsditch, with an inclination of his head. 'I wish you an excellent day.' He turned on his heel, and was almost at the door when the magistrate spoke again.

'It is my most fervent hope,' Legh said, 'that Miss Turner be restored to her family as quickly as possible.' Grimsditch looked back at him, but for the first time, he found the magistrate's expression unreadable. 'Let's pray that this unfortunate … incident can be put behind them swiftly.'

As Grimsditch made his exit from Mr Legh's fine estate, he pondered the man's response. Legh had never been married, to Grimsditch's knowledge, but it was plain to see that the gentleman was immensely attractive. With all that dark hair and his trim figure, not to mention his pedigree that went back centuries, his abundant wealth and his spectacular holding at Lyme, he couldn't possibly be short of female attention. What, then, was holding him back from finding a match? And why, when he evidently cared so fondly for Ellen Turner, did he shut down Grimsditch's words of encouragement? It was a conundrum. But judging from the sincerity of Legh's little speech just then, one thing was certain. From a purely legal point of view, Legh would be a good ally to the Turners.

★　★　★

## *Frances*

Frances sat in Jane Turner's parlour, patting her hand rhythmically as a mother might pat a baby's back. She wondered for the hundredth time if the woman would ever stop weeping. She'd never seen such a capacity for theatrics in her entire life, and quite frankly, it was giving her a headache. She thought, with just a hint of spite, that it was no wonder Turner and his brother had left the building with such haste. 'Come now, my dear,' she cooed. 'Perhaps you should retire to your room?'

'I could not possibly,' Jane declared, mopping in vain at her eyes with a lace handkerchief that had been soaked through for some time, and clutching onto Frances with her free hand. 'I must await news.'

'It could be days before we hear anything. If your husband is travelling to Gretna, that's … a long way from here.'

Jane nodded miserably. 'What will we do? If she has been abducted, what will we do? What about her come out?'

'Let's not worry about that now.'

'But I *am* worried, I am *desperately* worried.' She launched into fresh paroxysms of misery and Frances was forced to school her features into something resembling sympathy.

She hoped to God that Edward was moving swiftly to Gretna. Thanks to that damned Daulby woman's letter, he would have far less time than Frances had anticipated. She'd imagined that Ellen's disappearance would go unnoticed until the marriage was announced in *The Times*, when it would be too late to fail. But now, if Edward dallied, or if Ellen baulked and needed cosseting, Turner might just catch up with them in his new, fancy carriage.

Jane's sobbing intensified. She was now hiding behind her sodden handkerchief, so Frances allowed herself a roll of her eyes. From her calculations, Edward still had a day in his favour. She could only hope he'd make it count, and that this whole wretched escapade would be worth it.

# CHAPTER 16

*Earlier that morning*

*NEAR SHAP*

*Ellen*

The road to Shap was appalling. Ellen was used to hills around Shrigley, but these were monstrous in comparison.

The weather was against them too. It had been quite pleasant in Kirkby Lonsdale, but had taken a dramatic downturn, with grey skies, flurries of rain and an increasingly violent wind that howled around the carriage. All this was slowing their course to a crawl, and James had been forced to walk alongside the horses, to keep them calm and moving. Edward, meanwhile, was on the seat opposite hers, head lolling. He looked as though he was sleeping, but Ellen suspected he was not. She wondered what it might be like to be married to him.

She had been thinking about marriage for some time. What girl hadn't? Imagining a life away from her parents, away from Shrigley, was exciting and terrifying in equal measure. Having a household to manage, children … She swallowed at the thought of how one acquired children. Would Edward expect *that* if she married him? Not that she was at all certain what *that* entailed, but the thought of intimacy with Edward made her fearful. All she wanted at the moment was to be back at school with Hester and Lavinia, eating cake and laughing about pond-slime men. Men, she felt, were much easier to think about in the abstract.

Would her friends consider Edward a pond-slime man? Ellen was sure they would. He could be charming in the extreme, and when he went out of his way to make her laugh, she could scarce resist, but she'd no sense of the man beneath the charm. There was something about him that still unnerved her, though she couldn't put her finger on what it was. And since his proposal, James had been awfully quiet, which made Ellen worry that even Edward's own brother was unsure of him.

Edward's chin was on his chest now, and she suspected he really was asleep. Quietly, she pulled her book out of her reticule, made herself comfortable, and disappeared with Thomas. The more she read of Thomas's writings, the more she felt she was getting to know him. And she was fast forming the opinion that he was not only a brave, intrepid explorer, with huge curiosity about the world around him, but also a kind man. A man one could depend on, and trust. As she read, she tried not to wish most fervently that it was he who she shared the carriage with. Tried not to think about the fact that it was he, not Edward, she dreamed of kissing, and could imagine in her bedchamber undressing her. She could only pray that her papa would be in Carlisle, and he had a better plan to solve their troubles. One that didn't involve her marrying Edward Wakefield, and one that meant she might have a chance with Thomas.

★   ★   ★

## Edward

Edward slitted his eyes and watched Ellen as she curled up and read a book. Her reception of his proposal had been rather more lukewarm than he'd anticipated, particularly given the sense of peril he'd instilled. It was clear he needed to work harder at charming her.

She was clearly *thinking* about things, heaven preserve him. He had not expected her to say she would ask her papa's opinion.

He wondered what she was reading. Wondered what it was that held her attention. Most of the women of his acquaintance didn't read quite so avidly and with such absorption as she did. Really, it was most unladylike.

As Ellen read, her lips curled into a smile and her fingers went to her lips.

He shifted his position.

'You seem to enjoy reading.'

'I do,' she said, startled. 'I read a lot of things. Do you?'

'I rather enjoy philosophical and political works. One day I hope to enter politics myself.'

She put the book down on her lap and looked at him properly for the first time since his proposal. 'No wonder you are a friend of Papa's. He's always reading something political.'

'My cousin writes a great deal on the conditions of prisons and prisoners. She's quite the crusader.'

'Really? Might I have read anything of hers?'

'Elizabeth Fry is her name; she published a book recently on reforms for female prisoners.'

Ellen's eyes widened. 'I *have* heard of her.'

Edward nodded. 'My family appears to have an overwhelming sense of public duty, and I, I fear, am similarly afflicted.'

Ellen managed a wan smile. 'Hardly an affliction.'

Edward watched her. Tales of travel, political philosophy, and altruism were apparently the way to his little adventurer's heart. If she had an interest in politics, she may well make a good politician's wife.

'It's clear you enjoy your schooling, too.'

'I do. I'm glad Papa sent me to Miss Daulby's academy. I've learned a great deal and can't wait to return.'

Edward ignored the artless comment; if she imagined she might return to school, she'd not begun thinking of him as a husband at all. He stifled a feeling of irritation.

'I wasn't an attentive student at school,' he admitted, and it was the truth. He'd found education an unsupportable bore and had been branded wilful from an early age.

She nodded and appeared to give the matter thought. 'Perhaps that's because boys expect to be educated, whilst for girls education is the exception. Thus, we see it as a privilege, not a nuisance.' She shrugged.

Edward felt oddly put in his place. Not something he often experienced. 'I spent a lot of time with my grandmother as a child. She too was a writer.'

'A family tradition?'

'I think it must be. She wrote of social improvement and the connection between nature, God, and faith. She was sceptical about the role of imaginative fiction though. She argued one can easily make one's real life just as extraordinary.'

She sat up at that, clearly engaged, and gave him a sheepish smile. 'I do understand the sentiment, but I am rather partial to imaginative fiction.'

He smiled back. 'I confess I am, too.'

Her grin widened. 'Have you read Mary Wollstonecraft?'

Edward pulled a face. 'I have, and I fear you have too.'

She shook her head. 'Mama forbade me to read her and I've never been fortunate enough to happen upon a copy.'

'It is for the best, let me assure you.'

She appeared ready to end the discussion then, so he reached for a question to reel her back in.

'What sort of imaginative fiction do you like best?' he asked.

She smiled again, this time with animation. 'All manner of things. *Sense and Sensibility* was an absolute treat. Oh, and you must have read *The Castle of Otranto*!'

He settled against the seat. 'Tell me more.'

Although still a little wan, she rallied and regaled him with stories from the fictional worlds she had visited, and he had to admit he was surprised. Turner had clearly failed in spectacular fashion to control what his child read. Consequently, Ellen was a peculiar hybrid with one foot in radical politics and the other in romantic nonsense.

* * *

When they stopped at Penrith to water the horses, the weather remained foul. Keeping Ellen in the carriage, he clamped his hat to his head and sprinted for the inn, James jogging by his side. They tumbled into the stables, panting, and lingered there, sheltering from the lashing rain as the stable boy got to work.

'How is she?' James said.

'Much brighter. I think it's safe to say we are getting along famously.'

James pouted; still sulking, no doubt. 'What did you do to achieve that?'

Edward shook his head; *does a gambler know how his winning hand was dealt?* 'Talked about radical politics and romantic novels.'

91

James's eyebrows lifted almost to his hair. 'Truly?'

'Indeed. We discussed Mary Wollstonecraft and Jane Austen, almost in the same breath.'

'What?' James wasn't much of a reader.

'She's warming to me, and I think our next volley will pitch her nicely into my arms. And not before time.'

James frowned. 'Edward,' he hesitated. 'Are you … in love with her?'

Edward stepped back and gawped at him. 'In *love*? James, do you truly have bats in your attic?'

'What I mean is,' James winced, 'if you do marry her, you will be gentle with her, won't you?'

'You keep saying this,' Edward hissed. 'Exactly what is it you think I mean to do to her?'

Predictably, James had no answer to that. Instead, his brother recoiled back into sullen silence, just as a groom appeared at the stable door.

'We can change the horses if you like, sirs?' the groom said, running a hand down one of the mares' flanks. 'These ones look damn near done in.'

'We'll change at Carlisle,' Edward said curtly, 'but thank you.'

The groom nodded, but looked uncertain. 'Mebbe go easy on them. Want me to check your carriage?' He gestured at the equipage that was flailing wildly in the wind outside.

'No need,' Edward said; he'd had enough of James's ramblings for one day. 'We need to get on our way.'

With one last sharp look at James, Edward conveyed that the rest stop was over. Then he and his brother dashed back out into the rain towards the carriage.

# CHAPTER 17

## *CARLISLE*

By the time they arrived at Carlisle, it was almost 6 o'clock, and it was clear that there was something wrong with the carriage. The weather had continued to worsen, rain turning to sleet and snow, and the wheels were making a most unholy noise with every grinding turn.

They pulled up at the Bush Inn, and Edward directed Ellen and James inside for some refreshment, whilst he spoke to the groom. He sincerely hoped that this was something that could be fixed easily, because they most certainly could not spare any time to dawdle. Ellen had been game to come this far, but he suspected that her fortitude was wearing thin. Gretna was almost within touching distance. If only they could get there tonight …

As he waited for the men to look over the equipage, he cast about for ideas to propel Ellen into marrying him before dawn. She'd wanted to wait for her father's advice, so he needed to come up with something very compelling indeed. A reason she simply couldn't refuse.

The germ of a rather excellent idea was formulating in his head, when the sour-faced head groomsman sidled over to him.

'Well sir,' he said with a gravity that was positively funereal, 'You've got plenty of problems. The most pressing of which is the shafts.'

'How long will it take, and how much?' said Edward. He had no time to indulge the man.

'Well,' the groomsman scrubbed his chin and pulled in a breath. 'How long have you got?'

'Ten more seconds.'

The man shook his head, humourlessly. 'It'll take at least couple of days.'

'Then I'll leave with it as it is.'

The man's eyes bulged with concern. 'You heading for Gretna?'

'And if I am?'

'Well, you'd better spend a *little* time here getting it fixed. If you don't, you'll be wandering the moors with your lady friend screaming like a banshee in a carriage with no wheels. And that wouldn't be very romantic at all.'

Edward breathed out slowly, and restrained the urge to shake the man.

'How much?'

He named his price, so Edward doubled it. 'Only if I can have everything fixed and ready to go at first light.'

The man hesitated, but nodded.

Relieved, he strode into the inn to tell Ellen that she would have a good night's sleep before what she thought was the final leg of the journey. Excitement shivered through him at the thought of the actual destination.

★ ★ ★

Early the next morning, as he settled the ridiculously extravagant bill with the innkeeper, Edward felt refreshed and filled with anticipation. Ellen was in the carriage, believing that her father had found sanctuary in a house across town, and that they were about to take her to him. Meanwhile, his germ of an idea for how to coax her to Gretna was now fully formed.

'I think it should come from you,' Edward said to his brother as they walked briskly out into the courtyard. There was an altercation going on outside the inn – some rowdy louts throwing their weight around after too much ale – and with a flash of inspiration, Edward decided he would make good use of them.

'What? What do you mean?' James said, hurrying beside him.

'That night's sleep has sharpened Ellen's wits, and she's started asking *questions* again,' Edward said wearily. His heiress was *far* more malleable when she was tired. 'Plus, with all your sulking yesterday, I think she's having doubts about me. I need you to put it right.'

'I don't know why you think I'm capable of that. Edward, you know I can't lie so convincingly.'

Edward glanced at him. 'Yes, you can. All you need to do is say exactly what I told you to.'

His brother cringed. 'Edward, please …'

'You can't fail me now. Don't make me lose my temper.'

James looked at the ground. 'Tell me again what to say.'

That was more like it. He ran through the plan again, and when he could see that the horses were changed, and the carriage ready for departure, he took hold of James's arm.

'Look.' He nodded to the men outside the tavern who were now shouting and jostling.

'We do it now. Run!'

* * *

## Ellen

Movement made Ellen look out of the window and she was shocked to see Edward and James running full tilt towards the carriage, coat tails flying, arms pumping. James made it first and threw himself in; Edward barked instructions to the driver and then joined them. Both men were out of breath.

James slammed the door and Edward knocked on the roof. The carriage pulled away with a lurch, making Ellen grab the seat.

James pulled out a handkerchief and mopped his face. Edward looked grim.

'What? What has happened?' She looked from one to the other. 'We are going to see my father now, aren't we?' At this point, the knowledge that her papa was so close was all that was holding her together.

James took a long, slow breath, then looked up at her. 'I just saw him.'

'Then we must go back! You must take me back immediately.'

'We can't, truly we can't,' James said. He looked terribly upset. 'My dear Miss Turner, if I could take you to your papa, I would. On my life, I swear I would.'

'What happened?' Ellen felt an all too familiar panic start to rise. She looked at Edward, who shook his head.

'I don't know, I wasn't there; I was dealing with the groom. Speak, brother, tell us what took place.'

'Your papa came out of hiding to see you when he realised you were here, my dear. He was so filled with joy, but the sheriff's men were in pursuit of him. I'm sure you saw the commotion outside the inn.'

Ellen sat back in shock. 'Those uncouth people were looking for my *father*?'

James nodded, casting a swift look at Edward.

'He was in a back room, with another gentleman. A Mr Grimsditch?'

Ellen sat forward. 'Yes, yes, Mr Grimsditch is my father's legal advisor and very good friend.' She was glad her father wasn't alone.

'Well, Grimsditch took your father by the shoulders and led him away. Told him that they must leave immediately before the men pursuing them found him.'

'Oh no, poor Papa!' Ellen's hands went to her mouth.

'I did have the opportunity to speak to him about … about Edward's proposal. It was all very hurried, and I was worried that I had not represented it in the best light.'

'What did he say? What was his advice?'

James swallowed. 'Mr Grimsditch agreed immediately. He said it was the only thing that might save him.'

Ellen's mouth was dry. 'And Papa?'

'Oh, my dear, he considered it so very carefully, mindful of your tender years, and your future that he'd planned. But he did say … that if you had ever loved him, you would accept Edward's suit and marry him with all haste.'

*No*, Ellen's instinct told her. *Please, I can't*. But she'd vowed that she would, if her father said so. She felt bile rise in her throat.

James put his hand in his pocket and pulled out a hastily scrawled note. 'Mr Grimsditch wrote this for you, before they left.'

He handed it to her. It was the briefest of notes, but it couldn't be any clearer.

*My dearest Ellen, you are your father's last and only hope. I pray that you can show the same fortitude as him and take this course of action to protect him and your dearest mama.*

*Yours, etc.*

*Grimsditch*

Ellen screwed her eyes closed. For a brief moment, she wondered why her father hadn't written this note himself – hadn't he wanted to reassure her? But she knew that was selfish. Her papa was in the darkest days of his life. As she pictured him at his lowest, in the tavern she'd left only minutes prior, a sob escaped her.

Edward came and sat beside her. He took the letter from her and gave it back to James, who hesitated and then took something else from his pocket. She held her breath whilst he unfolded his hand.

'Your father also gave me this.'

On his palm sat her papa's signet ring.

'He pulled it from his finger as proof of his eternal devotion.'

'I need no proof of that,' Ellen whispered and picked up the ring she had seen so many times on her beloved father's hand. She had no idea what to say, what to do. Edward was the next to speak. His words were kind, his eyes filled with concern.

'My dearest one, if you are sure that you could wed me, we will move with all haste to Gretna. But, if you feel any sense of repugnance towards me, or that you simply cannot go ahead with this matter, I will return you to your mama forthwith.'

With that he took her hand, raised it to his lips and softly kissed the back. Then, ever so gently, he moved a lock of hair from her face, tucking it behind her ear, and looked directly into her eyes.

'Ellen Turner, would you do me the inestimable honour of becoming my wife?'

His face was very close; the carriage felt to be closing in. She didn't want to marry Edward, but how could she not? What else was there to do?

Ellen took a breath and did what her father needed her to.

'The honour would be all mine.'

# CHAPTER 18

*Earlier that morning*

*NEAR KENDAL*

## William

William held onto the reins with one hand, and peered at his pocket watch in the moonlight. Two o'clock in the morning. Beside him, his brother's head lolled then reared up as he jerked awake. The weather was improving, and he was sure if they pressed on, they could make Carlisle by first light. They had passed Kendal, pausing only to change the horses, and now he felt as though they were really making headway. At this rate, even with horse changes still needed, he could be in Gretna by breakfast. For the first time, it felt possible. They might find Ellen in time to stop any folly. To find out what on earth was going on.

William glanced at his brother. 'How are you holding up?'

Robert shook himself. 'Just fine,' he said. 'We're almost there.'

William heard the exhaustion in Robert's voice. He appreciated, now more than ever, that his younger brother had grown into a fine man.

'I'm glad you are with me,' he muttered gruffly.

'Couldn't let you do it alone,' Robert said, closing his eyes and speaking in an equally gruff tone.

William stared out into the darkness, and drove as hard as he dared. He had to make it in time. He simply *had* to.

# CHAPTER 19

*Later that morning*

*GRETNA GREEN*

*Ellen*

Gretna Green was undoubtedly the most talked about, most yearned for adventure for any girl. Ellen knew this because she'd talked of it often enough with Hester and Lavinia. She'd lost count of how many times they'd dreamed of dashing, daring, handsome men falling in love with them, sweeping them off their feet, and carrying them here through the dead of night.

The reality of it was significantly less exciting. In fact, it was terrifying and mortally uncomfortable.

For a start, it was cold, and the sky was murky. The horrendous rain had abated overnight, as had the wind, but it was gloomy in the extreme. All she had to wear were her wrinkled second-best school dress and sensible school shoes. They were perfectly pleasant and serviceable, but not what she'd imagined she'd be married in. She had no flowers for her hair, and no flowers to carry. No magnificent wedding breakfast, no ceremony in St George's in London. Instead, Ellen stared at the house that stood before her in the bleak Scottish drizzle. The place was where she would be bound to Edward Wakefield for the rest of her life.

She tried not to cry.

Edward led them into the parlour, and James rushed off to find the parson. She sat by the fire and held her reticule on her lap, feeling deeply uneasy. She knew that she should be proud to do what she was doing, proud to be saving her family home, but she didn't feel that way at all. She felt small and helpless and wished desperately that her papa would arrive. If he could just be with her, just hold her hand, and tell her all would be well …

The more she thought about it, the more she felt that he was near. He had to be. He'd been in Carlisle at the same time as them. Where had he gone from there? It was, she decided, entirely possible that he might follow them to Gretna. She couldn't imagine him letting her marry without him there to give his blessing. Especially under the circumstances.

In her heart, she wanted him to run into the miserable little chapel, demand all proceedings be stopped, scoop her into his arms and save her. But her head told her that this could never be. If things were as dire as James had said, her father would be somewhere closeby, hiding from those who hunted him. And this wedding – if one could even call it that – was their only chance to save Shrigley.

In her reticule, she could feel the sharp edges of Thomas's book. She touched her thumb to the corner, and remembered the gleam in Thomas's eye, the warmth of his hands and the hint of awkwardness when he'd given it to her. She knew, with a painful twist to her heart, that had her papa turned to Thomas for help instead of Edward, she would have married him at Gretna in a heartbeat.

She heard footsteps outside the door; no doubt James had located the parson. Edward came to sit down by her. He held out his hand in a peremptory fashion, and said:

'You should sit on my lap.'

Had he said, *you should leap out of the window*, she couldn't have been more surprised.

'Might I ask why?'

He winked at her. 'We need to look like we are in love.'

'Oh, I see.' Ellen wished she did. In her world, a young couple, even deeply in love, wouldn't be sitting on one another where people could see. In private, perhaps, but …

She took a deep breath and stood. He held up both arms, and with a restrained sigh, she lowered herself until she sat her bottom on his legs. She tried to perch delicately without settling all of her weight on him. However, he wrapped an arm firmly around her waist and dragged her closer to him so suddenly that she was forced to sit squarely on his lap and lean back against him. She could feel the hard, muscular warmth of him through her dress and she wanted to leap up. She forced herself to remain still.

He took hold of one hand and ran his thumb over the back of it, then squeezed her midriff, making her tense even more. The door opened, and it wasn't James who walked in, but a young woman who beamed at them as if what they were doing wasn't remotely embarrassing. Ellen tried to smile back, terribly aware of Edward's body beneath hers.

'Would you come with me?' the woman said, and Ellen got to her feet. Edward maintained his hold on her and lifted her hand to his lips before following.

Over the years, Ellen had envisaged a small cosy chapel when she thought of Gretna Green, but instead they were taken into a forge. An actual forge. Instead of an altar, stained glass windows, gently glowing candles, and choristers singing, there was a large anvil with a battered bible resting on it. The elderly parson moved them about bodily until they were beside each other in front of the anvil, picked up the good book, and said the requisite words in an accent so thick, Ellen struggled to follow. He bade her respond, then Edward produced her father's signet ring, and she couldn't prevent the tears that welled in her eyes as he slid it onto her finger. It was too big for her, so she held it in place with her thumb, stroking back and forth.

Ellen held onto her composure by looking over the parson's shoulder. It was too late now. Even if her papa made it to see her, she would be married.

Just then, an almighty bang shook the room. It was so loud that Ellen shrieked, and Edward grabbed hold of her. Panic and hope rose in her chest, all at once, as she twisted to look at the doorway.

# CHAPTER 20

*William*

William stumbled from the carriage at Gretna Green, and was forced to hang onto the door to stop himself falling over. He'd never been so exhausted in all his days. But right now, nothing in the world mattered but his purpose: saving his daughter. He righted himself, tugged at his waistcoat, and strode out towards a building that looked like the village chapel, with Robert at his heels. His pistol weighed heavily in his breast pocket, and his jaw was set.

'What do you intend to do?' Robert said, panting as he kept pace.

'Find out if they are there. If there is a wedding planned, it will be cancelled forthwith. And if it is already taking place, my preferred option would be to drag the bastard out here and tear him limb from limb.'

Robert hesitated, then nodded with a wry smile. 'Fair enough.'

It bolstered William that his brother would fall so readily in with this bullish plan. Truth told, he'd no idea what he would do if he did meet this villain, Thevenot. He wasn't even sure that it would be possible to catch him – but he'd damn well die trying.

They arrived at the nearest door, and he hammered on it. A young serving girl opened it a crack and peered out.

'Beg pardon, miss, but I'd like to speak to the parson.'

Eyes wide, she took in his and his brother's dishevelled state and swallowed. 'He's in the chapel.'

'And where might that be? Is there a wedding taking place?'

She nodded and emerged, pointing to look what looked like a forge. 'In there.'

Edward glanced at Robert, and they set off at a sprint. Edward reached the door first and rattled the handle. When the door failed to open, he beat it with his fist.

'Open up!' he barked. 'Open up, damn you!'

He was still yanking the handle when it twisted suddenly in his grasp and the door fell open to reveal a short, very annoyed looking elderly man.

'What?' he demanded. 'What are ye about hammering and banging?'

'Beg pardon, sir,' William said, only slightly more calmly. 'My name is William Turner. I've reason to believe that my daughter might be heading this way with a view to marriage. She is but seventeen, and I need to be absolutely sure that does not happen. Would you be able to reassure me that no such wedding has taken place?'

William's heart throbbed in his chest. His head pounded in time with it.

'Her name?'

'Ellen Turner.'

'About so high,' he held up his hand. 'Pretty thing with dark hair and dark eyes?'

The world receded to the thumping in his ears. He nodded, waiting, not wanting the answer. 'Yes.'

'She was married but half an hour ago in the chapel. Gave me twenty shillings and told me to get some gloves. Nice girl.'

Half an hour ago? *Half an hour ago?*

'Are you certain?' He felt Robert's hand on his arm.

'Aye. You can see the register if you wish.'

William tried to swallow. 'I do. Where were they headed from here?'

The man shook his head. 'No idea. I don't ask questions; I just marry them.'

William watched as the man began to shuffle back inside.

'Wait!'

The man turned.

'His name. What was the man's name?'

The parson hesitated, seemingly searching his memory, and then nodded. 'Wakefield. Edward Gibbon Wakefield.'

William remained motionless for some time after the man left to fetch the register. The name was meaningless. He knew only one thing.

He was too late.

He'd failed his daughter. Completely and utterly.

# CHAPTER 21

*Forty-five minutes earlier*

*Ellen*

Ellen slowly turned back to face Edward. Nobody was at the door. Her papa was too late.

The parson lowered the hammer he'd just used to bang the anvil, and pronounced them husband and wife. Before she had regained her composure, to cap it all, Edward leaned over and kissed her quite passionately on the lips. Nothing of the cautious gentleness he'd shown earlier was in evidence. She wanted to drag her mouth away; no one had kissed her like this before, so wet, so ... intrusive. But it dawned on her with painful clarity that, now she was his wife, he could do with her whatever he wanted.

She managed to smile and thank the parson, who introduced himself as Laing – or at least that's what it sounded like. He also told her that it was common for the bride to give him a gift. Embarrassed, she rummaged in her reticule and came out with a twenty-shilling note. She glanced at Edward, and only when he nodded, did she hand it over. She knew that any money she spent now would be Edward's money, and she would need his permission to part with it. As the parson tucked it into his pocket, she wondered too late, with a wave of panic, if that might have been her family's last twenty-shilling note.

'Perhaps you should buy some new gloves with it,' she said, blinking rapidly to quell the tears that threatened. 'It's chilly outside.'

So that was it? From schoolgirl to a married lady in a few muttered words and a clang of the anvil? If it was not so frightening, it would be hilarious. Hester and Lavinia would burst their sides laughing if they heard the story. Only Ellen wasn't laughing. At all.

Edward left her alone in the parlour whilst he finalised the payments and collected the marriage certificate. James, he said, was waiting for them outside in the carriage. When Edward returned, he took her arm and pulled her close to his side on the sofa.

'Is that everything?' she asked.

'It is.'

'We are married?'

He took her hand and kissed it, staring into her eyes as he did so. 'We are definitely married.'

Ellen nodded and tried to smile.

'How do you do, Mrs Wakefield?' he murmured.

'Very well, thank you.' *Not very well at all.*

'How does it feel to be Mrs Wakefield?' *Frankly, terrifying.*

'Mrs Ellen Wakefield ...' she tried repeating the name with a smile, but it sounded terribly wrong. She did not feel herself at all, as if she were watching this conversation from a distance. Like a scene read from a book. 'Very nice,' she lied politely.

Edward gave her another of his long looks, but she couldn't for the life of her think of anything else to say. Barely a few days ago she'd been happy in her home, with her friends, her family. She'd been planning her come out, thinking about court presentations, balls, parties … and now she was married to a man she barely knew with her family facing bankruptcy. It was inconceivable.

'What do we do now?' she asked him.

He frowned and tilted his head with a smile. 'What do you mean?'

'Where will we meet with my father? When can we return … to Shrigley, to see my mother?' She'd almost said *home*, but as the full import of her married status continued to hit her, she realised that she wouldn't live at Shrigley anymore; it wouldn't be home anymore. She swallowed, and all at once the floor seemed to dip and lurch beneath her feet like seawater. She'd no idea where home would be. Where had Edward said he lived, again? Lord, she just wanted to go home.

'My mother will be beside herself with worry, so the first thing is I'd like to go and reassure her that all is well. Or if not entirely well, then at least, Shrigley is saved. Her health is delicate, and she will be terribly ill with all the upset.'

Edward tapped a finger on the arm of the sofa and looked tense. 'I'm not sure that will be possible straight away.'

'Oh?' The seawater sensation was not receding. 'But Papa is safe now, is he not? We don't need to keep running.'

'He will be, but before we reach that point, there is much to take into account and much to arrange.'

Ellen cast her new husband an incredulous look. Couldn't he see how badly she needed reassurance from her family, after everything that had happened? Did he have no concept of how desperately worried her mother would be? 'I imagine there is. But, Mama …'

'Perhaps you can write to her?'

Ellen stifled a sigh. There was a polite but implacable look on his face that suggested the topic was now closed. She hadn't the strength to argue further right now, but the conversation was far from over. 'Where from? Will we go to your home now – in Cheshire, wasn't that what you said?'

'*Our* home,' he corrected with a smile, 'is in Paris.'

Ellen tried to digest this, but her mouth hung open. 'Paris? But I distinctly recall you saying that you were living in Cheshire.'

He nodded. 'I have been *staying* in Cheshire of late. With friends. But my home, as I am fairly sure I said, is in Paris.'

Ellen swallowed, and wondered if she would still be quite sane by the end of this rescue mission. 'How … lovely.'

'I've worked for the British Embassy there, and I'm good friends with the ambassador. Actually, we will need to head for Paris very soon, because that is where James's wedding is to be held. Will you enjoy Paris? I think you'll love it.'

'I'm sure I will.' She answered purely by rote. She'd dreamed of going to Paris, but not in this way. When would she see her parents? Her home? Her friends?

Before she could say more, Edward held up a hand and cocked an ear towards the door. She heard footsteps at the same time. He leaned over to wrap both arms about her waist, kissed her on the cheek and then nuzzled his nose into her neck as he held her tight against him, just as a maid walked in.

The maid giggled – Ellen guessed Edward had winked at her. He tucked Ellen's fingers into the crook of his elbow and kissed her temple.

'Come, my love.' He spoke louder now the maid was in the room, rather like he was on a stage, and this was all a performance. 'We must make all haste.'

Ellen did her best to smile as she walked with him, realising that they should probably keep up the pretence of being in love.

'I think we should make for Penrith. From there, we'll see if we can find your papa.'

'Oh, thank you, that would be wonderful.'

As they walked outside, James called to them from the carriage. 'Congratulations, Mr and Mrs Wakefield,' he said, doffing his hat.

Ellen smiled at him, and tried not to stiffen when Edward slid his arm about her waist again and tugged her to him. She stumbled closer, and Edward shifted and gave her a meaningful look. It took her a moment to realise that he wanted her to return his embrace. She swallowed and put her arm about his waist and they continued on towards the carriage.

'I know your mama will be sad not to have been present at our wedding, but perhaps we could have a celebration on our return? I'm sure she will be delighted to wish us happy,' Edward said as he handed her into the barouche.

Ellen thought of the extensive plans that her mother had made for her marriage. Plans for her to marry well above Mr Wakefield's station, all scuppered forever. To say that she would be disappointed to have missed the wedding was an understatement of gargantuan proportions. However, the alternative to her not marrying Edward was too awful to think about. It struck her with some force that, had Edward not been willing to wed her, and so swiftly, her family would have been cast out into the streets.

'Thank you,' she blurted. 'Thank you for helping Papa, for marrying me. I'm sure … I'm sure there are a lot of women you might have preferred as a wife.'

Edward settled in the seat opposite her, beside his brother, and they both looked at her with unreadable expressions. Then

Edward did something quite startling: he lifted a finger and tapped her lightly on the nose. 'I am delighted with my marriage, Mrs Wakefield. Never think I am not.'

She flushed and looked away. Why on earth would he be delighted about marrying *her*? He was much older, and had, it seemed, a successful life in Paris. She was but a schoolgirl. Had Papa's fortune been intact, she might have harboured some suspicion that he was a fortune hunter. However, that was impossible: the money was all gone.

He put a finger under her chin and brought her face back to his. His gaze was tender.

'When we reach Penrith, I will send a notice to *The Times* announcing our marriage.'

Ellen gasped. 'All my friends will see it.'

'And won't they be the picture of envy when they realise you've been swept away by a handsome man, made the object of his affections and his passions, then dashed to Gretna to be married over the anvil?'

'I suspect they will.'

He looked at the expression on her face and laughed. After a pause, she surprised herself by laughing with him, and James joined in. The whole adventure had been so surreal, so absurd, that they struggled to stop. So as the horrid little barouche pulled out of Gretna, all three of them were still in fits of giggles.

# CHAPTER 22

## *THE CROWN, PENRITH*

'I shall be pleased to settle in my bed tonight,' Edward murmured late that evening, as the barouche pulled up outside yet another tavern.

Ellen looked away and bit her lip. She had spent much of the journey to Penrith wondering what would happen when they arrived, and whether or not Edward would expect a wedding night. It had been a marriage of convenience, but it was a marriage, nonetheless. He would no doubt have ... expectations.

She swallowed as she recalled Hester's genuine question about what happens when one is ravished. They'd all been in hoots of laughter, but the truth was that none of them really knew what might happen in the bedchamber between a man and a woman. She had the sketchiest of understandings of anatomy and the necessity of placing certain parts in unmentionable places to procreate, but there it ended. Her mother had never discussed marital relations with her; there had been no need. Not yet.

'This way, Mrs Wakefield,' a young maid said with a smile, and Edward handed her over. She was shown to a comfortable-looking room, and although the maid was efficient and kind, Ellen couldn't relax. She perched on the edge of the large bed and fiddled with her gloves.

A tap came to the door and Ellen jumped, pressing a hand to her chest. 'Come in.'

Her relief when it was James who popped his head around the door was palpable. He came into the room and bowed.

'Would you like to eat in your room or join us in the parlour? They've very kindly rustled us up something to eat.'

'Would you mind enormously if I ate in here? I can scarce remember the last time I was this tired.' She emphasised the point with a delicate yawn behind her hand.

He gave her a warm smile. 'We don't mind at all. I'll tell Edward you are going to go to sleep. He and I have rooms down the corridor, so we won't disturb you when we retire.'

Ellen smiled her thanks and prayed that James's words meant Edward would sleep in his own room, not hers.

'I shall see you at breakfast.'

James bowed again and left her alone. She sat back cautiously and wondered what this evening might have been like had she been married to Thomas Legh. How might she feel if she lay here waiting for him to knock on the door, for him to come into her room wearing naught but a nightshirt or a robe? Ellen swallowed and shifted. She would, she realised, feel very differently indeed. There was a flutter in her stomach and her cheeks heated at the thought.

She closed her eyes and touched her fingers to her lips where Edward had kissed her, then imagined Thomas kissing her. She could recall the warmth from his body and the delicate scent of him from when she'd bumped into him at Lyme Park. It had been deliciously welcoming, enticing even. Edward had no such intriguing scent. Beneath all that cologne, there was something faintly, unpleasantly, starchy about him. His hands were not firm and warm against her skin; they were soft and sometimes damp. He'd certainly never smiled at her the way Thomas had. It felt as though Edward was going out of his way to charm her, which was kind of him, but when she recalled the way Thomas had given her a copy of his book, his awkwardness had felt more ... honest.

Ellen sighed. The inappropriateness of dreaming of another man whilst her husband lay in the adjoining room was not lost on her, and it occurred to her, with a jolt, that unless she ceased dwelling on Thomas Legh, her marriage was not going to be a happy one. She was, quite simply, married to the wrong man. But there was nothing that she could do about it. Duty and honour had dictated whom she should wed, and having done it, she now needed to reconcile herself to a life as Mrs Wakefield.

She hugged Thomas's book to her and decided that she would keep it with her, share in his adventures, until she reached her father and things were settled. Once that was done, and she was ensconced as Edward's wife and mistress of her own home, she would put Thomas's book, and put all thoughts of him, away for good. It would feel like laying aside a part of herself, but it would have to be done. That brief, incandescent moment when they met at Lyme Park would be consigned to the past and simply become a precious memory.

She blinked away tears and settled herself more comfortably. Once she got back to school, she would be able to ... She stopped mid-thought and squeezed her eyes closed. She wasn't a schoolgirl anymore; she was a married woman. There would be no returning to school, no more horseplay with Lavinia and Hester, no more midnight feasts, no more ... freedom. More tears swam in her eyes, and she wallowed in unhappiness for a moment before dashing them away. She would, she resolved, banish such girlish thoughts when she reached her new home, with her new – she swallowed – husband.

# CHAPTER 23

*The next day*

*William*

William stood outside his wife's parlour at Shrigley, Robert by his side. At this moment, he'd give anything not to tell her the awful tidings they'd brought. Judging from Robert's utterly dejected countenance, he felt quite the same way.

He clapped Robert on the shoulder, and they both braced themselves before striding inside to find Jane, Grimsditch and Miss Davis in attendance. Jane immediately threw her hands in the air.

'You are *here*! Tell me, is Ellen with you? Have you saved her?'

William clenched his jaw, and it took him some time to respond. He moved to take Jane's hand, and crouched beside her chaise.

'I'm so sorry, my love. We were too late.'

The silence in the room was dreadful. Miss Davis's eyes were on stalks, Grimsditch lost much of his colour and Jane, after regarding him for a second, wailed aloud.

'No … no … *no*! William, you promised me, you said you could do it … Do *not* tell me she is married! *Do not!*'

William screwed up his face and pressed his lips to the back of Jane's quivering hand.

'I'm so sorry,' he murmured again, then opened his eyes and stood up. He cleared his throat then addressed the room. 'Ellen married one Edward Gibbon Wakefield at 8 o'clock in the morning on the 8th of March. Robert and I arrived at eight thirty, by which time, they'd disappeared again.'

Grimsditch groaned. Miss Davis put a hand to her mouth, shock writ large across her countenance.

'Might I be of assistance, sir?'

Ackroyd, apparently hearing the commotion, had come into the room and was cautiously closing the door behind him. The small, neat man seemed remarkably calm despite the scene that confronted him.

William passed a hand over his mouth and was shocked to find that it trembled. He balled it into a fist and put both hands behind his back.

'Thank you, Ackroyd. Please send for Mrs Turner's lady's maid and arrange for a paregoric draught to calm her nerves. We have received some … difficult news.'

The man's eyes widened fractionally as though this was nothing out of the ordinary, and went out as discreetly as he had come.

'Who?' Jane shrieked, as soon as the door was closed. 'Who is this Wakefield? And where have they gone?'

'We have no idea,' said William. 'The chapel held no information beyond the marriage register.'

'I'm so sorry,' Grimsditch said, coming to stand beside him. 'But I do have one small lead. Thevenot was a servant at Lyme Park until recently, when he got the sack. Legh told me. He was very sympathetic to your cause.'

William nodded at him in appreciation. That was something, at least.

'But what about Almacks?' Jane whimpered, rocking herself back and forth. 'What of the viscount I had eating from my hand? I don't know how I'll face anyone ever again, as long as I live.' She stood up, and looked as though she wanted to pace the room, but then flopped back down, newly overwhelmed. 'How could she *do* this to us?'

William pinched the bridge of his nose, and sighed. Had his wife not reached the same conclusion he had? 'I don't think she did, my love.'

'What do you mean?'

William shook his head, and said gently, 'I don't think it *was* an elopement. I think she has been abducted.'

He waited for his words to sink in. '… Do you?' his wife said, as her eyes glazed over with fresh horror.

'Robert and I discussed this in some detail on our journey,' he continued. 'Someone told Ellen's headmistress you were ill, to get her out of school. That suggests a deliberate attempt to mislead her. And you must know, my love, that Ellen is a good girl who knows what she's about. She would never subject you to such distress. What's more, now Grimsditch has confirmed that the Thevenot fellow is a malingerer … It's the only plausible explanation.'

'You mean she … was tricked? Lied to?'

Jane's voice was still horribly shrill and nasal, and William rubbed a hand across his mouth. If only his beloved would cease crying for a *moment* …

'Indeed, my love. Why don't you retire to your chamber and rest yourself? All this upset is not good for your health. I promise you, I will take care of everything.'

Jane nodded, fresh tears falling as she stood to leave them.

'Will you send the announcement today?'

'Announcement?' William frowned, baffled.

'The announcement of the marriage, William,' Jane said slowly, as though he were simple. 'We need to have one in place for the newspapers, for our friends …'

William gritted his teeth, and fought not to roll his eyes as the Davis woman nodded along, her agreement absolute.

'No … I am going to Lyme Park this very moment to speak with Mr Legh.'

'Legh? Why?' his wife demanded.

William didn't have time to appease, he just needed to get on with things. 'Because if there's anyone who can help me stop the whole thing, it's him.'

Jane's mouth fell open and Miss Davis went very still. Robert looked impressed, and there was a conspiratorial twinkle in Grimsditch's eye.

William knew his grin was shark-like, but he didn't care.

'You didn't think I'd let some jumped up, pockets to let, nobody marry my child, did you?'

'William!' she spluttered. But William's mind was made up. He bowed to them all, and headed for the door, ignoring Jane's entreaties to stop.

# CHAPTER 24

*Edward*

'Good morning, Mr and Mrs Wakefield!'

Edward watched his wife flush as James joined them at the breakfast table. She'd been absorbed in writing letters to her little friends and her parents, and he'd been quietly looking forward to reading them. She'd taken the news that her papa was now bound for London reasonably well, but she had been quiet ever since. He couldn't blame her. The prospect of travelling so far again was indeed grim.

'I trust you both slept well?' James quipped as a maid laid a plate of bacon in front of him. Ellen's flush deepened.

'Very well, thank you,' Edward replied with a warning look at his brother and a smile for Ellen. 'I propose once you have eaten, James, we get on our way to Leeds. I must be punctual for Ellen's papa. After all, I am now his son-in-law!'

'Good idea,' James said, avoiding both his and Ellen's gaze.

'Indeed,' Ellen said. 'I shall go and gather my things. Will you have these posted for me, Mr ...' She paused, and corrected herself. 'Edward?'

*Good girl*, Edward thought. 'Gladly, my dear.'

'Are you going to post them?' James said when Ellen had gone, casting him a sideways glance.

'Of course not, but I need her compliant until the marriage is acknowledged.'

James nodded but said nothing. He set about eating his bacon. Edward casually opened the letter Ellen had addressed to her father and scanned the content. She was indeed a dutiful daughter. He put the others – addressed to Ellen's mother, a Lavinia, and a Hester – in his pocket, and turned back to his brother.

'She's a fetching little thing, isn't she?'

James set down his fork.

'From what I'd heard,' Edward went on, 'she wasn't considered a great beauty, but I think people have underestimated her. There is something rather fine about her countenance, and she has comported herself well under very trying circumstances.'

A muscle ticked in his brother's jaw. 'Am I to conclude that your wedding night was a success?'

'Brother!' Edward said in shocked tones. When James looked at him, he arched an eyebrow. 'A gentleman never tells,' he said and tapped the side of his nose. But at the mulish look on James's face, he relented. However much fun it was to taunt his brother, he still needed his help.

'Don't be ridiculous. Of course I didn't consummate the marriage. She's very young and inexperienced, and we have much to achieve.'

James sniffed and returned to his breakfast. 'I had no idea you were such a romantic.'

Edward refrained from making the comment he wanted to and continued in conciliatory fashion. 'Well, I do have *some* sensitivity, and besides, if this goes wrong, I don't want to add a felony charge against me. If I've treated his daughter with kid gloves, Turner is more likely to view me more as a good prospect than an out and outer.'

James seemed to have nothing to say to that.

'When we reach Leeds,' Edward went on, 'I need us to part ways. I want you to go to Shrigley Hall to speak with her father and mother. I want you to deliver them a letter from me, and convince them that we are already in love, and just waiting for them to acknowledge us. Frances should have been pouring fond words about me into their ears, so the ground will be well prepared.'

James nodded. 'I will do what I can, but I do need to get to Paris. If I don't pay more attention to my own wedding soon, I'm certain I'll be jilted.'

He slammed his knife and fork on the table, making James jump. 'James, I need you to do more than just *what you can*. I need you to convince Turner, quite thoroughly, that I am a good catch, that I will take good care of his daughter, and in short, that I am an extremely good prospect as a husband. Also, that should he not accept, then he, his wife, and his daughter will be utterly ruined.'

'Of course.'

Edward nodded and gave him a long look. 'You are crucial to the success of my plans, brother. Do not fail me.'

# CHAPTER 25

*William*

William Turner alighted from his carriage and hurried through the courtyard of Lyme Park. He had no idea how the meeting would go. Grimsditch had said that Legh seemed sympathetic when Ellen was a missing schoolgirl, but the deed was done. How would Legh feel about the whole fiasco now Ellen was married?

There was a lot at stake. Getting Ellen away from this Wakefield character wouldn't be easy, but he couldn't countenance his fortune – the product of his life's work, and Robert's – being handed out to some damned insignificant. Neither could he bear the thought of his dear, sweet daughter chained to such an objectionable tartuffe for the rest of her days.

If he was going to pursue the course he wanted to – taking Wakefield to court in a bid to free Ellen from him – he would need Legh's support. But in asking this of Legh, he risked losing Legh's support for *him*, as High Sheriff. Legh's endorsement of him was absolutely crucial to his position in society: for if the magistrate snubbed him, then all of Cheshire would follow suit. His investiture celebration, mere weeks hence, would become a circus of humiliation ... And then, Ellen's chances of a good marriage would be well and truly up the spout.

In his study, Legh greeted him in his typically reserved fashion. But beneath the firm handshake and placid smile, was that *nerves* William detected? Surely not.

'I won't beat about the bush,' he said, accepting the offered chair and brandy. 'I've come to see you because yesterday my daughter was married ... at Gretna Green.'

As his words hit Legh, William realised the man really was on edge. For the merest of moments, something gave way in Legh's eyes – there were flashes of shock, disappointment, and something else that William couldn't quite identify – but just as quickly, he recovered his mask of calm.

Legh took a drink – a rather large drink, William thought – before replying. 'Grimsditch told me she'd been taken from school,' he said slowly. 'I'm relieved to hear she is safe. But, who has she married? Surely not Thevenot?'

'No, not Thevenot,' William said, and Legh's shoulders dipped slightly in relief. 'Instead it was a jackanapes by the name of Edward Gibbon Wakefield.'

'Wakefield,' Thomas echoed, frowning. 'The name rings a bell. Do you know him?'

'I have no notion,' said William, 'but by God I intend to find out.'

'You haven't heard from him? Hasn't he made demands?'

'I've heard nothing from him yet. But the bastard will get a shock when he starts his ways on me.'

'How so?'

William sat back in his chair and smiled. 'Well, I won't be rolling over and accepting this, of that you can be certain.'

Legh looked unsure of his meaning.

'I'm not giving him anything whatsoever. Not a penny, not a farthing.'

Legh choked on his brandy. 'You mean, you'll let Ellen live in penury with him? You'd do that to her?'

William snorted at the man's innocence. 'Not at all, I intend to expose him, have him thrown in Newgate, and have the damned marriage annulled. I'm not having a child of mine shackled to an abuser, a seducer of children, a toadying mushroom. Frankly, if, nay *when* I get my hands on him, I'll fucking eviscerate the swine.'

A silence followed. Legh gave him a series of long looks, none of which William could decipher. 'Are you sure about this course?'

'Nothing will divert me. I assure you. If this … this Wakefield,' he spat the name with all the vitriol in his soul, 'abducted my Ellen, he will regret it.'

Legh licked his lips and took a breath, which indicated to William he wasn't going to like what the man said next. He was right in his assumption.

'You realise that if you do that, you will drag Ellen through the courts, and when the newspapers get hold of it …'

William stiffened. 'It will be worth it to have her free of him and able to marry the man she chooses.'

'Turner,' Legh spoke in the gentle tones of one addressing a small child. 'Turner, she will be ruined. There will be no grand society wedding even if she is completely and utterly innocent in all of this. She will be cast out, completely and irrevocably.'

William observed Legh carefully. The distress in his eyes was genuine, he was sure. He recalled how only a few days ago, Legh had made a point of bringing Ellen a copy of that book he'd written, and inscribing it for her. Had there been what his wife liked to call a *moment* between them?

'There may be *some* willing to overlook the scandal,' he ventured. 'Someone with enough standing, someone who understands?'

Legh's lips twitched. For a young man, he was remarkably quick-witted. In many ways, he reminded William of his earlier self.

'If you are casting in my direction, you should also know I have no intention of marrying.' He sighed; the sparkle in his eye dimmed. 'Nothing to do with what has happened to your daughter – let's just say, for me, that ship sailed a long time ago.'

Legh shrugged then, as if what he'd said was immaterial, but he wasn't fooling William. The way he'd said *a long time ago*, one would have been forgiven for thinking he'd lived a hundred lonely years, not thirty. What had happened to make such a young man so cynical about wedlock?

But before William could ask any questions, Legh cleared his throat. 'If you decide to go ahead and prosecute,' he said, 'might I suggest you enlist the support of the foreign secretary? He may lend weight to your cause.'

William nodded. 'I shall.'

'And,' Legh said tentatively, 'I could make some enquiries into Wakefield, try and determine who he is … If that would help?'

'I would be inordinately grateful if you would.'

Legh nodded thoughtfully, cradling his glass. 'I'll be honest with you, Turner. I have reservations about what you are proposing, grave reservations. However, what Wakefield did was wrong, and I am deeply sorry for the part my erstwhile servant played in it. If you seek reparation, for what it's worth, you shall have my support.'

William let go of a breath. 'I appreciate that. And I thank you for your candour.'

'Good,' said Legh, sincerely. 'Now, on a brighter note… Are you going ahead with the celebrations in April? Do you still want me leading the procession?'

William lifted an eyebrow slowly in response and offered a conspiratorial smile. 'What do *you* think?'

\*   \*   \*

Wedding Announcements, Friday 10th March:

On the 8th inst. Edward Gibbon Wakefield, Esq., to Ellen, only daughter of W. Turner, Esq., of Shrigley Park in the county of Cheshire.

Teacups rattled in their saucers as William slammed his fist onto the breakfast table. The bastard had announced it in the damned *Times*. Always one step ahead. Always seizing the upper hand. Well, not for long. Not for damned long.

He thrust a hand through his hair and gripped it tight. He just needed to *find* them. Find where they were, and then get Ellen away from him. He screwed his eyes closed, just as a knock came at the door.

'Come.'

It was Ackroyd. He cleared his throat. 'A Mr James Wakefield is here to see you, sir. I've installed him in the study.'

William blinked. Was he hearing correctly?

'Wakefield? James Wakefield?'

Ackroyd nodded, and glanced almost imperceptibly at the paper still open on the table. 'I believe he may be related to Mr Edward Wakefield, sir.'

William flew out of the breakfast room, ignoring Miss Davis who was passing on her way to sit with Jane, and ripped open the door of the study to find a tall, fashionably dressed young man with fair hair standing awkwardly by his desk.

'Who the hell are you,' William snarled, 'and where is my daughter?'

The boy blanched instantly and took several steps back, holding up a hand. 'Sir, I have come to give you the happy news of your daughter's marriage to my brother, and to assure you that she is safe and well.'

William advanced on him, watching the scoundrel edge around the desk as an antelope might back away from a tiger. 'Happy? You think I am happy? Do I *look* happy?' He didn't even try to disguise the northern notes in his voice: in fact, he gave them free rein.

'You think you can come into my home, with your hoity toity ways and your stupid shirt points—' he flicked a finger at the ridiculously high points, which were almost poking the fool in the face, '—and announce that *my child* is now married to your brother?'

Wakefield gulped.

'Well? Where are they? Tell me that! Where is this brother of yours, and what has he done to my daughter?'

'I can assure you, sir, that El … Mrs Wakefield … is in high spirits, and looking forward greatly to telling you … No! What are you doing?'

Wakefield yelped and leaped for the door, when he saw William stride to the sideboard and open the box that held his pistols.

'Sir, please, I beg of you to listen … We …'

William took out the weapon and Wakefield tore open the door and ran. William lunged after him.

'Tell me where she is, you lummox!' he roared.

The boy fished in his pocket and hurled a letter on the floor. 'It's there! It's all in there. For God's sake, don't shoot!'

William grinned, raised his arm, closed one eye, and looked down the barrel as the idiot threw himself out into the front yard. He heard him scramble across the gravel as he stalked after him to the door. He'd managed to get on his horse and was kicking the poor animal half to death to get it moving. William raised his arm again and heard a squeal of alarm as the horse reared and then careened down the drive.

William hesitated, then shot into the air. The scream he heard was deeply satisfying.

# CHAPTER 26

William picked up the letter that Wakefield had dropped and took it into the study. Ackroyd followed.

'Tea, sir?' the butler said, face straight, not mentioning a word about what just occurred.

'That would be splendid.' William turned away to clean his pistol so that Ackroyd didn't see him smirk.

It was only a matter of time before the rest of the household, namely his wife, would be along wanting to know why he was firing shots, so he opened the letter immediately and scanned the contents.

*Dear sir,*

*I cannot help feeling that I ought to write to you, and yet I am so completely at a loss to know what to say. I begin this letter, then, in the hope I will find the the words as I proceed. Nothing that I can say will give you pleasure, except that your dear child is perfectly well, and would be completely* happy but for her separation from you and her mother. I rejoice in being able to give you that assurance.

I know, sir, I have done you an almost unpardonable injury. I wager that in your situation I too would be furious with the man who had dared marry my daughter without my consent. Still, I hope that if I were ever in such a position as you are now, I would suspend my judgement till I had learned all the facts. It is in this spirit that I beg that you will take the trouble to know me, and learn from all my friends whether or not your daughter has made an unhappy marriage. I trust in God that she has not, and firmly believe that if I succeed in making her happy, you must be satisfied; at least that would be my feeling in your situation.

I acknowledge the full extent of the wrong that I have done you, but I may be able to repair it, unless you put reparation out of my power, by refusing to give me the opportunity. At all events, I have incurred towards your child the most sacred of obligations; and I feel that, come what may, even though you should entertain towards me the most unrelenting hatred, she has a claim upon my devoted tenderness, such as few women could ever make before.

Ellen and I shall soon travel to the Brunswick Hotel in London, where we'll eagerly await word from you. I must tell

*you that she pines to see you, and watches the arrival of*
*every packet as if her life depended upon it. She is a dear,*
*affectionate, excellent creature, and well deserves from you*
*as much affection as she feels towards you.*

   *I remain, sir,*
   *Your obedient,*
   *E.G. Wakefield*

William read it twice, keeping a tight rein on the fury that pulsed through him. Just as he thought. The brute was all but blackmailing him to accept the marriage to avoid a scandal. He wanted to throw the letter on the fire and watch it burn, but instead he folded it carefully and put it into his desk drawer. This was evidence. Evidence he could use.

He made for his wife's parlour and found her standing in the middle of the room, looking bewildered.

'What on earth was all the commotion?' she demanded as he walked in.

'My apologies, love. It was me.'

'William!'

She was wearing what looked like a new lace cap. It was pretty, and suited her well.

'Did I see Miss Davis heading your way?'

'You did, but it was only to tell me that her dear papa has been taken ill. She will not be able to visit again for a few days.'

'I'm sorry to hear it, my love. I have no doubt she will miss your company.' He hoped this didn't mean the Davis woman was a fair-weather friend.

He, guided her to her chaise, sat beside her, and took both her hands. 'How are you feeling, my love?' he said. At least he could speak to her without an audience this time.

'I really don't know what to feel, William.'

'Well, I have some news.' He braced himself for another bout of histrionics. 'Wakefield's brother paid a visit.'

Jane's eyes widened. 'Oh! Is he still here?' She fiddled to undo her cap, fussed with her hair, then re-tied it. 'I take it from your demeanour that Ellen is not with him?'

William shook his head, steeling himself for what would come next.

'Do you think we should offer him luncheon, or just tea?'

'Neither.' William said, more sharply than he'd intended. 'The pigeon-livered fool scarpered. He dropped off a letter from his brother.'

She put her head on one side and regarded him. He waited.

'That noise, William. Did you … you didn't … *shoot* him?'

He shuffled his feet. 'I might have shot *near* him. I didn't actually hit him.'

'For God's sake, William!' she cried. 'If you'd only made him welcome, he could have told us where Ellen is.'

She had a point, but he was damned if he'd admit it. 'In the letter, Wakefield said they're bound for London, and the Brunswick Hotel. Naturally, I intend to follow them there as soon as possible.'

Jane pursed her lips. 'What else did the letter say?'

'He wants money, and for us to acknowledge the match.'

'Oh, God,' Jane said, and fanned herself with her handkerchief before sinking back onto the chaise. 'Thank heavens, he's prepared to settle.'

'Beg pardon?' William tried to keep his tone level, wondering if his wife had lost her head entirely.

'That's what happens,' she said, almost matter-of-factly. 'When something like this occurs, the only thing is to do what Miss Davis said right from the start. Settle a generous sum on the couple, buy them a nice house, and establish them in society.'

'You want me to give in.'

His wife turned to him with beseeching eyes. 'William, you need to make this right.'

'But how can we possibly make such a marriage right?'

'*Just pay him!*' she shrieked, her tone filled with a savagery he'd seldom heard from her. 'If it isn't a love match, go to London and pay him to *pretend* it is. Then Ellen will be respectable, and we will all be saved!'

William clenched his teeth. He loved his wife, truly he did, but sometimes ...

'Jane, my love, we cannot allow this.' He squeezed her hands and tried to hold her gaze before her thoughts stampeded any further. 'I shall find out what happened and bring her home, and all will be well.'

'But how? She's a married woman now, you can't change that.' Her voice cracked, and once again she melted into tears. 'You need to make it *right*, William.'

William's gut clenched. 'You have my word that I will do all in my power to make this right, my love.'

But as he bent and kissed his wife, he had the strongest suspicion that his idea of *making it right* was not going to align readily with hers.

# CHAPTER 27

*The next day*

## THE BRUNSWICK HOTEL, LONDON

*Edward*

It was almost done. All he needed now was word from James that his visit to Shrigley had been a success. Then, with just a little time alone with his wife, he'd convince her that she loved him enough to forgive his deception, and his future would be assured.

It was late on Saturday evening when they reached the capital, and Edward led his wife into the entrance of the Brunswick Hotel. The little heiress had no doubt expected him to have a London residence, and was struggling to hide her disappointment at the temporary lodgings, but fortunately, a waiter approached them before she could complain.

'My good man,' he said jovially, 'the name is Wakefield. would you be kind enough to show me and my new bride to your best room?'

The man responded in a lowered tone. 'Might I have a word, Mr Wakefield?'

Edward blinked. This was not a good sign. Ellen was so weary, though, she hadn't noticed. Remaining calm, he steered her to a plush seating area in the lobby, which was out of earshot, before returning to the waiter. 'What do you want?'

The waiter started. 'Your sister is upstairs, sir. She asked me to direct you to her as soon as you arrived.'

'My *sister*?'

The man nodded.

A frisson tingled down Edward's spine. He didn't have a sister.

'Arrange refreshment for my wife and then take me to her.'

The man bowed and disappeared. Edward returned to Ellen.

'My dear, we seem to have a small issue that I need to resolve. The waiter will bring you something to eat and drink whilst I attend to it.'

Ellen's tired eyes widened. 'Might it be possible for me to enjoy the refreshment from the comfort of my room?'

'Of course, but first I must just …' He waved an arm vaguely as the servant came back with a plate of sandwiches, cakes, and tea. She eyed them with some interest, and he took advantage of the distraction to slip away from her.

He followed the waiter upstairs to a room, and rapped on the door. His heart sank when he saw who was behind it.

He walked in and closed it behind him. Paused for a moment, and then turned. 'I had not expected to see *you* here.'

Frances merely arched an eyebrow and went to sit on a chair by a small fire. 'You might want to thank me.'

'Indeed, if thanks are in order, you have them … Mama. How did you know where to find me?'

'I was at Turner's house when he received your letter.' She smiled at him. It was a predatory smile, and one he usually enjoyed seeing on her face. Today though, it was underscored with something else.

'Do you bring news from him?'

She nodded. 'I do indeed.'

He played along and moved closer. 'Anything you intend to share? Have you and my brother paved the way for the marriage to be accepted?'

'Oh, yes, James did his very best with Turner.'

Edward laughed. 'And …? What did he achieve? How is my dear father-in-law?'

She pulled a thoughtful face and spoke mildly. 'Well, I can tell you Turner is … incandescent. Yes, I think that does him justice.' Her eyes sparked. 'Incandescent with rage. He didn't give James any chance to speak, so James, in his wisdom, threw your letter at him and ran away down the drive whilst Turner shot at him …'

Edward was agog. '*What?*'

Frances's mild expression changed in a second. 'I *told* you. I warned you, but no, you thought you knew best. Well, I can tell you now that you need to gather up your pretty little wife and get her and yourself out of the country before you are apprehended. Turner has gone mad. Absolutely mad and he is coming for you.'

'Don't be hysterical, Frances. I'll talk him round,' Edward blustered. He needed to let Ellen rest. He wasn't sure how much further he could push her. He got up and paced the room, one hand smoothing his hair.

'Listen to me,' Frances hissed, coming to stand close. Too close. 'You either get yourself to the coast and get onto a ship for France, or you will be arrested. Trust me. I've seen him.'

Edward let go of a heavy breath. 'Where is James?'

'Leave James to me. Just get out of here, and off English soil.'

There were times for sparring with Frances, and times for action.

He decided the latter would serve him best. Edward ran down the stairs and headed for his wife, mind spinning. This was not how he had envisaged things turning out, not at all.

He found her sitting upright in her chair, sipping tea.

'Do you feel refreshed, my love?'

Ellen put the cup down. 'I'd like to go to my room, please. If I don't lie down soon, I may faint dead away.'

'Darling,' Edward began and saw her stiffen. He reached out and took her hand. 'Darling, I need to tell you something, but before I do, I need to remind you we are in a public place, in London.' He held her gaze until the import of his words registered.

'My love, your father has been forced to flee to France.'

'France?' Her lower lip began to tremble.

'Hush, hush,' he entreated, frantically searching for an explanation. 'Yes, love, France. It was the safest thing for him to do; his creditors were closing, apparently as yet unwilling to accept our married status because of your age. Things are going to take longer than we thought. We need to follow your papa, and when we are all together, presenting a united picture, no one will be able to challenge our arrangement. Once this is done, your father's creditors will be appeased, and your father will be a free man.'

He held his breath, but then saw that she believed him and congratulated himself. 'Of course,' she said, shaking herself. 'Do we leave first thing?'

Edward squeezed her hand and held her gaze. 'We need to leave now.'

Her face was positively ashen now. For a worrying moment he feared she might be ill. 'I need my clothes, my things. I ...' She gestured at her creased, dusty gown in exasperation, and he quelled a feeling of irritation with the girl's constant questioning.

'Hold fast, my love. We are so close now.' He touched her knee tenderly. 'In France you can shop to your heart's content, and we'll return for your things just as soon as it's safe.' He was mightily relieved when, at this, she pulled herself together. Edward rose to his feet and Ellen followed, like the incredibly stoic young lady she was.

'Let us make haste,' he said and folded Ellen's hand into the crook of his arm. 'You are the bravest of brave girls and your papa will be so unspeakably proud of you, as am I,' he murmured.

She swallowed and tears hovered again for a moment but did not fall.

# CHAPTER 28

*Two days later*

## William

William sat in the study of his London home on Parliament Street with Grimsditch and Robert. The atmosphere was more than a little tense.

'What news?' Grimsditch asked.

William drummed his fingers on the table. 'I made it to the Brunswick, and Wakefield had been there, but they had already left.'

Robert groaned. 'Every damned time …'

'I know, but I managed to speak to one of the footmen and he overheard them planning to leave for Calais. A place called the Hotel Quillon.'

'So, we go to Calais?' Robert said. William nodded, but Robert looked pensive.

'What? What is it?' William said.

Robert pursed his lips. 'Before we leap out with this, we need to be sure of the action we intend,' he said.

William scowled, but Grimsditch cut in. 'I agree,' he said. 'I've given the matter considerable thought, and whilst I completely understand that you want to get her away from the scoundrel … your wife's position does have merit.'

William groaned. 'For God's sake, I'm not letting him get away with this. How many times must I say it?'

'But Ellen's social standing will be destroyed,' Robert said. Of all of them, Robert was the most conscious of the aristocracy's ways. William had to admit that he didn't always appreciate the intricacies of society.

'I don't care about that. We can weather all of that.'

'Well, forgive me for saying so, but you should care,' Robert said. 'If you follow that path, your child will be ruined. All hopes of a great match will be dashed, and Jane will be utterly, utterly devastated. I doubt with her constitution she would survive the scandal.'

William glared at his brother. 'Would you allow your niece to be kidnapped in this fashion? Would you let everything you and I have worked for be handed over to some … some bacon-brained rattlepate? How can you even *countenance* it?'

Grimsditch leaned over and laid his hand over William's, surprising him into silence.

'William, we have been friends a long time, and trust me, I do not say this lightly. Yes, he may have kidnapped her, but *she* married him. She agreed to a marriage in Gretna, so there is a possibility that … she's happy with him. What else could have induced her to say yes? If he took her against her will, all she had to do was say no at the altar.'

'You think he threatened her?'

'I don't know; all we know is, she agreed. If you do as he says, pay him off, buy them a nice house in London, give them something to live on, they can be introduced to society, and all will be well. You will have your child back, and your wife will be able to hold up her head, but we will need to work fast and make sure that the newspapers are with us and spread the correct message.'

William was shaking. *It might be too late for that*, he thought. A newspaper man had already come knocking at his door, asking for his reaction to the marriage announcement. He had managed to keep his tone even as he feigned being late for an appointment, and asked the man to return another day. Had the fellow believed him? Or had he smelled a rat?

He looked at Grimsditch. 'I thought you were behind me.'

'I am. You will have my support regardless of what you decide, but I've had time to reflect on the journey here, and it would be wrong of me not to voice the concerns I have. Miss Davis could see the pitfalls, and it's often worth listening to the women on these matters.'

Grimsditch touched his arm again and didn't let up. 'I'm sorry to say this to you, my friend, but besides the fact that it will be damned difficult to bring him to justice whilst he's in France ... well, it's entirely possible he's ... deflowered her. There could be issue; there could be a grandchild.'

William shook off his hand, got up and paced the room. He couldn't even think about that.

Robert took up the pressure. 'When we get to Calais, you can knock seven bells out of him if you like, but she needs to come back as a respectable married lady. The match needs to be celebrated, and fast.'

William swallowed. He knew what they were saying was sensible. Knew that it was what his wife wanted, but he couldn't do it. He simply couldn't allow this lickspittle to take what was his. To take his child, take his fortune, and take everything he held dear. He couldn't allow it.

He sucked in a breath, put his hands on his hips, and looked at the assembled men.

'No.'

Grimsditch took a measured breath and gave him a look that spoke of resignation. 'Very well. But first, I think we need to visit Parliament.'

★   ★   ★

A week after his daughter's wedding, William slumped in a chair in his parlour on Parliament Street. Sadly, the advice of Robert and Grimsditch had been echoed in the shocked tones of Lord Canning, the foreign secretary. Grimsditch had managed to get them an interview, but when he'd explained his position and his intentions, the man had stared at him with something suspiciously like pity.

*My dear fellow, the child will be forsaken if you do not accept the marriage*, he'd pronounced. When William had tried to explain Ellen's innocence, Canning simply held up a hand. *It matters not. Believe me, she is ruined.* The utterly implacable statement had pierced his armour, found a chink in his faith, and it hurt. Perhaps they were all right.

He put a hand over his eyes. He needed to meet this Wakefield chap and assure himself that the man was at least decent. But how could he be decent and do what he did?

*Damnation.* He stalked to the decanter and filled his glass. He was taking a long drink when the butler tapped on the door and announced Mr Legh of Lyme Park. 'Show him in,' William grunted, surprised.

Legh came in looking extremely fine in London garb. He was the kind of man who had been brought up to instinctively know what was acceptable in society and what was not. And *he'd* told him Ellen was ruined too. *Damned aristocrats.*

'If you've come to hector me about accepting the marriage, I fear you are too late. I have been outnumbered.'

Legh frowned. He looked at the glass in William's hand then back at him. 'Beg pardon?'

'I have been outmanned, outgunned … out everything. Even the damned foreign secretary said she was ruined. Everyone says she is ruined. It doesn't seem to matter that she is completely innocent.'

Legh looked uncomfortable. 'Sadly, that is the way of the world. However, there is something you need to know. Something about Wakefield.'

'What?'

Legh looked at the brandy glass. 'May I have one of those?'

William's heart thudded in his chest as he poured and handed the glass to Legh. They sat in the leather armchairs facing each other beside the fire.

'What have you found?'

Legh took a long drink, inspected his fingertips, then looked up at him. 'He's done it before.'

\* \* \*

William scowled. 'What in God's name are you talking about?'

'Wakefield. He's done it before.' Legh took another drink. 'He abducted an heiress and persuaded the family to accept it and settle a significant sum to avoid scandal.'

'*What?*'

Through the bright red fury, he saw Legh nod. 'If it is Edward Gibbon Wakefield, he has done it before.'

William was out of his chair and pacing. 'Sweet Jesus … Tell me. Tell me everything.' He could barely stop his voice from shaking.

'I gather your daughter is a significant heiress?'

William stuck out his chin. 'A million pounds.'

Legh's eyes widened. 'That … *is* significant.' He cleared his throat. 'Well, it was ten years ago. Wakefield was young, and in dire straits. Creditors were chasing him, and he was completely at point non plus, so he abducted a sixteen-year-old heiress. A Miss Clara Pattle. He kidnapped her and—' Legh cleared his throat again '—compromised her, then demanded money from the family to keep the abduction quiet and claim it was a love match. He also demanded a large annuity.'

William was shaking.

Legh looked into his glass. 'They acquiesced and met his demands. Apparently, Miss Pattle gave every impression of being happily married to him. I understand there were a couple of offspring, but Miss Pattle died before she inherited her father's wealth, so he was back to the beginning. Expensive lifestyle, but not a feather to fly with.'

'So, he saw Ellen as an opportunity.'

'I fear so.'

William ground his teeth together. 'This changes everything.'

Legh hesitated, frowned, and again William knew he wasn't going to like what came next.

'Sadly, it changes nothing.'

Well, at least he knew he could rely on Legh for honesty. He smiled. He suspected it wasn't a pleasant smile.

'It changes everything,' he repeated. 'I'm going to get him, and I'm going to get my daughter back.'

Legh hesitated again.

'For Christ's sake, man, spit it out.'

Legh cocked an eyebrow and the faintest hint of a smile appeared on his face. 'Do you think it would be wise to see what your daughter would like to do? If she's happy with him

... *If* she's happy with him,' he repeated as William tried to interject, 'it might be kindest all round to let things lie. There are other ways to punish him that don't involve destroying your daughter, believe me.'

'Ask her?'

'A novel thought, but yes. Ask her what she wants. She will know what going through the courts will mean to her reputation. Ask her if she is prepared to do it, because if she isn't, she might just back Wakefield's story and make you look like a fool.'

*Christ!* William closed his eyes, took a long drink, and stared at the perceptive young man in front of him. He was sure that once Ellen knew the truth about Wakefield, she would not want to remain married to him. But of course, he could give her a choice – he *would* give her a choice ...

Legh cleared his throat yet again, and William rolled his eyes. *More honesty?*

'Am I right in thinking that you are bent on following them to France?'

William nodded and took another drink. 'Of course.'

'Might I make a suggestion?'

William's lips twitched. He really did like Legh. 'You can try.'

'What do you intend to do when you see him?'

William shrugged. 'Kill him?'

Legh smiled. 'I thought as much. If you are really going to try to prosecute Wakefield, you need to be whiter than white from now on. No more shooting at people, no ripping anyone limb from limb ...' he raised his eyebrows seeking acknowledgement.

William grunted.

'I suggest you let Grimsditch and your brother go and retrieve her. If she wants retrieving, that is.'

William wanted to shout, rail … but instead he put down his glass.

'Has anyone ever told you that you can be damned annoying when you're right?'

# CHAPTER 29

*Two days earlier*

*THE HOTEL QUILLON, CALAIS*

*Ellen*

Ellen arrived in Calais cold, exhausted, and in a foul mood. Edward tried his best to jolly her along, but she was beyond jollying. Her legs ached, her feet ached, and her rear ... well, the less said about that the better.

He took her to yet another hotel, the name of which escaped her. She was ushered to a small suite with what looked like a parlour and two bedrooms, where a beaming young maid in a large cap was waiting. As Ellen dragged herself to stand by the fire in her room, Edward came to her and put his arm about her shoulder.

'You look done in, love.' He squeezed her gently and kissed the side of her head. 'Why don't you retire, and we can talk more in the morning? I'm certain you will enjoy France when you are rested.'

Ellen nodded and leaned into his embrace for a moment before pulling away, anxious lest such demonstrations of affection might turn to more. 'Thank you, I will.'

Edward gave her a searching look before leaning in to give her a lingering kiss on the cheek. She had to force herself not to recoil – he had been drinking wine on the boat and his breath smelled unpleasantly sour. He reached up and cupped her chin, before kissing her again, on the mouth. She screwed her eyes closed and kept still.

He pulled away on a groan. 'What you do to me,' he whispered as he walked from the room.

Ellen shivered. She had no idea what she did to him.

The maid – Veronique – helped her undress, and when she was in her night-rail, with Veronique running a brush gently over her hair, she started to relax. She gave in to the rhythmic movement, as Veronique gathered it all together and plaited it swiftly.

Ellen smiled up at her. 'Thank you so much.'

Veronique bobbed a curtsy.

'Do you need anything else, madame?'

Ellen shook her head. 'No, that's perfect, thank you. You can go now.'

The girl bobbed a curtsy again, but as she turned to leave, there came a hard knock on the door. They both froze.

Ellen's heart exploded back into action, thundering like a jackrabbit. The door opened, and her husband came in. He was dressed for bed and wore what looked like a nightshirt beneath a silk robe in garish shades of emerald and puce. His feet were in slippers, but she could see his bare ankles, and he wore nothing at his throat. In only a night-shirt and dressing gown herself, and with her hair down, she felt horribly exposed. She gathered the edges of the robe together at her chin.

'I forgot to say that we will now be in time to attend James's wedding in Paris. We can purchase you some new clothes for it, to make sure you are fully up to snuff. What do you say?'

Ellen cleared her throat. The thought of more days in a carriage made her want to scream, even if the carriage was taking her to Parisienne modistes. She fixed a smile on her face. 'That would be very nice. When is the wedding?' If he said that they needed to leave on the morrow, she might just do bodily harm!

'It's on the 26th, Easter Sunday. So we have some time to get there.'

*Almost two weeks.* She nodded and smiled.

'Good, good,' he muttered, and his gaze travelled from her face down her body and to her bare feet. When he looked back up, he smiled slowly. 'I will introduce you to my very good friends, the British ambassador and his delightful wife. I'm sure you will love them.'

Ellen nodded. 'That sounds lovely.'

Edward took a step closer. 'You know, the ambassador's wife is the second daughter of the fifth Duke and Duchess of Devonshire.'

He left that comment dangling, and even in her exhausted state, Ellen perked up.

'The Devonshires? Are you part of the Devonshire set?' She'd heard outrageous tales of the old Duke and Duchess – they'd been at the very pinnacle of the ton.

'I am indeed,' he said, and licked his lips. 'And so shall you be.'

'Goodness,' she murmured. Paris with the daughter of the infamous Duke and Duchess of Devonshire? Her mother would be in alt when she heard about that!

Edward took another step closer and regarded her most fondly. She froze, and didn't breathe until he spoke again. 'We can talk more in the morning. Sleep well, my love.'

The door closed behind him, and as Veronique made to

follow, Ellen picked up the hairbrush and ran it through the end of her long plait for something to do. To her surprise, Veronique paused, laid a hand on her shoulder, and gave it a reassuring squeeze.

Ellen's gaze shot to hers in the mirror.

'All will be well, madame, you'll see.'

That was the kindest thing Ellen had heard in days. She nodded, too moved to speak, and hoped at least Veronique would sleep soundly tonight.

\* \* \*

A couple of days later, Ellen had to acknowledge that France was agreeable. Edward had assured her that her father was on his way now to see them, and this had helped her feel more settled. The weather was temperate; the hotel, whilst not top of the trees, was passable; and Edward had so far stayed in his own bedchamber. A visit to a stunningly talented modiste, Madame Jarnière, had furnished her with a small wardrobe of beautiful day dresses suitable for a young married lady, along with a pelisse, a coat, half boots, kid gloves, and matching bags. More exciting was an order for the most stylish evening dresses she had ever seen. She had to confess she was smitten with each item, even though Edward had been rather more involved in influencing her choices than she might have liked.

In all, it was pleasant. However, bouts of homesickness came upon her at times, strongly and with no warning. It was hard to explain why one suddenly became weepy, and in those moments, she wanted nothing more than to be laughing in the dormitory with Lavinia and Hester or curled up with a good book by her mother's chair.

She was also beginning to feel increasingly guilty about the time she spent lying in bed reading Thomas's book. She had finished it days ago, but since she'd only vowed to put it away once she was in her marital holding, she'd allowed herself to turn back to page one and begin again. When she felt that wave of sadness, that longing for home, escaping with him on his adventures was the only relief she could find.

This morning, though, she was as settled as she had ever been since leaving school. She was in the parlour of their apartment, adjusting a wayward lock of hair in the mirror, when her husband came into the room closely followed by a breakfast tray.

'You look lovely,' Edward said, kissing her on the cheek and flicking her nose with his finger. She was coming to dislike the way he did that, but she looked down at her new walking dress of blue figured muslin with a high neck, and remembered to smile.

'Thank you.'

'Are you planning to go out?'

'I thought I would take a walk.' Ellen sat and poured the tea. There was toast, butter, and jam on the tray – *tartines*, as Veronique called it – so she helped herself to a piece. Edward slathered two with jam and ate with gusto. In the sunlight streaming through the window, he did look quite dashing, his fair hair cast gold.

As she made to excuse herself, Edward surprised her by jumping up and coming around to her side of the table. He pulled her to her feet, his gaze appearing to roam all over her face and body as he kept hold of her hands.

'Our marriage didn't begin in the best of fashions, but we are good together, aren't we?' he said with disarming hopefulness.

'I hope I will be a good wife to you,' she managed to get out, not knowing quite where to look or what to say.

'You are a wonderful wife. I can scarce believe how lucky I am to have found you. And I have something for you.'

He fumbled in his pockets; could it be a letter from her father? But then he paused and gave her another of his persistent looks. 'It wasn't all bad, was it? Our journey to where we are now? We had fun on the way.'

Ellen struggled to recall having any fun, but it seemed churlish to argue, so she smiled and nodded.

'Remember Kirkby Lonsdale, when you and James slept right through our race across the Lake District? How, when you finally woke up, we all creased with laughter, then the strange maid brought us gingerbread and put it in your lap?'

Ellen recalled the moment and smiled. 'I do.'

Edward laughed. 'It was hilarious! James's face! And recall when Laing hit the anvil so hard, we both nearly fainted with shock?'

Ellen had to laugh at that. 'It was so loud!'

Edward pulled her into his arms and nuzzled his nose by her cheek. 'What tales we shall have to tell our grandchildren. What exploits!'

Ellen chuckled and let him hold her.

He squeezed her and then lowered his head to kiss her very gently on the lips. It was a better kiss than the last, and she wondered vaguely if she could prevail upon him to only kiss her when he'd been eating toast and jam. He deepened the kiss and Ellen's breath caught.

He pulled away and rested his forehead against hers. 'What you do to me,' he whispered. It really was awkward not knowing what he meant by that.

He took her face in both hands and smiled. 'I want you so badly, and I think you are beginning to want me too.' He kissed her again before she could reply, and slipped a hand back into his pocket. He brought out a ring box and Ellen's heart thumped a little harder.

He hesitated, and then handed the box to her. Her gaze shot to his, then back to the box. She opened it and gasped. 'Edward ...' It was a wedding ring set with square-cut emeralds. It looked like an antique.

'It was wonderful to be able to use your papa's ring in Gretna, but I thought you should have a wedding band of your own.' He took the ring and slid it onto her finger. 'We've been so happy here, I wanted to give you something. Something that would always remind you of our unusual, but marvellous, journey.'

'It's beautiful.' She held up her hand, tilting it this way and that.

# CHAPTER 30

Days passed, and Edward continued to be incredibly attentive and adoring as he squired her about the town. It was remarkably busy around the port, which gave the place a constant thrum of excitement, and there were some charming shops and cafes around the square. There was no sign yet of her papa arriving, but she could hardly claim this was a miserable way to wait for him. It was clear Edward was doing his best to entertain her.

However, each night, she lay wondering if he was going to come to her room. As the time to retire grew nearer, he would sit closer to her, hold her hand and kiss her in a most drawn-out way, and each night the length of the kissing grew. As it did, he became increasingly ardent and then appeared to be restraining himself. Every night she was sure he would come to her and claim his husbandly rights. Every night she lay waiting, flinching at every creak. She almost wished she could ask him about it, but she feared talking about it might precipitate the act. So, she remained silent on the subject and lived with the ever present, nagging uncertainty.

On the seventh day, she'd risen early. She was trying not to brood, when Edward smiled at her over the breakfast dishes. 'You look distracted, love.'

Ellen looked up. 'Forgive me, I was thinking of Mama. I do hope she will reply to my letters.' She'd written home a second time when they landed in France, signing off as *Mrs Wakefield*, as Edward had reminded her to. How would her mother receive this? Surely she would be delighted with her for saving the family home, but she would no doubt still be mourning the viscounts Ellen would never marry. She just needed to hear from her mother that everything was – and would be – well.

Edward reached out and touched her hand. 'Of course she will, love, just as soon as she knows where to reach us. In the meantime, rest assured that she knows you are happy. And if you're happy, your mama will be too.'

Ellen nodded, hoping that he was right in his estimation. 'What do your parents think of our marriage? You haven't spoken much about your family.'

Edward's gaze took a wistful turn. 'My father doesn't pay much attention to my personal affairs, I'm afraid, and my mother died a while back. She was a remarkable woman, and she would have loved you.'

Ellen poured them more tea. 'I'm so sorry to hear she is no longer with us.'

'Speaking of mothers,' he said, looking at his plate. 'I feel that we are … close enough now for me to … to talk completely openly with you.' He looked up in a beseeching way. 'Do you feel that way? May I do that?'

'Of course.' Ellen waited, wondering what on earth he could possibly say to surprise her now.

'Do you want to be a mother, Ellen?'

Ellen almost choked on her toast. Surely he didn't want to make her a mother at *breakfast* time?

'I do,' she said, taking a sip of tea. 'When the time is right, of course.'

He sighed. He looked unhappy. Was he growing impatient with her?

'I ask because,' he said, and she held her breath, 'when we arrive in Paris, I will introduce you to my children.'

Ellen doubted he could have said anything that would have shocked her more. She put her cup down clumsily, spilling tea on the tablecloth. 'Children? You have *children*?'

'I do.'

'You mentioned that you were a widower, but not that you have children.'

He was staring, unhearing, into the middle distance. 'Since Clara died, they've been my whole world. But my work drags me away from them all too often.' He swallowed and his eyes refocused. 'A dear friend of mine, Mrs Phyllida Bathurst, who is also a member of the Devonshire set, ensures they are cared for whilst I am away.'

'You must miss them abominably.' Ellen folded her hands in her lap and cleared her throat awkwardly. 'How many children do you have?'

He shook himself and attempted a smile. 'I have my dear Nina, who will be …' He apparently had to stop and think about the ages of his offspring. 'Nine years. And my Edward Jerningham, who is seven years.' His smile grew fond. 'We call him Jerningham.'

Ellen nodded: *one girl and one boy*. She tried to think of something else to say. Not only was she a married woman, but she was about to become a mother of … two?

'We had a third child, our dear elder Edward, who was born the year after Nina, but he passed almost immediately.'

'Oh, my sincere condolences. I can't imagine what it must be like to lose a child, and a son, too.'

He nodded and appeared to take a breath. 'Jerningham was born a couple of years later, but my … my wife, my Clara, died shortly afterwards.'

Ellen shook her head. 'I'm so, so sorry, that must have been dreadful for you all.'

'It was. I was cast down considerably for some time and the children were heartbroken.'

'Oh, Edward …' Ellen wanted to reach out to him, offer comfort, but didn't quite know how.

He offered her a small, sad smile. 'Thank you, my love. Your kindness does you credit.'

'You must have loved her a great deal.'

He nodded and inspected his thumbnail for a moment. 'I did. It was not until I met you that I could even consider remarrying,' he said, surprising her yet again.

'Really?'

He wiped his fingers under his eyes and Ellen wondered if he was weeping. She couldn't see any tears, but he looked so terribly sad. When his chin wobbled, she couldn't bear it anymore. She got up out of her chair and came around the table to sit beside him. She took hold of his hand.

'You don't need to talk about it.'

'But I do, you see … It's been so many years since my poor children had a mama, so many years since I've even felt that I might be able to love again, and now … here you are. Ellen …' He paused. 'Ellen, I love you.'

Shocked, Ellen held onto his hand tightly and tried to find something to say.

'Do you think … do you think you could find it in your heart to take on two motherless children?'

'Of course!' The words had left her mouth before she'd finished the thought. 'They've been through so much; you all have. I shall do my very best to … to look after them, to make them happy again.'

He shuddered and a choked sob escaped him. Ellen hesitated, but then gathered him awkwardly into her arms. He clung to her. 'I can't thank you enough,' he whispered. 'I love you so much, and I know Nina and Jerningham will love you too. And …' he snuggled closer, and she felt him crack a small smile against her shoulder, 'I can't wait for us to add to our little family.'

Ellen said nothing, but kissed the side of his head.

\* \* \*

After the revelations over the breakfast dishes were complete, Ellen set off with Veronique on their regular morning walk along the quay.

All that Edward had told her – his grief for Clara, his declaration of love for Ellen – was overwhelming. But it did make him seem more … human. Now that his eyes weren't urgently searching hers, she could think more freely, and she was beginning to ask herself: could she love him and his children? *Could* one learn to love?

And what might it be like when, one day, she and Edward had children of their own? She imagined a warm, sweet bundle in her arms and wondered if its hair would be dark like hers, or fair like his.

She smiled, and picked up her pace as Veronique trotted obligingly alongside. She was Mrs Edward Gibbon Wakefield now, for better or for worse, and it would do her no good to wish otherwise. And besides, Edward seemed so very ardent in his devotion, and there was no denying that he was spectacularly handsome. She'd seen the admiring glances he drew from other women when they were out in public, and that made her feel quite pleased to be on his arm.

She pulled her shawl closer about her shoulders against the spring breeze as she and Veronique walked along the quayside, past the market stalls laden with freshly caught fish, fruits and vegetables, cheeses, eggs, and baked goods. As much as she missed the toasted crumpets of home, the aroma of a French *boulangerie* was the most delicious scent she'd ever had the pleasure to encounter. Perhaps, she supposed, she needed to give Edward and their marriage more of a chance. Indeed, she needed to …

Ellen stopped. Behind the fish stall in front of her, the ship from England had moored, and the passengers were disembarking. She held up her hand to shield her eyes from the sun.

*It couldn't be, could it?* Her heart pounded as she stared. 'Uncle Robert?'

She clapped both hands to her mouth as tears sprang to her eyes and she trembled all over.

'Uncle Robert!' she shrieked, lifted her skirts, and ran.

\* \* \*

Ellen ran as fast as she could, whilst Veronique shouted after her. But as she dodged around the people milling about, she found herself quite unable to make progress past a huge cart laden with luggage. By the time she had circumnavigated it, her uncle was no longer in sight.

Frantic, she looked this way and that, and Veronique touched her arm.

'Madame, madame … what is it?'

'My uncle. Quick, Veronique, we must return to Mr Wakefield.' She managed to maintain a modicum of decorum as she made sure that Uncle Robert had definitely disappeared, then she and the maid hurried back to the hotel.

She burst into the room to find Edward in his shirtsleeves reading the newspaper. He looked up, and his eyebrows raised in shock at her flustered appearance.

'Darling, whatever has transpired?'

Ellen struggled to get her breath. 'Uncle,' she gasped. 'My uncle, he got off the ship from England. My Uncle Robert is here in Calais, but I lost sight of him. Will you help me find him? He must be here to meet my papa. Oh, Edward, I *saw* him!'

Edward put his newspaper down carefully. 'My dear, that is simply the most wonderful news. Didn't I tell you that you would hear from your family soon?'

'Will you help me find him?'

He stood up and pulled her into his arms. She clung to him, and he peppered the side of her head with small kisses.

'My love, calm yourself. I wrote to your uncle myself before we left England, and gave him our direction. He knows exactly where to find us.'

'Oh!' Ellen smiled. Edward had done that for her? It was the first nice surprise she'd had in weeks. She laughed at her foolishness, then cried a little. Edward drew her more tightly into his arms and rocked her gently.

'Why don't you stay here, gather yourself, and let me go and greet him? Then I'll bring him to you.'

'Can't I come with you?'

Edward laughed softly and shook his head as he let go of her. 'I doubt you want an emotional reunion with your dear uncle in the lobby of a hotel?'

Ellen felt her cheeks warm. He was right. 'Of course not.'

Edward nodded and squeezed her arm. Ellen was so thrilled she threw herself back into Edward's arms and hugged him. They swayed together for a long moment.

'Lord,' Edward whispered in her ear. 'I love you. I love you so much.'

Ellen pulled back to look at him and, leaning forward, kissed him shyly on the mouth. It was the first time she had initiated any such contact between them, and this time, his lips felt soft, his embrace warm – it made her heart race.

Edward groaned as he lifted his head. He pressed his forehead against hers. 'Please, please, my love, remember that kiss. Whatever happens.'

Ellen laughed, but Edward looked serious, probably more serious than she had seen him. 'Promise me you will remember that I love you so very, very much. How happy we are, and how lovely it was when you kissed me just then.'

She nodded, smiling into his eyes, wondering why he was so anxious. 'I promise,' she said, and stood on her tiptoes to kiss him again.

# CHAPTER 31

*Edward*

Edward ran lightly down the steps to the hotel lobby, not quite knowing what to expect. He had not, of course, written to Ellen's uncle, but if Frances's sniping had taught him anything, it was that the Turners were damned resourceful. Somehow, they already knew Ellen was in Calais; it was only a matter of time before they'd track her – and him – to the Hotel Quillon.

One thing was for sure, the Turners would need to fall in with his plans swiftly if they were to avoid the most appalling scandal. A scandal they could ill afford. The significance of their fortune had allowed them entrée into society, but only so far. If they gave anything at all for their social standing, they would need to embrace the marriage vocally and visibly.

Edward smiled to himself. He liked the idea of Ellen's uncle on the back foot. It would give him the right atmosphere to launch into his impassioned speech about his love and devotion. He had to admit, he really was becoming rather fond of the girl. She was kind, and her beauty was a taste he was fast acquiring. As for that bright young mind of hers … He intended to enjoy moulding it. Her almost unquestioning acceptance of his children had been positive in the extreme, and this morning he genuinely felt they were but days away from consummating the marriage. Then their relationship would be cemented for good.

He was still smiling when he entered the lobby of the hotel, boots ringing on the tiled floor. He spoke to the concierge and arranged for the use of a pleasant parlour where he would be able to talk to Robert Turner before allowing him access to Ellen. He was forced to acknowledge that therein lay the danger: what would Ellen say when she found out it had all been a ruse? He could hazard a guess at her fury, given the spirit she displayed. However, he had every faith in his ability to bring her under his thumb when he took her to Paris, and she saw the circles that she would be able to move in as his wife. It was a finely balanced plan, but all the more interesting for it.

He didn't have to wait long before no less than three imposing gentlemen entered the lobby. He immediately recognised Mr Grimsditch, which gave him his first qualm. He'd made enquiries about him when they'd planned the whole venture; the man was as ruthless as he was talented. And he presumed one of the other men was the uncle? God alone knew who the other chap was. But there was no William Turner.

Grimsditch strode forward, brows pulled down, a cold look in his eye.

'Wakefield.'

'Mr Grimsditch, how good of you gentlemen to come. I have procured us a room, as I doubt you wish to have this discussion in public?'

Grimsditch gave him a look that would have melted glass, but Edward returned it with a bland smile. 'This way.' He set off walking, making them follow.

'Is my father-in-law with you?' he threw over his shoulder and then turned his back on them again. If they thought they could scare him with this little ambush, they thought wrong.

'He is not.'

'Ah, a pity, my dear wife was so hoping to see him.' He led them into the small parlour and closed the door. He strode to the sideboard, where brandy and glasses were laid out, and lifted the decanter.

'Drink?'

'Where is my niece?' said one of the men. The tall one, with an air of superiority about him. So, he *was* a Turner.

Edward gave him a kindly smile and poured several glasses and handed them about. 'My *wife* is here, but I think we need a conversation before I allow you to speak with her.'

'Before you *allow*?' the man spluttered, turning red in the face and putting his glass on the table untouched.

'I don't believe we've met, sirs?' Edward waited for the gentlemen he didn't know to introduce themselves. They seemed content to glare silently, until Grimsditch said curtly, 'This gentleman is Ellen's uncle, Mr Robert Turner. And this,' he said, gesturing to the third man, 'is Mr Ellis Brown, a Bow Street Runner.'

Well, that was a turn up. Edward extended a hand to shake, but neither gentleman reciprocated. He let his arm drop with an exaggerated sigh.

'Gentlemen, might I suggest that we discuss this like the civilised men that we are? I know the circumstances of our marriage were unusual, but I can assure you that my wife is quite happy with our arrangement, as am I.'

'She may well be,' Grimsditch interjected, 'but her family is not. Ellen Turner is seventeen years old. She is not old enough to marry, not old enough to give consent to marry, and certainly not old enough to be subjected to the trauma that you inflicted upon her person.'

'I say ...'

Grimsditch warmed to his topic. 'You, sir, are nothing but a ruthless ravisher. Nothing but a jumped-up fortune hunter, and a callous, despicable seducer.'

'My dear man ...' Edward gave his best impression of bruised virtue.

'I can assure you, Wakefield, I am your dear nothing. We are not prepared to discuss this with you any further. I insist that we are taken to Miss Turner.'

Edward smiled. 'I am more than happy to take you to *Mrs Wakefield*. I would simply request the opportunity to—'

'Here,' Grimsditch said, pulling a paper from his coat with a flourish. 'Should you be in any doubt about Mr Turner's intentions, I have in my possession this document, which will ensure that the strongest possible measures will be taken to restore Miss Turner to her family. I have direction from the foreign secretary himself.' He spread the letter and read.

'*The act committed was a very atrocious one, that he has taken away Miss Turner, a mere child, by means of a forged letter, that he has struck a blow at the peace of the family, the effects of which he never could repair.*'

Edward fought not to roll his eyes; Grimsditch still hadn't finished.

'You are a fiend, Wakefield. You deserve to be shot. Now I command you to—'

'Mr Grimsditch,' Edward interrupted with a raised voice. 'I assure you I understand. I have a young daughter of my own; if anyone were to take her off, I would put a bullet in his head.'

'I don't give a damn for what you may or may not understand. Under English law, this marriage is not legal, and we are taking Miss Turner back with us to England.'

Edward sighed, and Robert Turner moved closer to him. Edward resisted the urge to step backwards.

'What in God's name possessed you?' Turner said. 'What on earth could induce you to carry off a child you have never met?'

It was clear that Robert Turner had never been in dire need of funds.

'Because I knew of her. And once I *had* met her, I was convinced that she was the only one for me. That only my dear Ellen—'

'Just like Clara Pattle was the only one for you? Or was it perhaps Ellen's fortune that attracted you to her, just like it was Miss Pattle's fortune you were seeking.'

Edward gave them an exaggerated pout. 'You wound me.'

At that, Turner and Grimsditch both spoke at once, gesticulating. Brown remained stony-faced and silent in the hubbub. Edward wanted to laugh. It would be folly to do so, but he had the upper hand. Or he would do, if he could just speak to Ellen before this rabble before him put poison in her ear. He felt sure that Ellen had a strong enough sense of self-preservation to do the sensible thing and lie in the bed she'd made for herself.

Turner moved closer still. Chin pugnacious, eyes glittering, fists balled. 'I demand to see my niece. Go and get her. Now.'

*Christ*, Frances was right. These Turners were different. Nothing but a pair of northern lobcocks with no finer sensibilities at all.

'Gentlemen, as besotted with me as my wife is, your sudden appearance here will no doubt excite her, and throw her emotions off kilter. I should like to be here when you speak to her, to reassure her of my love.'

'No!' The word was said in chorus by the three men; so Mr Brown wasn't mute, after all. It seemed he was fighting a losing battle: all he could do was hope that Ellen would stand firm.

'Might I beg you not to give her a poor opinion of me? She married me – that cannot be undone. If you make her unhappy now, you will make her unhappy for life. Is that what you want?'

In that moment, he saw it in the gentlemen's faces: they agreed with him. But then it struck him. *They* might see reason, but it was her father's thoughts on the matter that would count. And although absent, he clearly felt differently.

Edward licked his lips and pinched the bridge of his nose as though he were deeply affected. 'May I speak with you after you have met with her? Will you at least grant me that?'

Grimsditch stared at him for a long moment, and then nodded. 'Go and fetch Ellen. She and Mr Brown can speak with her uncle, and I will wait with you outside.'

Again, Edward wanted to laugh. Did they think he was going to abscond? That he was going to run from the best thing that had ever happened to him?

He headed back to their rooms, where Ellen was waiting. Grimsditch went with him. 'You know, I have treated her with the utmost deference,' he said as they walked side by side.

'I should damned well hope so.'

Edward hesitated a moment, then made a decision. 'I can assure you that your Miss Turner is the same Miss Turner as she was when I took her away.'

Grimsditch gave him a sharp look. 'The marriage is unconsummated?'

'My dear man, what do you take me for? I've told you, my attachment to Ellen is real. I hold her in the highest regard and would never do anything that might cause her a moment of distress. Despite what you might think, I am cognisant of her youth and inexperience, and I am not a brute.'

Grimsditch sniffed. 'No? Just a kidnapper?'

This time, Edward didn't even try to hide his roll of the eyes. He tapped on the door in front of them and opened it.

Ellen got immediately to her feet, her eyes lighting up when she saw Grimsditch. She ran to him, holding out both her hands. Grimsditch gallantly bowed over them.

'My dear Miss Turner, how relieved I am to see you.'

Ellen beamed. 'Oh, Mr Grimsditch, and I you. I can't tell you how much. Tell me, is Papa with you? Is he here?'

'No, my dear, he is waiting for you in London.'

Ellen flashed Edward a look and then turned back to Grimsditch. 'Is it safe for him there?'

'Safe?'

'Yes …'

'Shall we?' Edward interrupted.

Grimsditch paused, but acquiesced. 'Come, I have your uncle waiting for you. Let us go and greet him and then we can tell you anything you need to know about your papa.'

Ellen nodded. 'Oh yes, please, let's do that. I've been so terribly worried about him. When Mr Wakefield and his brother explained all about the collapse of the bank, of both banks, I couldn't believe it.'

They bustled out of the room and Grimsditch gave him a fulminating glare over Ellen's head. Edward suppressed a pang of anxiety at her referring to him as *Mr Wakefield*, took hold of her hand, and whispered, 'Remember, darling girl, what a marvellous life we have ahead of us in Paris. I love you.'

Ellen's lip quivered, and she nodded, but looked uncertain. Edward forced the gentle smile to remain on his face until she turned away.

# CHAPTER 32

*Ellen*

Ellen was trembling as she walked to meet her uncle. She gripped Edward's hand gratefully, because Mr Grimsditch's scowling silence frightened her.

They arrived at a door and Mr Grimsditch moved to open it, waving Edward back. Edward looked cross but remained at a distance, as Mr Grimsditch turned back to her.

'My dear Miss Turner, in here is your uncle and a Bow Street Runner. You can talk to them and tell them everything that this man has done to you in confidence. You need hold nothing back.'

'Done to me?' Ellen frowned as she looked again at Edward. 'I don't understand.'

Mr Grimsditch looked discomfited. 'They just want to talk to you so they can ascertain how you came to be married to this man.'

Ellen had an uneasy feeling in her stomach. 'I married him to save Papa. After Papa spoke to Mr James Wakefield, and sent a message. After I had your note begging me to marry him.'

At this, Mr Grimsditch's ears became red, and he made a strangled noise. He looked like he might explode.

She turned to Edward, baffled. 'Would someone care to enlighten me as to what is going on?'

Edward spoke softly; all the while, Grimsditch glared at him. 'Your uncle has asked to speak to you alone, and I have acceded to that request, my love. I'll be right here, and we can talk afterwards.'

Ellen looked from her husband to the man she knew her father trusted above all others. Edward appeared to be doing his best to remain calm, but there was something in his manner that unnerved her. Mr Grimsditch opened the door for her silently and, feeling entirely unprepared for what awaited her, she stepped inside.

'Ellen! My dearest child, it is so good to see you safe and well.'

Unable to contain herself, she flung herself into her Uncle Robert's arms. The smell of his coat reminded her so much of home, that she promptly burst into tears.

'Oh, Uncle Robert. I am so, so pleased to see you. How is Papa faring? Is he somewhere safe? Please tell me he is.'

Uncle Robert gently took her shoulders and looked at her closely. 'Safe? What do you mean, my dear?'

'From his creditors and the men who were pursuing him.'

Her unease increased when she saw the puzzled look on her uncle's face.

'Come, my dear, I think it would be enormously helpful if you could explain how you came to be in France, married to this … man.'

'You mean you don't know? Hasn't Mr Grimsditch, or anyone at the Blackburn bank, explained?'

'Explained what, my dear?' Uncle Robert said as he gestured to a small sofa. She sat on it beside him. Only then did she notice another man at the edge of the room, who she presumed was the Bow Street Runner. The man stepped forward, and nodded at her mutely.

'This is Mr Brown, who is here to help us clear all of this up,' her uncle said.

Ellen returned a polite nod to Mr Brown. *Clear all of this up?* Did they need a Bow Street Runner to finalise the transfer of Shrigley from her papa to her husband? Something told her it was for another, more ominous reason. Her sense of unease grew.

'Why have you left Mr Grimsditch and Mr Wakefield outside the room?' she asked. 'Why – beg pardon, Mr Brown – do you need to be accompanied by a Bow Street Runner? For goodness' sake, please tell me what's going on!'

'We need to speak to you without Mr Wakefield's influence, Miss. Get the facts straight,' Mr Brown said. His voice was very deep, and stern.

Ellen put a hand to her throat. A clock chimed softly somewhere, and she could hear noise from the road outside, but her world seemed to shrink to the small parlour.

Uncle Robert took both her hands and squeezed them. 'From the beginning, love.'

Ellen tried to breathe deeply, but it was hard. She squared her shoulders.

'Papa sent Monsieur Thevenot to school to collect me. He gave Miss Daulby a letter from Dr Hull, which said Mama was terribly ill and needed me to go home straight away.'

Her uncle nodded. Encouraged, she continued. 'We got to Manchester, where I thought I would be meeting Dr Hull before heading to see her, but then Mr Wakefield explained to me that the letter had been a ruse to get me out of the school without causing a scandal.'

'And why did Mr Wakefield think it necessary to do this?' Mr Brown said.

'Because of the bank collapse. Mr Wakefield told me that Ryle and Daintry had collapsed and with it, Papa's fortune. He explained he was an old friend of Papa's, and since Papa was fleeing from his creditors, we needed to follow him.'

'Follow him? Why did you feel the need to follow him, miss? Why not go home to your mama?'

Ellen thought for a moment, disconcerted by Mr Brown's question. She remembered the desperate sense of urgency, the fear and panic that had assailed her, making it seem imperative that she go with Edward to find her father. 'Well … well, because Mr Wakefield told me that was what Papa wanted.'

Uncle Robert nodded. 'So, you followed him?' he asked.

'Yes. We went to Halifax, but we missed Papa, and then we were forced to head for Carlisle. That's where we heard that the Blackburn bank had collapsed, and the loan Papa had arranged meant that Shrigley would be lost.' She wasn't explaining it all very well, but Uncle Robert was still nodding at her to continue. 'So, Mr Wakefield came up with the idea to save Shrigley by marrying me. Even though the money was gone, the property could be transferred to me, and Mama wouldn't be flung into the streets.'

Uncle Robert let go of her hands, put a hand over his mouth, and closed his eyes for a moment. It frightened Ellen.

'Did I do wrong?' Her voice felt small.

'No, my love, you did nothing wrong,' he said, looking at her again.

Mr Brown's expression was steely. 'Go on, please, miss. What happened in Carlisle?'

'Well, Mr Grimsditch and Papa were there, but being pursued by an awful crowd of ruffians, and they had to flee. Edward's brother, James, managed to speak to Papa and Mr Grimsditch, and they said that if I had ever loved Papa, I would marry Edward and save him. They gave me the note that Mr Grimsditch wrote, and the ring that Papa gave me for the wedding. I knew then that it was the only thing to do.'

'And how do you feel now about Mr Wakefield?' Robert said.

Ellen looked at her uncle, unsure of what answer he expected. She sighed. 'Grateful?'

'So that's why you went to Gretna and married him? You thought it was the only way to save your mama and papa.'

Ellen nodded.

'Are you in love with him?'

Ellen blushed. She shook her head. 'I am … trying to get to know him. Trying to … love him.'

'Darling, I'm sorry, but I must ask. Has he … has he behaved as a gentleman towards you?' Uncle Robert said.

Ellen frowned. 'He's been very kind.'

Uncle Robert bit his lip for a moment, then spoke very softly. 'Has … has the union been consummated?'

Ellen's heart beat so hard it made her feel queasy. She felt colour flare in her face as she tried to form words that she never thought to say to a much-loved uncle.

'No, he has been a gentleman in that way.'

'He hasn't touched you, or hurt you?'

Ellen stared at the floor as the heat in her face intensified. 'He … he has kissed me. Quite a lot.'

'I see.' Uncle Robert took hold of her hands again. 'My dearest, dearest Ellen, you know I love you very much.'

'Of course I do.'

'Well, I have something to tell you, and it's not going to be easy for you to hear.'

Fear shimmered in her belly and crawled up to her throat. 'What?'

'It was all a lie. Everything Edward Gibbon Wakefield said to you was a dreadful lie.'

# CHAPTER 33

Ellen laughed. What Uncle Robert said was so absurd, she couldn't not laugh. 'Beg pardon?'

Her uncle was looking at her, with varying expressions of sympathy, unhappiness, and … wariness.

'What do you mean it was a dreadful lie?'

Her Uncle Robert took hold of her hand. 'My love, the banks are fine. Ryle and Daintry is in good health, the Blackburn bank is thriving. Your mama and papa are perfectly well, aside from worrying about you.'

'Papa is not bankrupt?' Ellen felt like she was floating. This couldn't be real.

Uncle Robert shook his head. 'He is, and continues to be, one of the wealthiest men in the area. Wakefield is not your papa's friend; they've never even met. Wakefield lied to you about the whole thing from start to finish.'

Ellen felt tears rise. 'It wasn't true?'

Uncle Robert nodded, and his eyes looked damp. 'I'm afraid not.'

'But why?' Ellen burst out. 'Why did he tell me all that? Why would he *do* that to me?'

'Oh, love,' Uncle Robert murmured and rubbed her arms. He blinked rapidly. He cleared his throat and appeared not to be able to continue for a moment. 'Edward Gibbon Wakefield is a … a fortune hunter. He's done this before. He abducted a young heiress and married her ten years ago, but she died before he could inherit her papa's fortune. He's hoping that now you are married to him, your papa will settle a house and a living on him so you can take up your place in society, in the knowledge that on your papa's passing, the entire Turner wealth will become his.'

Ellen stared at him. Edward, a fortune hunter? Could he be that cruel?

'I was abducted?' She looked at Mr Brown, the Bow Street Runner.

He nodded. 'I'm afraid you were, Miss. I'm here to make sure that we are able to uphold the law and ensure your safety.'

Her uncle swallowed. 'You were abducted, my love. On the pretext that you were saving your papa, when in fact there was nothing at all wrong.'

'I see.' Her stomach rolled. She felt sick and unspeakably stupid.

'Ellen?'

Shock gave way to fury, and it burned through her with the realisation of what Edward had done, the full import, the reality of it.

She put her hands to her cheeks that now blazed. 'He's ruined me, hasn't he.' She was shaking. All her plans, all her dreams, all up in smoke because Edward Wakefield decided he wanted her papa's fortune. Any dreams she might have had of falling in love were gone, any dreams of Thomas were gone … It was so unfair. So unspeakably unfair. 'I feel so stupid,' she whispered.

Uncle Robert passed her his handkerchief, and she realised she was crying. 'You are not stupid, my dear, not at all. Remember, he has done this before, and he used the people you love the most to terrify you into doing his bidding. He's a clever and cold-hearted man.'

'He said he was a widower with children.'

Uncle Robert nodded. 'He is. Her family paid him to keep quiet, the marriage stood, they were able to rejoin society, and they had a family.'

'Is that what will happen to me?'

He made a sound of distress. 'It's one option open to you.'

'What do Mama and Papa think?'

'You will be able to talk to them about it when you come home with us. Would you like to do that?'

'Am I able to? Will I need his permission?'

Uncle Robert grunted something she didn't catch and ran a hand through his hair, disordering it entirely. But she feared she already knew the answer.

'I'm married to him. I'll always be married to him. I am now his to control, aren't I? He owns me.'

Uncle Robert took her hand again. 'Your papa has some thoughts about this. If marriage is really not what you want, he thinks there might be another way. But first, Wakefield wants you to talk to him.'

'Must I?'

Ellen had never thought of herself as fragile, or the kind of girl to have the vapours, but at this moment – as shame, misery, and humiliation flooded every inch of her body – she felt faint and understood why so many women took to their beds.

Uncle Robert smiled. 'I will be with you, my dear.'

Ellen got unsteadily to her feet. She took a deep breath, smoothed her skirt, and nodded. 'Then bring him in.'

★　★　★

Ellen watched as Edward and Mr Grimsditch came through the door. Edward came straight for her, arms outstretched, his face a picture of worry. For a moment, she wanted to let him embrace her. All she needed to do was accept him, and they could be man and wife in the eyes of the world, exactly as Uncle Robert said. If she did that, this would all go away.

But knowing what he'd done to her, how could she let him touch her, ever again?

She stared at him for the longest time, then left her hands by her side.

He looked genuinely anguished by the rejection. But then he would, wouldn't he? He stood to lose a fortune.

'Ellen, my dearest love, will you give me leave to explain?'

'How?'

He tilted his head and tried to look into her eyes. 'Sweetheart,' he wheedled, 'remember what you promised?'

Ellen returned his stare, defiant, trying hard not to appear afraid. 'I promised to remember that you said you love me.'

He smiled and captured one of her hands in his. He ran his thumb over the back of her hand. 'That *we* love *each other*. I love you so very much, and you love me – I know you do. We can have a good life together. We can be so happy.' He tried once again to pull her into his arms, but she resisted, and snatched her hand back.

'You lied to me. You made me believe that my family was ruined.'

'Darling ...'

'Well, I am ruined now, aren't I!'

'Not …' He gave her a tender smile, but his words held an undertone of threat that rang as clear as day. 'Not if we stay together. If we present a united front and explain that it was a romantic elopement.'

Something snapped in Ellen then. It struck her that he was exactly as her first instinct had told her. Untrustworthy … unnatural … sly …

She gave him a smile, one that made his eyes gleam with anticipation. Then, with all the strength that she could draw upon, she slapped him across the face.

His head snapped to the side then he rounded on her, a cold, dark anger in his eyes that momentarily he couldn't conceal. Then he recovered himself and laughed, holding his cheek. 'My, my, Ellen. You have fire, I'll give you that. I think we are going to be very good together.'

Ellen ran into her uncle's arms, palm stinging, cheeks burning.

Mr Grimsditch looked Edward up and down with absolute contempt. 'Mr Wakefield, you have practised upon this child the most extraordinary deception I have ever heard of. We will be taking Miss Turner back to England now, to be with her family. If you fail to comply, Mr Brown here will place you in custody.'

Far from being chastened, Edward simply lifted an eyebrow. 'My dear man, we are on the wrong side of the water for that. You and your worthy Mr Brown have no jurisdiction here.'

Ellen felt her Uncle Robert's fists clench. She looked over at Mr Brown, hoping he would correct Edward, but the man shifted awkwardly and said nothing. Mr Grimsditch, however, looked utterly determined, and with something of a flourish, he pulled papers from his coat.

'In addition to the letter from the foreign secretary, I have here a warrant for your arrest. The French police will aid our cause. And for the last time, I am *not* your *dear man!*'

At this, Edward smirked. Actually smirked ... Ellen couldn't believe it.

'The gendarmerie will do nothing of the sort,' he said. 'The French understand passion, and they will have no interest in separating a pair of runaway newlyweds. You see, you might know all about English law, but I understand international law. And I repeat, your documents have no use whatsoever here. Ellen is my wife ... *my wife*' – the way he emphasised both words made Ellen's stomach churn – 'and you have no authority over what happens to her. *I* have that authority, *my dear man*, and if I say she is staying here with me, *she stays.*'

Edward gazed at Edward in horror, as her Uncle Robert held her tighter. Edward had nothing to hide anymore; he really was a monster. Mr Grimsditch retorted, loudly, but Edward countered even louder, and as the two gentlemen stood toe to toe and shouted at each other, debating who had legal entitlement to her person, she grappled with the choice she had to make. She could attempt some sort of life with Edward and his children, where she might have a modicum of respectability and a place in society. Or she could try and have the marriage annulled as Mr Grimsditch seemed to be suggesting in his raging at Edward. Did she want that? How likely was it to work? And would she have any reputation left at the end of it, either way? She doubted it.

What it boiled down to, though, was: should she let Edward Gibbon Wakefield get away with what he had done to her and to her family?

She pulled away from her uncle's embrace and cleared her throat.

Both men stopped shouting to look at her. Edward's hair had fallen over his brow and he pushed it back.

'I am not your wife. You tried to make me believe you loved me, but all you love is money. I will not stay here, and I will never go near you again.' She took off the emerald ring that he had given her and put it on the floor between them.

She would have liked to make a dignified and sophisticated departure from the room then, but it was all too much.

She burst into tears again.

Her uncle gathered her up once more, and she peeped out at Edward through her tears. Something changed in his demeanour then; his shoulders sagged, and his whole person deflated, as if all the malevolence had been sapped from him. She could still see the imprint of her hand on his cheek. He stared at the ring on the floor with such sadness, and for such a long time, that she almost believed he was truly hurt.

'Forgive me, my love,' he said shakily. 'I'm being an absolute ogre. The most important thing in all of this is your happiness.' His voice was soft, and he looked at her with yearning.

Ellen felt a single tear drop onto her cheek as she awaited his next words.

'You should have the chance to talk to your family. I should have given you that sooner.' He sighed and put his hands in the air. 'You've caught me, Ellen. The way I've misled you is despicable. And believe me, I despise myself for it. When we first set out on this adventure, I hoped we might rub along together well. I never imagined I was capable of falling in love with you, after everything I have been through in the past. But then …' He reached out as though to touch her and then let his hand drop. 'But there you were. Unspeakably brave, beautiful, courageous, witty … Ellen, you changed me. For all my deceit, I swear on my life that's the truth. I love you.'

She hesitated, then looked up at him. And as she did so, she caught the calculating look she had seen before. He was still playing with her, and she remembered just how much he had to lose. How much he'd frightened her to get what he wanted.

He swallowed and glanced at her, sad eyed. 'Do you still wish to return home? Or would you like to come with me to Paris first, and see for yourself the life we could have?'

Robert, Mr Grimsditch and Mr Brown were silent. It seemed they were all holding their breath. Ellen lifted her chin at Edward, but her reply was aimed at anyone but him. 'Let us leave on the next boat.' She knew people would think her foolish, but she couldn't countenance remaining here any longer. 'I do not, and cannot, accept that this is now my life.'

Grimsditch's look was faintly admiring. 'You are your father's daughter,' he said, with a shake of his head. 'Right you are: let's get you home.'

\* \* \*

## Edward

Edward Gibbon Wakefield sat in his room, tapping his fingers on the desk. All was not lost. Despite the altercation with Ellen's odious uncle, the singularly annoying Grimsditch, and that useless prop of a Bow Street Runner, all was not lost. Turner had far too much to lose by allowing this to become public knowledge. Far too much to lose by admitting that he had been foolish enough to allow his only child to be abducted and married from under his nose. He was a proud man, a vain man. He would come around when the prospect of her ruin, and the damage it would do to his own reputation, became real.

He had come to the conclusion that he needed Ellen to leave with his blessing. That she needed to know his love was true and steadfast. It would make it easier for her to return, once she realised that her life as she knew it was over. He suspected she had no idea how savage the *on dits* could be, how they'd relish taking down a family with a background in trade. Once she learned that, a life in Parisian society with Edward would be more tempting than ever. *Especially* once he was as comfortably ensconced in its highest echelons as he'd let on … which he was firmly convinced was only a matter of time.

So, he put pen to paper, and wrote with all the passion that he could muster to his new father-in-law. This time, he was even more extravagant in his expression of guilt, accepting even the cruellest insults that had been thrown at him during the storming of his honeymoon in Calais, abasing himself thoroughly. He begged Turner to speak to anyone who knew him, as they would vouch for his love for Clara. He reiterated, quite strongly, his forbearance in not pursuing his rights as a husband, that Ellen was still unsullied and pure.

Then he again threw down the gauntlet, carefully disguised as an olive branch. He reminded him of the delicacy of Mrs Turner's health, and the damage that a scandal could do to her, to him, to his child. He assured him that despite the nature of the methods he employed to persuade Ellen to the altar, he remained a man of honour and couldn't bear to see the family thrown to the wolves, with their lives wrecked by the scandal that would follow should he refuse to acknowledge the marriage.

He finished with a flourish and skimmed the letter with satisfaction before sealing it. Immediately this was done, he picked up another sheet of paper and penned a missive to his brother, apprising him of the developments. He would meet James in Paris to attend his wedding on Sunday, and whilst he was there, he'd cement his position within Parisian society. He was already friends of friends with the British ambassador; all that remained was to charm him at one or two more parties. Then, by the time he returned to England as the toast of the Devonshire set, the Turners would be begging to welcome him to the family. Just as the Pattles had done.

# CHAPTER 34

Edward arrived in Paris on Thursday 23 March and was delighted to find that, as good as her word, his dearest friend Phyllida Bathurst had prepared his children well. They were disappointed not to meet their new mama – they had already gathered flowers to make nosegays for Ellen – but he reassured them that they would see her before long.

Tonight, Phyllida was hosting a dinner party in her luxurious townhouse on the Boulevard Saint-Germain. The *crème de la crème* of Paris would be there, including the British ambassador and his wife, and it promised to be a sparkling soirée. Phyllida had played no small role in ingratiating Edward in these circles already: she was the Bishop of Norwich's daughter, and widow to a noted diplomat Edward had once had the good fortune to work for. Phyllida had taken Edward under her wing, and her generosity in sharing her connections had been exceedingly useful to him.

With the children safely in the nursery, he straightened his sleeve, made an infinitesimal adjustment to his cravat, and ran a finger down the side of his hair before heading for the oak-panelled drawing room. He was the last to arrive, and took a moment to survey the room, noting the people he would most need to charm this evening. Phyllida was fussing over the ambassador, Lord Granville, whilst his wife, Harriet – 'Harryo', as she was known to her bosom bows – chatted to some French aristocrat or other. James stood sipping champagne in the corner with a friend of Phyllida's late husband, and seemed intent on not meeting Edward's eye.

Lord Granville tipped his glass in Edward's direction, and he seized the opportunity to join them. Phyllida looked resplendent in jade green, emeralds at her throat and a feather in her hair, and Lord Granville, as always, was impeccably dressed and exuded masculine elegance. Both looked over the party with fashionable languor.

'Our darling Phyllida tells me you are married again, Mr Walkley,' the ambassador said. 'Congratulations.'

'Wakefield,' Edward corrected the man quickly, adjusting his cravat again. 'And thank you, Lord Granville. I am quite smitten.'

'How sweet,' said Lady Granville, who had materialised by her husband's side. 'Where is she?'

The lady had an uncanny ability to detect the best gossip in the room, as a wasp detects an open jam jar. Edward wondered if she felt that this knack made up for her lack of classical beauty. Somehow he doubted it. Her pairing with the devilishly handsome ambassador would surprise many, were she not a duchess' daughter. But Harryo's wit was sharp as glass. Edward knew he must treat her with caution.

He offered her a deferential smile. 'I intend to introduce my lovely bride to you as soon as I can, my lady. Sadly though, this evening she is detained in England.'

'Such a shame,' Harryo made a faux sad face, and quickly recovered. 'I'm sure she'd love us.' She and her husband then both took a sip of champagne, peering thoughtfully at Edward over their flutes.

'I for one,' Phyllida said, breaking the silence, 'am *most* disappointed in Edward.'

Edward quelled a nervous urge to adjust his cravat once more, and raised an eyebrow. Harryo's eyes widened, hungry for tittle-tattle.

'As you know, I rather fancy myself as a mother to him and James,' Phyllida continued, 'but they both had the absolute gall to find beautiful brides, without any help from me at all!'

She laughed, and the group merrily joined in. Edward let out a breath.

'I heard,' said Harryo, leaning in, 'that your bride is something of an heiress.'

'She is indeed. Between us, though, it's not as exciting as it sounds: her father is an industrialist from the North of England. Tell me, how are your delightful children? Young Frederick must be starting school any day now—'

'Christ!' exclaimed Granville, brushing aside Edward's attempt to change the subject. 'You married the daughter of a *northerner? From industry?* Brave man.'

Edward swallowed, ignored the ripple of laughter that arose, and gave them all a coy smile. 'We fell in love; what can I say.'

'Oh, you romantic soul!' Phyllida leaned over and kissed his cheek. 'Let's raise a toast, to the new Mrs Edward Gibbon Wakefield!'

They all drank to Ellen's health, and Edward would have felt a sense of triumph, were it not for the exaggerated northern vowels the Granvilles attached to *Mrs Wakefield*, and the fact that they were still splitting their sides with laughter.

\* \* \*

By the time dinner was called, James still hadn't bothered to come and greet Edward. A shame that his brother was choosing to give him the cold shoulder, so close to his wedding. No matter though: Edward had bigger fish to fry. He offered Harryo his arm to escort her to the table.

The lady accepted with a gracious dip of her head, and, as they filed slowly out of the drawing room behind the other guests, he made every attempt to dazzle her. The evening had not got off to the finest of starts, but as Harryo giggled politely at his jokes, and invited him to sit beside her at the dinner table, he felt, once more, at liberty to relax. He allowed himself to imagine the gatherings the Granvilles would invite him to in future, and the fast friendships that Nina and Jerningham would form with their children. It was only a matter of time before Harryo would fall head over heels for Ellen, too, her industrial roots notwithstanding …

He was so pleased with himself, he missed Harryo's comment. He turned with an apologetic smile.

'My most humble and abject apologies, what was that? I'm afraid I was wool-gathering. Dashed impertinent of me, I know.'

Lady Granville gave him a beatific smile, and leaned towards him in such a conspiratorial fashion that he chuckled, and leaned closer himself. It was then she went for the kill.

'I asked if you kidnapped your child— beg pardon, bride. After all, that's what the newspapers seem to suggest.'

\* \* \*

18th March 1826 – *Macclesfield Courier* – Macclesfield

The announcement of the marriage of Miss Turner of
Shrigley to Mr Edward Gibbon Wakefield has excited a
very considerable sensation in this part of the country ...
from every enquiry which the friends of Miss Turner have
been able to make, there appears to be no proof of any
previous acquaintanceship between the two parties.

21st March 1826 – *The Times* – London

We learnt by an evening paper of Saturday, that the
affair which had given occasion to so much joy, was in
actual fact a cruel case of abduction; the child who was
carried off being only 17 years of age.

24th March 1826 – *Stockport Advertiser* – Stockport

Sources say the rescue mission was a success, and that
Mr Turner's daughter was returned home safely on
Wednesday the 22nd of March. In spite of this
diabolical attempt upon the peace of his family, the
High Sheriff will now, as planned, celebrate his
investiture on Saturday the 1st of April at 12 o'clock. The
occasion will be marked with a grand banquet and
speeches, followed by a procession from Shrigley Hall
to Chester.

★　★　★

## Lord Granville

The celebrations of both Wakefields's weddings were barely over when Lord Granville, the British ambassador to France, sat in his office staring at a clutch of letters on his desk. He'd read them with interest and a deepening sense of unease. He'd never claimed to be whiter than white himself in his dealings with the fair sex, but with every word, it became more apparent that the elder Wakefield brother took things to new heights.

There was a highly emotional missive from a Mr Turner, Wakefield's father-in-law, and a strongly worded one from a magistrate named Mr Thomas Legh. The heftiest letter, though, was from Lord Canning, the foreign secretary. As he combed through the flurry of correspondence, three things became clear: Edward Gibbon Wakefield was a fortune hunter of the worst kind; there was a warrant out for his arrest; and the foreign secretary urgently desired Granville to withdraw all protection from him, and his accomplice brother, forthwith.

It was extraordinary. What in God's name were they thinking? He felt a prickle of annoyance that Phyllida had ever brought him into association with this … rabble. In his opinion, they needed to return to England forthwith to face up to what they had done. To face justice for the damage they had wrought upon an innocent child, no matter how vulgar her family.

With that in mind, he pulled out a clean sheet of paper, dipped his nib in the inkwell, and with a sense of distaste that curled his handsome lip, wrote. His wife's bosom bows would no doubt have words for him, but *c'est la vie*. Wakefield had been hanging on Phyllida's sleeve for long enough; he sincerely doubted that the man would be flitting around their social circle any longer.

# CHAPTER 35

*The previous Wednesday*

*Ellen*

The horses struggled up the hill on the road to Shrigley Hall, as always. Ellen sat with her Uncle Robert in the carriage, which was significantly more comfortable than the wretched barouche she'd been dragged about in for so long. As the horses crested the hill, and the house that she loved so much loomed into view, Ellen was struck with how little time had passed since she was last here. It was hard to believe how much had happened, and changed, since then.

'Here we are, my dear,' her uncle said as he leaned over to pat her hand. 'Your mama and papa are quite desperate to see you.'

Ellen nodded. She was desperate to see them too. 'Have you told Papa what happened?'

He nodded. 'I sent him a letter from London confirming what Wakefield had done. He'd already written all about it to the foreign secretary, and the British ambassador in Paris.'

'But Mr Wakefield is good friends with the ambassador; won't he come to Edward's aid?'

Her uncle scratched his neck. 'We can only hope he won't, once he hears the extent of Wakefield's treachery. I understand that Mr Legh of Lyme Park wrote to him, too, in the strongest terms.'

Ellen blinked. 'Mr Legh? Mr Legh knows what has happened?' Ellen felt a headache forming.

'Indeed, he has been an enormous support to your papa, and being a magistrate, his words will lend weight.'

'Oh,' she managed in faint tones. Thomas knew. He knew what had happened, knew what she'd done. Her uncle bounded out of the carriage, oblivious to her distress.

She clamped her jaw tight as he helped her down, and looked at the magnificent facade of her dear Shrigley; how proud they all were of it. In the spring sunshine, it looked particularly beautiful. The warm brickwork looked butter-soft in its glow and it was as if a fire glinted from every window. It looked like a fortress ready to receive her, ready to protect her. She shook her head at her fancy.

The door opened, and Ackroyd beamed at her as he hurried forward.

'Miss Turner, I can't tell you how good it is to have you home. Your mama and papa are inside waiting for you.'

Ellen rather thought that her father might have run out and scooped her up in a huge hug, but when he failed to appear, she set her shoulders and made her way inside, her uncle's boot heels ringing on the floor behind her. The renovations were complete now, the hallway empty of workmen and sawdust. The place looked and smelled so different from only two weeks ago. She wondered if she, too, was a different Ellen now. She suspected she was, because previously, she would probably have run into the house like a hoyden without a care.

She stopped and looked at her uncle.

'What is it?' he asked, a frown wrinkling his brow.

'I think he has changed me.'

'Wakefield?'

Ellen nodded. She closed her eyes and took several deep breaths. 'I don't think I want to be changed.'

'Then don't let him.'

She nodded, turned to Ackroyd, handed him her reticule, picked up her skirts, and ran.

She skidded to a halt, one hand on her hat, panting, as she burst through the doorway of her mother's parlour.

'Ellen!' Her father's shocked declaration made her heart clench. He stood by the mantel, staring at her like he'd seen a ghost.

'My love!' Her mother held out a hand from where she sat, but Ellen had already launched herself into her father's arms. He held her tightly then put her away from him so he could look at her.

'My dear, you look,' he swallowed, '... well?'

She could only presume he was being kind.

Her mother held out her hand again, so she quickly unlaced her bonnet and tossed it on a chair before kneeling beside her. She laid her head on her mother's lap, closed her eyes, and let her mother pet her hair with one hand as she wept into her handkerchief with the other. Robert poked his head around the door to greet her parents, but when he saw the emotional scene, mumbled something about leaving them to their reunion, and backed out of the room with a smile.

'This has been such an ordeal for you,' her father said as he stood back, shaking his head. 'You must be very glad to be home.'

'I am,' Ellen said. 'So terribly glad, Papa. I've missed you both abominably. In my letters to you I tried to sound happy, because he told me that I must, but really, it was awful.'

'Letters?' her mother sniffed. 'What letters?'

'We didn't receive any letters, love,' said her father. 'Perhaps Wakefield intercepted them somehow.'

'Oh,' said Ellen faintly. She wouldn't be surprised if he had. How many more times had that man tricked her?

'You were awfully, awfully brave,' said her father, rubbing her back. 'But we now need to get this … this idiot thrown in gaol and this nonsense annulled.'

Hope blossomed painfully in her chest. *Could* one annul a scandal? But above her head, she heard her mother tsk loudly.

'William,' she said in shrill tones, chin and lace cap wobbling together. 'We spoke of this. I told you specifically I had a letter from a Mrs Bathurst in Paris, telling me that Mr Wakefield is *not* an idiot and *actually* a rather wonderful gentleman, when you get to know him.'

Ellen pulled away and stared at her mother, heart pounding. If her mother thought the marriage should stand, why was she crying so much?

'She was very complimentary about his devotion to his first wife, which *was* a true love match.' her mother went on. *A true love match?* Ellen didn't know what to say to that. Somehow, though, she doubted Edward was capable of loving anyone but himself.

'But Mama,' Ellen said, her voice tight, 'Mrs Bathurst is Edward's friend. Of course she'd say—'

'Jane,' her father cut in sharply, 'What Mrs Bathurst says is of no consequence to us. Our *daughter* has come to know the man and *she* says he is a fiend!'

*Had* Ellen said that? She'd certainly thought it.

'What's more,' her mother ploughed on as if she hadn't been interrupted, 'you *know* how difficult it is to secure an annulment, William. Why put such a madcap notion in

Ellen's head? We need to stop dreaming, and acknowledge the match.'

Ellen's heart sank as her mother confirmed her worst fear. She knew in her bones now why her mother was so upset; much as it hurt her to say these brutal words, every one of them was true. The only sensible course – perhaps the only possible one – would be to paper over this disaster. What she couldn't understand was *how* it could be so sensible, when it was also such a wretched injustice.

'He has remarkably good connections with the British ambassador in Paris, and even the Devonshire set,' her mother was saying now, trying to put a positive spin on things. 'How much higher do we need to reach? I know there is no title, but he will elevate us magnificently.'

Her father came to stand by her mother and gently placed an arm about her shoulders. But when he spoke, there was anger beneath his words. Ellen had never heard him speak to her mother that way before.

'I don't give a flying fig who the ambassador is married to, Jane; all that matters is being rid of this scoundrel so that our daughter can be free of him. I'm damned if he's going to inherit everything that my family has worked for.'

Her mother primmed her mouth at his language, and both hands wrung at her handkerchief. 'But remember, William, our own dear Ellen is a married woman now, and she will have a view on how she would like to proceed. Indeed, you said that you would ask her opinion before making a decision, didn't you?'

Ellen's mouth went dry as she looked from her father's furious face to her mother's stubborn one. They rarely argued, but when they did … She cleared her throat, but her father cut in again, this time through gritted teeth.

'Our dear Ellen, our only beloved child, my heir, was kidnapped, lied to, and forced into a marriage that she did not want. I'm sure she *does* have a view on that.'

'Mama ... Papa?'

'Well, love,' her mother shot her an austere look, 'I would counsel you to think very carefully. One's reputation is not something easily repaired.'

'Jane!' her father snapped, making both Ellen and her mother jump. 'I will hear no more of this.'

'William!' Her mother's cheeks went pink, and fresh tears welled in her eyes.

This was not how Ellen had imagined her homecoming. *Lord*, she would need Hester and Lavinia to visit soon, and give her some good advice. Apparently, that wasn't going to be forthcoming from her parents.

\* \* \*

Later, as Ellen opened the door to her bedchamber, she was relieved to find that nothing there had changed. Everything was just as she'd left it, just as the night when Lavinia and Hester had bounced on her bed, laughing and eating cake, when she was nothing more than a carefree girl.

She undid her boots, kicked them off, and threw herself onto the bed. It was lovely to have nice things around her again, lovely to be comfortable, and lovely to be able to breathe without the worry that Edward would come knocking.

Just then, a tap at the door heralded two of the maids, who came in with wide smiles and curious eyes. One handed Ellen her reticule, the other put a tray of sandwiches, cakes, and tea on her table.

'Thank you,' Ellen said and dropped the reticule on the bed.

'Is there anything else you need, ma'am?'

Ellen was shocked when the other maid elbowed her companion and hissed, 'Miss!'

'Sorry, miss.'

'Nothing else, thank you.' It rather seemed that her father had given instructions to the staff to ignore her status as a married woman. She realised it was entirely possible that her mother had given instructions to the contrary.

They both bobbed curtsies and scrambled away, leaving Ellen staring at the closed door. Was this how it was going to be? Had Edward ruined not only her reputation, but her parents' happy marriage?

She sighed and poured herself some tea before piling pillows up and then settling on the bed with the plate of food. She popped a small egg sandwich in her mouth and was still chewing when her father came to see her, looking sheepish.

He closed the door behind him and came to sit on the bed, much as he had done when she was little.

'How are you?' he said. It was first time anyone had asked her that since she'd arrived home.

'I'm not sure,' she said, truthfully.

He nodded and looked out of the window. 'I'm sorry you got caught in the argument with your mother.'

She nodded. 'You seem to have very different ideas on how best to proceed.'

Her father sighed. 'We do … Some of what your mother says has merit. But I can't stand the thought of him getting away with this.'

Ellen swallowed, and pushed her plate away. 'Is it possible to have him thrown in gaol and the marriage annulled?'

'I believe … I hope so.'

'Do you think that my reputation would withstand that? A court case and an annulment?'

He looked at the bed. 'I don't know.' He cleared his throat. 'Do you love him?'

Ellen shook her head. 'I don't. I don't even like him.'

'Well, as I see it, if we *can* get the marriage annulled, you might get a second chance and marry a man you do love. And if we don't at least try ... I'll have failed you.'

'Nonsense!' She leaned against him. 'Uncle Robert told me all about your efforts to rescue me. That was beyond what many fathers would have done in your situation. It was positively heroic.'

Her father smiled sadly. 'Made a mull of it though,' he mumbled.

'One thing I don't understand ...' Ellen reached over to her reticule. 'When Edward told me he'd seen you, he gave me your handkerchief. The one I embroidered for you. That's how I knew, or *thought* I knew, that you were in trouble. Then, just before Gretna, when he said that the only solution was for us to be married, his brother gave me your signet ring. He said that you sent it to me with a plea that I marry Edward with all speed.' Both beloved items were carefully stored inside her reticule, next to Thomas's book. She pulled them out and showed them to him.

Her father was quiet for a long time as he turned the items over in his hand, again and again. 'He gave you these?'

Ellen nodded. 'How did he get them?'

'That's something I should like to know. Small wonder he convinced you.'

They sat in silence for a little while, each lost in thought, until her father put an arm about her shoulder.

'Our next move is yours to decide, love. What's it to be?'

Ellen wasn't sure why she was giving it any thought. If there was even the tiniest chance that she could be rid of Edward ...

'I want an annulment.'

Her father let go of an enormous breath. 'That's my girl.'

'Mama will be apoplectic.'

He pulled her into his arms and hugged her, kissing the top of her head.

'Leave Mama to me.'

# CHAPTER 36

It took an age for Ellen to feel even the tiniest bit settled back in her family home. Luckily, there was plenty going on to distract her. Her father was now wrapped up in anxieties about the impending celebration of his investiture, and although her mother was still bewailing their position on Ellen's marriage, the excitement at hosting such a once-in-a-lifetime event had gradually taken over the household. Ellen took comfort in this, and was beginning to detect small signs that the tension between them would not last forever.

The nicest distraction, however, would arrive today. Hester and Lavinia were now on their Easter holidays, and were coming to visit. Ellen had bolted from the house the moment she heard Hester's family carriage drawing up in the drive, and she now leapt at her friend, seizing her in a way that was, frankly, hoydenish.

'Lord, I cannot believe what happened to you,' Hester said, sounding like she could hardly breathe.

'Neither can I,' she whispered, loosening her hold enough to let Hester fill her lungs. 'How did you first find out? Was it my letter from Penrith, or did you see the announcement in *The Times*?'

Hester looked momentarily puzzled – clearly, she hadn't received her letters either – then shook her head. 'Miss Daulby told us when she read it in the paper. She was beside herself, nigh on throwing herself under the wheels of the nearest carriage she was so distraught.'

*Poor Miss Daulby*, Ellen thought. It wasn't her fault Edward was such a fraudulent cad. 'And what are the other girls saying?'

Hester's lips twitched and her eyes lit up. 'Oh, Ellen, their noses are positively dropping off with curiosity,' she said. 'Honestly, they are absolutely agog. It's the most outrageous thing that has ever happened in the history of the school.'

'You mean I'm notorious?'

Hester gave her an impish grin. 'Notorious, scandalous … I think you've reached a level of infamy that would enable you to pick your own superlative.'

Ellen laughed, then sighed. 'I was distraught when I realised that I could never come back for our final term.'

'I don't see why you couldn't,' Hester grumbled.

'I don't think married women go to school.'

Hester arched an eyebrow. 'You are not married, Ellen, you were tricked.'

Ellen squeezed her arm, unspeakably grateful at Hester's unshakable belief in her. 'Thank you.'

Until Lavinia had joined them, Ellen didn't want to say much more on the matter – she planned to give them every gory detail once they were all together. So Ellen and Hester sat in the drawing room, twiddling their thumbs impatiently, as Ellen's mother presided over tea and gushed about inconsequential things with Hester's parents. They spoke at such length about her mother's choice of napkins for the investiture banquet, that soon it was obvious (to all parties, Ellen supposed) that the adults were studiously avoiding the topics that truly held their interest: namely, elopements, marriage, scandal, and carriage races from Gretna Green to Calais. Ellen also thought she sensed a coolness in Hester's mama's manner towards her, which hadn't been there previously, but she could only pray that was her imagination.

By the time Lavinia's carriage drew up outside, Ellen couldn't sit it out any longer. 'I'll meet her at the door!' she blurted, and rose abruptly from her seat. 'Hester, shall we …'

'… Go for a walk in the sunshine? That would be famous!' Hester replied, catching on to Ellen's intentions immediately.

'Take care you don't catch a chill, and don't go far,' was all her mama said. Her mama lived in mortal fear of chills.

They both hurried from the room before anyone could decide they wanted to join them. They fell upon Lavinia – positively yanking her from her carriage – and ran together over the grass the short distance to the summer house. Ellen rattled the door, and to her enormous relief, it opened. She ushered Hester and Lavinia in and slammed the door behind them, leaning up against it with a heartfelt sigh.

'Thank God,' she breathed.

'My love,' Lavinia said with gravitas, 'You shall not remain married to that *oaf!*'

Ellen looked at her dear friend, overcome to be finally in the company of two people who were *completely* in agreement with her on the whole affair, and let it all out. Hester and Lavinia huddled close to her on the sofa as she told the whole story from start to end, so rapt that they only remembered to remove their gloves and bonnets after she'd finished speaking.

'Oh, Ellen, what an absolute out-and-outer,' said Hester. 'And as for his behaviour around the bedchamber, keeping you guessing like that was evil. *Certainly* not the actions of a gentleman.'

'They were the actions of an absolute shag-bag!' Lavinia chimed in.

Ellen's eyes filled as she nodded. Both friends groaned and reached over to pull Ellen into their arms. 'I knew you'd have a sensible view on it,' she whispered. 'There were times when I was just ... so frightened and so alone. But the worst of it is ...' she swallowed before confessing what she hadn't been able to so far. 'There were other times when he nearly won me over, and that makes me feel terribly foolish. There were parts in France that I ... I liked. He treated me like a lady, not a school-girl. He promised to take me to Paris, said he'd introduce me to the Devonshires ...'

'He was doing everything he could to manipulate you,' Lavinia said. 'It's no wonder he succeeded in beguiling you a *little*. *Especially* if he was very well-looking.'

Ellen hugged her, nodding. 'Do you think so? I'm not ... horribly shallow?' she whispered.

Hester patted her back. 'Not even a tiny bit, love. It sounds to me that he said all those things in the hope you would accept him. If you did that, your parents would follow suit. I don't think he loves you at all.'

'I know that now,' Ellen said with a watery laugh, 'but he was frighteningly persuasive. He was so constant and ardent in his devotions it was hard to think.'

Even as she said it, it was clearer than ever to Ellen that Hester was right. Every single thing Edward did, right from the start, had been to persuade her she loved him. Just as he did his first wife – he probably used exactly the same lines on Clara Pattle. The thought of how much planning he must have put into the whole performance made her skin crawl.

'What about Wakefield's brother?' Lavinia said, snapping Ellen out of that unpleasant reverie.

'James? He was harmless, quite gentle really. He's getting married in Paris on Sunday.'

Lavinia arched a perfectly shaped brow. 'Yet he supported his brother in his desperate scheme? Not so harmless when you consider that.'

'True, and it was James who told me that my father and Mr Grimsditch begged me to marry Edward. That's what made it so believable. He seemed so genuine.'

'It sounds like when you look at the whole,' Hester said with a frown, 'they are both *irrefutably* pond-slime men.'

'Inexcusably slimy,' agreed Lavinia. 'I'd go so far as to call them pond-slime *animals*.'

'As for men who are not pond dwellers,' said Hester, 'Have you seen Mr Legh since your return?'

They both looked at her expectantly. Ellen groaned. 'I haven't yet, but he's going to be one of the magistrates who hears my case. I'm going to have to stand up in court and tell him how foolish I was to be tricked so easily. It's awful! He's going to think I'm a complete lackwit.'

Lavinia grimaced. 'I know it won't be easy, but at least he will hear the absolute truth of it. Do you know when this will happen?'

'In a week's time, the day before Papa's celebration. It could hardly be worse timing.'

'And is that it? If they find Wakefield guilty, is it all over?'

Ellen shrugged. 'Almost, at least that's what I'm hoping. I think if he is found guilty, we can then petition for an annulment so that I am free to marry again if I wish it.'

'And …' Hester seemed to be suppressing a note of excitement in her voice now, 'did you think of Mr Legh whilst this was all going on?'

Ellen put her hands over her face for a moment and then lowered them with a sigh. 'Yes, I did. I thought of him a lot, in fact.' She told them of how Thomas's book had helped her through some of the darker times, and saw her friends exchange a knowing glance. 'I know there can't be anything between us now, but for a little while, I thought there might be.'

Hester spoke next, appearing to choose her words carefully. 'How do you know there can't be anything between you?'

'Well, for a start, I'm not sure I'd have been good enough for him even without the scandal. And with it ...' She shrugged.

'Don't sell yourself short, my love,' Lavinia said.

Hester squeezed her hand. 'If he's half the man you think he is, he won't care about the backbiters.'

Ellen hugged her friends, but she knew that he would care. He would care a great deal. What man wouldn't?

'First though,' Lavinia said, 'you just need to focus on getting through the trial. You will be the scandal *du jour* for a little while, but the world has a very short memory. The wolves will move on to someone else before long. Mark my words.'

*Wise words, or wishful thinking?* Ellen thought. 'I sincerely hope you are right.'

# CHAPTER 37

A week later, Ellen walked into the imposing building that was the Ram's Head in Disley, at the gates of the Lyme Park estate. She walked in, chin held high, with her father and Mr Grimsditch, staring straight forward and trembling. She immediately spotted Thomas, sitting beside two other magistrates, looking terribly stern and solemn. She'd known it would be awful having him hear the case, but seeing him there was more than awful: it was mortifying.

Her stomach flopped as she recognised James, standing at the front of the room, waiting to be tried. She'd discovered from her father that Edward had not yet returned to England; she would be forced to sit through his trial separately. But given that Edward would be arrested the moment he set foot on English soil, she doubted he would come back in a hurry.

James glanced up at her now, and swallowed as he shifted in his seat. She'd spent days trying to forget the abduction. Days arguing with Edward in her mind as she thought of all the things she should have said. Things she should, and shouldn't, have done. And just as she was starting to feel some peace, the letters she'd written to her parents from France had arrived, and raked up all her regrets again. Reading her own account of how *kind* and *gallant* Edward had been to her was unbearable.

Looking at James's weaselly face, now, she had to take a deep breath and force herself to keep moving towards her allotted seat, and not run away.

'Look him in the eye,' her father whispered. 'Show no weakness.'

But James had already fixed his gaze deliberately on the floor.

Her parents had kept the newspapers from her, but she now knew the case had been widely reported, that all and sundry were talking about it. As she looked about at the sheer number of strangers crammed into the Ram's Head and clamouring outside, she realised just how much interest there was in her situation. It was, frankly, disturbing.

She took a seat with her father and Mr Grimsditch, and as they waited for proceedings to commence, more and more people squeezed into the room until someone closed the door and a scuffle ensued. Ellen felt a headache take hold and thump unpleasantly behind her eyes, as Thomas murmured something to the other magistrates, then announced it was time to begin.

★  ★  ★

Ellen's statement was brief, to the point, and factual. She had practised in her bedchamber, but nothing had prepared her for the reality of reading it aloud in front of Thomas, and all the other people who craned their necks to see her.

She read, but her voice trembled, and several times she stumbled over the words. All the while, she felt two men's eyes on her most keenly: James's, whose gaze was slippery, and

Thomas's, whose expression was controlled to the point of being unreadable.

Once she had finished, Thomas thanked her politely, and then the questions began.

'Miss Turner, had you ever met this gentleman prior to this incident?' He indicated James, but Ellen kept her eyes on the paper in her hand; she couldn't bear to look at either of them.

'No, sir, I had not.'

'Would you have consented to marry Mr Edward Gibbon Wakefield had it not been for the artifices you describe?'

'No, sir, I would not.'

He asked her to sit down. She was still shaking as she listened to Mr Grimsditch's testimony. He told the magistrates categorically that he had never been in Carlisle, that at the time James said he'd spoken to him, taken a note from him, he was in London and could prove that to be the case.

When it was her father's turn, Ellen wanted to put her hands over her ears. He was so furious, so angry at James. He talked about how the whole affair had almost killed her mama, about how it had affected them all … It was frightful having one's dirty laundry aired so publicly.

Her papa turned and looked at James, a vicious scowl on his face. 'You, sir, are a villain!' he bellowed like a rhinoceros, and pointed at him so ferociously his coat tails flapped.

Ellen watched, agog, as James shrank back into his chair. When his eyes slid closed and he lost all vestige of colour, Thomas intervened, speaking in a low, calm voice, lest her father have some kind of apoplectic turn.

Finally, her father threw himself into the chair beside Ellen and folded his arms, and Thomas turned to James. 'Mr Wakefield,' he said, 'is there anything that you would like to offer in reply to the evidence that has been set forth today?'

James looked at Ellen. There was something almost pleading in his gaze before he sat up and turned to the bench.

'No, sir,' James said quietly. Thomas looked surprised, and Ellen breathed a sigh of relief.

Thomas sat down, and conferred quietly with the other two magistrates. Ellen's sense of relief dwindled as she wondered what would happen next. Had they provided enough evidence to condemn James? What did Thomas make of it all? She could only pray that they were not about to announce James's acquittal.

The deliberations between the magistrates ended, as they appeared to reach a solution. Thomas stood to address the assembly, and Ellen held her breath.

'The case is adjourned,' Thomas said in a clear, even tone. 'We shall continue on Monday the 3rd of April at 2 o'clock.'

* * *

Ellen let her father shepherd her quickly from the room to the waiting carriage. Outside, there were so many people wanting to speak to her. Jostling, pushing, shouting questions. Someone, in bellicose tones, demanded to know if they'd eloped, and everyone laughed at some of the more ribald comments.

Her father tucked her into his side and shouldered his way through the baying crowd. Ellen just closed her eyes and stumbled along beside him. Somehow, he got her into the carriage, slammed the door, and rapped hard on the roof with his stick. They set off with a lurch and Ellen fanned herself, open-mouthed with shock at the vociferousness of the rabble who had accosted them.

'Who are they all?' she whispered. '*The Shrigley Abduction*? Is that what people are saying?'

Her father ran a hand over his mouth. 'I'm afraid so, my dear.'

Ellen nodded, stunned. She rubbed her temple and closed her eyes. 'At least they're not calling it *The Shrigley Elopement*.'

Her father stared at her for a moment. Then a mischievous smile lit up his face. He nudged her, winked, and what he said next made her feel, at last, that everything was going to be all right.

'My thoughts *exactly*.'

# CHAPTER 38

*William*

The morning of the grand celebration of William Turner's elevation to High Sheriff of Cheshire dawned clear and bright. As he cast a final eye over the preparations, he tried to recapture some of the pride, some of the sense of achievement that the day represented. Shrigley had been cleaned and cleaned again, festooned with flowers and garlands, and the kitchens were going full steam ahead with the magnificent repast his wife had planned. This was the day that the whole of the region would see him honoured and fêted. Him, an industrialist from Blackburn, taking a place amongst the aristocracy and the well-heeled of the county. They might look down their noses in London, but here in Cheshire, as of today, he was *officially* well regarded. And he had more money than all of them put together. He refused to let any of what had happened interfere with that.

The magistrates' first hearing for the younger Wakefield boded very well. He'd expected a spirited defence from the boy, and when he'd put up none at all, it had given William hope that all would go in their favour. They just needed to hold fast and stay firm, until the other brother came crawling back.

He took a deep breath and pulled out his pocket watch, as his wife bustled up and gave him a playful push. 'Don't just stand there – get ready to receive your guests. You need to be ready! Are you ready?'

He leaned down and brushed his lips against her soft cheek, pleased to be on speaking terms again. 'Don't I look ready?'

She chuckled. 'You look splendid, and you know it.'

'The whole *place* looks splendid, my love. You are nothing short of a miracle worker.'

She blushed prettily and adjusted her cap as she cleared her throat. 'Mr Legh has arrived,' she said. 'He is in the parlour with Mr Grimsditch, Ellen, and the girls. You should probably go and rescue him.'

\* \* \*

## Ellen

Ellen perched on the edge of her chair in the parlour with a fixed smile on her face. She had been happily chatting with Hester and Lavinia, but when Mr Grimsditch had arrived with Thomas, she had apparently forgotten how to breathe.

Thomas looked magnificent. He wore a dark blue coat over a waistcoat embroidered with gold and silver, and his cravat was held by a resplendent sapphire pin. His dark hair was curled to a nicety, and his breeches fit his muscular legs like a second skin. A long ceremonial sword hung in its sheath by his side.

Something, however, about Thomas's comportment today perturbed her. He was terribly serious, and when she greeted him, he didn't smile.

'Miss Turner,' he said, offering a cursory bow.

What followed was perhaps the most awkward conversation of Ellen's life thus far – except the one she'd had with Uncle Robert about her virginity. Mr Grimsditch and her friends attempted to engage Thomas in small talk about the role he would play in the parade that afternoon, but Thomas was remarkably stiff in his responses. His usual reserve had been pushed to the extreme, and he was presenting as even more austere than he had in court. It seemed the others had all noticed this too, and it made the atmosphere in the room most peculiar. He looked like he didn't want to be talking to them at all.

Meanwhile, Ellen sat there, mute as the stuffed bear at Lyme Park. She kept trying to meet Thomas's eye – all the blue of his outfit gave them a smoky, azure tint that was spectacularly fetching – but she was sure he was avoiding her gaze. All the gentle humour he'd shown her the day they met, all the bashful candour in his eyes when he gave her his *Narrative of a Journey in Egypt*, were gone. He was now, it seemed, a closed book. Was it because of what happened?

'Tell us, Mr Legh,' she blurted, then fumbled for something to say. 'What is the … sword for?'

Lavinia and Hester looked at her as if she were an utter coot. Even Mr Grimsditch blushed on her behalf.

'It is purely decorative,' Thomas said humourlessly, then changed the subject. If at that instant the chandelier had fallen on Ellen's head, she might have preferred it.

Of course he was behaving this way because of what happened. Lavinia and Hester had been naive to think Thomas could still see her in the same way; it was a miracle that *they* could. She should have known that when it came to the world of respectable men, her mother knew best.

Her father joined them, and the three men took their leave. Ellen tore her gaze from the back of Thomas's head as he hurried away. At least he hadn't called her *Mrs Wakefield*.

\* \* \*

The sheer number of people who came to the celebration was breathtaking. Ellen stood beside her mother as they took a moment out of the crowd and watched from the top of the staircase. It was a public event, and Ellen had fretted that no one would attend because of the palaver about her in the papers. It would have been unbearable if she'd inadvertently made her father a persona non grata, after everything he'd worked for. But apparently, all the talk about their family had had the opposite effect. The scale of the numbers that poured down the drive and into the house was beyond what they could have anticipated. It was relentless.

'It's quite a remarkable turnout,' her mother murmured, staring at the throng, fanning her rouged cheeks.

'I know. How we will fit everyone in!' Ellen said. 'Perhaps you should speak to the caterer, Mama?' Mr Lynn from Liverpool had done a sterling job of preparing the banquet. The house was filled with the most delicious-looking food, including a baron of beef which sat on the sideboard, with the family crest in what looked like butter above it. But would it be enough?

Her mother nodded and opened her mouth, but as another eight or ten guests piled into the hallway below, all she could utter was an astounded squeak.

\* \* \*

Ellen found Lavinia and Hester in the crush. They teamed up to act as gracious hostesses, and were busily greeting guests, directing the serving staff, and ensuring everyone knew the itinerary for the occasion, when a familiar voice distracted Ellen. 'Well, aren't you popular,' Miss Davis said above the hubbub.

'Indeed, it seems father is Cheshire's most wanted!' quipped Ellen. 'I was just speaking to Mama. It's quite … swarming in here.'

Miss Davis was looking elegant as ever. The four of them chatted and exclaimed about the extensive preparations for the day, which Miss Davis had kindly helped her mama to carry off. Miss Davis also complimented Ellen's dress, which lifted her mood somewhat; her bungle in the parlour with Thomas had left her feeling most ungainly. She'd worn her favourite new cream gown from France for the occasion: nipped at the waist, with full sleeves at the shoulder and tiny rose-coloured flowers on the bust, it paired well with the satin bows in her hair, and had sent Lavinia and Hester into spasms of envy.

As the servants darted about bravely, drinks began to flow. Miss Davis sipped champagne, whilst Ellen and the girls drank copious amounts of lemonade, and from the level of noise in the house, it seemed the guests were enjoying themselves mightily. They met interesting people from all over the county, from farmers' wives to viscounts to little children. Each visitor effused about how marvellous a reception it was, and how excited they were to meet Ellen's father in person. It made Ellen's heart balloon with pride for him. As she turned away from a few guests, Ellen *could* feel the weight of their eyes on her back, but was content to pay them no heed. People were bound to be curious, after all.

By the time it was announced that the banquet would be served shortly, Ellen had lost sight of Lavinia and Hester. Miss

Davis had disappeared too, and so Ellen was making her way out of the parlour unaccompanied, when a large, well-dressed matron stopped in front of her.

'Are you Mrs Wakefield?' she demanded, as though she had every right to accost Ellen thus in her own home. *How rude!*

Ellen's eyebrows lifted and she tried to maintain a regal aplomb, but her heart sped up. 'I am Miss Ellen Turner. I don't think we've been introduced.'

The woman sneered – there was no other word for it. 'I don't think you need introduction, my dear. I'm surprised your mama has let you out of your bedchamber. I doubt your father wants his special day tainted by your shocking behaviour.'

The woman turned on her heel and Ellen stared after her, speechless. What in the name of all that was holy …

She carried on her way towards the dining room, still stunned at the woman's rudeness, but it made her listen more closely to some of the conversations that flowed in the lines of people jostling to get to the feast. The fragments were enough to make her remove herself from their company with all speed.

'Gretna Green! They went to Gretna Green. If she didn't want to get married, all she had to do was refuse,' one man was saying, laughing to his friends. 'She was pretty keen if you ask me …'

'… and he let her come back? How ridiculous. No wonder he's celebrating his investiture on April Fools' Day …'

'… well, they've had a wedding night, so …' The laughter that followed was as unpleasant as the comments. Ellen could scarce believe what she was hearing. She put her head down and ducked into the drawing room. There, she crossed paths with a group of young women who exchanged glances at her approach.

'Why, Mrs Wakefield, how nice to see you,' one of the girls said. 'Tell me, is a wedding over the anvil at Gretna as romantic as they say?' They all giggled, and Ellen wanted to slap them. She ignored them without qualm and hurried back into the hallway.

It was utterly shabby. How *dare* they.

She wriggled her way through the crowds to the staircase, and tried to ignore the speculative looks of those who watched her ascend. Some actually turned their backs on her. The cut direct in her own home! It was exceedingly rag-mannered.

It was also what her mother and Miss Davis had said would happen. And they were right. She all but ran to the sanctuary of her room, slammed the door behind her, locked it, and threw herself on her bed.

She rolled over to find a letter there with her name on. She hesitated, wondering what on earth it could be.

When she read it, she almost tore it in frustration. It was a hastily scribbled note from Hester. She and Lavinia had been collected by their parents and forced to go home early, on account of the *revelations* printed in one of the regional papers that morning. Apparently the article was filled with stories of the wedding, the wedding *night*, and Ellen's *secret tryst* in France.

> *... I'm terribly sorry, dear one. Our parents are being quite hysterical. We shan't be allowed to write for a while, at least until this slander is disproved, but please know that we adore you forever, and you will get through this ...*

She let the letter fall into her lap, put her face in her hands, and wept.

*   *   *

Ellen managed to make it to the dining hall in time for the speeches. She had splashed her face with water, and could only hope it wasn't hideously blotchy. She avoided looking at anyone as she hurried to find her mother.

Her mama took her arm and yanked her down into her vacant seat at the table. 'Where on earth have you been? They are about to start!'

Ellen glanced at her mama's proud face and could only conclude that her parents had not heard the whispers, seen Hester and Lavinia being bundled away, or been rudely accosted ... yet.

Her father sat at the head of their table, Thomas on his right-hand side. Her father looked stately and terribly proud, as he had every right to be. They had come so far as a family, and Ellen had been so blissfully confident that their good fortune would simply continue. However, as she looked at the assembled company, it scared her just how unspeakably fragile their position in this world really was. How easily it could all come crashing down around them.

When the room was settled, and everyone in place, Thomas cast a glance at her father and nodded almost imperceptibly. Then, he stood and tapped his pastry fork against a crystal wine glass.

A hush fell, and Thomas held a dignified pause before speaking.

'My lords, ladies, and gentlemen. It gives me the greatest pleasure ...'

Unlike his standoffish mien in the parlour, Thomas was awfully commanding in this setting. There was something about him that made people stop and listen, something vibrant and interesting. He talked animatedly, extolling her father's virtues and making people laugh with his witticisms.

She felt that even if he didn't care for her, Thomas's faith in – and friendship for – her father was genuine. It occurred to her that it was the support of pillars of society like him that would be needed if they were to emerge from this scandal unscathed.

When the speeches were done, and all had eaten their fill, it was time for her father to begin the procession to Chester. Ellen followed her mother outside, where seats had been laid out in rows for the spectators, as those taking part in the parade got into position.

Ellen would have liked to watch from her bedroom window, where she'd be able to see much farther, without being seen herself. She'd imagined she'd do this with Hester and Lavinia, squealing and pointing out how wickedly handsome Thomas looked after his costume change. But instead she sat quietly, with her back straight and her hands in her lap.

Within minutes, the procession set off. Thomas was seated on horseback beside her father, in a riding coat embellished with gold, with hundreds of Thomas's tenants behind them. Following them were the javelin men with the Turner crest on their halberds.

'Doesn't your father look happy,' her mother said, in a bright tone that sounded oddly forced.

'He does indeed, Mama.' Ellen could still hear the whispering about *Turner the April Fool*, and the change in her mother's voice told her that now, she could too. But her mother didn't need to say anything; Ellen could feel *I told you so* in every line of her body.

Her father's new red carriage, which he'd procured expressly for this event but which had already travelled to Gretna and back, gleamed in the sunshine. Ellen watched in awed silence at the magnificence of the parade that would make its way to the tiny neighbouring village of Pott Shrigley, and all the way to the county capital.

As the last of the marchers disappeared down the drive, and the sound of hooves and footsteps grew quiet, Ellen felt a cold sense of loss. Without the distraction of the ceremony, she was left to the mercy of the tattle mongers. She cast a last glance down the drive. It felt like the happy, confident, cheerful part of her was disappearing too as she braced herself to turn back and face the crowd.

\*　\*　\*

## Frances

Frances watched the distress settle on Ellen's face as she listened to the rumours that swirled around her. Watched the colour drain from Jane's as people turned away from her, and whispered about the fact that her daughter had married Edward quite willingly. Spent days in an enclosed carriage with him. Enjoyed a wedding night.

That morning's exposée was just the beginning. Soon, the national press would be printing story after story. At first, there had been some sympathy for the plight of a schoolgirl being whisked away and coerced into marriage, but she had worked hard at ensuring that the other side of the story was also heard. And what she had to say – anonymously, of course – was far more salacious, far more newsworthy, and far more damaging.

The tide of public opinion was turning, of that she was certain. She accepted another glass of champagne from a passing footman, and made her way over to Jane, painting on a sympathetic smile. It was *such* a shame her husband had refused to acknowledge the match. It was a rash decision, no doubt, and one he would regret very soon.

# CHAPTER 39

*Ellen*

The Ram's Head in Disley was as unwelcoming as before. Ellen sat with her father and watched as the group of men before them discussed whether her kidnapping was a capital offence or a misdemeanour.

Mr Grimsditch was trying to persuade the magistrates that it was a capital offence, because that would mean that if convicted, James would receive a serious prison sentence, or even face transportation to Australia. But this time, James Wakefield had brought a lawyer with him to speak on his behalf, a Mr Harmer, and *he* was suggesting in strident tones that the matter should be dealt with as a misdemeanour.

'What will it mean if they decide it is a misdemeanour?' Ellen whispered to her father.

'It would be a disgrace, that's what,' her father murmured back, hotly. 'He'd get sureties for good behaviour, a fine, or a short stint in prison at best.'

The proceedings had been dramatic, with James's lawyer dredging up everything that had been dealt with at the previous hearing. The man seemed determined to paint Ellen a willing accomplice in the Wakefields's plan, almost quoting word-for-word a series of false or twisted *bulletins* from the latest evening papers.

Keeping her chin up through the onslaught had been painful. Her parents hadn't let her read the articles that were multiplying by the day, and now she understood why. As Mr Harmer described her *girlish wiles* with gusto, she sensed her father's breathing hitch, and saw a muscle in Thomas's face twitch. It was the first semblance of an emotional response Thomas had given since the trial began, but it came as no surprise: he was obviously scandalised.

The justice system couldn't be as fickle as the *on dits*, could it? She was amazed James had the gall to suppose that it would. He knew; he *knew* what he and Edward had done, yet he stood there, all blond hair and innocence, pretending butter wouldn't melt in his mouth, whilst his boor of a lawyer alluded to her eagerness to participate in the *adventure*. When he looked up and accidentally met her gaze, at least he had the grace to appear embarrassed.

Mr Harmer was now asserting that James's misdeeds were harmless because, since her father was still young enough to produce a son, Ellen was not his *proper* heir but only his *heir apparent*. She thought her father might have crossed the room and smacked him, had the magistrates not called an end to the arguments there, and retired to reach a decision.

Thomas had studiously avoided looking at her throughout the proceedings, just as he had on Saturday. If she wanted this trial to be any less torturous, she would need to find a way to stop wishing otherwise. But in that moment, as he and his two po-faced colleagues went about determining her future, she would have given anything to see that smiling glint return to his eye.

\* \* \*

As she and her father waited in stony-faced silence, Mr Grimsditch came to join them. 'Newspaper men everywhere,' he murmured to her father. Ellen's heart sped up. She peered over her shoulder but couldn't really see anything.

'Turns out that our young miscreant is related by marriage to some damned poet or other, and that's set everyone atwitter.'

'Poet?' her father said, brows drawn down. 'Which damned poet?'

'Chap called Shelley.'

Ellen hadn't known that James's new wife was related to Mr Shelley, but could see why that would engender more interest in the trial. She sighed.

Mr Grimsditch spoke quietly. 'Apparently, James Wakefield also has a wealthy new brother-in-law who is expected to die without issue. That means his wife – or rather, *he* – stands to inherit thousands.'

Her father's jaw jutted out as he clenched his teeth. 'Another damned fortune hunter. They are both cut from the same cloth.'

Before Mr Grimsditch could vouchsafe any more interesting snippets, there was a commotion as the magistrates returned to stand before them. It was not Thomas who made the pronouncement, but another magistrate; Mr Grimsditch had told her his name was Newton.

He rambled on for a little while, but eventually got to the point.

'This court finds the defendant, James Wakefield …'

Ellen closed her eyes.

'… guilty …'

She snapped them open.

'… of a misdemeanour.'

There was a sharp intake of breath around the room, and her father went rigid beside her. Ellen swallowed. Another fracas ensued and she tried to follow what was being said, but before she could make sense of it, James was led away.

'What will happen now? Is he allowed to go free?' she asked Mr Grimsditch.

'No, my dear. Whilst Wakefield was only found guilty of a misdemeanour, bail was not granted, and as such a warrant will be drawn for his committal to Lancaster Castle. He will be held there until he can be sentenced at the Lancaster Assize in August.'

Ellen fidgeted with her hair, trying to take it all in. 'We must do this again but in Lancaster? And wait until *August*? Even though it's just a misdemeanour?'

Mr Grimsditch looked at her, and she could see sympathy in his eyes. 'I'm afraid so. And I'm sorry to say that before he is sentenced, Wakefield will also have the opportunity to appeal the magistrates' decision.'

'So he might still be acquitted?'

'Not if we present an impenetrable case against the appeal. At the Crown Court everything will be more formal: the sentencing trial will be held in the courthouse at Lancaster Castle rather than an inn, there will be a judge and jury, and I shall have to testify as a witness, because of the letter Wakefield forged from me. Thus, your father will need to instruct another solicitor to represent you there. But rest assured, I will be with you every step of the way.'

Ellen nodded as though that was all perfectly fine. As though she wasn't crumbling inside.

# CHAPTER 40

*One week later*

## Edward

'You should consider America, you know,' Phyllida said late one evening, as they sat comfortably in her salon on the Boulevard Saint-Germain. Lord and Lady Granville were notable by their absence.

Edward smiled at his friend. 'You are not the first to suggest it, my dear, but I'm not sure it would be the right thing to do.'

'You should think of the children. You could take them with you and make your fortune. I'm told it's a marvellous place, and it would be the easiest thing for a man of your calibre.'

Edward laughed. 'If I can persuade Ellen that I'm not the devil incarnate, I won't need to make my fortune.'

Phyllida swatted him on the arm and took another sip of champagne.

'Besides which,' he said, 'I can't abandon James.'

Phyllida gave him a lovely pout. 'Poor little James,' she said. 'What will happen to him and his darling Emily? They've been married mere moments and he's been spirited away from her. She's distraught!'

'Well, he's been denied bail and consigned to Lancaster. I've arranged for someone to see if we can't get him out before too long so they can be reunited. It's his own fault really: I did advise him to remain here with me.'

Phyllida put down her glass and gave him a searching look. She shook her head. 'You're going to do it, aren't you?'

Edward smiled, and then nodded. 'I am. I'm going to go to England to bring James and my wife home.'

Phyllida groaned theatrically. 'Darling, I admire your confidence, truly I do, but you are safe here. Your children are safe here. I fear that Turner is going to be a formidable opponent if he is prepared to drag his daughter through the courts *and* the papers just to thwart you.'

Part of Edward knew there was some truth in what she said, but the other part couldn't resist seeing the whole thing through. Could he pass up the chance to win the prize once and for all? Should he?

He laughed; of course he shouldn't.

'You know me, dear,' he said, 'I just *hate* to leave things unfinished.'

\*   \*   \*

It felt good to be back in England. On Thursday the 13th of April Edward strode along Piccadilly, cane in hand, and tipped his hat to various people as he walked. He'd no idea who they were, but it served to create a fabulous illusion for anyone caring to notice. He was unafraid, unrepentant, and above all, utterly assured of his success.

He'd noticed with no small amount of glee that the right words had leaked into almost all the newspapers. The word *abduction* was gradually being replaced by *elopement*, and the romance of it all seemed to be attracting more and more public interest ... He intended to cast himself as a lovesick hero, hopelessly pining for his beautiful wife. Star-crossed lovers being kept apart by a wicked and vengeful father. He chuckled – it was such a compelling story, he almost believed it himself.

He headed towards Mayfair, and the home of his solicitor, a reliably cut-throat polymath by the name of Scarlett. He had arranged to meet with Scarlett and Frances, and if his bail had come off as planned, James would be there too. He smiled and held his face up to the sun, taking in a deep breath.

When he arrived, he surrendered his hat and gloves to the footman and was ushered into Scarlett's study.

'Always a pleasure, Wakefield,' Scarlett said, and shook his hand firmly. Frances sat in a chair by the fire. James was standing at the edge of the room, and remained there as Edward greeted them all.

'Brother, I'm so pleased you are here.'

James did not smile. 'It's nothing short of a damned miracle that I am,' he said, tapping his fingers on the mantel.

Edward suppressed a sigh. 'Well, praise be for miracles then. Are you able to bring me up to snuff with developments? Our friends at the newspapers seem to be reporting much in our favour.'

It was Frances who answered. 'They are. The public are gobbling it up.'

'Gratifying indeed.' Edward could see that she was dying to say more, but the presence of his legal representative was no doubt stifling her. 'Well, whoever was able to give them the truth of the matter has my undying gratitude.' He nodded his head in a brief bow.

'You know you will be arrested, don't you?' James said.

Edward turned to Scarlett who nodded. 'I fear this to be the case.'

'Then fear no more. I intend to hand myself over to the magistrate and avoid the ignominy of arrest.' Edward enjoyed the stunned silence that filled the room.

'What? Are you run mad?' James said.

'James, cease carping, I know exactly what I am doing.'

'Well, given what you do will impact directly upon myself, I'll own to a modicum of worry!' he yelped. 'I've just married and have no desire to conduct the early stages of my nuptial bliss from behind bars. Emily is already rapidly forming an unsavoury opinion of me.'

'As I said,' Edward continued, ignoring him, 'I intend to hand myself in to the magistrate, and beg an audience with my father-in-law.'

'Edward …' Frances's tone held a warning note.

'You *are* mad,' James said, gaping at him then pacing the room and running his hands through his hair. 'I assure you, Frances was right, the man is a savage. If he were a gentleman, you would even now be settling into married life. As it is, he will most likely attempt to shoot you too.'

Edward couldn't help the smile that grew, particularly as it made Frances's eyes spark with anger. He turned and looked at Scarlett who was following the exchange with interest.

'Might you have any advice to offer, Mr Scarlett?'

Scarlett scratched his head. 'My advice would have been to remain in France and to keep your beloved wife with you. As things stand, though, I agree that handing yourself in is preferable to being arrested. However,' he paused and looked at Frances and James, 'I also see that meeting with the bride's father might … inflame the situation.'

'Perhaps it will. Or perhaps I will persuade him that marriage to me is his family's only option.'

Frances adjusted her gloves. 'Might I remind you that we all have a great deal to lose here. You have already underestimated Turner once. A second time would be sheer folly.'

'But it might just get us all out of this difficult position and allow us all to get on with our lives. Lives that will be considerably enriched by my bringing dear Ellen into the family, *with* her father's blessing.'

James groaned, slumped into a chair, and put his head in his hands. Frances was visibly restraining herself, and Scarlett … Well, the lawyer looked both alarmed and thoroughly entertained.

'Any final words, Mr Scarlett?'

'Tread carefully, Wakefield. I intend to win this case, and I can only do that if your father-in-law doesn't murder you first.'

\* \* \*

This next part of his venture was going to be the most challenging and the most interesting. He had found directions for the residences of all three magistrates that stood for James's trial and would most likely hear his case too. His intention was to hand himself over to one of them. He suffered the gravest temptation to submit himself to Thomas Legh at Lyme Park, largely because Ellen had seemed so transported by the book Legh had given her, but partly because he seemed to be a staunch supporter of Turner. It felt quite poetic. However, he knew that the next part was likely to be filled with a good deal of emotion and anger, and it seemed foolish to fan the flame unnecessarily. With that good sense uppermost in his mind, he decided upon the worthy Mr Samuel Newton, who had signed the warrant for his apprehension.

He rapped upon the shiny black door to the magistrate's residence, and waited. His heart thumped in his chest and sent a shiver of excitement through him. He could do this. He knew he could. If he could secure a few moments of Turner's time, Ellen would be his, for better and for worse.

# CHAPTER 41

*The next day*

*William*

William Turner paced the study in Samuel Newton's pristinely spartan home.

'So, he simply arrived on your doorstep and presented himself for trial?'

Newton could do no more than nod stiffly. 'He did. I wasn't even aware that he had returned to the country, but he says that he wants to put an end to the gossip. Wants to ... save your family from being the object of speculation, or that was the inference. He wants to talk to your daughter and you so that this can be resolved amicably, and so that they can be ... ah, reunited.'

'I'm going to kill him with my bare hands.'

Grimsditch was now looking at him with thinly veiled horror. 'I would trust that you'll restrain yourself, William,' he said nervously. 'You are, after all, a gentleman.'

William gave him a smile that bared his teeth. 'Don't bank on it.'

'Turner,' Newton said, 'listen to me. We have him. We have him, and he will be here any moment. There is no doubt that he will be taken to Lancaster, there is no doubt that he will stand trial. Not after what he did. However, Wakefield is not the dilettante you think him to be. He is a shrewd and intelligent man. You would be wise to remember that.'

William snorted.

'You might not like to hear it, but he is. At the moment, he is still hoping to convince you that marriage to him is the best option for Ellen and for your family. He is hoping to win you over and claim you as his father-in-law.'

'That will never happen.'

'I know that and so do you. All you need to do is remain calm and sensible. Do not play into his hands.'

William snorted. 'Calm? You expect me to be calm with that … that … *bastard?*'

Newton raised a brow and gave him an intent look. '*Are* you a gentleman?'

*No*, William thought. He wasn't born a gentleman, and he knew that on some level, he'd never be seen as one. But saying that to the magistrate would do him no favours. 'Of course I'm a gentleman.'

'Then kindly behave as one, and not as some thug from the slums of Blackburn.'

That bit. It bit deep. So deep, William was tempted to plant Newton a facer.

'You will give Wakefield no end of pleasure if you lay into him,' said Grimsditch quietly. 'If he leaves here with a black eye and a fat lip, who will look like the scoundrel then?'

'Christ!' William balled his hands into fists, and resumed pacing.

At that moment, Newton's butler announced Wakefield's arrival. William squeezed his eyes tightly shut for a moment.

'Are we ready, gentlemen?' Newton asked. William did not miss the subtle emphasis on *gentlemen*. He might be many things, but he wasn't stupid.

He stood by the mantel, slipped one hand casually in his pocket, unclenched his other, and waited. Newton's butler brought in a youngish man of thirty or so. He was taller than his brother, and most certainly had more countenance. Tall, with fair hair and dressed in a dandyish fashion, he could see how the ladies would like him. Could see how *Ellen* might like him.

He had a solemn look on his face, and in his eyes he could see remnants of uncertainty.

Newton made the introductions, and William made his face as neutral and disinterested as he could.

'Mr Turner, we meet at last. I heard a good deal about you from my wife on our travels.'

William bit the inside of his cheek at the word *wife*, exactly as Wakefield intended. Newton and Grimsditch were right. The man was playing with him.

'I'm sure you did. Strange, she's barely mentioned you since her return home.' His tone was perfectly civil, he made sure of it.

'You must know, Mr Turner, that my feelings for my … for your daughter, are honest and true. Our journey began in the strangest of ways, but somewhere along the way …' he shrugged and gave a good impression of a man lost to love, 'we fell in love with each other.'

William looked at him but gave him nothing.

'Mr Wakefield, you realise that we must now make arrangements for your hearing,' Newton said briskly.

'Of course, I am fully prepared for that. I was just hoping for some time to assure my father-in-law that Ellen was loved and cared for this whole time. That her every comfort was paramount in my mind, and that the days we spent in Calais were some of the happiest of my life.'

More than anything, William wanted to hurl his fist square in the trickster's gut, then, when he doubled over, smash him in the face. But Newton was right. Gentlemen didn't do such things; gentlemen wouldn't touch scum like Wakefield with a ten-foot pole. He could see that his lack of response was starting to confuse the young man.

Newton was speaking to Grimsditch and preparing some documentation, so Wakefield took the opportunity to continue his offence.

'I would also very much like to speak with Ellen,' he said, eyes down, demeanour chastened. He was good, he would give him that, but William had spent a lifetime clawing his way up through the aristocracy and he had learned to spot an accomplished liar.

'Perhaps, perhaps not,' he said without emotion. 'I will speak to my daughter and see if she has any appetite for your company.'

Wakefield was startled, and it showed. 'You are very, very generous. Just as she described. And I assure you, this problem now facing us is eminently solvable. It is my most fervent wish to spend the rest of my life caring for Ellen and making her happy. If she can see that, we could do away with all this dreadful nonsense and simply be together in harmony.'

William pretended to consider the proposal. 'I must admit, there have been some who feel that settling something on the pair of you would make the whole debacle disappear.'

'It would indeed,' Wakefield said, with a gleam in his eye that William suspected was excitement as well as avarice. The imbecile thought he was wearing him down, thought he was winning. It felt extremely gratifying at last to have the upper hand.

Wakefield continued. 'All this brouhaha would be over, and you would be able to enjoy your elevation to High Sheriff without further interruption. I'm sure that the past weeks have been utterly infuriating for you.'

'They have, they have indeed. It has been very … difficult.'

'If I could but spend a little time with you, your wife, and Ellen, you might see that I am not the scoundrel that I have been painted. I am a decent man, a good man, and I love your daughter to distraction. I am not without ambition; I shall strive to enter parliament and make Ellen, and you, proud.'

William smiled. So that was how the land lay. He wanted a seat in parliament but didn't have the blunt to secure one himself. William was spared from answering though, as Newton finished his discussion with Grimsditch and cut in.

'We will hear the case in Disley in two days,' he pronounced and proceeded to give Wakefield the details. Wakefield nodded his agreement.

'I shall be very pleased to see Ellen there, even if it is under such trying circumstances,' he said softly. 'But if you could find it in your heart to let me speak with her beforehand, we might be able to bypass all this fuss.'

Turner rubbed his chin as though he were pondering. Newton was staring at him; Grimsditch looked lost, and more than a little worried.

He turned to Wakefield, patted him on the shoulder, then turned to the magistrate.

'Mr Newton, thank you so much for your support in this matter. I can assure you that I will be available for the hearing, as will my daughter, and we will be ready to impart the full detail of this man's villainy.'

'But Mr Turner, sir,' Edward said in his most placatory tones yet, 'just a moment with Ellen ...'

He turned to Wakefield, gave him a broad smile that he hoped was as dark and furious as he felt.

'Over my dead body.'

# CHAPTER 42

*Ellen*

The day of Edward's hearing dawned, and Ellen sat in her bed, drinking chocolate and thinking. When she'd attended James's hearings she had been scared and flustered. She'd even felt *sorry* for James. But no more. She was angry with Edward. Angry with him for what he put her through, for what he was putting her parents through. For thinking even now that he could just walk back into the country, hand himself in, and pick up with her. What a swollen-headed ghoul he was!

There had been many reports in the newspapers now: some had taken to casting her as a silly schoolgirl, others as being vulgar and ignorant. When she appeared at James's second hearing it was said that she wasn't terribly clever; that although she had been tricked into marriage, she was too simple to remain unhappy with the union. But Ellen was determined to sway public opinion back and show them that she was no fool. And she had a plan in place to achieve that.

Mr Grimsditch had suggested that today, she should show the world that she was intelligent, well educated, and not one given to flights of fancy. Not someone who might be easily coaxed into an ill-advised elopement.

There should be no shaking, no trembling, no fumbling of words … Edward Gibbon Wakefield had done the family wrong, and justice must be done so Ellen could be free of him. It was as simple as that.

Today, she knew she could do herself proud.

She dressed carefully, paying particular attention to her appearance this time. She was tall, and many took her for older than her years. She intended to use that to her advantage.

Her gown was black and startling in its severity. It complemented her figure beautifully. Her hair was pulled back and hidden beneath an austere but stylish high poke bonnet. All in all, her outfit exuded cold elegance, and this time, she was ready to do what needed to be done. She would not be thrown by Thomas's presence. She would not be cowed by the whole rigmarole of the courtroom. She would most certainly not give Edward Gibbon Wakefield the satisfaction of seeing her distressed.

She gathered her things and went to say goodbye to her mother, who was in the breakfast room. She went in, and her mother stared.

'What?' Ellen said, patting her hair. 'What is it, do I have a smudge somewhere?'

'No … no, not at all. You look … you look …' Her mama smiled mistily. 'Stunning. And terribly grown-up.'

\* \* \*

Flanked by her father, Uncle Robert, and Mr Grimsditch, Ellen approached the Ram's Head. All of them were in black. They almost looked as though they were in mourning. Which in some ways, they were.

Mr Grimsditch had told her that Edward would be inside, so as they reached the entrance, she arranged her face as icily as she could. Then they walked in as one, a warrior queen and her entourage.

Edward was ready and waiting, dressed to the nines in a forest green jacket over a gold striped waistcoat. She looked away before he had a chance to see her; otherwise she was sure he would try and smile at her, or signal to her in some way. She was surprised at the jolt it gave her, seeing him again. When she sat down her hands trembled, so she clutched her reticule, and stared haughtily ahead.

When Thomas came in, his face was calm and blank. As usual, he didn't look her in the eye once, and as usual, he was so unjustly handsome, Ellen wondered if *that* ought to be a misdemeanour. She tried to emulate his calmness, and her papa must have divined she was struggling, because he reached across, captured both her hands in his large one, and squeezed. It helped.

Eventually, proceedings began and Mr Grimsditch presented her case. He really was exceptionally good at it, and eventually, when it was her turn to be asked questions, she was exceptional too. She stood on the required spot, held her hands loosely in front of her, put her chin in the air and pretended to be the calm lady of quality that she resembled. She answered questions as succinctly as possible, never moving from her position that she married Edward because she had been lied to, despite provocation from the searching questions asked of her.

Thomas looked at her. 'Would you have married Mr Edward Gibbon Wakefield had you been aware of the true circumstances? That your mother was perfectly well, that your father's business was intact, that your family did not stand on the brink of penury. Would you have run away with him to Gretna?'

Ellen looked him in the eye and lifted her chin. When she spoke, it was with clarity and the faintest arch of her eyebrow.

'I would not have. If I might say, I did not run away. I was taken. I was taken from my school and taken to Gretna Green under false pretences.'

She caught Mr Grimsditch's fleeting look of satisfaction and felt pleased.

An argument ensued between Mr Grimsditch and Edward's lawyer, much as it had done with James's about the nature of the crime, and whether it was a capital offence or a misdemeanour.

This time, when the magistrates came back into the room after lengthy consideration, it was pronounced that this was a capital offence, and Edward would receive bail until his sentencing at Lancaster Assize.

Ellen looked to the ceiling as a wave of relief consumed her. She heard a hiss of satisfaction from her father and her uncle, and Mr Grimsditch looked, like his name, grimly delighted. Edward wore an expression of anguish and moral outrage; his lawyer looked inconvenienced, but not very surprised. The only person she didn't dare look at was Thomas.

# CHAPTER 43

A few days later, a letter arrived from Lavinia. Ellen fell on it immediately. It was the first time she had heard from her since the hurried departure from her father's investiture celebration. With shaking hands, she broke the seal … but then she dropped it. What if Lavinia was writing to break off with her? Had her parents decided they couldn't remain friends? That would be unbearable … But not knowing was worse. She snatched up the envelope and tore it open. When she read the content, she laughed, then cried a little.

*My darling Ellen,*

*I sincerely hope my letter finds you in good spirits, and that you are managing to rise above the challenges you face. In case you might be wondering what the world is thinking, I've enclosed some cuttings. Poor Papa simply cannot understand why his newspapers keep disappearing!*

A heap of press cuttings spilled out, all about the latest hearing at Disley. She scanned them all anxiously, and was relieved that the *Liverpool Mercury* now described her countenance not as *juvenile*, but *grave*. Meanwhile, the *Manchester Gazette* said that she had a figure that was *peculiarly commanding*, and a manner that bespoke *more than an ordinary share of intelligence*. They went on to say, *Her countenance is pale, but the fine expression of her eye adds considerably to her personal beauty, which is heightened by a set of perfectly formed white teeth which ornament a gracefully turned lip.*

Ellen chuckled at that. *A gracefully turned lip?* She picked up a cutting from *The Times* and scanned the content, noting that they thought her *enlivened by two piercing eyes and teeth a fine contrast to her ruby lips*. She put her hand to her mouth, nay, to her gracefully turned ruby lips, and giggled, wishing Lavinia and Hester were there to share her reaction to the ridiculous comments. Then gasped as she read on. *The Times* said that her manners were *those of a highly finished lady without the slightest trace of gaucherie ... there is something fascinating about her.*

She put the newspaper down, hesitated, but couldn't resist going to the mirror and looking at herself. She turned this way and that, smiling then not smiling, then broke out laughing. How on earth they had come up with such puffery, she had no idea. But as the corners of her critically acclaimed lips turned upwards again, she decided that she rather liked it.

\* \* \*

The next few weeks were quiet. Hester and Lavinia were now allowed to write regularly again, but they were in school, and Ellen felt the loss of her own schooldays enormously. There had been little company, and Ellen wasn't sure if the lack of invitations and callers was because of the trial. It was hard to tell, and she didn't really want to know the answer.

It came as a surprise, then, when she was invited to join her parents at a dinner party that evening. Even more surprisingly, said invitation had come from Thomas. Why would he want her darkening his door, after all the distasteful things he'd heard about her in court? Perhaps, as her father's friend, he was just being polite. In any case, *she* wanted to see *him*, and at this juncture was grateful for any social engagements she could get. She only hoped that his other guests would not be beastly, and that he would not avoid her eye all evening.

'Penny for them?' her father said as the tooled along in the carriage towards Lyme Park.

'Not even worth that, Papa,' she said, fiddling with the ribbons on her gown of mauve gauze. It had been one of the dresses she'd acquired in Calais, which she hadn't the heart to part with. 'Just wool-gathering.'

'Well, it will do you good to get out,' her mother said. 'We need to start planning for after the trial. Did I tell you that the viscount I've been working on, Lord Longton, is still willing to get to know you?'

'You did, Mama ...' Ellen tried not to sigh; could she not shake off the husband she had, before another was thrust upon her? The carriage jerked and her mama held on to her hat.

'In fact,' her mother continued, with some umbridge directed at her papa, 'if Lord Longton wasn't coming this evening, I'm not sure I would be.' She sniffed and turned to look out of the window. Ellen exchanged a glance with her father. He gave her a tiny shake of his head so she didn't ask her mother to expand.

She gave her mother a pointed smile. 'Perhaps if Lord Longton doesn't fall in love with me, I could be an old maid and live at Shrigley forever, with you and Papa? I'd rather enjoy that.'

'Stuff and nonsense,' blustered her mother. 'You will marry, of course you will.'

'I could be a desert nomad?' Ellen wasn't sure what imp of mischief was making her provoke her mother today. 'I could travel the world like … like Lady Hester Stanhope.' She almost said *like Thomas*, but restrained herself.

Her mother's mouth fell open and she quivered with shock. 'Ellen … please! You cannot seriously …'

Her father put a hand over his mouth and looked out of the window, but his eyes were dancing.

Her mother spent the rest of the journey staring at her, as if she had grown another head.

\* \* \*

Thomas's party was an informal affair, and by the time they'd finished eating, it was clear he'd put some thought into the guest list. To her relief, no one had snubbed her or even mentioned the dreadful court case. Thomas had seated Ellen beside her mama's Lord Longton, which was a tad mortifying, but he turned out to be a most affable young man whose silky chestnut hair flopped about increasingly, the more engrossed he became in conversation. Ellen wondered briefly if her mother had influenced Thomas in his choice of place settings – Ellen wouldn't put it past her to write ahead – or if this was simply Thomas's way of confirming that he himself held no interest in her. Thomas was seated at the other end of the table, as far away from her as the small gathering would allow.

After dinner, the small party retired to the saloon. Like all the rooms she had seen, it was magnificent. She could see her mother eyeing the detail on the wood panelling, the grand rococo ceiling embellished with gold, and had to smile. Several huge floor-to-ceiling windows graced the large balcony for a splendid view over the lake and parkland. She sat with her parents and listened to her mother extol the virtues of such balconies, trying to look nonchalant, whilst she watched Thomas work his way around the guests.

'Miss Turner,' he said when he reached them. To her amazement, he not only met her eye, but smiled. 'I hope you are enjoying this evening?'

'Oh yes,' she said, wishing she could think of something waggish or interesting to say. 'Thank you, Mr Legh.'

'I wondered,' he said, 'have you noticed the carvings on the walls in this room?'

Ellen had, but she glanced at the wood panels again; the engravings were extravagant and quite masterful, depicting cascading leaves intertwined with violins and cherubs.

'I'd be happy to show you them,' he said mildly. *Goodness*, she thought. Did the man who'd given her the cold shoulder since her return from France now want to be friends again?

'Yes.' Ellen stood up rather too quickly. 'Please. That would be most kind.'

'Don't take up too much of Mr Legh's time, dear,' her mother said, somewhat dampening the moment.

As Thomas escorted Ellen to the other side of the room, apart from everyone, he launched straight into the history of the carvings. 'They were made from lime wood, around 1680. They depict the four seasons, art, science, and music.'

'My word,' Ellen said, peering more closely at the ornate work, and wondering why he was speaking like a tour guide.

'I'm led to believe they were by Grinling Gibbons.'

Ellen felt a twinge of anxiety at the name that made her think of Edward. She crushed the thought. 'They're lovely.'

'The whole house was redesigned in the early seventeen

hundreds by Giacomo Leoni,' he went on, 'and then I remodelled much of it more recently.'

'And you did it so beautifully,' Ellen said. 'I'd love to hear all about the process. But … Pardon my impudence, Mr Legh. Did you really just want to talk to me about the walls?'

Thomas looked at her, and there it was. The spark of amusement in his eyes. Her heart pounded.

'How are you holding up?' he said quietly.

*So, he does care.* She felt suddenly rather vulnerable, and steeled herself. 'Much better, now the hearings at Disley are over. Thank you for asking.'

'Good to hear it.' There was a pause, and the next time he spoke, it was so low she was almost convinced she'd imagined it. 'I was glad you came this evening.' He was looking at the carvings, rather than her.

'Really?' she asked in genuine surprise, realising too late that this too was a rather forward thing to say. 'I thought you'd written me off as a ninny. One couldn't blame you if you had.'

He looked at her askance and raised an eyebrow. 'What gave you that impression?'

'Well, you know …' she stiffened her spine, and did her best imitation of Thomas's frowning face.

He spluttered out a laugh, then cleared his throat. 'Whilst I'm in the process of hearing a case, I have to keep my distance from the complainant and the accused, to ensure a fair trial. But now that yours has been elevated to the Assizes …'

Ellen pieced together Thomas's strange coldness before the investiture banquet, his apparent indifference to her in court. His manner had been so different from before her abduction, and so different from the warmth he was extending to her now. A wave of relief washed over; it made sense. '… Here we are,' she said.

'Here we are,' he echoed, shyly. There was a tinge of sadness too in his voice, but she couldn't quite pinpoint the reason. 'I've every confidence it will go your way. The trial at Lancaster should be a formality.'

'Do you think so? Some of the newspapers are still calling me a silly child, who thought marrying some ne'er-do-well I'd never even met before would be a great wheeze. Others are claiming it's a grand love match and that I'll be flinging myself into his arms 'ere long.'

He glanced sideways at her again, that small smile tugging at his lips. 'I suspect anyone who was at the most recent hearing will be disabused of any such notion.'

'Thank you.'

'I really would be surprised if he wasn't convicted. And once that's done, your father will press ahead with the annulment and you can go back to being who you are.'

'And who, exactly, am I?'

He looked directly into her eyes. 'You are Ellen Turner.'

To her surprise, her eyes filled with tears. She looked away and nodded.

'Never forget that,' he murmured. 'Ellen Turner, wrangler of fearsome bears!' His smile was wicked, and it made her snort with laughter. He chuckled with her as he accompanied her back to the group.

# CHAPTER 44

It felt like a lifetime, but August finally arrived, and with it, the trial at Lancaster Assize of Edward Gibbon Wakefield and James Wakefield. In the interim they'd been notified that two accomplices were to be tried in the same hearing: Monsieur Thevenot, and one Mrs Edward Wakefield.

'Who is Mrs Wakefield?' Ellen asked her father over dinner.

He pulled a face. 'I believe she is married to Wakefield's father.'

'Edward never mentioned her.'

'That's probably because she was his accomplice, darling. It rather sounds like she helped them to plan the escapade. It will be interesting to see what she has to say for herself.'

Ellen frowned. 'Do you think she helped Edward to steal your handkerchief and ring?' They still hadn't got to the bottom of that mystery.

'Impossible,' her mother said. 'We've had no ladies by the name of Wakefield in the house.'

'Perhaps she bribed someone else to pilfer them? A servant, maybe?' Ellen suggested.

Her father grimaced, and her mother quivered with outrage. 'What mother would do such a thing?' she seethed. 'What is the world coming to when mothers plot and scheme to secure a bride for their children?'

Ellen blinked and hesitated. Her father choked on his bread roll.

'I'm sure we will find out more,' her father said, once he'd stopped coughing. 'Are you ready for the journey to Lancaster?'

Both Ellen and her mother nodded. Her mother would not attend the trial itself – the risk to her health was too great – but her father had rented a house for them to stay in, a little way out of the city. The best part though was the fact that Hester and Lavinia's parents had relented and allowed them to accompany her. And they weren't just coming for moral support. Mr Grimsditch had devised the most astonishing role for them to play, which would make Ellen's entrance to the court one the papers would not forget …

★   ★   ★

Arriving at Lancaster Castle, Ellen was bubbling with excitement. Mr Grimsditch's plan to fox the newspaper men was genius. She sat in the carriage with Hester and Lavinia, and giggled before schooling her features. Although, because of Mr Grimsditch's marvellous plan, no one could see them.

They were dressed identically. All in black, all heavily veiled. No one would be able to tell which was Ellen – so if they wanted to ask her impertinent questions, they wouldn't know where to begin. It was perfect!

'Are you ready?' Hester said, clutching her hand.

Ellen nodded. 'I am now. I couldn't be more ready.'

Lavinia laughed. 'We are your handmaidens. The newspaper men and the public will be frantic!'

Ellen's chest squeezed at the thought; for the first time, she felt as though they were in control of the proceedings.

'What should we say if anyone speaks to us? Asks us who we are?' Hester said.

Ellen was transported back to Thomas Legh's saloon for a moment, and it made her smile. 'There is only one answer.'

She took both girls' hands and held them tightly. '*I am Ellen Turner!*'

A roar went up as the three of them exited the carriage and made their way through the castle gates. People shouted, laughed, shrieked … It was exhilarating. Ellen stood tall as she entered the building, then hugged Hester and Lavinia tightly before they had to part, confident that she could now meet what lay ahead.

The cavernous vaulted ceiling gave the hall of justice an air of grandeur, but the atmosphere was no less stifling for it. There was a pungent smell of ancient dust, old books, and too many people. The judge, a portly older gentleman with a bald head that accentuated his bushy eyebrows, was already seated at his podium.

She took up her place beside her Uncle Robert, on a raised platform before the ladies' box, and looked out over the crowded courtroom below. Hester and Lavinia were seated with their parents, near the back of the room, and at the front were her father, Mr Grimsditch, and her father's new counsel, Mr Cross. She hadn't as much affection for Mr Cross as she did for Grimsditch – he was a fantastically pompous man with an imperious chin and a belligerent nose – but his credentials were second to none, and she trusted him.

As she continued to look out over the room, spying familiar faces in every direction – friends, acquaintances, scribblers, and a few mean-spirited spectators she recognised from the investiture celebration – it occurred to her how long she'd spent being *watched*, and how heavily it had weighed on her these past months. All the scrutiny she had endured was building to this final hearing, and now, she was well and truly centre stage. It seemed that right now, the only person not staring at her was Thomas, who was sitting alone in the stalls, apparently deep in thought. She took a series of steadying breaths.

'Chin up, old thing,' Robert murmured.

Ellen nodded, and held her breath as a rumble of noise resounded from the back of the hall. A second later, Edward Gibbon Wakefield swaggered in, sporting a black handkerchief, yellow waistcoat, and a dark brown buttoned up frock coat. He moved as though he owned the place and everyone in it. Edward looked straight up at Ellen and, without an ounce of shame, gave her a flirtatious smile and a wink. She shuddered before throwing him a withering look in response.

Edward took his seat next to Thevenot and a man she presumed was their lawyer. The lawyer apparently did not share Edward's mood, and a hurried discussion took place between them. Voices were quickly raised, and something of a buzz set up about the courtroom.

She leaned a little closer to her uncle. 'What's happening?' she whispered. 'Are we going to begin?'

'I don't know,' he murmured.

'Where is James?'

'I don't know,' he said again, and Ellen heard the first note of uncertainty in her uncle's tone. The first crack in his confidence. 'He should be here by now.'

Moments later, Mr Cross hurried over with her father and Mr Grimsditch in tow. All three looked a little out of breath.

'Well,' said Mr Cross with exaggerated chagrin, 'we have two problems. Firstly, young Wakefield hasn't arrived, neither has Mrs Wakefield. The judge is concerned they may have absconded. Secondly, a technical point, but an important one, Edward Gibbon Wakefield was found guilty of a capital offence at the magistrates' hearing, but seemingly, due to some clerical error, all the defendants are now being judged for a misdemeanour. Wakefield's solicitor is claiming he is unprepared to appeal against that, and needs more time.'

Uncle Robert snorted. 'That's nonsense. What more does he need to prepare for? Edward Wakefield is not even taking the stand!'

Mr Grimsditch and her father were nodding vigorously in agreement. When they'd first learned of Edward's decision to not take the stand, they'd all been confused. Edward was such a fluent manipulator, they couldn't imagine him fearful of being caught out under interrogation. But then they'd understood: he wasn't afraid. It was his supreme confidence, his arrogant certainty that everything would go his way, that led him to believe he had no need to participate in his own trial.

'I'm tempted to concur,' Mr Cross said stuffily, 'but unfortunately, his solicitor is within his rights.'

'But why would the Crown Court do that, if it was an error? The magistrates have already decided he deserves a harsher sentence.' Ellen said.

'The Crown Court overrules the magistrates, I'm afraid,' said Mr Cross. 'And once an error like this has been made, it would be an administrative nightmare for them to alter it.'

Ellen gasped. Could her assailant's sentence really be so drastically reduced, to save these men some paperwork? She was expecting Edward to be sent to prison, or even transported, for what he'd done to her. Now, it seemed he might receive no more than a slap on the wrist. And rather than thanking the

Lord for it, Edward was complaining that this was unfair on *him*? Her blood boiled; she didn't know whether to weep or scream.

'This is ridiculous. It's an absolute shambles!' Ellen's papa huffed as he sat down next to her and crossed his arms.

'Remember to keep up a dignified front,' Grimsditch reminded them softly. Ellen unclenched her fists dutifully, and tried not to cry. Her confidence drained as she watched the judge conclude his whispered conversation with the court official, then address the room.

'The counsel for the defence has not been given adequate opportunity to prepare their case,' he proclaimed. 'For this reason, the sentencing is adjourned until two weeks hence, at 9.30 on the 21st of August. Bail will be collected for the defendants Mr James Wakefield and Mrs Edward Wakefield Senior, who have failed to present themselves on time.'

Ellen could only listen in horror as the judge dismissed the court. She had been so ready. Everything had been so perfect to launch her boldly into the proceedings. And here they were. Brought to a halt entirely by a slip of a clerk's pen. It really was the edge of enough.

She heard her father and Mr Cross protesting; in the stalls, Hester and Lavinia looked ready to storm the pulpit, and Thomas was shaking his head in disbelief. But in the absence of half the defendants, there was nothing else to be done. The last of her morale trickled away.

By the time they'd gathered themselves and stood to leave, Edward, Thevenot, and their lawyer had already disappeared from the room.

★ ★ ★

## Edward

Edward strode into his lodgings in Lancaster, tossed his hat and cane at a startled maid, and opened the door to the parlour. As he expected, James was sitting idly by the fire. His brother swallowed and tried to look defiant.

'Well?' Edward said quietly. 'I'm waiting.'

James shrugged. 'What is there to say?'

'I'd like an explanation for your behaviour today. Where were you when I needed you? Where was Frances?'

James thrust his hands in his hair. 'I can't bear it. She can't either ...' he shook his head and turned away.

Keeping a tight rein on his temper, Edward grabbed James's shoulders and dragged him out of his chair. He closed in on him so their faces were inches apart.

'Not this nonsense again.'

Colour flooded James's face, but he put his chin up. 'I don't want to go to prison, Edward. I *told* you this was a bad idea. It's not my fault.'

Cold fury gripped Edward. He took hold of his brother's throat and squeezed. 'You will do what we agreed. After all that talk about how much you *care* about Ellen, you will not ruin her and leave me – your *brother* – in the lurch.'

James's eyes were wide. 'But, but Emily says—' he choked.

'Emily needs to learn,' snarled Edward, keeping his hold tight, to ensure James would remember every word, 'that it is not *wives* who wear the trousers. Frances does too. Now locate your manhood, brother, or my pistol will locate it for you.'

# CHAPTER 45

*Ellen*

'Stand still …' Lavinia tilted Ellen's head to an impossible angle, and she fixed a particularly recalcitrant curl for her. She let go gingerly, and Ellen righted her head slowly. 'Done!'

Ellen laughed and moved her head about. 'What would I do without you?'

'I'm not sure, my dear, but you would do it looking bedraggled.'

'Pay her no heed. You look lovely,' Hester said, giving her arm a squeeze.

They stood together before the full-length glass in Ellen's room and linked arms. 'We do look rather ravishing, don't we?' Lavinia said, and then turned to Ellen. 'Speaking of which, we never did establish exactly what ravishment entailed, did we. Ellen, you have reached the grand old age of eighteen without finding out.'

'Despite being married!' Ellen quipped.

'Anyhow,' Lavinia said, turning this way and that to check that her own fair curls bounced in exactly the right fashion, 'I'm relying on your mama to have invited a whole host of delightful gentlemen to your birthday party.'

'She assures me that we won't be thin of company,' said Ellen. 'I do hope that this time, people won't come simply to stare.'

'If they do, we shall stare back until they simply wither away. Won't we, Hester?' Lavinia gave a fabulously devastating glare and Hester tittered nervously. Ellen played along, but secretly she was worried. For her parents, the summer had been a lesson in separating their true friends from their false ones, and one that continued to surprise them. All in all, society had been … awkward, and throwing a ball for her eighteenth birthday felt rather like gambling with their reputations.

'I believe the Earl of Wincanton will be here tonight. He definitely likes you, Lavinia,' she said.

Lavinia flushed and pirouetted about the room. 'He does, doesn't he.'

'Will Lord Longton be here? He seems to be taking a shine to you,' Hester said with an arch look at Ellen.

'Mother is most … hopeful he will be. She has been cultivating him quite shamelessly.'

'And are *you* hopeful?'

Ellen shrugged; her future was still so uncertain that right now, any kind of romantic hopes made her feel tired. Especially with all the sleep she was losing, thinking of a certain tour guide at Lyme Park.

'More importantly, what about Mr Legh?' Lavinia said, as if reading her mind. 'Has he gaoled any more enemies for you recently?'

'Only when they deserve it,' Ellen said, coyly. 'And I'm reliably informed we *might* see him this evening.'

Lavinia squealed and they danced about the bedroom, linking arms and laughing, until their hair pins came loose and their curls needed to be tamed all over again.

\* \* \*

'How is your dance card looking, my love?'

Ellen smiled weakly at her mother, then looked at the card in her gloved hand. 'Very well, thank you,' she lied. In fact, she had only a couple of dances marked, which alarmingly did not include the first. But admitting this would only lead her mama to foist her onto someone awful, so she scurried away to escape further questioning.

It was a lovely party; the ballroom at Shrigley glowed in the light of hundreds of candles, in part thanks to Miss Davis, who had helped her mother make everything just so before travelling to a family engagement of her own. So far no one had given Ellen the cut in the way they did at the investiture. However, her face was already aching from smiling at people as they milled about, drinking, laughing, and watching her.

The orchestra had almost finished tuning their instruments, and if she didn't want her mother to start flapping, she needed to find a partner for the first dance sharpish. She might have easily relied upon the dashing Lord Longton, but alas, he was nowhere to be seen. She was starting to contemplate running away and hiding in a cupboard, when the voice of a new arrival spoke nearby.

'Good evening. May I say you are all looking very elegant tonight?'

Ellen whirled, a smile blossoming, at the sound of Thomas Legh paying his respects to her friends and her mother. He turned to her and bowed gallantly. She dropped a curtsy in return.

'You came!'

'Happy birthday, Miss Turner. Might I claim a dance, or am I too late?'

Ellen laughed, but it was a brittle sound. 'You can take your pick; I'm not exactly overwhelmed.'

Her mother looked mortified, her mouth opening and closing like a codfish, as Thomas gave Ellen his small smile and took her dance card. He looked it over and frowned before looking back up at her with that distinct glint in his eye she'd come to think about … a lot.

'Would it be presumptuous of me to claim your first dance?'

*Dear Lord*, she wanted to hug him. 'I'd be honoured,' she managed, with some semblance of sophistication, she hoped.

He winked at her, actually winked at her, and after a beat of hesitation, wrote his name by the Galop … *and* the waltz. A waltz! Her very first waltz was to be with Thomas Legh. She felt hot all over, her heart was thumping, and were she not so intent on acting the lady, she really could have grabbed him.

'Thank you, that is so terribly kind of you.'

He gave her an odd look. 'I'm not being kind.'

'Of course you are, and I love you for it.' She snapped her mouth shut. *Sweet Jesus!* Had she just told Thomas Legh she loved him? She had! Ellen wanted to cut out her tongue, run away, never to return. She stood, cheeks flaming, waiting for the ground to open and swallow her, but of course it didn't. The music started, and with a smile that turned into a laugh, Thomas shook his head and held out his hand.

\* \* \*

'You said *what*?' Lavinia exclaimed in delighted outrage, as they took cover afterwards with Hester by the refreshment table.

'I know,' moaned Ellen. 'It was foolish, but he has been so kind, and I do love him for it.'

'Are you in love with him?' Hester whispered.

Ellen flushed. 'I like him a lot,' was all she felt she could admit to, before she spotted Lord Longton bounding towards them.

'Miss Turner, might I have the pleasure of this dance?'

Ellen dipped a curtsy and offered him her hand, just in time for the Cotillion. He was a pleasant and undemanding dance companion – save the few times he trod on her foot – and with his unusually long lashes, he was very handsome. As they whirled around the floor, they had little breath to spare for conversation, so Longton entertained her by telling her snatches of jokes and laughing loudly at his own silliness. She couldn't resist joining in: for although he had told her the same jokes at Thomas's dinner party not so long ago, she was charmed by how much he amused himself.

When he returned her safely to her friends, she thanked him, and he disappeared.

'Your mother is pink with joy. I suspect she has already drafted the invitations to your wedding,' Lavinia said.

Ellen groaned and avoided her mother's eye. 'He is far too young to be thinking of marriage,' she said. Or at least, she hoped he was, as she wiggled her bruised toes.

The evening wore on, and she danced with several more gentlemen: some handsome, some charming. But she found herself counting down impatiently until the musicians finally gathered themselves for the waltz. With perfect timing, Thomas bowed before her once more.

Her pulse raced as he placed one hand gently on her waist and held her hand in the required position. She placed her other on his shoulder, and they were away. He guided her effortlessly across the floor, and she relaxed into the warmth of his embrace.

'You know,' he murmured close to her ear, 'I've been thinking of the outfit you wore that last time at the magistrates'
court.'

'You have?' Ellen asked, her face growing hot. She'd been
convinced he hadn't looked at her once that day.

'I have,' he said, and she could hear that he was smiling. 'It
was most effective. Might I suggest that you wear something
equally severe at the Assize next week?'

She laughed as he twirled her with one hand, and swept her
off in the opposite direction. 'I have my outfit planned,' she
confided, 'and it is severe in the extreme. I shall look like a
maiden aunt who has never had a moment's fun in her entire
life.'

He leaned back and looked at her wryly. 'I sincerely doubt
that.'

'Now you are *definitely* being kind,' Ellen teased, wondering
how pink her cheeks were. After a beat, she said sincerely, 'I'm
sorry your trip last week was wasted.'

'You saw me at the courthouse?' His gaze intensified, and she
looked away.

'I did. It means a great deal to me that you came all that
way.'

'It does?'

She glanced back at him and for a moment he looked charm-
ingly awkward, then he turned her around and was at her ear
again.

'It does. It seems fitting: after all, you have been with me
throughout this whole debacle.'

He fell silent then, evidently confused. Was he waiting for
her to elaborate, or hoping she wouldn't? She looked around
them, and when she saw that no other dancers were close
enough to hear, she decided to risk speaking.

'If you recall, a day or so before I went to school for the last time, you were kind enough to give me a copy of your book.'

She felt him nod, very close to her cheek. *Lord*, he smelled divine. 'Go on.'

'Well, before I left the school with Monsieur Thevenot, I was told to pack a bag. So, I put your book into my reticule and I read it on the journey: up to Gretna, down to Calais, and again when we got there. When things were really bad, I was able to lose myself in your travels, and it felt as though you were keeping me company. So thanks to you, I didn't feel quite so alone.'

The music was drawing to a close. She felt his grip on her waist tighten briefly, before they stopped spinning and he stood back to face her. When he spoke, his voice was gruff.

'I am glad that I was able to accompany you in some small way, and make your journey less frightening.'

He really meant that, she could tell. Touched by his candour, she nodded. 'You did. And besides,' she offered a smile, feeling suddenly that it was important she lighten the mood, 'I was terribly jealous of all the places you visited. Except the mummy pits ... They sounded terrifying!'

She was expecting him to shudder theatrically and join in with the joke, but instead he was still staring into her eyes in a way that seemed keenly felt, but was hard to decipher. She realised then that he was still holding her hand, and she feared they would attract attention.

'Thomas ...'

He blinked in shock, and when she realised what she'd said, she knew her face was crimson. 'Mr Legh, I—'

He dropped her hand. 'I am indeed fortunate that I'm able to travel so widely. It is one of the things I enjoy most about remaining unmarried.'

Ellen's heart gave a painful thump. She swallowed. 'You enjoy remaining unmarried?' she repeated stupidly.

'I do.' His words were said softly. Carefully. 'I decided a long time ago that marriage was not for me.'

There was no doubt about it: he was telling her, kindly, that her affection for him was misguided. 'I see,' she murmured, blinking rapidly. 'I see.'

'Enjoy the rest of your party,' he said warmly, as he handed her to her next dance partner: some lord or other she had never met before this evening. Then he bowed nicely and strode from the room, leaving her reeling, and with nowhere to turn.

# CHAPTER 46

A week later, Ellen arrived at the hall of justice again. It was difficult to feel the same sense of triumph she had enjoyed last time, when Hester and Lavinia had been with her. She did, however, feel confident in her stylish black gown and her narrow bonnet trimmed with red ribbon. She had refused to fall into the dismals after the debacle of the last visit to court, and was now ready.

Hundreds of spectators were squashed into the courtroom, just as they had been before, and the sense of anticipation was palpable. But anticipation of what? Of Edward's conviction, or of Ellen's sentencing to a life married to her kidnapper?

Again, she was ushered to a seat before the ladies' box, opposite where the jury would be, and her Uncle Robert sat beside her. Below, a lot of men with white wigs were milling about, looking at papers, rustling them together. They murmured to one another before taking up their positions with solemn seriousness. Her father, Mr Grimsditch, and Mr Cross were seated down there too, and Hester and Lavinia were in the ladies' gallery, craning their heads to give her reassuring smiles.

At first Ellen couldn't make out Thomas, and she was afraid that after their mortifying exchange at her birthday, he had not come. But then she spotted him near the back of the room, and – *oh Lord* – he was staring straight at her. He looked terribly serious, but when he saw her looking, he nodded, then winked at her. *Heavens*. Did he have any idea how her heart pounded when he did that?

She was still reeling from his declaration that he would never marry. It had been several days, but she could not shake the incongruity of it, alongside the memory of his hand tightening on her waist, and his breath tickling her ear as he murmured that he'd admired her dress in court. Had she imagined the crackling intensity between them? She wanted to return his smile, but conscious of her surroundings, she simply gave him a regal inclination of her head. His smile faded.

Not long after, Edward arrived with his lawyer, Mr Scarlett. Edward looked impassive, clearly playing the part of the elegant man about town. She looked around to see if James was there too, but he was not. With a pang of anxiety, she wondered again: will he arrive at all? She was sure she'd expire with worry if he didn't, and they had to delay the trial again. She had a brief glimpse of Monsieur Thevenot looking pale and unhappy, but she had no idea if Mrs Wakefield was in attendance.

The judge appeared, and after a little toing and froing, things settled, and a hush fell over the courtroom. Robert had begun to fidget beside her, and she could see her father, Mr Grimsditch, and Mr Cross frowning. Even Edward's face darkened as he whispered urgently to his lawyer. They were doubtless all thinking the same fretful thought: where was James?

All of a sudden, a loud shout went up at the back of the room. Ellen could barely believe it when James Wakefield threw open the doors with a clatter, strode across the floor, climbed over the barrier, and pushed himself in so he was seated between Edward and Scarlett. He cast a pleading look in Ellen's direction that she couldn't begin to decipher.

The room went wild. So many people had come to watch, so many people were waiting to see what was said, and James's dramatic entrance gave them the spectacle they'd been waiting for. Newspaper men pushed and shoved, observers shouted and cheered, and the lawyers were all yelling when the judge stood and brought down his gavel several times with significant feeling.

'Silence!' he roared.

Everyone settled back down with much shuffling and scraping of shoes and chairs. James slumped in his seat, tugging on one ear. Edward and Scarlett were both turned to him, looking frankly furious, but he appeared not to notice, staring sullenly at his shoes. He looked unkempt and miserable, and Ellen couldn't help but wonder what his poor wife thought about this whole wretched affair.

They were waiting now for the arrival of Mrs Wakefield. The wife of Edward and James's father who, allegedly, had masterminded the whole wretched plan. Ellen was more than interested to find out who she was. What manner of woman would engineer the downfall of another in such a way? She looked at her Uncle Robert, her father, Mr Grimsditch, and Mr Cross, and they were clearly interested too.

Nothing could have prepared any of them for what happened next.

It took long moments for the court to settle after her father lunged to his feet, face contorted with fury, shouting at the woman who walked into court, cool as you like, chin held high. She wore a beautiful poke bonnet that was horribly familiar to Ellen, allowing her dark ringlets to frame her face and fetching eyes. Ellen couldn't believe it. Simply couldn't believe it.

Mrs Edward Wakefield Senior was none other than Miss Frances Davis. Her mother's closest friend and confidante.

Her father was still shaking his fist when Mr Grimsditch took his arm and urged him to silence, lest he be thrown out.

'Did you know this?' Ellen asked her uncle, barely able to form the words.

'Most certainly not.'

Ellen's heart squeezed. Her mother would be beyond devastated. *She* was beyond devastated. How could Miss Davis have done this to her? Why? Why not just introduce her to Edward in the normal way?

Her father demanded to be able to speak with Mr Cross and the judge allowed it. Ellen watched as the two men muttered furiously, presumably wrapping their heads around how to prove the duplicity that had taken place. They knew that Mrs Wakefield had orchestrated much of the initial plan, but had no idea just how close to the family she was. Everyone was agog when they realised what had happened, what her father's outburst meant.

Her uncle reached over and took her hand. She clung to it.

'It must have been her who stole the handkerchief and my father's ring,' she said, still barely able to believe what was before her.

A hush fell again over the court, and the jury were sworn in. Ellen wished she could glean something from their countenances, but she couldn't. She wished that ladies were allowed to be on the jury because she felt sure that another lady would have much more of an understanding of her predicament. As it was, several stony-faced men stared back at her.

Another man stood and read the indictments. Ellen listened and was pleased that it told the story exactly as things had happened. It was said in a terribly roundabout way, but essentially held the truth of the matter.

Mr Cross then stood to deliver the opening statement for the prosecution.

'Gentlemen,' he boomed. 'By another statute, stealing away an heiress against her own consent, and afterwards marrying her, whether with her consent or not, is a capital felony; and if that offence had been committed on English ground, at least two of these defendants would, in the due course of justice, be condemned to an ignominious death, and executed upon the walls of this castle!'

He held on to his gown at his chest with one hand and looked about the courtroom, lingering on Edward and James. Apparently it was true – if Edward had married her in England, they would have hanged. However, they did not. They took her to Scotland. And that made it all very different.

Mr Cross then spoke about Frances Wakefield, or Miss Davis, in tones of stern disapproval, nay horror; about how she had pretended to befriend Ellen's mother, all the while plotting with Edward and James to acquire the Turner fortune. He talked of how Frances, James, and Edward planned the whole thing from start to end. To abduct an heiress, exactly as Edward had done before with Clara Pattle, and blackmail her father into accepting the marriage and settling funds on him.

As he talked through all that had happened in the finest of detail, it filled in a lot of the gaps in her understanding of how it had all come about, how it had been meticulously planned. The feeling in the courtroom seemed to be one of shock and horror too.

'He was magnificent,' Ellen whispered to her uncle when Mr Cross had ceded the floor. How could the jury believe anything else other than the tale as he told it?

'Very impressive,' Robert agreed.

Next was Edward's counsel, Mr Scarlett's turn to make an opening statement for the defence. He raked Ellen with a contemptuous look and sniffed in a dismissive manner, then began.

He went on for a great deal of time without, to Ellen's mind, appearing to say anything. Eventually, she realised he was talking about Frances. Saying that the notion Frances had schemed to gain entrée to Ellen's world was ridiculous; that it was only natural of her to want to meet the family of the man who had just been sworn in as High Sheriff of Cheshire. He spoke with awful disdain as he completely rebuffed the allegations that Mr Cross had so carefully outlined, and Ellen wanted to shout out that he was a liar. Sensing her agitation, Uncle Robert took hold of her hand and squeezed it.

'Pay him no heed,' he whispered. 'His job is to try and make us look bad.'

'But he isn't telling the truth!'

'Hush, my dear.'

Ellen hushed, but cursed the man silently, as every time he turned her, he seemed to sneer a little more.

Next, Monsieur Thevenot was brought forward, and he told the court that he simply did as he was paid to do: deliver a note to the school and escort a young lady to Manchester.

'And tell the young lady in question that you worked for her father, when in truth you did not?'

'Yes.' Thevenot shrugged, indifferently.

'Did you know that the letter you delivered was also a lie?' Mr Cross asked him.

'Yes.' Thevenot shrugged again.

'And you knew for what purpose it was forged?'

'I knew Monsieur Wakefield had romantic intentions,' he said. 'And when I saw the mademoiselle, I could see why.'

Elle shuddered.

'Did you know that Mr Wakefield planned to coerce Miss Turner into marriage, via deceit and intimidation?' said Mr Cross, in acid tones.

'Bah …' Monsieur Thevenot scratched his head, then shook it. 'I don't remember hearing that. What happened after Manchester was none of my business.' He shrugged a third time, and was dismissed from the stand.

Next, Mrs Frances Wakefield moved to take up her place. Ellen clutched her uncle's hand tightly. Frances now exhibited none of the calm she had exuded before the jury walked in. She stood, head bowed, a light tremor visible in her hands. Ellen was sure it was for show.

Mr Cross began. 'Mrs Wakefield. Or should I say Miss Davis? That *is* how you introduced yourself to Mr and Mrs Turner when you befriended them at Shrigley Hall, is it not?'

She blinked and looked down at her hands. 'Mrs W— Wakefield, sir. I am M—Mrs Wakefield.'

Frances was speaking in a voice that was not her own. Her usual sharp wit and easy charm were masked completely by these quivering, faltering, reedy tones. Ellen looked at Robert in astonishment, and she could tell he was thinking the same thing. Frances was playing the part of a simple, feeble, middle-aged woman, so the jury would underestimate her capacity for cunning. She was nothing more than an actress!

'To whom are you married, Mrs Wakefield?' Mr Cross went on.

'Mr Edward Wakefield Senior.'

'The father of these two gentlemen?'

'Yes.'

Mr Cross looked about the courtroom, one eyebrow raised. 'And is your husband here today, to testify on behalf of you and his sons?'

Frances's lower lip wobbled. 'No, he is not.' At that, she burst out sobbing, and made a production of dabbing at her eyes with her handkerchief. Ellen's hatred for the woman intensified: the way she was crying, the mannerisms she was feigning … they were Ellen's mother's. When Frances's treachery had laid her mother so low, had Frances then studied her pain, so that she could imitate it here today?

'When Mr Edward Wakefield the younger found himself in financial difficulty,' Mr Cross went on, 'he came to you and your husband for money, did he not?'

Frances nodded weakly, and blew her nose.

'Speak up, Mrs Wakefield,' the judge said.

'He did!' she cried shrilly.

'So you suggested to him that he abduct a wealthy heiress and marry her, in exactly the same way that he abducted Miss Clara Pattle ten years ago.'

A murmur went around the court. Ellen saw Edward sit up.

'I did not. He came to me and asked if I knew of any wealthy young ladies in need of a husband. I … I told him that I knew Miss Turner was *allegedly* an heiress, and he might want to consider paying his addresses to her.'

At this Edward went rigid. Frances hadn't denied that he'd abducted Clara Pattle. Ellen's gaze bounced between the two of them.

'I see,' said Mr Cross. 'And on the day Mr and Mrs Turner received word from Miss Daulby that their daughter had left school with Monsieur Thevenot, where were you?'

'I was at their house,' she said.

'And in the days following this news, what did you do?'

'I remained at Shrigley, comforting my dear friend Mrs Turner ...'

Ellen's father scoffed loudly at this; Frances flinched, and Mr Grimsditch shushed him.

'... until I was called away to care for my sick father,' Frances said with bruised dignity.

'Caring for your sick father ...' Mr Cross echoed. 'Then why, Mrs Wakefield, were you sighted meeting with the defendant Edward Wakefield at the Brunswick Hotel in London, only moments before he fled for France?'

Frances looked like she'd been slapped. She lifted plaintive eyes at Mr Cross and began to blink rapidly. Ellen slapped her uncle's arm in excitement.

Mr Cross laughed softly and shook his head. 'Oh, Mrs Wakefield, do not try to suggest that you were innocent in all this. The moment you heard that Mr Turner did not intend to accept the marriage, you travelled with all haste to warn Edward Wakefield to leave the country. I also put it to you, madam, that it was *you* who stole these items—' he produced the handkerchief and signet ring with a flourish, '—from the Turner household, so that Edward Wakefield could deceive Miss Turner into thinking her father wished her to marry him!'

'You cannot prove it!' Frances cried.

'You are right,' Mr Cross said, 'it cannot be proved that you are guilty of theft in addition to conspiracy to abduct a child, Mrs Wakefield. But only because you were clever enough not to mention your thieving in the letters the police have recovered, in which you wrote to Edward and James Wakefield your instructions on when and where to carry out the kidnapping!'

Gasps rent the air; the entire courtroom was rapt.

'We've got her now,' murmured Uncle Robert, and Ellen squeezed his hand.

'It was also in those letters,' Mr Cross went on, 'that you admitted to forging the letter Monsieur Thevenot delivered to Miss Turner's headmistress on the 6th of March. I have that letter here, Mrs Wakefield. Will you kindly read it out to us?'

He brandished the letter that Ellen had stolen from Miss Daulby. But as he held it out to her, Frances Wakefield's eyes rolled back into her head, and she crumpled forwards. Ellen almost laughed: was she pretending to *faint*? What kind of woman was she?

But when Frances did not sit up again, to Ellen's astonishment, sympathetic murmurs soon began to ripple through the hall. A court official helped Frances to stand, and she sobbed pitifully as she was led on unsteady feet from the room.

'That performance will have got her nowhere,' Robert murmured reassuringly. 'Her guilt is patently clear.'

Ellen nodded, still a little stunned, as James Wakefield took Frances's place at the stand.

Edward's teeth were gritted now. James looked utterly defeated before the questioning had even begun; he stared at his hands, sullen as a schoolboy who was about to face the rod.

'Were you aware of the letter that Mrs Wakefield forged?' Mr Cross asked him.

'Yes.'

'At whose behest did she write that letter?'

James swallowed. 'My brother's.'

'Your brother, Mr Edward Gibbon Wakefield?'

'Yes.'

'Were you aware of the lies that were told to Miss Turner about the collapse of Mr Turner's banks?'

James nodded and stared at his hands. 'Yes.'

Ellen watched, spellbound. Edward had clearly expected James to say more, to say that Ellen had gone willingly, but James remained oddly silent. Every question that was asked, he answered simply, and made no attempt to lie. He just confirmed everything that was put before him. Meanwhile, Edward was glaring at him, apoplectic, and completely powerless to do anything about it.

Mr Scarlett now picked up the questioning.

'Mr Wakefield. Let's keep the questions nice and simple. Did Mrs Ellen Wakefield travel willingly with you and your brother to Gretna Green?'

'Yes.'

'Did she marry your brother at Gretna Green willingly?'

James licked his lips. 'She did.'

'Well then,' Scarlett said smugly, 'no further questions.'

'I have one more question, if I may, your honour?' Mr Cross chimed in.

The judge nodded, and Mr Cross drew himself up to his full height. James gulped, evidently wishing the interrogation was over.

'Was Miss Turner at any point on the journey, or at Gretna Green, coerced?'

James hesitated. 'Not at Gretna Green.'

A hush fell over the room.

Mr Cross smiled broadly, and repeated James's words slowly. '*Not at Gretna Green*. How enlightening ... No further questions, your honour.'

There was a buzz about the courtroom as James was led away. Ellen looked at her uncle whose mouth was hanging open.

'He basically admitted that you were coerced at the start of the journey,' Robert breathed. 'I think he may have just knifed his brother in the back.'

Ellen looked down at Edward and smiled. From the murderous look on his face as he muttered to Mr Scarlett, she knew it was true. Was he regretting his choice to not take the stand, she wondered? It mattered not, either way: Mr Scarlett was shaking his head. It was too late for Edward to change his mind.

* * *

Each of the defendants who had elected to speak had now done so, and Ellen's father was called as a witness. Her heart swelled as she watched him approach the stand. She held on to her uncle's hand and listened as he answered Mr Cross's questions, telling the court that he was her father, and that he had never met James or Edward before the abduction. He was then handed over to Mr Scarlett for cross-examination, and Ellen gripped tighter.

'Mr Turner,' Scarlett said, in what Ellen felt was a very sly way. 'You were elevated to the position of High Sheriff of Cheshire in January of this year, were you not?'

'Yes,' said her father, puffing out his chest.

'I suppose that,' Scarlett went on, 'in the months that followed, a good many gentlemen in the neighbourhood paid their respects to you?'

'They did.'

'Called upon you?'

Was Scarlett trying to imply that he might have met Edward and forgotten? Ellen waited.

'Naturally,' her father said coolly. 'But no gentlemen called on me to pay their respects, other than my friends, before I held a celebratory gathering in April. *Well after* Ellen's return from Calais.'

Ellen wanted to clap and cheer. She exchanged a smile with her uncle.

Next, they brought in Miss Daulby. Ellen felt for her – she had clearly been deeply affected by this whole debacle, and she didn't look terribly well. One of the court gentlemen asked if she could speak up.

'This is the important bit,' her uncle whispered as they were getting her settled.

'It is?'

Uncle Robert nodded. 'This is where we will hear about when Miss Daulby received the forged letter. This was what set the whole thing in train. It is incontrovertible. Everything that you did after that was because you believed your family to be in peril because of this first lie, and then the other lies. It is the foundation of the case against Wakefield.'

Ellen nodded and waited.

# CHAPTER 47

Ellen listened, breathless, to Miss Daulby as she answered the questions quietly, but with authority, every inch the firm headmistress that Ellen adored. Mr Scarlett's line of questioning focused mainly on Ellen and her talents. Ellen was thrilled when Miss Daulby described her as a very clever girl, with great quickness and sagacity – although she wasn't entirely certain what *sagacity* was. Miss Daulby also described her as having a good temper and disposition. It was pleasing to hear such a description after many of the newspapers had branded her a featherbrain. She did say though that Ellen was very confiding and trusting, and Ellen wasn't sure if that was a compliment or not.

Next, Mr Cross asked Miss Daulby questions about Miss Greenaway, who was taken out of the school because of the collapse of her father's business interests. He seemed to be laying the foundation to show that Ellen would have reasonably understood the disaster that could befall a family if their bank collapsed.

He then squared his shoulders and asked about the arrival of Monsieur Thevenot.

'Do you recollect on the morning of the 6th of March, Monsieur Thevenot arriving at your academy?'

Miss Daulby nodded, mouth prim. 'Yes.'

Mr Cross handed a letter to Miss Daulby. 'Is this the letter that he delivered to you?'

'Yes, that is the letter.'

'What did Monsieur Thevenot say, at the time he delivered it to you?'

'He said that he came from Shrigley Hall; he was sent to collect Miss Turner because Mrs Turner was very ill.'

'Did he mention, madam, at the time, any particulars respecting Mrs Turner's illness?'

'Yes, sir, he said she was taken ill the night before whilst at supper. He said that the knife and fork dropped from her hands.'

Ellen glanced over at Thomas who was murmuring to the man beside him. Then she looked down at her father, whose face was thunderous.

'Miss Daulby, if that letter had not been delivered, if you had known that Mr Wakefield desired to take away Miss Turner, should you have given your consent to her going?'

Miss Daulby lifted her chin. 'Certainly not.'

Before dismissing Miss Daulby, Mr Cross asked her to read the letter aloud, since its author had been unable. She did so slowly, solemnly, enunciating each word. Ellen didn't dare breathe. When she'd finished, she folded it carefully and handed it back to Mr Cross, who regarded it for a moment before looking up.

'The order was to preclude any other person going with Ellen, for had she been accompanied, the object of the parties would have been frustrated ...'

The courtroom was graveyard-silent, and Mr Cross had the jury's undivided attention. Uncle Robert was right. This was a very important point. Ellen was more relieved than she could say that she'd had the good sense to keep that letter, tucked in the front of Thomas's book. She glanced at Thomas, and he nodded at her.

⋆  ⋆  ⋆

Next, Mr Cross called forward Dr Hull and Mr Grimsditch, who each confirmed that they were not the authors of the letters Miss Daulby and Ellen received. He also summoned the waiter from the Brunswick Hotel, who identified Frances as the woman who'd posed as Edward's sister before his escape to France. Then, he asked the judge's permission to call Ellen to the stand.

Quelling her nerves, Ellen exchanged one last bolstering look with her uncle. But before she'd risen from her seat, Mr Scarlett interjected.

'Objection!'

Scarlett had approached the bench, and was talking in legal terms so dense that at first she didn't understand what he was saying. Then she grasped the crux of it: the man was suggesting she should not be allowed to take the stand and give evidence against her husband.

Stunned, she looked over at her father, then at Mr Grimsditch. Both looked grim.

Apparently, Scarlett's reason was that Ellen's participation in the hearing might occasion implacable animosity between man and wife. Surely they couldn't do that to her. They couldn't gag her, could they? Was she simply her husband's property, with no entitlement to a voice of her own?

She leaned forward, hanging on every dramatic word with dawning horror. Scarlett paused and looked around a courtroom so silent it was eerie.

The judge did not respond immediately. He was clearly thinking carefully, and by the time he opened his mouth Ellen was positively blue from holding her breath.

'Gentlemen, I have the highest opinion of the discretion of my learned friend, Mr Scarlett, the Attorney General for this County Palatine, who acts for the defendants. I cannot bring myself to believe that he will be guilty of so gross an outrage to common sense, and to all the principles of the law and justice, as to make that attempt, which has been bruited about the country, of disabling the young lady from giving evidence. Objection overruled.'

Ellen wanted to leap up, clap, and shout *bravo!* But instead, she rose from her seat with poise and walked at a dignified pace to the stand. Until just a few minutes ago, she'd felt ready to tell her story, but now the weight of expectation sat heavily on her. Swallowing, feeling horribly on display with every spectator's eyes on her, she tried to emulate Miss Daulby's firm resolve and repeated Grimsditch's advice in her head. *Answer calmly and clearly. Give no more information than was asked for.* She risked a glance at the stalls and her eyes went straight to Thomas, who gave her his small smile and another brief nod of his head.

Mr Cross gave her a steadying look, and then began. 'Miss Turner, could you confirm for the court that you are the daughter of Mr Turner, of Shrigley?'

Ellen cleared her throat. 'I am.' Her voice was clear and true.

'Did you depart from Break House boarding school on the 6th of March?'

'I did.'

Ellen continued to answer the questions as succinctly as she could, as Mr Cross allowed her to tell the jury exactly why she had embarked on the chase across the countryside in the company of the Wakefield brothers. She gained in confidence as she went on.

When Mr Cross asked her what had induced her to agree to a marriage to Edward, Ellen felt tears sting the back of her eyes at the memory. She took a breath. She would not cry, she would *not*. She looked at her father who was nodding along with her; she looked at the stalls and this time found Hester and Lavinia, whose faces were glowing with encouragement.

'He told me that an uncle of his, who was a banker in Kendal, had lent my papa sixty thousand pounds, and that his uncle had demanded security for the loan.'

'Did he say what the security was to be?'

Ellen nodded again and looked at her hands before lifting her chin and looking out at the court.

'Shrigley Hall.'

'Did he say anything more?'

'He said … he said that his uncle was demanding Shrigley Hall, and my mama would be turned out of her home any day unless I married him.'

There was a rumble around the court at that. Ellen felt bolstered by it.

Mr Cross asked a lot of questions about their movements on the way to Carlisle and the Scottish border, and the events that had occurred in Carlisle that had persuaded her to accept Edward, and she answered them easily because, by now, it was more than clear in her head just how badly used she had been. How Edward had manipulated her love for her family. Mr Cross noted that she had travelled overnight and that she had barely had any sleep.

Mr Scarlett stood up. 'Would you allow me to add two or three questions?'

Ellen glanced at the judge, who nodded.

Mr Cross and Mr Grimsditch had both gone to great lengths to prepare Ellen for this moment. They'd warned her to take care when talking to Mr Scarlett, because no matter how safe his questions might make her feel, his job was to make a liar of her, make a fool of her, and to try and prove that she'd wanted to marry Edward. Mr Scarlett moved closer to where she was and seemed to ponder the questions greatly. His long, thin face looked troubled. Ellen felt queasy.

'Mrs Ellen Wakefield,' he said, and Ellen flinched at the use of her married name, 'the court has heard that when you married Mr Wakefield it was with your father's ring.'

Ellen wasn't sure why he was repeating this, but nodded. 'Yes.'

He smiled at her, but it wasn't a real smile. 'Yet, later, you accepted another wedding ring from Mr Wakefield. One that he bought for you in Calais?'

'Yes.'

'A romantic gift,' Scarlett simpered. 'And when you accepted this second ring, you believed yourself to be the lawful wife of Mr Wakefield?'

'Yes. I returned the ring to Mr Wakefield when I learned of his treachery.' Out of the corner of her eye, she saw Mr Cross shoot her a warning glance. Had she said too much?

'After the wedding, did you write a letter to your mother and father?' he continued, ignoring her comment.

'Yes, I wrote several.'

'In those letters, did you use the name Mrs Wakefield?'

Ellen hesitated but had to answer honestly. 'I did.'

Mr Scarlett gave a long, lingering look to the jury, eyebrows raised.

'Thank you, Mrs Wakefield. And during your time in Calais, Mr Wakefield also purchased several garments for you, did he not?' continued Mr Scarlett.

'Yes.'

'Would you tell the court exactly what those garments were?'

Ellen thought for a moment, then reeled off the list.

'And Mr Wakefield bought these items for you at his own expense?'

'Yes.'

'Not yours?'

'I hadn't any money of my own.' His line of questioning was beginning to unnerve her.

'I see. And when you returned to England with your uncle, did you leave those garments behind along with the ring, or did you keep them?'

Ellen faltered. She'd been wearing one of the dresses, the shoes and the shawl when she left France, and she'd packed in such a hurry. What good would it have done to leave them?

'I kept them.'

'Lucky lady!' Mr Scarlett exclaimed. 'A second wedding ring *and* an entire new wardrobe, all at Mr Wakefield's personal expense. And you kept every single gift, except the ring. Remind me, Miss Turner, who has been cheating whom of their fortune, here?'

Ellen was stunned. Was this man really trying to insinuate that she'd swindled Edward, for the sake of a few *dresses*? She looked right at him and he returned her look with no discernible discomfort at the lie. It made her wonder if there was something wrong with him.

'I had only two other dresses with me,' she said slowly, 'and I needed *something* to wear. I thought—'

'You *thought*,' Mr Scarlett interrupted, triumphant, 'that *before* you abandoned your husband and vilified him before all these good people, you would enjoy spending his money at the most fashionable modiste in Calais!'

Someone in the jury tutted. Whispers stirred amongst the stalls. Ellen tried to protest. 'No, that's not—'

'It seems, gentlemen,' Scarlett said with a flourish, turning away from her, 'that my client's wife wishes to have her cake and eat it.'

Mr Cross stood up and cleared his throat.

'Miss Turner. Might I ask how many dresses you owned before you met Mr Wakefield?'

'Perhaps twenty,' she said, 'maybe more.'

'And as the heiress to a million-pound fortune, Miss Turner, it seems unlikely to me that you would give much thought to a gift of five more gowns. Is that correct?'

Ellen breathed a sigh of relief. 'That is correct.'

'And if Mr Edward Wakefield desperately wanted his dresses returned, I'm sure you would be more than happy to adhere to his wishes?'

'Of course.'

'One last question: you have been asked about a letter that you sent to your mama, which you signed with the name Wakefield. Who dictated that you should do that?'

She lifted her chin. 'Mr Edward Gibbon Wakefield told me that I must.'

She was allowed to resume her seat after that, and she sat, trembling all over, heart fluttering in her chest. She'd known Mr Scarlett would be sly, but his angle of attack had taken her completely by surprise. First the newspapers savaged her for appearing too much like a schoolgirl; then when she dressed in her more grownup French clothes, she was accused of fortune hunting. Was there any way a lady could win, in this setting?

Mr Scarlett stood again. 'Gentlemen,' he said to the court, 'you observed I did not ask the young lady many questions. My instructions were not to do so.'

Ellen frowned. What did that mean?

'I asked her whether she did, until she received that intimation at Calais, believe that she was the lawful wife of Mr Wakefield, and she certainly did.'

He gave her a knowing look and cast the same look at the jury. 'There she was, at Manchester. The question was, what was to be done?' He shrugged and held up his hands, looking about the room. 'What was she to do?' He said the words with false puzzlement. 'Return to her father's house? Return to school? Or ...' He looked around again, this time with a smirk. 'Or, was she to go off and be ... married to Mr Wakefield. A very handsome, well set-up young man who promised to buy her fashionable dresses and jewels, to introduce her to Paris society. To introduce her to the Devonshire set, no less.' He huffed a laugh. 'What a choice for a young girl to have to make.'

Ellen rolled her eyes. The man was repeating himself. But at his next words, her mouth went dry, and her stomach turned over.

'Gentlemen,' he boomed. 'I will now show to you, that from the very first stages of this adventure, my client's wife was full of gaiety and alacrity. That from Manchester, to Gretna Green, to London, *and Calais*, she never ceased in her expressions of pleasure and satisfaction to all those persons who saw her on her way, and ... they are numerous!'

Ellen's breathing faltered as she recalled Edward's instruction to remain jolly, to appear to be simply on a journey and not fleeing to save her father. She looked over again to see a small smile play about his mouth. He glanced up at her and blew her a kiss.

Scarlett had not finished.

'I shall prove that moments before the wedding at Gretna Green, she sat on Mr Wakefield's knee with an appearance of great fondness; that the marriage was contracted, not as some kind of … of martyrdom, but instead, with a degree of eagerness and impatience that is seldom witnessed at that place.'

Ellen felt ill. Thomas was frowning and leaning forward in his seat, and her father's ears were purple.

Mr Scarlett was unrelenting, his voice ringing out in the courtroom, making the jury sit up and take notice. Several of them were looking at her as he spoke. She set her chin and tried to resist the tears that threatened.

'Gentlemen, I will demonstrate that, from first to last, there was no indication of dejection, of intimidation, or of violence done to her feelings. As the prosecution has taken pains to emphasise, she is a very intelligent girl; she was well grounded in education – she must have known which way the carriage was going. Indeed, to all persons who witnessed it …' – he paused and looked around – 'they were a very loving couple.'

Ellen was aghast. The horrific possibility that she might lose this case now loomed large in her mind, and it was overwhelming. She was going to be attached to Edward forever. She would never be free of him. She would have to live with him, bear his children … She made a choked sound and Uncle Robert reached over and squeezed her hand again.

Scarlett droned on a little more before eventually sitting down. The judge decided to speak, and she didn't dare listen to what he said, but when her uncle nudged her, and nodded towards him, she paid attention to his words.

'I am of the opinion that the evidence you have opened, except that which goes to show the validity of the Scots marriage, is quite immaterial to the present indictment.'

Ellen held her breath. Immaterial? Was he going to ignore what Mr Scarlett had said?

'I consider the offence stated on the record, if it be satisfactorily proved to the jury, was committed first at the school, and then when they were at Manchester. Once they had left Manchester, it really did not matter what inducements were used.'

Ellen leaned close to her uncle. 'What does he mean?'

'Hush.' The entire court hung on his words.

The judge continued. 'The young lady's own evidence proves decisively that she did consent to marry. She did acquiesce, at Gretna Green, to the proceedings that took place there. But ... that is not the offence with which these defendants are charged. If you feel there is anything in it, Mr Scarlett, I will hear the evidence.'

That sounded ... positive? Hopeful? Was he saying that no matter how she behaved afterwards, this issue they were considering was whether or not she had been lied to, because everything she did after that was in response to the lie? The murmur around the courtroom supported this notion. Her father looked amazed, and Thomas made a gesture with his fist that looked ... triumphant!

*Oh God*, she couldn't bear it. 'Is this good?' she murmured.

Uncle Robert smiled down at her. 'I think it might be, but it depends on what Scarlett turns up now.'

# CHAPTER 48

Before long, it felt like Mr Scarlett had found just about every innkeeper, parlour maid, boot boy, groom, waiter or waitress from Manchester to Gretna Green, and he paraded them all into the courtroom, one by one. All of them said that she was laughing and happy when she arrived at their respective establishments.

'Edward *told* me to appear jolly,' she whispered to her uncle, feeling a strong sense of ill usage. 'He told me that if I aroused suspicion by looking drawn and haggard, it might put Papa in further jeopardy. Why doesn't Mr Cross mention that?'

'I suspect,' Uncle Robert said, 'that he is going to let this rabble speak for themselves. Look at them. They are hardly reliable witnesses, are they?'

He had a point. As each new witness came forward, it became more and more plain that whilst they'd been waiting their turn to give evidence, a good deal of alcohol had been consumed. The inn keeper from the White Lion in Halifax had slurred his words considerably, and the head groomsman from the Bush Inn in Carlisle had fallen over on his way to the stand.

'Besides,' said Robert, 'if we take what the judge said, it's unlikely anything they say would matter even if they weren't up the pole.'

Ellen could only hope he was right. She watched as Mr Scarlett carried on valiantly, if a little red-faced. Mr Cross offered the occasional comment, highlighting the most farcical aspects of the situation. It was almost like watching a game.

Now it was the landlady from the Rose and Crown in Kirkby Lonsdale, one Ann Bradley, who swayed slightly from side to side, as Mr Scarlett lifted his nose in the air and prepared to question her.

'Madam, on the 7th of March, you say you recollect two gentlemen and a lady passing through?'

She folded her arms under her ample bosom and nodded. 'Yes, sir. *Hiccough!* 'Scuse me, sir.'

'Did you see them in the carriage?'

'I did see them, *hiccough!*, by the light of a lantern.' She nodded sagely and looked vaguely about the court.

'Was the lady in good spirits?'

'She was. Very good spirits,' she said. 'My maid gave her some *hiccough!* gingerbread,' she added, as though this was somehow important.

'What makes you say she was in good spirits?' Mr Scarlett asked.

'I heard her laughing in the carriage.'

'And where were you when you heard her laughing?'

'I was in the bar.' She gave another knowing nod.

A murmur went around the court at that, and Mr Scarlett looked discomfited at the unlikely statement.

Mr Cross stood and was allowed to question the woman. He smiled and waved his hand at her as though she was standing far away. She waved back heartily. Titters rippled through the court.

'My friend has asked you every question, but whether the gingerbread was good. Was it good?'

The woman beamed at him and nodded vigorously. 'Very good!'

The court erupted in gales of laughter and Ellen didn't know whether to laugh with them or cry. However, the tone changed once more when Mr Scarlett started examining the staff from Gretna. When the landlord's daughter talked about how happy Ellen had appeared on Edward's lap, she shuddered, and couldn't bring herself to look at Thomas. The witnesses went on and on, describing every look, every touch passed between Ellen and Edward at a tortuous pace, until the judge intervened.

'Is this the whole of the evidence that you have of the wedding ceremony?'

Ellen sat up straighter.

Mr Scarlett's face puckered. 'I will very soon call a gentleman who will give further evidence.'

The judge raised his eyebrows pointedly. 'Are you going to carry these parties from this place to Calais?' There was a warning tone to his voice. 'I really must rely on you to exercise your discretion in your use of the court's time.'

Mr Scarlett looked affronted. 'I understand it is a corroboration of such a marriage, that the parties are before *and* afterward appearing to be hanging on each other as man and wife.'

The judge looked at him for a long time before he sighed. 'Be it so.'

Ellen cringed as Mr Scarlett brought out Monsieur Quillac from the hotel in Calais and quizzed him about whether or not they had behaved like man and wife, even going as far as to produce a drawing of their suite so the jury could see the proximity of their bedchambers.

'Sheer nonsense,' her uncle muttered, but Ellen could see it provoked a good deal of interest in not only the spectators, but the jury, too. She felt ill.

Then Mr Scarlett really did shock Ellen. He brought out Veronique. Ellen stared at the maid who had been so kind to her, and her heart plummeted.

'Mademoiselle,' Mr Scarlett said, 'you were maid to Mrs Wakefield during her stay at the Hotel Quillac, were you not?'

'I was, monsieur.'

'And during that time, how did Mrs Wakefield appear?'

Veronique swallowed. 'She was a good wife.'

'In what way was she a good wife, mademoiselle?'

Veronique's shrug was gallic and brief. 'She obeyed her husband.'

'Did she appear happy in her marriage?' Scarlett looked at the jury with the air of a man about to present a denouement.

'She appeared to be happy …'

'Thank you, mademoiselle, that—'

'She appeared happy, but she was not,' Veronique said, interrupting Mr Scarlett's speech. He turned and eyed her askance.

'You said she appeared happy.'

'With respect, monsieur, appearing happy and being happy are not one and the same. Madame Wakefield was unhappy when she was alone.'

Silence.

'You say she was unhappy *when she was alone*,' Scarlett said, disdainfully aping Veronique's French accent. 'But how could you possibly know her innermost thoughts? Are you a clairvoyant, mademoiselle?'

At this, Veronique looked Ellen in the eye. 'I am sorry, madame. I read it in the letters she wrote to her friends shortly after she was married.'

Edward's head whipped around, nostrils flared. Ellen's hand went to her mouth. *What?*

'I was responsible for cleaning both madame and monsieur's rooms, and in the latter, I happened upon a bundle of letters which had been torn open and read, but never posted. I admit it was a little, how you say, nosy of me, but because I found this suspect ... I read them.'

Ellen gasped. The letters she'd written at Penrith, which never arrived! Edward had read them, and kept them? Frantically, she racked her brains to remember what had been the content.

Mr Cross leapt to his feet. 'Mademoiselle,' he said, 'to whom were these letters addressed, and were they dated?'

'Objection!' cried Mr Scarlett.

'Denied,' said the judge flatly. Mr Scarlett looked like he wanted to kick someone.

'There was a letter addressed to a Lavinia, and another to a Hester,' Veronique said. 'Both were dated the 9th March, from Penrith.'

'The day after the wedding,' Mr Cross breathed.

Robert drummed his hands on Ellen's knee. 'This is marvellous,' he whispered. 'They're being assassinated by their own witness!'

'Indeed,' Ellen said. But something was deeply bothering her. So why did she feel so uneasy?

'And what did these letters say?' Mr Cross said.

Veronique looked awkward for a moment. 'Actually,' she said, 'I have them here. I can read one out, if you like?'

Mr Scarlett was ... scarlet. Mr Cross nodded eagerly. 'Please do.'

Veronique looked at Ellen again, and all of a sudden, she understood why she felt wrong. Why Veronique had apologised when she took the stand. *No, no, no* … But it was too late; she was already reading.

'My dearest Lavinia,' Veronique read, 'You will not believe me, but I am writing to tell you that I am, as of yesterday, a married woman. I cannot explain all the details here, but it's my dearest wish that one day soon I will be able to tell you the whole strange – and frankly, terrifying! – story. My husband's name is Mr Edward Gibbon Wakefield, and I think he is a kind man, although I only met him two days ago … Lord, I must sound quite mad.

'I had to write this to you and Hester, because I cannot tell anyone else. Please promise me you will keep this secret for me: I have had the most awful and frightening time, and I have married not for love but purely to save my family from certain ruin. Again, I cannot tell you more at present, because the situation is still too delicate and must remain absolutely secret, but the worst part is that when I was told I must marry Mr Wakefield, I knew in my heart that I was already in love with someone else …'

*Lord!* Ellen wanted to crawl under her chair and hide; she had never been so exposed in her life. Her father and her Uncle Robert were gaping at her, open mouthed. She didn't dare look to the stalls, in case she accidentally locked eyes with Thomas.

'… However, please know that I am safe, and that without Mr Wakefield's kind offer of marriage I would be in a far worse position. I miss you terribly, and I will write again when the danger is gone. All my love, from your friend, Ellen Turner.'

Ellen sank into her chair as the court erupted in a cacophony of shouts, jeers, and whispers. Everyone – truly, everyone – was staring at her. Thomas was visibly shocked. Hester and Lavinia were gawping so widely she was sure she could see their tonsils.

Her father, Uncle Robert, and Mr Grimsditch still looked baffled, and Edward ... Edward was absolutely livid. The look he sent her was one of pure vitriol.

The judge had to bang his gavel several times to get the court to come back to any semblance of order. When it did, he thanked Veronique for her testimony, and as Mr Scarlett and Mr Cross seemed to have no more questions, she was allowed to sit down.

Ellen kept her gaze in her lap, her cheeks blazing. It appeared that thankfully, all the evidence was now over. The judge invited the counsel for the defence to summarise his case for the jury. Mr Scarlett spoke at great length, and with great emphasis on Ellen's willingness to marry Edward, just as he had done throughout the entire trial. In fact, he seemed in danger of re-iterating every word and had to be hurried along.

It was then Mr Cross who stood before the jury. He looked very solemn as he calmly, and succinctly, stated that the crime was committed in Liverpool, when Miss Daulby was handed the letter containing the lie. Then he coolly dismantled the case for the defence, declaring it a mishmash of irrelevant information, inaccuracies, and falsehoods, as proven by the testimonies given by the witnesses for the prosecution, together with that of the defence's own final witness and the judge's interventions.

*Bravo, Mr Cross*, Ellen thought.

The judge thanked both lawyers and proceeded to summarise. Ellen drew in a breath and listened.

He began by reminding the jury that all defendants had been found guilty at the magistrates' courts of conspiring to take Ellen against her will. He then proceeded to discuss in some detail the roles of Monsieur Thevenot and Frances Wakefield, before returning to the case against Edward and James.

'With reference to the other two persons, it is for the jury to say how far they can entertain any doubt upon the subject, because it appears to me, if you believe the evidence of Mr Cross, that the whole of the charge is distinctly and unequivocally acknowledged by Edward Gibbon Wakefield and James Wakefield.'

Ellen swallowed. Did this mean …? She didn't dare hope.

The foreman of the jury stood, and the judge indicated for him to speak.

'My lord, we the jury think it is not necessary to go further.'

The judge nodded. 'Then, gentlemen, you will take into your consideration the circumstances of the evidence as far as it relates to the different parties – Jacques Thevenot, Frances Wakefield, James Wakefield, Edward Gibbon Wakefield – and you shall say whether they are, or are not, guilty.'

The members of the jury conferred for a moment, and then expressed a wish to retire to consider the verdict.

They walked from the room slowly, and Ellen tried to breathe evenly.

'Well,' Robert said, 'I don't think that could have gone any better.' He was beaming.

Ellen wasn't entirely sure she agreed – had he not *heard* her most intimate expressions of desire for a mystery would-be lover, read out to hundreds upon hundreds of people? There was no doubt about it now: she would be infamous forever. And even worse, the man she'd written about in that letter now knew that she loved him, and she knew that he didn't love her. But in terms of the case against Edward and James, it did seem to have gone well. She even dared to hope it had gone very well.

'It rather sounded to me that the judge agrees with us,' she said. 'When will the jury come back?'

Uncle Robert shook his head, still smiling. 'I don't know, my dear; hopefully before too long.'

★　★　★

In the end, it took less than an hour. Ellen was shaking as the jury filed back in, and they all sat down. The rest of her life depended on what the man who was standing up to represent the jury said.

The judge welcomed them. 'Have you reached a verdict upon which you are all agreed?'

'We have, my lord.'

'And how do you find the defendant Jacques Thevenot?'

'Guilty.'

'And the defendant Frances Wakefield?'

'Guilty.'

'And the defendant James Wakefield?'

'Guilty.'

'And the defendant Edward Gibbon Wakefield?'

The juror seemed to pause a moment, and, trembling all over, Ellen held her breath. She glanced at Edward. There was no discernible emotion on his face, only a flicker of irritation as the juror pronounced the verdict.

'Guilty!'

# CHAPTER 49

Ellen didn't know whether to laugh, shout, cry, or … what. She pressed her hands to her mouth and leaned forward in her seat, eyes squeezed tightly shut. Her uncle was on his feet, as were most of the people in the courtroom. The shouts that went up on hearing the verdict were deafening. When she uncurled and dared to open her eyes, her father was pumping Mr Cross's hand, Mr Grimsditch was laughing, and Hester and Lavinia were dancing. It started to hit her that this was her first step back towards freedom. Very soon, she could go back to being Miss Turner again, just as Thomas had said.

She steeled herself to look over to where Thomas sat. He was talking to the man next to him, but quite suddenly, he looked her way and caught her gaze for a moment. He didn't smile, and it was clear: he knew.

Immediately Ellen looked away, utterly unable to look at him again. Just then, amidst the cheers of congratulations, she heard a woman she didn't know shriek that she was a harlot: a harsh reminder that whilst she was almost free of Edward, she might never be free from the scandal. Only time would tell how high the price would be for this victory, and it was all too much. She grabbed her Uncle Robert's arm. 'I want to go home. Now.'

Getting out of the courtroom was something of a trial in itself. There were so many people, all pushing and jostling, trying to see her, trying to reach out and touch her. As they pressed in on her, in her state of heightened emotion, she'd felt unbearably hemmed in. So much so, an unfamiliar panic set up in her and she was afraid she was going to scream at them all to get away from her. She caught sight of Thomas once more in the crush, but she looked away before he saw her and clung to her father and uncle. Neither had spoken yet of the revelations that Veronique made. She had absolutely no idea what they might think or say. All she wanted was to be away from the court, away from people, and away from Thomas.

She sat in her father's carriage, as he and her Uncle Robert celebrated over her head. *Congratulations, my dear*, they said, *you were marvellous*, and then proceeded to discuss the entire case in all its dizzying twists and turns. Ellen rode in silence and tried not to listen. She didn't want to rehash the entire thing. She never wanted to think about it again as long as she lived.

# CHAPTER 50

Ellen sat in the parlour of the Lancaster house with her parents, and exchanged a pained look with her father. Her mother looked so pretty in her lace cap, her eyes sparkling with happiness for Ellen. But now, it was time for them to break her heart again.

Her father smiled tightly and rubbed the back of his neck. 'Jane, dear ... Although the trial was a success, there is something we need to tell you before it comes to you through another source.'

Her mother looked at both of them, bafflement plain on her face. 'Whatever happened?'

Ellen sat closer and took hold of her mother's hand.

'When the court asked Mrs Edward Wakefield – Mrs Wakefield Senior – to step forward, we had something of a shock,' her father continued. 'You recall that Mrs Wakefield was the one who planned the whole thing? Selected Ellen as a good victim, and set the brothers off on this diabolical course?'

'Yes, I gathered that from what you said last time. What is the matter? For goodness sake, William, spit it out.'

He sighed, closed his eyes momentarily, then opened them.

'My love, Mrs Wakefield, Mrs *Frances* Wakefield, is actually none other than Miss Frances Davis.'

Her mother looked blank. 'You are talking nonsense.'

'I wish I were, my love. She used her maiden name. She *was* Miss Davis of Pott Shrigley, but she married Edward Wakefield Senior a little while ago, and she simply didn't use her married name in our company, to try and avoid being implicated.'

Her mother's gaze sharpened. 'Are you saying that … she weaselled her way into my confidence? That she used the information that she gleaned to help this … this … *demon* steal my child away?' Her voice was rising. She groped for her handkerchief and pressed it to her mouth, trembling.

Ellen squeezed her hand tighter. 'It was a monstrous thing for her to do, Mama. Absolutely monstrous,' she said.

Her mother nodded, and cast Ellen an anguished look. 'It was she who told me it was imperative that the match be recognised. That you remain married to that evil man …' She put her hands to her mouth as tears spilled over. 'Oh, my darlings. I'm so sorry I believed her!'

'Oh Mama!' Ellen held her mother and kissed her forehead. 'Please don't be sorry. It wasn't your fault.'

But it was no good; her mother was inconsolable. Her hand was on her chest, and her breathing was becoming more and more irregular, and it was frightening. 'I can't talk about it now,' she gasped. 'Send for my maid, love. She will know what to do.'

Ellen was shaking. Of all the abuses that the Wakefield family had heaped upon them, this was the worst. Seeing what that wretched woman's betrayal had done to her mother was beyond anything. Tears stood in her eyes as she got to her feet to call for the maid. Her father's face was locked somewhere between fury and agony, and as Ellen headed for the door, he moved awkwardly, clumsily, to her mother's chair, then kneeled beside her and gathered her close.

* * *

Days later, back at home, everyone was still talking about the trial. Ellen nibbled a piece of toast in the breakfast room at Shrigley, alone with her parents, since Uncle Robert had gone home to Manchester. She was only half-listening to them, she was so tired of it all.

'I still can't believe they let *that woman* go with no prison sentence,' her mother said, for what felt like the hundredth time, and with no less vehemence. 'Nothing but sureties for good behaviour! Can you *countenance* it?'

Edward and James had both been sentenced to three years' imprisonment, and Monsieur Thevenot had been handed a petty fine, but it had been decided that Frances had, in the judge's words, *suffered enough* simply by being convicted. As such, she was freed with no sentence. She had wasted no time in disappearing from their lives without a trace, which was perhaps a good thing. Her mother was, as a consequence, beside herself with indignation. Ellen tended to agree, but luckily, her mother's health was improving: she was loath to add fuel to her fire.

'Well, at least Edward and James were gaoled,' she said, helping herself to another piece of toast.

'I do wish you wouldn't call them that, dear,' her mother said, dabbing her handkerchief to her eye. 'It's most unbecoming.'

Ellen said nothing, just buttered her toast.

'And what about the Lords? Do they not realise that these men and *that woman* were tried and found guilty? That our dear Ellen is innocent?'

Her father looked up from his newspaper and grunted. He had lodged a petition with the House of Lords the day after the trial to have the marriage annulled. He put the paper down.

'The Lords have decided,' her father said, 'that they must debate whether or not it will be legal for Ellen to give evidence against her husband at the annulment.'

Ellen jumped so violently she knocked the jam pot over. 'But Papa!' At the trial, the judge had already decreed that she could give evidence. *A judge!* Surely they couldn't throw that back at her?

'I know, love.' He sighed and ran his hand down his face. 'God alone knows why they want to go over it all again. But they think they might need an act of parliament to prove that you can.'

Her mother's eyes filled with more tears. 'I fear that this is never going to end,' she declared in tragic tones.

'We will fight this, and we will win,' said her father firmly. 'Have no fear, my loves.'

Ellen wished she could share her father's optimism. She sighed and propped her chin in her hand, only to have her mother tap her elbow irritably. She sat up straight and put her hands in her lap.

'Well, once that is done, we can then get on with finding our dear Ellen a suitable husband,' her mother said.

Ellen's eyes widened, astonished. 'I think, perhaps, I might like to wait a little while before embarking on matrimony again.'

'Whyever would you feel that way?' her mother said, genuinely at a loss.

Ellen opened her mouth to respond but closed it and took a calming breath. Her mother still didn't know about Veronique's little announcement in court, *thank God*. 'I've just … had enough of husbands for a little while.' Her father squinted at her, but she ignored him – she had been successfully avoiding discussing Lavinia's letter with him, too.

'Nonsense!' her mother declared. 'Your father and I have talked about this. Although we *had* thought you might be utterly ruined, if we move quickly, we can take advantage of the fact that you are quite the *cause célèbre*! And if we apply ourselves to the task before the interest dies down, a title might not be out of the question.' She nodded sagely. 'The Egerton ball next week will be a perfect opportunity. Viscount Longton will be there, and you are definitely a hit with him.'

Ellen sighed. The Egerton ball was one of the most prestigious in the area, and she knew she was lucky to have received an invitation. She bit her tongue and mustered a smile. 'Mama, I fear suitable men would not want to shackle themselves to someone with a reputation such as I now have, even if I am momentarily infamous.'

Her mother gave her an arch look. 'Men will overlook a great deal for a million pounds.'

Ellen maintained her smile with enormous difficulty at this. 'Perhaps you can include me in your deliberations? I rather fancy marrying someone who simply likes me for who I am.'

'Miss Turner?' Ackroyd appeared at the door. 'A letter has arrived for you.'

'Thank you, Mr Ackroyd.' Ellen took the envelope, thankful for the interruption, and broke the seal. When she saw who had sent it, she almost dropped it. She had to fumble to keep hold of the paper.

'Who?' her mama asked, immediately on the scent.

Ellen's head was swimming. She wanted to run from the room and read the letter in private, but she managed a casual smile. 'It is from Mr Legh.'

'Hmph,' her mother said, and her father sent her a questioning look. But Ellen's eyes were drawn to the carefully written missive. She read it silently, keeping the paper close to her chest so her parents could not see.

*Dear Miss Turner,*

*Firstly, may I offer my sincerest congratulations on the success of your court case. The judge drew exactly the right conclusion, and it is my fervent hope that you will now be free of the man who treated you so cruelly. You presented yourself at all times with courage and dignity, and are to be commended.*

Ellen swallowed. It was awfully stiff and formal. She read on.

*I feel it incumbent upon me to offer my sincerest apologies that, if at any time, my actions made it appear that I was trying to lay claim to your affections. My position on marriage is unchanged. A disappointment in my past and circumstances surrounding my family make such a union, for me, impossible.*

*I trust that your father's plan for the annulment will go as smoothly as the trial, and that you will be free to select your own husband in the very near future.*

*Yours etc.*

*Thomas Legh esq.*

Ellen folded the letter and looked up, unable to hide the tears in her eyes.

'What?' her mother said, looking from Ellen to her father. 'What on earth has that man said to upset you so?'

Her father shifted awkwardly in his chair, and rubbed the back of his neck. 'Ellen, dear. Something one of the witnesses said in the trial made me and your uncle wonder if you might harbour a ... a tendre for Mr Legh?'

Ellen's mortification was complete. So *they* knew, too? Was it that obvious? There was no further to sink. Her stomach contracted into a tight ball of misery.

'A *tendre*?' her mother exclaimed. 'I knew it! For goodness sake, Ellen. Was this revealed in court? Did people hear it?'

Ellen managed to look at her mother and avoided answering her demands. 'What is it about Mr Legh that you object to mama? Do you dislike him?'

'I dislike his attention to you, my girl. He has no business making advances.'

'Mama, Mr Legh is not making any kind of advance.' *Quite the opposite*, she thought with a pang, as she stared at the folded letter in her hand. 'He was simply congratulating me on the success of the trial.'

'Well!' her mother blustered, lace cap wobbling with outrage. 'The Lyme Park scandal is nothing I can speak of. It is not for the ears of ladies.'

Ellen blinked. Was Thomas the subject of scandal himself?

'I have never heard anything other than praise and kind things spoken about him,' she ventured.

'Precisely! It is too scandalous to even repeat.'

Ellen drew in a breath and turned to her father. 'Papa?'

He shook his head, bewildered and apparently amused. 'Do

tell, Jane. It will be quite the luxury to hear a scandal that isn't about us.'

'William!' her mother shouted, but her father gave her his best coaxing smile, and she relented.

'Well. This is *not* something I would normally say in polite company, but since you are *hounding* me so ...' her mother dropped her voice to a stage whisper. 'Mr Legh's father was something of a ... colourful character. He had seven children by ...' – she wobbled her cap again – '*seven different women*, and didn't marry a single one. Can you *imagine!*' Then she covered her lips with her handkerchief. Seemingly, she had enjoyed saying that out loud but was now ashamed of herself.

Ellen was stunned. 'Thomas is illegitimate?'

'Ellen!' her mother shouted. 'Language!'

'My, my,' her father said, leaning back in his chair, a small smile playing on his lips. 'And yet, he is one of the most well respected men in Cheshire!' He looked more awed than horrified.

Was *this* why Thomas had sworn off marriage? Because he thought no woman would want him? He also said that he had been disappointed ... Ellen tapped the letter against her lips. Had somebody rejected him before because of his parentage?

'Well, at least that is cleared up,' her mother said. 'I don't have to worry about attention from that quarter any more.'

'For heaven's sake, Jane,' scoffed her father. 'Mr Legh is a dear friend of ours. And all your bosom bows like him perfectly well, don't they?'

Ellen watched her mother falter. 'Mama ... Who was it that told you Mr Legh was beyond the pale?'

'Why, it was Miss Davi ...' her mother let the sentence trail away.

# CHAPTER 51

The Egerton ball was a magnificent affair, and Ellen was dressed for the occasion. She had kept her French clothes in the end – she called them her trophies of war – but tonight's outfit was new: a light green confection, trimmed with gold, that whispered against her skin. Her dark curls were tamed and pinned, and pearls were threaded throughout. Elbow-length white gloves completed the ensemble, and she felt quietly pleased with the result.

Hester and Lavinia were both dressed to the nines, too: Lavinia in the prettiest pale blue that highlighted her eyes, and Hester in flawless white, trimmed with the palest pink.

'He does have the most splendid whiskers,' breathed Hester. The proprietor of said whiskers, Captain Hugo Tremayne, had just asked her for two dances, and seemed a superb prospect for more reasons besides.

Lavinia, meanwhile, had not conceded a second dance to any of her suitors. *Why waste a slot?* she'd argued. *One must sample all one's admirers as swiftly as possible. It's the only way to sort out the riff raff.*

'Viscount Longton seems frightfully keen on you, Ellen,' she said now. 'What do you think?'

It was true. Lord Longton had danced with her most enthusiastically and was now interspersing his usual comedic patter with a growing number of compliments about her dress, her eyes, and even, in a moment of lapsed inspiration, her nose. There were no two ways about it: he was definitely attempting to flirt.

'He's terribly … sweet.'

Hester cast her a knowing smile. 'Not for you?'

Ellen shook her head. 'Mama would be overjoyed if he offered for me. But I am still smarting from Mr Legh's letter. Actually, more than smarting …'

'Don't look around,' Hester said, sharply. Immediately she wanted to look but remained still.

'He – *Mr Legh* – is heading this way,' she mouthed, wide eyed.

*Oh God.* Lavinia gasped theatrically and Ellen tried to hide her alarm before turning at the sound of Thomas's voice.

He bowed and she inclined her head. 'Mr Legh, how lovely to see you.' It was no word of a lie. He looked so terribly handsome in his black evening wear, with his sapphire pin nestling in the white of his cravat. But his beautiful grey eyes were guarded, and he wasn't meeting hers.

Before he spoke again, she could have sworn he swallowed. 'Might I request a dance?'

'I think I might have one left,' she said. She'd meant it in jest, but it came out sounding boastful and absurd.

He simply nodded and waited, clearly in no mood to joke.

As the musicians struck up for the next dance, a waltz, she sighed. *Best get this over with.* 'In fact, I'm free for this one.'

He hesitated, then held out his hand. She exchanged one last helpless glance with Hester and Lavinia, then Thomas's strong fingers curled around hers, and he led her expertly into the dance. His touch was gentle yet firm, and he whirled her about the room as though they'd been partners forever; she was close enough to catch that wonderful smell that was uniquely him, and she found it hard to breathe.

'Thank you for writing to me,' she said quietly.

Without missing a beat, he nodded. 'I trust you were not offended?'

Ellen looked up at him. 'If I had been offended, I would not be waltzing with you.'

He looked directly at her, at last. 'You understood?'

'I made my mama tell me about the ... scandal of your parentage. Which I am in no position to judge you for, by the way.'

He stiffened at that. But then some other dancers veered too near and he swiftly regained control, twirling her out of their path.

'What I don't understand,' she went on, 'is the disappointment you mentioned in your past. Have you suffered a rejection because of the scandal?'

She felt his pulse quicken next to hers. He gave a small nod of admission and said gruffly, 'It was years ago, and thankfully, she is now happily married to someone more suitable.'

'Do you still love her?'

They turned in the other direction and, to her surprise, he chuckled.

'You're kind to ask, but don't worry about me. She and I had little in common, and we would never have been happy together. Besides the differences in our backgrounds, she was a stay-at-home type, whereas I'm...'

'... an adventurer.' Ellen completed the sentence for him, and they turned again in the other direction. 'I am glad you are not still hurting.'

'Thank you,' he said, and they moved in silence for a moment. She could feel the warmth of his body, and it made hers tingle in response. There was a tension between them, she was sure of it. Could she be imagining that he wanted her to break it?

'If you don't love her,' she ventured, '... and I hope you don't mind my asking, but ... do you like me?'

He lost his footing. She hadn't been expecting that. She helped him remain upright and as he found his way back into the steps, he looked her straight in the eye. There was an intensity in his gaze that she hadn't seen before, in his eyes or anyone's.

'We are friends, are we not?' he asked.

'You are avoiding my question,' she pressed. Gently, she dared to rub her thumb against his hand, and his grip tightened around hers.

'Miss Turner,' he said, 'please. I cannot. I asked you to dance, because I wanted to tell you that I have invited your parents next week to join me on an expedition with you and Viscount Longton. I see how much he admires you, and I see the wonderful life he would be able to give you. It would be my honour to assist in bringing you closer together. Just ... I hope that if it pleases you, we can remain friends.'

As the music ended, she sank into a curtsy, grateful to hide her disappointment. He wanted to set her up with *Longton*? *Lord, have mercy*. But when she looked up into his eyes, she could see that everything she'd hoped he'd say was silently, sadly, there. He didn't want her to marry Lord Longton; he didn't just want to be friends. But he was too honourable to pursue her, because he felt he could not offer her anything permanent. Her heart ached for him, but then a spark of hope lit within her. Might there be a way to change his mind?

As he bowed gallantly and escorted her back to her friends, her mind raced, and on an impulse, she said, 'I might have another dance free.'

'Then I would be glad to claim it.' There was a tiny waver in his voice, which he masked with a cough.

'The supper dance?'

He looked down at her and smiled. 'Of course.'

Ellen squeezed his arm, and he bowed and left her with Hester and Lavinia. An idea was forming in her mind. It was outrageously bold, but it might just work.

'Well,' Lavinia said, 'if he is sworn off marriage, he doesn't dance like it.'

Ellen was forced to agree.

★   ★   ★

When Thomas came back to her at the time they'd agreed, Ellen's nerves were singing. It was now or never.

'Ready?' he said.

'I'm terribly sorry,' she said, 'but I'm tired of dancing. I don't suppose I could prevail upon you to take a walk with me instead?'

She noticed a muscle ticking along Thomas's jaw, and wondered if he was clenching his teeth.

'A walk?'

'Yes, please.'

'Of course. Shall I accompany you to the refreshment room?'

Ellen faltered. She'd planned to lure Thomas away from the crowds so she could ask him once and for all how he felt about her, but the refreshment room would be packed. 'I don't imagine there is anywhere quieter, where we could talk privately?' she asked sheepishly.

His eyes flashed and he looked surprisingly anxious. 'What are you up to? Have you been drinking the punch?'

Ellen had to laugh at that. For a moment she marvelled that, while Edward had successfully coerced her to travel hundreds of miles with him, she could not keep this man hoodwinked for one hundred feet.

'I have had some, but I assure you, I am not in my cups.'

'Well, why are you dragging me off? People will talk, and I've gone to inordinate lengths to ensure that I don't inadvertently attract attention to us.'

'You've been trying to avoid drawing attention to us?'

'Yes!'

Ellen's heart stuttered. 'Then, is there is an *us* to draw attention to?'

Thomas stopped and stared at her.

# CHAPTER 52

E llen waited, barely breathing, whilst Thomas floundered. They were now walking out of the ballroom as quickly as they could without being remarked upon.

'Ellen, please,' he hissed, looking around anxiously.

'Perhaps if you would just talk to me about how you feel …'

'I thought you understood. I am not in a position to offer you anything so any kind of … of flirtation is absolutely out of the question.'

'But don't you want to know for sure who I was writing about? In that letter Veronique read out in court?'

He blanched and looked around. They were in the corridor just beyond the refreshment room, and in the hubbub of nearby conversations, nobody had heard them. He tried the nearest door and, when nobody was looking, he ushered her inside, to an empty parlour.

He shut the door behind them with shaking hands. 'I can't believe we're doing this.'

Ellen stood firm and crossed her arms. 'I need to know where I stand, and I think you do too.'

He looked at her, exasperated. 'Fine. Who was the letter about?'

'You. Do you like me?'

He groaned and put his head in his hands. 'You shouldn't like me.'

Ellen took a patient breath. He was such an honourable man; too honourable for his own good.

'Mr Legh. I'm sorry you've been disappointed before, but you must know that I am no stranger to scandal. If there's anyone who can understand how you feel, surely it's me?'

'Your scandal was not your fault.'

'Neither was yours.'

'Yours can be undone; mine is in my blood.'

She put a hand to her temple. The poor man was convinced he was untouchable. But was he really so naive that he believed she was in a better position?

'Do you really want me to marry Lord Longton?'

He winced. 'We should go back to the ballroom.'

She stepped a little closer. 'Lord Longton is a lovely young man, but I don't feel I can quite be myself around him. He doesn't make me feel … the way you do.'

His gaze shot up to hers, despite himself.

'I think that's because,' she continued, 'whether you admit it or not, you *seem* to like me just as I am.'

His eyes sparked, and a corner of his mouth twitched. 'There's a lot to like,' he said in a low voice.

'So you *do* like me!' She stepped closer again and he seemed to bristle, as though he was about to lean in too. Then he screwed his eyes closed.

'Miss Turner. I will not take advantage of you.'

'How would you be taking advantage of me?' she whispered. They were inches apart now, just as they had been during the dance. He swallowed. Which way would he turn this time?

He hesitated, then slid his large hand along her jaw. The heat from it burned into her and she turned her cheek into it. 'I would like it very much if you kissed me,' she said.

He seemed about to argue, but then she pressed against him and with a groan, at last, he kissed her.

Ellen moaned softly against him. So *this* was a kiss. The softness of his lips, the firmness of his hands on her back, in her hair, made her shiver inside. She kissed him back, and with a low noise of pleasure he opened her mouth with his and touched his tongue to hers. It robbed her of breath, but when he did it again, and began a hot, aching rhythm, Ellen followed with all the adoration that was pent up inside her. He whipped around with her until her back was against the parlour wall, but still she leant into him as they moved as one.

He tore away from her, panting, and flushed. 'Ellen ...' he croaked. 'Ellen ...'

'Hush,' she said, placing a trembling finger over his lips. 'Don't say it. Don't ruin it.'

His eyes slid closed, but not before she glimpsed the pain in them. 'Can't you just talk to me?' she whispered.

He shook his head. 'This isn't right,' he murmured.

'I doubt it could be more right.'

He opened his eyes and looked down at her, jaw tight. 'Making love to you in the Egertons's parlour would most definitely be wrong.'

Ellen laced her fingers through his. 'I don't care about the scandal,' she said. 'I just want you.'

For a moment, she thought he might relent. But he closed it down and shook his head.

'We must go back, before someone discovers us.' He ran his hands over his hair, smoothing it, then tugged at his waistcoat. 'You'll have to go first.'

'Why?'

'I'm in no fit state.'

'What do you mean?'

He looked at her and there was a gleam in his eye. 'One day you will understand.'

'Can you not just talk to me and stop talking in riddles?'

The glint in his eye slowly disappeared and he shook his head 'No.'

Ellen sighed. She wanted to say so much to him. But instead, she stood on tiptoe, and kissed him swiftly on the lips. 'Then write to me. I will see you next week.'

She could feel his gaze burning into her as she slipped out of the parlour, and back to the party.

\* \* \*

Just days before the hearing for the annulment in the House of Lords, that would hopefully make Ellen a single, unmarried woman again, she readied herself for the most unusual expedition that Thomas had organised.

Admittedly, any jaunt a married woman could make with her parents, her suitor, and the man with whom she had shared a passionate, secret liaison, would be unusual. But when her father had told her what they were to be doing, Ellen knew the day ahead would be truly outlandish. They were going to the site of the gasworks in Macclesfield, to witness … a hot air balloon ascent!

'I have absolutely no idea what to expect from this,' said her mother, as they donned their coats and shoes in Shrigley's hallway. She was resplendent in a dusky rose-patterned gown and large-brimmed hat, tied firmly beneath her chin with gauze to prevent any mishaps.

'Neither have I,' Ellen said, and it was true – she had not heard from Thomas since their encounter at the Egerton ball. 'But I am most excited to find out. I've read of ascents taking place in London, but never from Macclesfield.'

'Indeed, my love.' Her father rubbed his hands together and beamed down at her.

They made the journey, and Ellen tried to focus on the thrilling spectacle ahead of them and not on what Thomas might, or might not, say to her.

Her mother proceeded to give Ellen a potted history of all the eligible men who would be there, including Lord Longton. (Thomas, she noticed, did not feature on said list, but her mother had been considerably warmer towards Thomas since she'd traced her dislike of him to Frances Wakefield … and since Thomas had started helping her to match Ellen with a viscount.) Fortunately, her mother's delighted account was so enthusiastic that they arrived in Macclesfield before Ellen was required to respond.

They exited the carriage, and Ellen gasped when she saw the balloon sitting in splendour at the gasworks. There were an awful lot of people running around, holding ropes, shouting and tugging the enormous, surging beast.

It was quite the largest thing Ellen had ever seen. Fabric that looked like silk, painted in glorious shades of blue, turquoise, and green that rolled and shivered with the wind. Air seemed to be inflating the body of the balloon and sending it upward, but as it was not yet ready to ascend, the men were working hard to keep it firmly attached to the ground.

Her father put his hand to his eyes to shade them, and watched. 'My God,' he breathed.

Even her mother appeared transfixed at the sight and had to remember to close her mouth.

A gust of wind moved the balloon and the men around it louder; one man was dragged along the ground before they were able to pin him down.

'It looks remarkably dangerous,' her mother said.

'It's actually not too dangerous if one knows what one is doing,' a voice behind them replied, and Ellen whirled to find Thomas smiling, with a wariness in his eyes. The memory of his body pressing hers hard against the wall in the Egertons's parlour rushed back, and brought colour to her face.

She dipped a long curtsy, hiding her blush, and he bowed to them all.

'It looks remarkably good fun,' she said when she'd recovered. 'Have you been in one?'

'Not yet,' he said with a twinkle in his eye.

'*Yet?* You mean you intend actually getting into one of those things?' her mother said, clearly appalled.

'I should definitely like to try it. Imagine, drifting so high over the roads and fields. Finding out what Lyme Park and Shrigley Hall might look like from high above in the air?'

'I feel quite nauseous thinking about it,' her father said with a shudder.

'It would be wonderful,' Ellen breathed, as she dragged her gaze from the shimmering beast to smile up at Thomas. 'We should embark upon a journey in a balloon at the earliest possible opportunity!'

Her parents made a chorus of horror, but Thomas didn't play along. 'Perhaps Longton will offer to take you.'

'Perhaps, if he is brave enough.' Her riposte sounded more cutting than she'd intended, but she was getting tired of everyone foisting her onto Longton simply because he was a lord ... and because he was the only man who seemed genuinely interested in marrying her, who wasn't in prison.

'Brave enough for what?' As if Thomas had conjured him, Lord Longton bowed graciously over her mother's hand, then hers, and shook hands with her father and Thomas. 'I say, what a marvellously big *bag* it is!'

'You mean *that*?' Her father smiled genially, nodding towards the balloon. 'My hoyden of a daughter was wondering if you were brave enough to ride one with her.'

'Golly,' said Longton, looking faintly horrified before laughing it off. 'Good to see you as ever, Miss Turner.'

As Ellen greeted Lord Longton politely, she risked a conciliatory glance at Thomas. His expression was unreadable.

At that moment, they were jostled as people surged to get a closer look. Thomas began to share what he knew of the balloonist – a Mr Green, who was now famous for the number of ascents he had achieved, and most notably survived – but Lord Longton bellowed over him.

'Hoi hoi!'

'Ah, what are you doing?' Ellen said, nervously, as Longton gesticulated towards the men taming the balloon.

'You said you wanted to ride one,' Longton said brightly, 'so I'm going to see how they do it. Tally-ho!' And with that, he bustled forth.

'Don't get too close!' her mother cried as he disappeared into the crowd. She tucked her hand under Ellen's arm, singularly puffed up at this development. 'He's quite the daredevil, isn't he?'

'He is indeed.' Ellen refrained from pointing out that only moments ago, Longton had been terrified of the balloon.

'It's almost ready to go now,' Thomas said. 'Mr Green will need to do the final check.'

As Thomas predicted, a small, ordinary looking man hurried about checking things, and gave a brief, but exhilarating speech about the perilous adventure he was about to embark upon.

Then, with two men beside him, Mr Green clambered into the basket that hung beneath the huge balloon, and with a shout and a wave, the balloon was unleashed, and it began to rise.

Ellen screamed with everyone else as it left the ground and lifted into the air.

'Extraordinary,' her father breathed as he watched. 'Simply extraordinary.'

A single, long rope still trailed along the ground beneath the enormous vessel, as it began to float up over the surrounding buildings.

Thomas stood beside Ellen, at last. 'Breathtaking, isn't it?'

Ellen nodded, still looking up at the rising balloon, trying not to turn her face to his; perhaps if she didn't move, he'd stay by her side for longer. Too soon though, Thomas pulled away and frowned. 'What on earth does Longton think he is doing?'

Ellen snapped back down to earth. She scanned the crowd and spied Longton running full pelt after the trailing rope. Two balloonists were chasing after him, shouting urgently.

'The man's not a daredevil, he's a nuisance,' Thomas muttered. Did Ellen dare to read a hint of dislike in those words? 'If he's not careful, he'll end up going with it.'

'No!' Her mother shrieked.

'Apparently, it's happened. If the men don't leave go of the ropes at the right time, they risk being lifted with it, and very quickly it's too far to jump safely. One young boy had to be pulled up and dragged into the basket before he fell.'

'Oh my,' her father shuddered. They all watched on help-lessly as Longton gained on the rope, and lunged for it; fortunately, one of the balloonists caught up with him in the nick of time, and pushed him out of the way. He stood, brushed himself down and returned to them at a jog, quite oblivious to the fact that the balloonist was still shaking his fist at him.

'Damned remarkable,' he said when he reached them, trying to catch his breath.

Ellen raised an eyebrow at his language, but he didn't notice.

Thomas cleared his throat pointedly, and Longton flushed. 'Beg pardon,' he said, hurriedly.

They all looked upwards as the balloon drifted elegantly, far above the height of the houses and the trees. It was still rising.

'Can they control the descent?' Ellen asked after a little while. 'It looked like they were using some kind of gas.'

'My word, a bluestocking in our midst?' Longton said with a laugh. Everyone joined in the joke except Thomas, who looked irritated on her behalf. Ellen wanted to hug him.

When the excitement subsided, and they made their way back to the carriage, Lord Longton walked beside her, chatting about inconsequential things. Ellen couldn't help glancing at Thomas. His face was impassive. Stony, one might say. She wondered if he might not be the tiniest bit jealous of the match he'd been eagerly helping her mother to make. The thought was gratifying, but she couldn't refine too much upon it. Until she had been to the House of Lords for the annulment hearing, she was still very much married to Edward. And if things did not go well, she would remain married to Edward forever. That was the thought that kept her awake at night.

When Lord Longton fussed over handing her into the carriage with a good deal of bonhomie, Thomas simply stood back leaving her to wonder if his earlier reaction had been wishful thinking. Only days ago, when he'd kissed her so thoroughly and comprehensively, she'd felt as though she were in heaven. But when she peeped out of the carriage window now, he had already moved away and was chatting to a lady she hadn't met before. As they pulled away, she sat back and wondered how *she* would control her descent.

# CHAPTER 53

In the intervening days since the balloon ascent, she had seen nothing of Thomas. No word whatsoever, not even a note. And now here she was, in London, about to be thrown to the lions again.

Ellen arrived with her father at the House of Lords, and as they waited for the hearing to begin, any hope she'd harboured that interest in her case might have waned was dashed. The Lords Chamber was packed, and people were fighting to get in. The doors had to be barred to stop people pouring through, because, she discovered, it was all in the newspapers again. She was sure Frances was up to her old tricks, trying to garner public sympathy. *That woman*, as her mother now called her, was frighteningly good at whipping up support for Edward's position as a wrongly convicted, lovestruck husband.

The House of Lords had an air of magnificence and opulence, all red leather seats and dark gleaming wood, but she wasn't in the mood to appreciate it. She looked at all the solemn faced, solemn robed men sitting on both sides of the room, and thought how dispiriting it was that her life, her fate, her future, were entirely in their old, aristocratic hands. Would they believe her, or even care about her predicament? It was hard to breathe amidst all the masculine tradition, curiosity, and disapproval in the atmosphere.

She took her place beside her father and Mr Grimsditch, and Edward arrived to stand opposite her. The gentlemen of the Lords all strained for a good view of him; Ellen could barely bring herself to look.

Mr Grimsditch stood up and made the case that Ellen's testimony at Edward's trial had been legal, because, quite simply, the judge had decreed it so. He went on to argue that the marriage should be annulled, keeping matters brief and straightforward.

When her father was brought forward to testify as a witness, Ellen looked over at Edward. He didn't have anyone representing him today; instead, he appeared to be taking notes himself, frowning as his nib flew over the paper. When he was asked if he wanted to cross-examine the witness, he stood, and Ellen saw her father tense.

'Gentlemen, whilst I am more than willing to refute all the allegations that have been made against me in this … bill …' Edward said the word bill with icy contempt. 'I am completely unprepared to do so! I was not advised that the hearing would take this form. I will, however, prove beyond any doubt that my wife, Mrs Edward Gibbon Wakefield, married me of her own free will, that she was—'

'Mr Wakefield,' the Lord Chancellor said patiently. 'The question is, at this time, would you like to take the opportunity to cross-examine the witness?'

Ellen's gaze bounced from the man speaking to Edward, as she held her breath.

'I would, but I am not prepared to do so. I need access to my notes, to the evidence that was given previously—'

'Mr Wakefield, I'm afraid we cannot wait. Either you cross-examine the witness now, or you lose the opportunity.'

There were further similar exchanges, and eventually Edward relented. But his failure to halt the hearing entirely did not dishearten him. Far from it ...

Instead, every time Edward was invited to speak – which was often, since he'd apparently dispensed with Mr Scarlett's services – he threw himself into undermining Ellen's credibility as a witness. He raked up all the moments from the trial that had filled her with shame, in order to paint her as a stupid child now, and then a jezebel. He added new embellishments, too: speaking at length of how much she had adored him, and how she'd begged him to shower gifts upon her in exchange for kisses in Calais. The memory of those kisses made her feel ill, now she knew what she could have had with Thomas.

It was only when Edward was quoting a witness from the trial about the knee-sitting incident at Gretna Green – *he had no need of his notes after all*, Ellen thought – that one of the lords spoke out.

'Reciting the transcript of a trial is not bringing evidence to us,' the lord said.

But this comment was swiftly rebutted by another lord. 'The gentleman before us has every right to read to us the evidence that he feels will challenge the charges of fraud and force that have been brought against him. He should demonstrate to us why he feels he should not have been convicted.'

Echoes of *hear, hear!* rumbled about the chamber, and Edward was allowed to go on humiliating her.

This was awful. It was not going at all how the trial had gone. It dawned on Ellen gradually that this was not a judicial setting but a political one, and that here, the rules were grossly different. Edward had spoken to her of his political ambitions, and she could see now that those ambitions were not delusional: he was in his element, and he held the lords rapt as he spouted his lies about her, uninterrupted and unchallenged. When Ellen dared to look up at the lords, she could feel their eyes bearing down on her: some questioning, some amused … None sympathetic. She could feel in the air that her father and Mr Grimsditch were worried.

When at last Edward was finished, the Lord Chancellor cleared his throat to make his pronouncement on the affair. Ellen wanted to run away. Simply jump up and run. She couldn't bear to hear these pompous old men tell her that she would have to remain married just because they took Edward's word over the evidence that she had been cruelly lied to. Over the outcome of the trial that convicted him.

Her father surprised her by taking hold of her hand and squeezing it. 'Chin up,' he murmured. Ellen took a breath and braced herself. At least Edward had been led out of the room and she wouldn't have to see his triumphant face when the outcome was announced. Well, she wouldn't live with him, she'd run away. She'd run away to … to … Egypt.

The Lord Chancellor spoke, his tone low and serious. 'My lords, I feel it incumbent upon me to state that during the ten days that Mr Wakefield was allocated to call witnesses to support his statement, he singularly failed to do this.'

Ellen blinked and stiffened, and when the gentlemen in the chamber started murmuring in agreement, she looked up at her father. He was breathing rapidly. He took her hand again and crushed it in his.

The Lord Chancellor continued with his criticism of Edward and his evidence, and the calls of *hear, hear!* – though tentative at first – grew and grew. It didn't take long before the atmosphere in the room shifted entirely from how Ellen had perceived it when Edward held the floor. Soon, the chamber was resounding with jeers and roars that were aimed, almost unanimously, at … Edward!

*Oh God*. They … they … believed her!

The Lord Chancellor now called for silence and continued. 'It should be noted that once Miss Turner was apprised of the deception that had been practised upon her, she had nothing further to do with Mr Wakefield. She has lived entirely separate from him with no contact whatsoever, and her father refused to bow to his entreaties, rather subjected himself and his family to the proceedings to exonerate his daughter.'

The cheers to this were deafening.

The words after that were lost in a blur, but when her father stood and embraced her, she knew that the bill would be passed, knew that her sham of a marriage would be annulled. These wonderful, frosty old men had believed her.

She was free.

# CHAPTER 54

*William*

A few days later, William Turner sat at the dinner table in his London home, his wife and daughter by his side. They'd invited a large circle of friends and esteemed acquaintances to celebrate what was, finally, the end of their ordeal with Edward Gibbon Wakefield. As always, his wife had performed miracles and created a magnificent feast, with flowers in abundance. She'd also pressed him to invite a number of eligible and titled young men, chief amongst whom was Viscount Longton. His daughter, however, appeared supremely uninterested in the gaggle of beaus, only showing any emotion at all when Thomas Legh arrived.

The meal concluded, and William tapped on the side of his glass with his pastry fork. When the conversation subsided, he stood.

'My dearest friends, would you raise your glasses in toast to my beautiful daughter, Miss Ellen Turner?'

Everyone in the room cheered, and all stood to raise a glass. Ellen flushed in the candlelight and smiled.

'Miss Turner,' he said, and raised the glass to his lips.

'Miss Turner,' was the echo and all in the room drank.

There were a few kind speeches, and Ellen received them graciously. He had to admit, he was very pleased with the way that she had acquitted herself during the entire debacle. She had been calm, gracious, and poised throughout in a way that belied her want of years.

He sat back down and took hold of his wife's hand as conversation flowed again.

'She's done well,' he said quietly.

'Extremely well,' his wife said with an arch look. 'Though I'm still not sure her reputation has survived, nor ours.'

'What? Look at all these people!'

'Most of them have come because they want to gawp at us, husband.'

He had to admit his wife had a point. The interest in them had been ridiculous. Sometimes it felt as though the entire country was talking about them.

'I think it imperative that Ellen marry as swiftly as possible. The entire world now knows exactly how much I am worth, and we will be beset by dandies and idiots with pockets to let, trying to romance her,' he said.

'I agree wholeheartedly, but I still maintain that we should aspire to a title for her,' Jane whispered.

He looked down the table just as Ellen offered a tentative smile at Thomas Legh. Legh simply looked tortured for a second, then dipped his head in response. 'I'm not entirely convinced that we need a title,' he murmured to his wife.

'Nonsense! What about young Longton? He's shaping up nicely.'

William glanced at the flighty young man further down the table, and shrugged. 'You married me without a title.'

She flushed. 'Well, you were terribly handsome and had good prospects.'

William didn't respond. He looked at his only child. It grieved him to admit it, but his wife had been right. She had been irrevocably damaged by the publicity from the trial. They all had. He knew that now. He was relieved the Wakefields were behind bars, but the cost had been high. He had a room full of people who had accepted his hospitality, but they both knew the number of people who had declined. He watched as Ellen looked at Legh with unhappy eyes and could only pray it had all been worth it.

*   *   *

## Ellen

Conversation flowed around her, and Ellen risked another glance at Thomas. He was seated across from her, further down the table, and too far away for them to converse. He was always well turned out, but tonight, in his London finery, he looked good enough to eat. The cut of his clothes bespoke the most expensive tailoring, the precision of his neckcloth, the elegant simplicity of the sapphire pin setting him above all other aspirants to fashion in the room. His dark, wavy hair was tamed into his signature Brutus, and Ellen wanted badly to run her fingers through it again. He, on the other hand, showed absolutely no desire to repeat such scurrilous goings-on, no matter how much he'd enjoyed them the first time. She'd hoped that the outcome of the hearing in the Lords might have softened his demeanour, but if anything, he now seemed even more remote.

'You're a funny one.' Lord Longton's voice at her elbow snapped her out of her daydream.

'How so?' She'd quite stopped listening to the poor man some time ago. He must think her dreadfully rude.

'All that *reading* you do! I can't fathom it,' he said, waving his hands in an abstract way until his blancmange fell off his spoon, making Hester laugh.

Ellen rolled her eyes at him. 'But I love to read. Don't you?'

'Lord no, gives me a pain in the head. My original estimation was right, you *are* a bluestocking.'

He said it with affection, but it still rankled. 'What do you like to do?' Ellen asked.

'Horses,' he said immediately. 'I'm developing the stables and have some grand plans, I can tell you …' Ellen smiled as he rambled on about the work he wanted to do to his country home and the horses that he'd bought and trained. He waxed lyrical about Tattersalls and somewhere else she'd never heard of. She forced herself not to look over at Thomas again.

'He's very funny, isn't he?' Hester said, joining her as the ladies retired to the drawing room and left the gentlemen to their port. It made Ellen feel sad. He *was* funny. Friendly, charming, nice … all those things. And at the hot air balloon ascent, he might have easily mangled himself trying to impress her. Lord Longton didn't deserve her indifference. But how could she offer him more, when she knew Thomas?

She stole one more glance at Thomas as they left the room – he was holding up his glass and had evidently just said something that made her Uncle Robert laugh.

'Your Mr Legh is looking positively dashing tonight,' Hester said.

'He does, doesn't he.'

'He's also been spending a lot of time looking in your direction.'

Ellen's eyebrows shot up and she avoided turning to look. 'Really?'

'Most definitely.'

Ellen went quiet after that, lost in thought. She knew she should leave Thomas alone. She knew she should let go, because it was what he said he wanted. But she couldn't shake the memory of something Veronique had said in the courtroom: *appearing* to want something, and *actually wanting* it, were two different things.

\* \* \*

Later that evening, when the gentlemen had joined them and dancing was underway, Ellen's mood had not improved. Lord Longton had accidentally kicked her shin during the quadrille, and Thomas had not asked her to dance at all. Indeed, she hadn't seen Thomas dance with any of the ladies, and it seemed he intended to spend the entire soirée deep in conversation with the other gentlemen at the edges of the room. She longed to speak to him, to find out once and for all where she stood, but she knew that was impossible. It was clear that eyes were on her. Some mamas still steered their daughters away from her, and some of the gentlemen had looked at her tonight with a level of speculation that made her uncomfortable.

Ellen couldn't dwell on the matter for too long, though, as a rather dapper gentleman bowed to her and claimed a waltz. He wasn't overly tall, but he had a nice smile, and nice teeth too. When he introduced himself as *Lord* Tomlinson, and Ellen saw her mother watching from across the room, eyes wide with anticipation, she knew she must accept.

'I hope you won't mind my saying, Miss Turner,' he said as he twirled her around the dance floor, 'that you look wildly stylish this evening.'

Ellen laughed at the compliment, secretly relieved. She had donned one of her French dresses, the ones she had come to think of as her war trophies: this time a delicate green gown edged with ruffles of lace, with a low waist. The modiste had claimed that it was all the rage, and she'd put it on hoping it would help her to maintain an air of sophistication in the face of any curious stares. 'You are every bit as pretty as they said you were,' Lord Tomlinson went on.

Ellen's smile faded a touch. 'Who said that, pray?'

He twitched a shoulder in a shrug. 'It's what all the newspapers said.' He kept casting her extremely admiring glances in such a way that Ellen wondered if he'd been drinking. 'Is it right you are looking for a new husband?'

The feel of his hand on the small of her back was suddenly uncomfortable. Ellen tried to divert his comment.

'Aren't most unmarried young women?'

'Well, I have to say, if things were different, I'd be tempted to throw my hat in the ring, so to speak.' He looked down at her with eyes that darkened suddenly. 'But as things stand ...' He left the comment hanging, but the hand on her waist tightened and he pulled her closer to him.

'As things stand? What things?' She tried to move away, but he simply twirled her and maintained his hold, fingers pressing harder.

He tilted his head close to hers. Too close. 'If you'd consider an arrangement, I could make you very, very happy.'

'Beg pardon?'

He gave her a lopsided smile. 'Well, my father would skin me if I offered for you, but I think we could have a rather splendid time together.'

Ellen was so horrified it took a moment for her to form words. 'Are ... are you offering me ... carte blanche?' She'd heard of it, laughed about it with her friends, but never, ever, imagined she would receive such an insulting offer.

He looked mightily relieved that she understood the notion of being someone's mistress and carried on with enthusiasm. 'You'd want for nothing. Your own home, carriages, horses … I'm a very wealthy man. I could take you to France, Italy, anywhere you like.'

'How kind,' she said, trying to find her voice. So this was what it was to be notorious. Men making obscene propositions instead of proposals of marriage. Was that what she could expect from now on?

Something kindled in his eyes, something like excitement. 'Just say the word and I'm all yours. I could promise you fidelity for as long as it lasts.'

The music came to a halt, so she looked up at him, cocked her head on one side, and smiled, though she doubted there was any amusement in her eyes.

'I've given your kind offer careful consideration, and my answer is …'

His breathing quickened and he smiled.

'Not if you were the last man on earth.'

She walked away, head held high, and tried not to cry.

# CHAPTER 55

Ellen had no idea where she was heading, she just knew she needed to get out of the room and away from that odious man. Thomas had clearly spotted her hurried departure, because he arrived by her side.

'Miss Turner,' he said, with grating formality, 'it's been a while since we spoke.'

'Has it?' she said flatly, not stopping or trying to hide her sarcasm.

He looked momentarily embarrassed, but ploughed on. 'Might I offer my congratulations on the outcome of the hearing in the Lords.'

Ellen couldn't even raise a smile. 'Thank you, that's very kind.' She carried on walking.

Thomas kept pace and cleared his throat. 'May I escort you somewhere? Forgive me, but you appear … upset?'

She looked up at him, and when she saw nothing but concern in his eyes, she felt her icy resolve begin to melt.

She was forced to blink again. 'I am, but please don't be kind to me in public. I'm holding on to my composure by my fingertips.'

He took her hand and tucked it into his arm. 'Your parents have made some alterations to the house since I was last here,' he said. 'Perhaps you could give me a tour, and tell me all about them?'

Ellen managed a laugh. There hadn't been any alterations, but she pointed out some fictitious ones as they walked, and when it seemed that no one would notice their departure, led Thomas to her father's study.

She closed the door behind them and locked it.

'Ellen,' he said, a warning note in his voice. 'You shouldn't do that—'

'It doesn't matter though, does it!' Ellen burst out.

He looked shocked, and she put a hand to her mouth. But once she'd said it, she was certain that it was true. Locking herself in a room with Thomas was reckless, but what of it? All her efforts to detach herself from Edward had fallen short: she couldn't change the way the world saw her. And when a lady's reputation lies in tatters, what more has she to lose? She put her hands to her flaming cheeks and squeezed her eyes shut, as tears overwhelmed her.

'Ellen?' Thomas said again, but softly this time. 'What is it?'

She took a deep breath and squared her shoulders. 'Someone offered me carte blanche. He said I was beyond the pale, but pretty enough that he'd still be willing to buy me anything I wanted.'

Thomas's nostrils flared, and a muscle ticked along his jaw. 'Who?'

'I'm not telling you that.'

'Why not?'

'Because you look angry.'

'Angry? Damned right, I'm angry. How dare anyone address you so. I'll murder him!'

'Please stop,' Ellen said, putting her hands to her ears.

Thomas groaned, and he did stop. He stopped his pretence of politeness, and pulled her into his arms. She went willingly and buried her face in his neck. They stayed that way for some time, gently rocking against each other.

'Have you had any other trouble?' he murmured.

'A few stares and comments, but nothing I can't deal with. I didn't want to make a fuss. Thomas … I—'

But he was already pulling away from her. She'd been wanting to touch him like this, to speak with him like this, for days, and now she was wasting her chance. He was turning for the door … She had to say something …

'Aren't you going to kiss me again?' she blurted, and when he looked back at her with mingled shock and regret, she knew that was *not* the right thing to say. Could she be more maladroit if she tried?

He placed his hands gingerly on her shoulders and held her at arm's length. 'You know I can't. You wouldn't want people thinking I had a claim.'

Ellen wanted to throw herself back into his arms and tell him he could have any claim he wanted. But as she opened her mouth, he brought a finger to her lips and fixed her with a look so complex, she wasn't sure what he'd do. Was he about to lean in? Was he angry with her?

He shook his head and abruptly dropped his hand. 'I'm sorry, Ellen. I just can't.'

'Don't worry, you don't have to say it.' She was unmarriageable. Ellen couldn't bear to hear it from Thomas too, so she turned and tried to leave in dramatic fashion, but the door lock was stiff. He came up behind her, crowding her, and she could feel the warmth of his body from head to toe. Again, she thought he might whip her around, kiss her, tell her everything was going to be alright, but instead she watched his hand close over the door handle and open it for her.

'You go first. I'll wait,' was all he said. So she stumbled dumbly out into the corridor, feeling as though she'd been pushed, decisively, out of his life.

&ast; &ast; &ast;

A couple of days later, Ellen sat through morning calls with her mother. Under normal circumstances she would have enjoyed it, but word of Tomlinson's horrendous proposal had reached her parents, and as the visitors seemed more interested in ogling her than talking, she could only assume it was now common knowledge. It was appalling. On top of that, the conversation with Thomas simply wouldn't leave her. They had parted awkwardly and at first she'd been convinced that if he called on them, she would find a way to make things right. But as she sipped through cup after cup of tea, and the hours slipped by with no visits from Thomas, she slowly faced the reality: there was nothing to put right, because there was nothing between them. Not for him, anyway.

During a brief lull in visitors, she sat alone with her stitching, and was trying to think, when a tap on the door made her sit up. A footman handed her a letter with a bow. She took it, and her heart sped up. It was Thomas's distinctive hand.

She took a breath, then broke the seal and spread the paper before her.

My dear Miss Turner,

When we had a conversation at the Egerton ball, you asked me to speak to you honestly. I was unable to do so. You also bade me write. I think this might have been said in jest, but perhaps you rightly saw that I sometimes find it easier to put pen to paper than I do to form words in person.

Firstly, may I say that I hold you in the very highest regard. Your good opinion is singularly important to me, and I was horrified that you had been told of the circumstances of my birth. It shamed me to think that you were forced to hear this. I know that you feel this is of no matter, but it matters to me. It pains me to tell you that I was rejected by someone who professed to love me because the scandal was too much for her to bear. I couldn't live through that again and for that reason, decided never to marry.

You have been through so much. It is clear to me that you need someone with a spotless reputation to sweep you off your feet and wipe out the scandal you have been forced to endure, not be troubled by someone like myself who will simply add to the burden you already bear. However, I am not arrogant enough to think I can dictate your desires or decree where your affections should lie.

*I find that in your company, my decision not to marry is constantly put to the test. I have no right to ask this of you, but if you could find it in your heart to give me a little time, if we could return to being friends, perhaps we can work out whether or not we could be adventurers together in this life?*

*Would you, could you, wait for me?*

*Your humble servant.*

*Thomas Legh esq.*

Ellen's heart was racing. What was he saying? That he wanted to give what was between them a chance? Was he afraid that she would reject him and break his heart again? *We could be adventurers together in this life …* A sob escaped her and she put her hand to her mouth.

She shoved the letter into her reticule and scrubbed at her eyes when the door burst open and her mother flew in, all a flutter.

'Ellen, Ellen … tidy yourself immediately.'

Ellen looked down at her gown. It was trimmed with yellow, and more than respectable.

'Your hair, your hair!' her mother shrieked and started prodding at the curls by her ears.

'Mama, please, whatever is the matter?' She batted her mother's hands away and stood up.

Her mother paused, cheeks pink, and sucked in a breath. She flapped a hand over her chest. 'The viscount.'

'Which viscount?'

Her mother gave her an astonished look. 'Lord Longton.'

'Yes?'

Her mother paused, lifted her chin, gave her a very knowing look, and took in another deep breath. 'He … Lord Longton … is with your father.'

Ellen was lost. Whatever Longton wanted with her papa had clearly … Oh …

'What is he asking?'

Her mama squealed. Actually squealed and grasped her hands. 'For your hand! You have done it, my love. You have done it. Against all the odds, despite everything the *on dits* said, despite what the newspapers said, you, my love, have captured an aristocrat. You have raised us into the upper echelons of society, you have … you have succeeded!'

'Hardly, Mama … I really—'

The door opened, and Longton appeared in the doorway. Her mama gave her a long look and left them in a flurry of lace cap and quivering excitement.

Ellen's head was spinning. Surely not? Surely not *now*, of all moments?

'Lord Longton, how kind of you to call.' It was all she could think of to say.

This was the culmination of all her mama's hopes and dreams: an offer of marriage from a member of the aristocracy. A marriage that would bring a title for her, and for her children. As she stared at the pleasant young man in front of her, whom she liked but most definitely did not love, the thought that struck her forcibly was that this was very much her mother's dream. She'd gone along with it until now – what dutiful child wouldn't? – but the last few months had shown her that marriage was not something to be undertaken lightly. If she married unwisely again, it would be for good. There would be no going back this time.

He bowed low over her hand, and took a breath.

'My dearest Miss Turner, I have just spoken to your papa, and he has given his permission, his consent, for me to ask for your hand in marriage.'

*Oh God …*

He licked his lips. 'Would you make me the happiest man and marry me?' His eyes were shining brightly, and he recovered himself enough to grin at her.

'Lord Longton, you do me such an … an … honour. I … well …' She cleared her throat. It really was an honour, and just as Thomas had said in his letter, he was the man with the spotless reputation who could sweep away all the scandal from her life. This was exactly what Thomas meant. What her family wanted. Needed.

Could she throw away this opportunity, on the slim chance that Thomas would relent? That he might acknowledge that the passion between them could be forever … and trust that she wouldn't break his heart?

She looked again at the hopeful lord in front of her.

'I've come to think of you as a dear friend … I can … I can't …' She looked up at him, mortified, as she realised the truth of it. 'I'm so sorry,' she whispered, 'but I don't think I can accept.'

*God*, her mother was going to *kill* her.

He looked mildly put out. 'Oh, really? I thought we might rub along together nicely.'

The fact that he wasn't devastated was an enormous relief. 'I think we probably would rub along extremely well, but don't you want to marry someone you love?'

He grinned, then laughed. 'No! Who's going to fall in love with me?'

She felt an odd pang in her chest. 'Someone will! I'm sure of it. You're a lovely man.'

'Thank you, that's awfully sweet of you to say. That's why I thought I'd try and marry you. You seem to like me.'

Ellen wondered what on earth people had been saying to him. He continued, 'I might not be the brightest button, but I want to marry someone I can laugh with.'

'An admirable ambition,' she said and felt instantly sorry that she couldn't accept him. He really was lovely, and she wanted him to be happy.

'You're sure?' He tilted his head and gave her an encouraging smile.

'I'm sure.' And she was. He could have given her everything that her mother and father wanted, but not what she wanted.

'No hard feelings?' He gave her another wide smile and she smiled back.

'Not a one. I hope that we can still be friends.'

He bowed gallantly over her hand, paused, then brushed her cheek with a brotherly kiss. 'Always,' he murmured, and left.

Ellen stared at the door for a long time.

She pinched the bridge of her nose with thumb and forefinger. She wanted to marry someone that she could talk with, laugh with, love with. She wanted someone she could enjoy kisses and passionate moments with. Longton was very nice, but she didn't want passion with him like she wanted with Thomas. She didn't yearn to see him like she did Thomas, didn't ache to feel his arms about her and his lips on hers … like she did Thomas.

Thomas.

The man she loved.

She sat down and put her hands to her cheeks. She loved him. It was as simple, or as complicated, as that, and she couldn't marry another man whilst she felt that way. It would be unfair to both of them.

But then … what if Thomas didn't love her? What if he never offered for her? What if she'd just turned down the chance of a home, a title, children, and a place in society, respectability, for … nothing?

What had she done? She closed her eyes when she thought of what her mother might say. When the door opened, her heart sank so low she wondered if she might faint. The relief when her father entered the room rather than her mother was … huge.

'Well? Are congratulations in order? Should I pen an announcement to *The Times*?' He looked so pleased. She hated having to disappoint him, and she didn't know how to say it, how to break it to him.

Something inside her firmed, and she stood up and went over to him, and patted his arm. 'I received a lovely proposal from Lord Longton, but I'm afraid I said no.'

'No?'

Ellen nodded and waited.

'By all that is holy, Ellen. Why would you say no?'

Ellen held her composure and took a breath. He looked so crestfallen, but somehow, she knew he already understood her answer.

He heaved a deep sigh. 'You were lucky to get an offer from him. He's a decent boy too and … darling, I'm not sure if the alternative is possible.'

Ellen flushed as she realised what he meant. 'I know. But Longton *is* a very decent boy, and that's why it would be wrong to marry him.'

Her father opened his mouth but closed it again, then put a hand to his forehead. 'Your mother will be apoplectic.'

Ellen's chest squeezed. 'I know that too, and I'll do all I can to support her. I'm sure you wouldn't want me to marry the wrong man just to maintain her health?'

He frowned at her. 'Of course not.' He rubbed the back of his head and looked less certain. 'Of course not.'

★ ★ ★

It was some considerable time later when her mother breezed into the parlour and swept her up into a warm embrace.

'Congratulations again, my love. Have you come back down to earth yet?'

'Have you not seen Papa?' Ellen was sure that by now her papa would have broken the news.

'No, love, I've been busy celebrating. We must arrange to see the dressmaker and the milliner, and I've begun planning your betrothal party. Of course, it will be here in London, and the guest list ... oh, Ellen, the guest list will be stellar ...' Her mother stopped when she realised that Ellen wasn't rhapsodising with her.

'What? What is it?'

Ellen took a breath and gathered every shred of her courage. 'Mama,' she began, but her voiced quailed. She cleared her throat, stared at the floor, and spoke all in a rush to get the awful words out. 'Mama, I'm so sorry, but I declined his offer.'

Her mother was silent, so Ellen risked a peek. Her mother stared at her for a moment, shook her head, and observed her with a puzzled smile. 'I'm sorry, what did you say?'

'I turned Lord Longton down. I said no to his proposal.'

'But ... but ... why?' Horror was creeping into her mother's face, reddening her cheeks and making her eyes shimmer.

'I'm not the right woman for him, and he's not the right man for me.'

'But he's a *viscount*,' her mother said, as though Ellen was slow.

'I know.'

'He's a *viscount*!' she shrieked. 'He's everything we've been working for, planning for. Marriage to a viscount will put us right in the middle of society and consolidate your father's position. Are you holding out for higher? Is that it? Because let me tell you, you won't do better!'

'I'm not holding out for higher.'

Her mother went very still, the horror apparently mounting. 'But I've told people. Told the high in the instep matrons who came and looked down their noses at us ...'

It was Ellen's turn to shriek. '*What?* Why would you do that without first speaking to me?'

'Because it never occurred to me, not for the smallest second, that you would be stupid enough to turn him down. You foolish, foolish, ungrateful girl.'

'Well, you must tell them. You must tell everyone that I am *not* marrying Longton.'

Her mother made an exasperated noise.

'Mama, promise me! *Promise* me you will.'

# CHAPTER 56

The return to Shrigley the day after the argument was even more dreadful than Ellen imagined it might be. Her mother didn't speak to her for the entire journey. It was completed in total silence broken only by the occasional sob from her mother and sigh from her father.

Ellen felt awful, but as the journey dragged on, she gradually felt a sense of irritation creeping in. It was almost as though her mother herself had wanted to marry Longton, she mourned his loss so deeply.

By the time they arrived home, Ellen was limp and exhausted. She wanted nothing more than to ride over to Lyme Park and be with Thomas. She had not found the words to reply to his letter – nor the chance, with the eagle eye her mother kept on her – but all she knew was that she needed to see him. If not to talk, just to sink into his arms and breathe.

She stripped off her gloves and handed her hat and coat to the waiting footman as she walked across the hallway of her home. Light streamed in from the domed ceiling window, casting the whole room in golden light.

Her mother walked past her, headed straight for her sitting room and slammed the door behind her. Ellen's father put a hand on her shoulder.

'She'll come around.'

Ellen wanted to cry. It felt so unspeakably unfair.

She made her way to her bedchamber and then lay on the bed looking at the rain that began hammering against the window. Any thoughts of venturing out quashed, she closed her eyes and wondered what Thomas was doing. Wondered if he was back from London. Wondered if he had realised yet how he felt about her. She was sure that he felt something. What she was not sure about was whether or not anything would ever come of it.

★ ★ ★

The next day, word came that Thomas and his party had returned. Her mother was still not speaking to her with much civility, but by a stroke of luck, some of her mother's friends were paying a call to Lyme Park that morning, and Ellen was allowed to join them. She had no idea how she would manage to speak with Thomas alone, but she ached to see him. To be in the same room as him, to look in his eyes and decipher whether he really meant everything he'd written in that letter, would be enough. As they exited the carriage, and her mother fluffed out her cap and her skirts, they went through the arch and into the courtyard to be greeted and shown to the drawing room.

It never failed to surprise her how beautiful and welcoming Lyme Park was, but as she admired the saloon yet again, it eventually dawned on her that the atmosphere in the room might be just a little … chilly.

Her mother's bosom bows were already in attendance, and she immediately sank into the comfort of their company.

Thomas stood by the fireplace, and as she looked at him, he immediately looked away. He was still for a little while before coming to stand before her. She smiled up at him, but he didn't return the smile. What on earth was wrong?

'Miss Turner, how very nice to see you,' he said, but his voice was flat, his eyes dull. It was as if he didn't know her. Without another word, he turned away, leaving Ellen blinking. Could this really be happening? Did she *imagine* Thomas's letter?

A terrible possibility occurred to Ellen then. A possibility so heinous, so utterly ... revolting, it made her feel as though the room were spinning.

What if the letter hadn't really been from Thomas? What if, like the letter that had set off this whole chain of events, it had been written by someone who wanted to keep Ellen unmarried for their own devilish agenda?

*Wait for me*, the letter had said. What if the letter was a ploy designed to persuade Ellen to remain unmarried, waiting on a proposal that would never come, until Edward found a way to get her back into his clutches? Frances Wakefield was not in prison, and she'd heard in court that Ellen had her heart set on someone ... If her father and her uncle had worked out who that person was, it would have been the easiest thing in the world for someone with her cunning.

Could Frances have played the same trick on Ellen *again*, and succeeded?

Uncertain, and horribly confused, Ellen sat with her mother and her friends, and listened to their conversation. She wasn't required to contribute much, so it was a safe place to be. She tried to catch Thomas's eye, but failed dismally, and sat wondering what on earth she had done to warrant such ... such coldness from him. Perhaps their last meeting in London really did show his true feelings for her – or total lack thereof.

Eventually, he joined them again and there was no evidence of any thaw in his demeanour.

'I wasn't sure we would see you so soon,' Thomas said, looking not at Ellen but at her mother.

'Oh?' Jane said, confused. 'Did you think we were still in London?'

Thomas gave her an odd look. 'I imagined that wherever you were, you would be busy planning your family's celebrations.'

Ellen couldn't stand it any longer – she replied before her mother could. 'What celebrations?'

Thomas looked at her properly then, and she saw it: hurt was writ large in his eyes. He took a breath, as if to steady himself, then gave a forced smile. 'To celebrate your betrothal, of course. I hear congratulations are in order?'

Ellen froze. 'Betrothal?'

'Yes, to Lord Longton.'

Ellen looked at her mother, whose face had gone an alarming shade of fuschia. 'Ah,' her mother said, her voice shrill and tight. 'Now, Mr Legh, I'm afraid—'

'Why does Mr Legh think I am engaged to Lord Longton, mother?' Ellen asked, trying to keep her voice even.

Thomas looked baffled. Her mother shot her a ferocious glare.

'Don't embarrass me any more than you already have, darling,' she hissed under her breath. 'Mr Legh, I'm afraid there's been a misunderstanding. Wherever did you hear that our dear Ellen was engaged?'

'It was the talk of the ton,' Thomas said, still bewildered. 'I heard from Mr Grimsditch *and* Lord Tomlinson that you'd told them yourself.'

'Mother!' Ellen hissed. 'You *promised*!'

Ellen was beyond mortified, but then it struck her. Did this mean ... Thomas's letter was real? That it was a misunderstanding? That he really did ... want her to wait for him?

'This is horribly embarrassing,' her mother said, squirming in her chair. Ellen had never seen her mother look quite so flustered. 'You see, for a moment I thought Ellen *was* engaged to the viscount and it was such wonderful news – or *would have been*,' she shot Ellen another glare, 'that I suppose I started celebrating too soon.'

*Unbelievable*, Ellen thought. 'Lord Longton was kind enough to offer for me,' she said to Thomas, 'but I turned him down. I wanted to wait for the right man.'

Thomas looked at the floor, taking this in. 'I see,' he said. There followed an awkward silence.

He cleared his throat. 'Ah, Miss Turner, have you seen the recent alterations to the Bright Gallery?' He said. 'Might you wish to ... take a tour?'

Ellen looked at her mother who seemed like she might object, but she stood. 'I would be delighted.'

\* \* \*

Ellen followed Thomas in silence down the hall, past the giant stuffed bear, until they reached the door to the library. She paused at the door and closed her eyes. This was where it all began.

He closed the door behind them quietly, and it was a moment before he turned around to face her. He ran a hand over his mouth momentarily before he pulled it away to respond. 'You're not betrothed? You turned down an offer from Longton?'

Ellen nodded. 'I did.'

Thomas nodded.

'You thought it had happened again, didn't you. Thought that I had abandoned you because of the scandal surrounding your family.'

He looked tortured, but he nodded.

'And that letter ... You meant it?'

'Every word,' he said, his voice choked. He moved towards her and Ellen moved too. She threw herself into his waiting arms.

He held her tight and buried his face in her neck.

'Thank God,' he murmured. 'Thank God.' She held him all the tighter.

He pulled away and looked at her. 'I can't tell you ... I've been so ...' Then he leaned in, and kissed her. She kissed him back, heart singing. 'I thought I was doing the right thing by staying away,' he said when he drew breath. 'But the truth is, I was also afraid. And when I thought I'd lost my chance ... I couldn't bear it.'

'Truly?' He wanted a *chance* with her! 'Even though I am even more notorious than you are?'

'Truly.' He put her from him, and there was something solemn in his gaze. 'The moment you said that you *weren't* marrying Longton, I realised something. Asking you to wait for me ... it was foolish, selfish. It's about time I faced up to how I feel. To offer you *all* of myself, not just parts. If, of course, *you* don't need more time ...?'

Ellen almost laughed. 'Your timing may be unusual, Mr Legh, but it is no less perfect for it.'

'Well then,' Thomas said with an anxious laugh, dropping to one knee whilst looking unwaveringly into her eyes. He took hold of her hand. His fingers were cold.

'Miss Ellen Turner of the Shrigley abduction scandal. Would you marry me?'

Ellen threw herself down to kneel before him, thinking her heart would burst. 'Mr Legh, of the Lyme Park scandal,' she said, 'nothing would make me happier. Let us be utterly scandalous together, for as long as we both shall live.'

She kissed his hands. He groaned and swept her into his arms. Then, still kneeling on the library floor, he kissed her like she'd dreamed he would. His arms were strong and warm, and she plunged her hands into the rich darkness of his hair as she held him to her, savouring the feel of his lips on hers.

He pulled away. 'I love you. God, how I love you.'

Ellen's heart thudded so hard in her chest it hurt at his admission. When she said *I love you too*, the widest grin split his face as he let out a yell, pulled her to her feet, and lifted her up to swing her around. She clung to his shoulders, laughing.

He stood her back down, then kissed her again, this time even more wildly.

He pulled away and rested his forehead against hers. 'However will we convince your parents of my suitability?'

Ellen wanted to laugh but kept a straight face and looked up at him. 'We'll think of something. And if we don't, we can run away to some far-flung place until they calm down.'

He laughed. 'Adventurers together … We shall go wherever we dare!'

Ellen leaned in and touched her lips to his, making him moan softly. She loved it when he did that. He deepened the kiss, and Ellen felt that she was learning the art of kissing very quickly, for their embrace then spiralled into something fierce and … wonderful. When he pulled back, they were both panting. He ran his thumb down the line of her neck and over her collarbone.

'This is unfair,' she whispered, kissing his jawline.

'How so?' he asked, as his thumb continued to explore.

'You are all covered up.' She tugged at his shirt collar.

Something warm kindled in his eyes. 'You *are* feeling adventurous.'

She grinned, and he held her gaze as she unwound his cravat, unbuttoned his waistcoat and loosened his shirt strings. She ran a finger from his throat down, and gasped. 'I was right the first time we met.'

He shook his head and raised an eyebrow, confusion and delight in his eyes.

She ran her hands over the hair on his chest, marvelling at its softness over hard muscle. 'You *are* a bear!'

He growled, then captured her mouth again, and kissed her until the world slipped away.

# HISTORICAL NOTE

On the 14th of January 1828, Ellen Turner married Thomas Legh at the church in Prestbury. The wedding party returned to Shrigley Hall to celebrate with a wedding breakfast and then Mr and Mrs Legh travelled to Lyme Park. Ellen went from scandalous schoolgirl to being the wife of one of the most prominent men in the area.

It would appear from newspaper reports that Ellen and Thomas were active in local society and participated in local fundraising events, including the building of an infirmary. They took part in London society too, as Thomas was an MP, but appear to have spent most of their time at Lyme Park.

Edward and his brother served their sentences and on release were both thoroughly discredited. However, Edward Gibbon Wakefield had written pamphlets on proposals for colonising Australasia during his incarceration, and he went on to establish himself as an authority on the colonies. In 1836, he became one of the founding fathers of New Zealand!

Shrigley Hall is now a hotel and spa, and Lyme Park is owned by the National Trust.

The Rams Head, where the magistrates' court was held, is still a public house and is situated on the A6 through Disley.

Thomas and Ellen's first son was stillborn in November 1828, but in 1830 she gave birth to a daughter – Ellen Jane Legh.

In 1831 Ellen went into labour with their third child, but tragically, both she and her son died.

Her death was reported in the newspapers, and the account in *Bell's Life in London* read: *Mrs Legh, the lady of T. Legh Esq. MP, died last week. This was the lady about whom so much interest was excited four years since, in consequence of her abduction by Mr Wakefield.* Ellen was unable to shake the notoriety, even in death.

# ACKNOWLEDGEMENTS

My wonderful family for their unfailing support, and who kept me going when things were tough. Emma, Ian, Evie, and Willow. Mum and Angie. Richard and Nigel. Helen, Simon, Adam, and Melissa. Special mentions to Maya, Madge, and Sophie dog.

The incredibly detailed research done giving the full story of Ellen, Thomas, and Edward. Both books make fascinating reading:

*The Shrigley Abduction* – Abby Ashby & Audrey Jones

*Abduction The Story of Ellen Turner* – Kate M. Atkinson

Harper
North

# BOOK CREDITS

HarperNorth would like to thank the following staff
and contributors for their involvement in making
this book a reality:

Hannah Avery
Fionnuala Barrett
Claire Boal
Charlotte Brown
Sarah Burke
Cherie Chapman
Alan Cracknell
Jonathan de Peyer
Anna Derkacz
Tom Dunstan
Sarah Dronfield
Kate Elton
Mick Fawcett
Simon Gerratt
Alice Gomer
Monica Green

Elisabeth Heissler
Graham Holmes
Mayada Ibrahim
Taslima Khatun
Nicky Lovick
Megan Jones
Jean-Marie Kelly
Alice Murphy-Pyle
Adam Murray
Genevieve Pegg
Rob Pinney
Agnes Rigou
Florence Shepherd
Emma Sullivan
Katrina Troy
Daisy Watt

For more unmissable reads,
sign up to the HarperNorth newsletter at
**www.harpernorth.co.uk**


or find us on Twitter at
**@HarperNorthUK**

Harper
North